W9-ACI-387

KILLER OF WITCHES

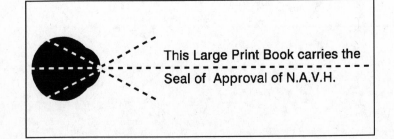

This Large Print Book carries the Seal of Approval of N.A.V.H.

KILLER OF WITCHES

THE LIFE AND TIMES OF YELLOW BOY, MESCALERO APACHE

W. MICHAEL FARMER

THORNDIKE PRESS
A part of Gale, Cengage Learning

GALE
CENGAGE Learning·

Farmington Hills, Mich • San Francisco • New York • Waterville, Maine
Meriden, Conn • Mason, Ohio • Chicago

GALE
CENGAGE Learning

Copyright © 2015 by W. Michael Farmer.
Map of the Apacheria about 1875 © 2014 by W. Michael Farmer
Interior sketches were created by Jim Trolinger at jtrolingerart.com
Thorndike Press, a part of Gale, Cengage Learning.

Thorndike Press® Large Print Western.
The text of this Large Print edition is unabridged.
Other aspects of the book may vary from the original edition.
Set in 16 pt. Plantin.

LIBRARY OF CONGRESS CATALOGING-IN-PUBLICATION DATA

Farmer, W. Michael, 1944–
    Killer of witches : the life and times of Yellow Boy, Mescalero Apache / by W. Michael Farmer. — Large print edition.
        pages cm. — (Thorndike Press large print western)
        ISBN 978-1-4104-8545-8 (hardcover) — ISBN 1-4104-8545-5 (hardcover)
    1. Apache Indians—History—Fiction. 2. Mescalero Indians—History—Fiction. 3. Mescalero Indian Reservation (N.M.)—Fiction. 4. Bosque Redondo Indian Reservation (N.M.)—Fiction. 5. Large type books. I. Title.
    PS3606.A725K55 2015b
    813'.6—dc23   2015030667

Published in 2015 by arrangement with W. Michael Farmer

Printed in Mexico
1 2 3 4 5 6 7 19 18 17 16 15

For Corky, my best friend and wife.

ACKNOWLEDGMENTS

A project of this magnitude is not done alone. I owe a debt of gratitude to many friends and associates who have supported and encouraged me in this work. There are several who deserve special mention.

Melissa Starr provided editorial reviews and many helpful questions, suggestions, and comments to enhance manuscript quality and to help bring to life Yellow Boy in a way I had not seen him before. Her work is much appreciated.

Bruce Kennedy's knowledge of the southwest and invaluable commentary made many helpful contributions to this story. I thank him for his support.

Lynda Sánchez's first-hand knowledge of Apache culture and history provided guiding light and clarity on many details. Her insights and comments on this story were invaluable. I owe her a debt of gratitude.

Jim Trolinger provided the illustrations for

the text and helped bring the major characters to visual life. His help and encourage-
ment will be long remembered and appreciated.

Pat and Mike Alexander have graciously
opened their home to me during return
visits to New Mexico for research and book
tours, and they provided company on long
roads across endless deserts and prairies
and tall mountains. Friends such as these
are rare and much appreciated.

Excellent descriptions of Apache culture,
beliefs, and methods of raiding and war in
the mid- to late-nineteenth century are
provided by anthropologists, linguists, and
historians. Some of the ones I found most
helpful are provided in Additional Reading
at the end of the story. The work by Eve
Ball and her associates Lynda A. Sánchez
and Nora Henn provided especially valuable insights into Apache life because they
faithfully recorded the stories Eve's Apache
friends remembered of the old days, and
they remembered those days very well.

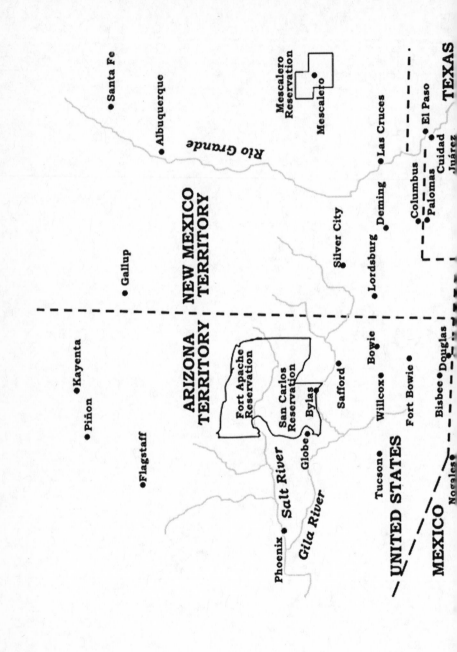

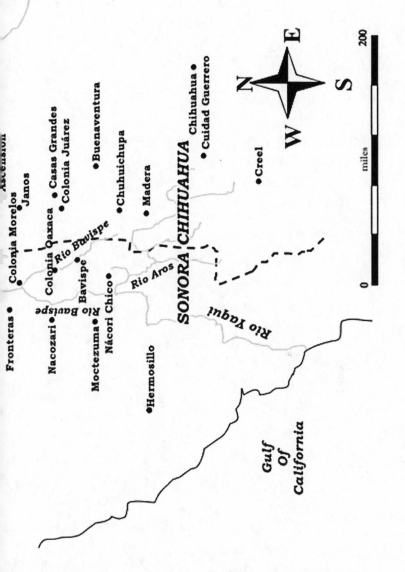

**Map of the Apacheria About 1875
(Towns appearing after 1875 have been
added to aid reader orientation.)**

CHARACTERS

Fictional Characters

Beela-chezzi (Crooked Fingers) — Yellow Boy's friend, a warrior

Caballo Negro (Black Horse) — Yellow Boy's father

Carmen Rosario — Sangre del Diablo's slave

Deer Woman (aka Gah) — Yellow Boy's childhood friend

Delgadito — Yellow Boy's competitor

Gourd Girl (aka Lucky Star) — a Mexican slave child adopted by Sons-ee-ah-ray

He Watches — Yellow Boy's adoptive grandfather

Juanita — Yellow Boy's wife

Kah (Arrow) — Yellow Boy's friend, a warrior

Klo-sen (Hair Rope) — a warrior

Ko-do (Firefly) — Yellow Boy's friend, a warrior

Maria — Juanita's mother

Moon on the Water — Juanita's little sister

Porico (White Horse) — Juanita's father

Rufus Pike (aka Roofoos Peek) — Yellow Boy's mentor

Sangre del Diablo (Blood of the Devil) — Mexican-Comanche *Witch*

Segundo — Comanche *Witch*

Socorro (Corn) — Yellow Boy's adoptive grandmother

Soldado Fiero (Fierce Soldier) — Chiricahua Blue Coat Scout

Sons-ee-ah-ray (aka Ish-tia-nay) — Yellow Boy's mother

Sons-nah (Corn Tassel) — Deer Woman's father

Yellow Boy (aka Ish-kay-neh, aka Nah-kah-yen) — The Killer of Witches story teller

Historical Characters

Al Sieber — Chief of Scouts under General Crook

Cadete — Mescalero Chief

Cha — Mescalero Chief

Colonel Edward Hatch — Commander of the Disarming

Dr. Joseph Blazer — Owner of the mercantile store and sawmill on the Mescalero Reservation

Fred C. Godfroy — Agent, Mescalero Reservation

General James Henry Carleton — Commanding General, New Mexico Territory 1862–1866

Juh — Nednhi Apache Chief

Kah Tensakes (Crooked Arrow) — Ancient Mescalero hunter who hunts elk on ice-covered snow

Kit Carson (aka Keet Kah-sohn) — Scout, Indian Fighter, and Colonel, New Mexico Volunteers

Lorenzo Labadie — Agent, Bosque Redondo Mescalero Reservation

Nana — Mimbreño Apache leader

Roman — Mescalero Chief

S. A. Russell — Agent, Mescalero Reservation

Santana — Mescalero Chief

Victorio — Mimbreño Apache Chief

APACHE WORDS AND PHRASES

Aashco — friend
Búh — owl
Dánt'e — greetings
Enjuh — good
Gaagé — raven
Googé — whip-poor-will
Haheh — a young girl's puberty ceremony
Idiits'ag — I hear you
Indah — white men (literally the living)
Indah Lickoyee — white intruder
Indeh — Apache name for themselves (literally the dead)
Ka dish day — goodbye
Klitso — gold
Ndolkah — cougar
Nakai-yi — Mexican
Nakai-yes — Mexicans
Nish'ii' — I see you
Pesh — iron
Pesh-klitso — yellow iron or gold
Socorro — corn

Tiswin — a weak, beer-like drink, brewed from corn

Season of Little Eagles — early spring

Season of Many Leaves — late spring, early summer

Season of Large Leaves — midsummer

Season of Large Fruit — late summer, early fall

Season of Earth is Reddish Brown — late fall

Season of Ghost Face — lifeless winter

CONTENTS

PREFACE

Eighty years of information on Apache life gathered by anthropologists, linguists, and historians is often ignored in novels and movies featuring Apaches. These stories fail to capture an understanding of Apache ways and beliefs as they were in the years when their raiding and roaming were disappearing, washed away in conflict by the unending flood of "White Eye" invaders filling the *Apachería*. Those were brutal, hard-fought years on both sides, and it is easy to overlook the humanity of the Apaches who fought without quarter, and expected none against the ruthless, steely determination of the White Eyes to claim the land, despite the horrors of Indian warfare.

In 1955, Paul Blazer, whose father and grandfather had run a store and a sawmill on the Mescalero Apache Reservation from about 1868, told Dr. C. L. Sonnichsen, the great chronicler of the southwest, "I hate to hear people talk about those Apaches as savages . . . if an Indian is a savage, a lot of white men are savages, too . . . Teddy Roosevelt was a savage. Some of the Mescaleros *were* savages . . . but they were no worse than the white men who 'hit them in the rear with a saddle.' They used to come into the store where I worked. I would give them a smoke, and they would sit around and tell me stories — folk tales. There was poetry and beauty in them. That was when I began to see that they were folks just like us."

This novel is an attempt to understand what Paul Blazer meant when he spoke with Doc Sonnichsen in the middle of the twentieth century from a perspective that stretched into the last years of the free Apaches. The story is an imaginative autobiography of the warrior and cavalry scout, Yellow Boy, a major character that appears in "The Vanishing Trilogy," a mythical story of the survival, revenge, and odyssey of Henry Fountain after the true-life murder of his father, Albert, near White Sands, New Mexico Territory, in 1896. I have used Yellow Boy to paint a picture of Mescalero Apache life and times from about 1860–1951, a period when the Mescaleros went from nomadic, horse-mounted raiders and hunters, to White Eye prisoners of war, to reservation residents dependent on White Eye largess, to proud, independent people, making their own way in the white man's world.

Language is a window into the culture of a people. Apache, its root language, Athabaskan, is a beautiful and complex tonal language with many variants between Navajo, Chipewyan, and Apache groups. It is difficult to learn to speak correctly, and its spelling using tonal marks difficult to write. I have attempted to give the reader a sense of Apache culture by using a few Apache words in the manuscript. Their spelling without tonal marks, except simple accents, depends on the source from which I referenced them, mainly from *Life Among the Apaches,* by John C. Cremony, and the *Western Apache-English Dictionary,* edited by Dorothy Bray.

Killer of Witches is the first volume in three that forms the story of Yellow Boy and a history of a people with the same hopes and fears shared by "folks just like us" in a time when their freedom was disappearing and the terrors on the dark side of this life, *Witches* and other evil spirits in the flesh, had to be neutralized or destroyed to enter the next life unscathed.

W. Michael Farmer
Smithfield, Virginia
May 2014

PROLOGUE

"You are stronger than we. We have fought you so long as we had rifles and powder, but your arms are better than ours. Give us like weapons and turn us loose, we will fight you again; but we are worn-out; we have no more heart; we have no provisions, no means to live; your troops are everywhere; our springs and waterholes are either occupied or over-looked by your young men. You have driven us from our last and best strong-hold, and we have no more heart. Do with us as may seem good to you, but do not forget we are men and braves."

— Mescalero Chief Cadete
to General Carlton, 1863

At the time Cadete spoke his words to General Carlton, the Mescalero Apache, Yellow Boy, my mentor and close friend for over fifty-five years, was three years old. He saved me from certain death in the winter desert after the murder of my father, Albert, in 1896; helped me avenge Albert; and taught me to survive in the hard country of the southwest. In 1950 I persuaded him to tell me his life story. Over the course of many afternoons and pots of coffee, I wrote it down as he told it in a mixture of Mescalero Apache, Spanish, and English in the whispery rasping voice of a vigorous old man. At the beginning of each session I read back to him what I had written from the previous session, and after explaining the meaning of some of my fancy words, he usually agreed I had captured the essence of what he had said. When I missed what he meant, I rewrote until he said I had captured his meaning. This is his story as he told it and meant it to be heard.

–Dr. Henry Grace, 1953

CHAPTER 1
ISH-KAY-NEH

Bosque Redondo, New Mexico Territory,
  October 30, 1865

My people were Mescalero Apaches, the Shish-Indeh, the People of the Woods. In the time when *Indah Lickoyee,* the White Eye outsiders, kept my people prisoners of war in Bosque Redondo, a chief called Cadete came to speak with my father. My life had not been long then, only five years, and my father still called me Ish-kay-neh (Boy), my true name not yet given.

The night Cadete spoke with Caballo Negro (Black Horse) by the little fire in our ragged tipi, my mother and I sat nearby eating a nasty-tasting stew, made from the worthless meat and worm-filled cornmeal the White Eyes gave us, which she had boiled in bitter water from the river the White Eyes called Pecos. We listened to Cadete and my father speaking in low, secret-filled voices.

My mother's eyes were bright with the heat of sickness, and her slender body trembled under the thin blanket draped over her shoulders. There was little stew in her bowl. She gave most of her food to me and to Caballo Negro. I wanted to spit it out, but she said I must eat to live, no matter how bad it tasted.

My mother's eyes followed every move Caballo Negro and Cadete made as she listened and waited to serve them. My father called her Ish-tia-nay, which meant "Woman." It was a sign of affection and respect among my people for a man to call his first wife by this name. Her true name was Sons-ee-ah-ray (Morning Star), for she was always out of the blankets before the morning star left with the dawn.

Listening to the words between Cadete and Caballo Negro, my mother looked at me and smiled. I understood their words gave truth to the stories the other women had told her while they dug mesquite roots for firewood far out on the *llano* (dry prairie). She had told me those stories. They said our people were leaving Bosque Redondo.

The words between Caballo Negro and Cadete filled my head with questions: *Why are we leaving Bosque Redondo? Haven't the*

Shis-Indeh stayed with the Blue Coats here since before my memories? Why will we take many different paths? Will my friends go to the same place I go?

I hoped Sons-nah (Corn Tassel) would go with Caballo Negro. That would mean I'd have a friend in the strange camp. I had a good time playing with the other children, especially Sons-nah's daughter, the girl with the big, bright eyes. I called her Gah (Rabbit) because she could win races, and no one ever caught her when we played tag. She was very fast dodging anyone who grabbed for her. There was no shame in her winning. We were friends. I felt she ought to win sometimes.

I had often wished I could help watch the horses and mules with the older boys, but my mother had said no when I asked. She had notched her memory stick for each new Season of Many Leaves I had lived and did not let me dispute it, even though I was big for my age. She said I had not lived long enough to work with the horses. The horses might step or fall on me, and I would never grow to be a strong warrior like Caballo Negro. I wondered if I could look after horses with older boys in the new camp. I did not want to work for my mother like a little child. In the new camp with no White

Eyes nearby, maybe I could begin my warrior training and become a keeper of horses sooner. I thought this change might be a good thing.

My wandering thoughts were cut short when Caballo Negro nodded farewell to Cadete and motioned my mother and me closer. Then he stared into the fire, holding it in his eyes, and spoke as a man in a trance. "In five suns, the *Shis-Indeh* will leave this place. We'll go at night in many different directions and follow many paths. The Blue Coats will know not who to follow. They can't follow all of us. Some will get away. The ones the Blue Coats follow will hide, and they'll fight if they're found, fight to the last man, woman, or child. We'll never come back to this place of bad crops, bad meat, bad water, slavery, and sickness."

He stopped speaking, and I heard a child whine nearby. I wondered if I would live to see the next Season of Many Leaves.

Caballo Negro held his hands over the fire, rubbed the cold away, and continued, "Cadete says it's best we go south to the camp of Cha, the brother of Cadete, Santana, and Roman. Cha raids the wagons on the *Indah* road running from sunrise to sunset near the mountains the *Nakai-yes* (Mexicans) call Guadalupes. Cha's camp is in the Guadalupes. The Blue Coats have looked for him many times, but they've never found him. With Cha, I can raid the *Nakai-yi* villages and ranches along the great river and the wagons on the *Indah* road. Caballo Negro will be a man again, a warrior, not a slave."

He frowned and stared at us so we would not forget what he said next. "There are *Indah* spies in the camp. Don't speak of leaving to anyone. A spy hears you, and we'll have to fight our way out rather than slip away.

"Ish-tia-neh, take all the supplies you can. We don't go to Cha's camp with empty hands. Prepare by working as if you're making ready for the snows in the Ghost Face Season. All the women will do this. Be ready in four days. We'll leave in the night under the noses of the Blue Coat soldiers."

My mother crossed her arms and nodded. "Uhmmph. This worthless tipi cover, it goes too?"

Caballo Negro clenched his teeth. "I hate to take it. It's falling apart, but we don't know how long we'll need it on the trail south."

From the tone of his words, I knew it was a good time to ask him a question. He might answer it rather than ignore me. I said,

"Father, will you hear a question?"

"Uhmmph?"

"How did our people come to this place?"

He looked at me with sad eyes, and his mouth turned down. "You're very young and know no better time. But Cadete, to save us from all being killed at Canyon del Perro when the Blue Coats surprised and attacked us, surrendered to Keet Kah-sohn (Kit Carson), who brought us here. You were barely off the cradleboard then.

"Now, the *Indah* tell us where we can go and when. They won't let us leave to hunt. They give us less and less to eat. There's nothing left here but dust in the air. The Blue Coats make us share this country with the Navajos. Keet Kah-sohn drives them before him in the north, and more come here every day. The *Indah* made us give our land to the Navajos after we worked like slaves digging ditches for water and planting seeds, though we were here first. The Navajos ought to be feeding us. The meat the *Indah* give us is no good. It makes us sick. Even the iron tools they give us to plant our crops break. The blankets we are given are thin and cold, not thick and warm like those of the *Indah* or *Nakai-yes.*"

Caballo Negro leaned toward our fire and stirred the embers with a stick, and I

34

watched the sparks rise before he added, "We must leave because there is nothing left to feed our fires. We have to ride half a sun just to dig firewood out of the ground. The water here makes us sick. Many, including your mother's father and mother, have become sick because of bad meat and bad water and have gone to the land of the grandfathers. Labadie, the agent who fights for us, the Blue Coats run off and listen to his words no more. The *Indah* have not kept their word, so we will leave this place. Even if we die naked and starving on the *llano,* we will be free. Do you understand my words?"

"Yes, Father. They pound my ears." I stared into the fire and tasted the anger awakened by his words. It rose in my throat like burning stomach water. I wanted to rise up the next morning a warrior and avenge the *Shis-Indeh* for their suffering. The fire was burning low, and I shivered as I thought of my friends and what we had to do when we were grown. "Father, another question?"

He raised an eyebrow.

"Will the warrior Sons-nah go to the camp of Cha?"

Caballo Negro smiled.

"Sons-nah will go to the camp of Cha."

I looked in the fire and asked no more

questions. At least my friend Gah would go to the new camp with me.

I shook my fist and said what I felt, *"En-juh!"* (Good!)

CHAPTER 2
THE FIFTH DAY

On the fifth day after Caballo Negro spoke with Cadete, I left my mother's tipi as the sun began to bring the morning, and I lifted my arms in the prayer to *Ussen,* the great god of the Apaches, which my mother had taught me to sing for the new day. With outstretched hands, I looked to the east and sang,

"Come Sun of the morning,
"Come bright light of *Ussen.*
"*Ussen* give us its Power.
"Give us the Sun of the morning."

On that day, my friends and I went to a corral and picked through the mule and horse apples for *socorro* (corn) or oats, whatever they were fed that had survived passing through their bellies. We did this to help our fathers and mothers find enough food to stay alive. I was lucky and found a few grains. I wrapped them together in a rag for my mother to wash and use in her stews.

The women worked as they did every day. Some went in the Blue Coat soldiers' wagons to dig in the dirt like badgers for more firewood (mesquite roots). Others gathered where the Blue Coats gave us food, and others patched the rags of their men and children.

After I returned from the corral, my mother fed me before we walked three miles to Fort Sumner to claim our weekly rations. At the place where rations were given, my mother waited in a long line while I played with the other children.

At last, she was near the door where the Blue Coats were to give us our food for the week and maybe some other things. I left my friends to stand with her. Soon, a soldier waved us inside, and we stood before a fat, ugly Blue Coat with hair on his face, who was sitting behind a table. He used a little spear with a sharp iron point dipped in black water to draw tracks on thin, white skins in front of him.

I already knew many of the words the Blue Coats used. It made them laugh when I used the words "Damn it," which they said so often. Apache children are taught very young to remember well what they are told and see. Many times our lives depended on it and we had no training to make tracks on the thin white skins like the *Indah* to help them remember. While I didn't understand the meaning of everything the *Indah* said then, I remember exactly the words the fat Blue Coat said and what happened that last day my mother took rations from the Blue Coats at Bosque Redondo.

He looked at the *Indah* card given my mother hanging around her neck and muttered, "Number three hundred ninety." He made tracks on a white skin and turned to another pile of white skins already covered with tracks while she stared at the wall behind him, her chin tilted up.

"Let's see, three ninety . . . three ninety, okay. Caballo Negro, his woman, and a child age five." He lifted his eyes and looked us over and then nodded. "Okay, Mrs. Negro there's three of ya, so ya git five pounds of meal, two pounds of meat, and three new blankets." He turned to a soldier behind him and said, "You git that, Private?"

The soldier said, "Yes, Sergeant," and went through a door to the next room. He returned with a small cloth sack tied off at the top, a piece of dry meat, dark and covered with mold, and three thin blankets.

He laid them on a board beside the Blue Coat who made the tracks on the white skins.

The Blue Coat turned a white skin with tracks toward my mother, held out the little spear for making tracks, and pointing to a place on the white skin, he said, "You know the drill. Make yore mark and you'n take yore rations."

My mother looked at the little sack of meal and the little piece of meat that was supposed to feed us for a week and shook her head, whispering words she'd learned in the last year, "No good. More."

The Blue Coat squinted at her and shook his head.

My mother said the words again, only louder, "No good! More!"

The Blue Coat said, "General Carlton says that's all we can give ya. Take it or leave it, I don't care. They ain't no more."

She stared at the Blue Coat who stared back, then she looked at me, and finally at the white skin with tracks lying on the table before her. She took the little spear he offered and made a cross mark. He made tracks beside hers, pointed to the supplies, and then waved toward the door, saying in a loud voice, "Next!"

My mother motioned for me to carry the

sack. She took the piece of moldy meat and blankets and stepped out the door with me behind her.

The sack, not so hard to carry at first, got heavier as we walked back to our tipi in the cold, bright air, but even at that age, I would never admit it. *I'm a big boy,* I thought. *I have to do my share of the work.* Most of the way back my mother sang softly, "*Ussen* has Power, give us your Power, take us from the Blue Coats."

I left the sack of meal in the tipi. My mother wanted to finish packing and sent me to play with my friends. The sun teased me, knowing I wanted it to bring the night quickly, the night we left the *Indah.* But the sun crawled across the sky like a little baby rather than running like a warrior. It had moved only a little each time I looked toward the west. I worried it might decide to sit there in the blue, play with the clouds, and not give the *Shis-Indeh* the darkness we needed to leave.

In my time, little Mescalero children played war games, ambushing and shooting reed arrows at each other. Although the arrows didn't stick in us, there was pain when they struck us, but we never risked blinding an opponent by shooting at his head. Every day, I practiced with the little bow and arrows my uncle had given me. The bow was not hard to pull, and the arrows, only dry stalks. Still, from the time I was barely able to walk, I had carried them everywhere and practiced against any and every target.

On that day, after every strike with an arrow from my bow, I looked at the sky, but the sun had barely moved. Gah, who also had a bow and reed arrows, hid with me behind a rock waiting to ambush two boys in our game. When we heard a horse snort behind us, we froze perfectly still, as our mothers had taught us. I slowly turned my head and saw a Blue Coat and a scout sitting in their saddles watching us. The scout spoke to the Blue Coat. "Little bastards start young don't they?"

The Blue Coat laughed and the scout said to us, "Practice with them bows all you want now, you little heathens. Use them against the Blue Coats when you're older, and you'll git wiped out."

I did not know where the words came from, but I shouted. "Damn it! The day comes when all the White Eyes and Blue Coats will run when they hear my name!"

The scout laughed. "What is your name?"

I held up my fist and yelled, "Ish-kay-neh!"

The scout laughed and told the Blue Coat I had said my name was Boy. The Blue Coat roared with laughter as if he had heard a funny story and, pointing a finger at me, as if it were a pistol, yelled, "Bang!"

I was so angry I was trembling as they turned their horses and rode back toward Fort Sumner. Gah whispered, "You are very brave, Ish-kay-neh. One day all the *Indah Lickoyee* will run at your name." She took my hand and said, "Forget the Blue Coats. Come on. Let's race with the others."

We often ran long, hard races of endurance, boys and girls. Sometimes we ran all the way around the great loop of Bosque Redondo. The dust on the path covered us, leaving grit, hard and crunchy when we closed our mouths, and making it hard to breathe. By the time we passed the pile of smooth river rocks marking the end of the race, we were wheezing, and we all looked as if we had been pulled from an *Indah* flour bin. After each race, I checked the sky; still, the sun had not moved much.

I washed the dust from my body and hair in a freezing little inlet in the banks of the river. Afterwards I carried jugs of the sour water to my mother. Little by little, the sun edged toward the distant, western mountains. When my mother asked me to bring wood for the night, I at last saw long shadows pointing east. The sun was going to its hiding place, and night was sure to follow.

At the great pile of mesquite roots used for community firewood, I pulled an armload of the black, hairy roots, which were twisted and gnarled at crazy angles. As I worked to get the roots out of the jumbled mass, I thought of being in Cha's camp, watching horses and never doing woman's work again. *Woman's work is too hard. Besides, it is not what a man does.* At the tipi, I used my mother's hatchet to chop all the roots into pieces small enough for a little cooking fire. It was enough wood to maintain our fire for two or three nights, and I smiled at the thought of how the extra wood would deceive the Blue Coats into thinking we would still be there days later.

I carried the wood into the tipi and, squatting by the fire, watched Mother cook and do other chores. Around the tipi fire, her pots and baskets and our blankets looked normal. Still, the order of things wasn't exactly as it had been the day before. After a while, I realized she had organized her things east to west from the door in packages of decreasing weight. She packed our heaviest gear first, carrying it or loading it on a mule or horse, and then added the lighter items next to make the load stable. I smiled. Clever and wise woman was my mother. No Blue Coat would ever recognize her preparations to leave. She was teaching me much.

Caballo Negro entered the tipi, sat by the fire, folded his hands, and waited for Mother to serve him. As she ladled the gruel out of the pot, she raised her brows and said, "All is well?"

He nodded as he leaned toward her to take the bowl and grunted, "Uhmmph." It was a good answer.

I heard him and smiled. After my night chores, I went to my blanket. Shivering against the cold outside and from excitement inside, I could not sleep as I watched the fire slowly die and listened to the words between Caballo Negro and Sons-ee-ah-ray. My eyes grew heavy, and, despite the very cold air and my excitement, I dozed off.

Sons-ee-ah-ray shook me awake and whispered for me to help her. The tipi cooking fire was gone, only a few bits of charcoal and white ashes left. It was dark and cold, and the air was filled with much dust and the sounds of many shuffling feet and horses and mules snorting and stamping their hooves. I shivered, and my teeth chattered as I looked up and saw stars between the bare lodge poles of our tipi. The ragged tipi cover was already down. I hurried to help roll it into a tight bundle.

From under the noses of Blue Coat guards, Caballo Negro had taken two boney horses and a mule from a corral and tied them to a lodge pole. One horse had a blanket across its back, and the mule carried a pack frame. I remembered seeing that frame astraddle the fence around the same corral where Gah and I went to search for grain. I knew it was the same one because of the marks painted in black on one of the front crosspieces.

My mother grunted as she threw the tipi cover on the pack frame, tied it tight, and then loaded her two big baskets, already filled, on opposite sides of the frame for balance. She looked closely around the floor of the tipi, making sure everything she owned in the world was on that mule. She told me that less than two fingers (finger widths above the horizon) of the night had passed since she had crawled from her blanket. She was ready to follow Caballo Negro.

She kneeled in front of me and tied a blanket around my shoulders so I wouldn't lose it. While she worked, I whispered,

"What trail will lead us to Cha's camp?"

"We'll run and lead the horses and mule toward where sun disappears behind the far mountains and then turn south. Caballo Negro knows the way. Watch what he does on the trail, and you'll learn many things. Your bow and arrows are in my big basket on the right side of the mule when you want them."

I slipped out of her arms and ran to the basket. She handed me the sack she had made from rags to carry my bow and bundle of reed arrows. I slipped it on and felt like a grown warrior.

"Why don't we ride the horses instead of running?"

She whispered, "They're too weak to go far if we ride. For three or four days, they must have their fill of grass and only carry a little weight. Then they'll be strong enough to ride. Now you must be very quiet until your father returns. If the Blue Coats hear us, they'll try to chase us back or kill us if we fight."

Caballo Negro appeared out of the night's gloom, and, grabbing me under my arms, swung me up on the boney gray mare and tied me on so if I went to sleep I wouldn't fall off. Suddenly, it seemed as if there were no others around us. The sound of shuffling feet had faded away.

Caballo Negro led the two horses out of the village of bare lodge poles, skeletons pointing toward the star-filled sky in the black, dust-filled air and supporting nothing except each other. Mother took the lead line for the mule and followed my father. Our people had left a few of the tipis at Bosque Redondo covered and sitting at the edge of the camp closest to Fort Sumner to fool the Blue Coats into thinking we were still there when the dawn sent the sun.

I held on to the horse's mane and bounced on its warm withers as Caballo Negro and Mother walked to a low bank and waded across the river to the high banks of the western edge. They led the animals up the western bank to the *llano* and began running west at a pace that covered many miles and saved the animal's strength. It was strange for me, but it felt right, riding in the cold darkness with only the light of stars and hearing Mother and Caballo Negro breathing deep gulps of air as their moccasins flew over the dead, dry grass. A quarter moon did not come until the night was more than half gone. But even in the deep darkness, with only stars lighting the *llano,* Caballo Negro led the way as if he saw as well as he did in the light of day. I thought, *No Blue Coat will ever catch us.*

CHAPTER 3
ON THE *LLANO*

Sons-ee-ah-ray and Caballo Negro ran west for many miles the night we left the Blue Coats and Bosque Redondo. They stopped three times, more to rest the horses and mule than themselves. They stopped first when the moonlight finally fell on the *llano,* and it was much easier to see in the dark and shadow-filled distance. Sons-ee-ah-ray led the animals into a shallow arroyo while Caballo Negro crept to the top of a rise and looked back toward the east, toward where soldiers would come. He watched and listened with his ear to the end of his knife handle, the blade stuck in the ground, and he sniffed the air. He saw nothing, heard nothing, and smelled nothing of the Blue Coats.

My mother allowed herself two swallows of water and gave me one after holding up one finger to be sure I understood that's all I could have. When I nodded, she gave it to me, and then waited for my father to return. He reappeared like a ghost floating out of the *llano* brush shadows and sat down on the arroyo bank, shaking his head at Sons-ee-ah-ray's questioning stare. Without the warmth of the horse under me, I soon grew cold and shivered until Sons-ee-ah-ray and Caballo Negro sat together, and Sons-ee-ah-ray, holding me on her lap, wrapped a thin blanket around us all. We drank a little more water and ate what Sons-ee-ah-ray had made in the past week for us to eat on the run, dry meat pounded together with meal, nuts, and dried cactus fruit. It was something like what the warriors carried when they went on raids and couldn't risk revealing themselves with cooking fires. It had taken her over a year, scrimping and saving every bit of food she could preserve, every special gift of nuts or dried fruit given her by other women, to gather the delicacies she had needed to make it. She hadn't doubted we would need it when we escaped Bosque Redondo.

In the deep stillness of the night, I drifted off to sleep huddled in the warmth of my father and mother. When I awoke, tied again on the gray horse jogging behind Sons-ee-ah-ray and Caballo Negro, I looked out over the dark, rolling plains that were covered

51

with never-ending dry, crackling grass and felt confused, disoriented, and frightened. I felt the wind on my hands and face and saw the occasional cactus and mesquite bush casting black shadows in the dim quarter moonlight. The night air was freezing cold, and bouncing on the boney horse made my bones feel like they rattled in every socket, but soon I realized we were far from Bosque Redondo and felt comforted, thinking the freezing air and boney horse worth it to leave the place of the Blue Coats with my warrior father and beautiful mother running in front of me.

We came to low rolling hills rising out of the *llano* like big bubbles in a pot of stew. They were covered with many bushes and separated by dry arroyos that passed around them like trails to be followed. We wound our way among the arroyos until we came to a black pool of water with a skim of ice around its edges, surrounded by grass and a few round boulders clustered on one side, where water dribbled, filling the pool.

Sons-ee-ah-ray and Caballo Negro stopped again. He crept to the top of the highest hill next to the pool and studied the way we had come. He seemed to be gone a long time as I sat with mother after we had filled our water bladders, emptied our own, and let the animals drink. She looked very tired and hung her head like a jaded horse, and her moccasins looked ragged and in need of repair. I asked why she didn't fix them. She said we needed to put more distance between the Blue Coats and us, and then there might be time to fix them when we stopped at daylight. When my father returned and again shook his head at her look, she seemed to regain her strength and, smiling, opened our blanket to him and motioned him to sit with us.

We rested there by that pool longer than we had at the first stop. Before we started running again, Caballo Negro went to the animals hobbled in the grass surrounding the pool. He ran his hands over their muzzles and legs, removed their hobbles and looked at their hooves, rubbing his thumb over one or two of them before he let the horse drop it. When he was satisfied, he nodded, came back to us, picked me up and put me on the gray mare again, and, pointing with his nose in the direction he wanted to go, led us farther west.

The coming dawn cast light on a line of cliffs and low hills in front of us, and Caballo Negro began turning south as he led us toward them. The sun was barely above the horizon when we moved into the shadows behind a high hill in front of the cliffs. After unloading the horses and mule, Sons-ee-ah-ray and I made a place to sleep in a small grove of piñons while Caballo Negro (who was often called "Caballo") climbed to the top of the hill and stared east. When he returned, we ate and he said, "The Blue Coats are not coming. Let's rest and let ponies graze until the sun hides again. I'll watch from the top of the hill until the shadows are short, and then you come to watch, Sons-ee-ah-ray."

My mother nodded. The last thing I remember before falling asleep was watching Sons-ee-ah-ray fixing the ragged places in her moccasins and those of Caballo Negro.

The wind was calm, the sun warm, and I slept all day. The second night, Caballo Negro and Sons-ee-ah-ray ran south along the sides of the hills and cliffs to the west. Before the moon cleared the eastern horizon, we came to another pool of water, drank our fill, and rested. Soon after leaving the water, the way south became much harder. It crossed a series of hills and deep arroyos, and Sons-ee-ah-ray and Caballo Negro had to run up and then race down, making it hard to keep the steady rhythm that had carried us far the night before. As the moon rose, we came down from the hills, and the land was flat again. They ran until the moon was high, and we found water made by a little spring dribbling out of a rock formation stuck there without rhyme or reason. Even as young as I was, I saw my mother was very tired. She stumbled often, and after we stopped to drink and rest, she was slow to rise, but she never complained.

Leaving the pool, we did not run far. The moon had barely moved when Caballo Negro held up his hand for us to stop. He pointed directly in front of us. We were approaching the white ruts of a wagon road that disappeared west behind a high ridge. He sniffed the air and then turned west, running toward the high ridge behind which the ruts disappeared. He tied off the horses in a small grove of piñons, took me down, and spoke to my mother and me in a low voice. "Do you smell the wood smoke? The wagon tracks in front of us say maybe there is a ranch on the other side of the ridge. A ranch means horses and food. Maybe I can take some, and we will run no more, eh, Woman?"

She smiled, nodded, and, trembling from

JAMES RIVER VALLEY
LIBRARY SYSTEM
105 3RD ST SE
JAMESTOWN ND 58401

the cold wind, said, "I know you are a strong warrior. We'll wait."

"If I do not return, ride these animals south toward the next water as far as they can make it. If they fall before the next water, leave them and run on. Wait there. Sons-nah and another warrior with their families will meet you within a day and take you on to Cha's camp with them. Be strong, Woman. Now we live free."

He turned to me.

"Ish-kay-neh, take your bow and guard your mother. Always help her if you leave without me."

I wanted to wail for him not to go, but I kept my mouth shut and nodded. My mother had taught me from the time I was off the cradleboard that Mescaleros do not cry. No matter what comes, they know how to suffer, how to endure.

Caballo Negro took his bow and quiver of arrows and disappeared into the night, running up the ridge. My mother and I squatted together by the biggest piñon tree, and she wrapped a blanket around our shoulders. I had my bow, a weed arrow nocked against its string. Tensed for action, I was ready to fight if it would help Caballo Negro. The night was quiet, the only sounds from the restless piñons in a gentle wind. I smelled the weak trace of wood smoke, of which Caballo had spoken. The moon rose to the top of its arc and fell toward the southwest horizon.

We heard a small pop in the distance, a rifle shot, then another and another. I started to rise, but my mother, her teeth clenched, grabbed my arm and looked at me with narrow eyes, telling me to be still. A woman screamed. I thought at first it was Cougar's war cry like we sometimes heard near Bosque Redondo, but I soon understood it was a woman's cry of fear.

There was another pop and then no more. Orange and yellow light filled the night sky on the other side of the ridge, and my mother and I stared at it, wondering if it meant we did not have to run anymore.

We heard horses running across the ridge before we saw Caballo Negro in the moonlight. He led six horses, and rode with a saddle on the seventh one, a large feed sack filled with supplies, and several blankets, rolled and tied, on the back of the saddle. His bow and quiver of arrows hung across his body. He guided the horse with one hand and carried a long soldier rifle with the other. It was the first rifle I remember seeing in the hands of my father.

He rode to my mother and me and slid

out of the saddle, smiling. "Woman, we will no longer shiver under thin blankets, and we will ride fast and far. These are good, strong ponies."

Though she should have been happy, she frowned. "Are you wounded anywhere?"

"I am not. But the *Indah* did not let me take these horses without a fight. He came firing this rifle at where he thought I stood in the shadows. I killed him with two arrows. Then his woman came out screaming, trying to take the rifle and shoot some more. She looked weak and sick. I decided she would not last as a slave for you. I killed her with another arrow. I filled a sack with things we need from the house and then set it on fire after I dragged them inside and pulled my arrows from their bodies. I took only the best horses from the corral and left others. With those horses left in the corral, it might take awhile for other White Eyes to realize the ranch did not accidentally catch on fire. Maybe the *Indah* will never understand this was an Apache raid."

My mother laughed, and shaking her fist high said, *"Enjuh!"*

I thought, *My father is a great warrior. His story will be told around Mescalero fires for many years.*

We loaded the fresh horses with supplies

off the boney horses and mule and drove the boney animals off toward the burning house. Caballo Negro set a steady pace that ate up the miles with the fresh, new horses. My mother and I rode together on one and led the rest. We stopped only once to rest before we reached the waterhole where Sons-nah and his family with my friend, Gah, and another warrior and his family were to meet us.

Caballo Negro let the animals drink and scouted the ground around the water. He led us to a low hill a bowshot from the waterhole and hobbled the horses in an arroyo behind it. He told Sons-ee-ah-ray to make a small shelter on the side of the hill away from the water so anyone stopping there would not see us. Caballo made a place for himself at the top of the hill to watch the waterhole. We ate more of Sons-ee-ah-ray's trail food, and then she and I crawled under the blanket-covered brush shelter to sleep while Caballo guarded the waterhole and waited for Sons-nah and the others.

The sun was high when Sons-ee-ah-ray left our little shelter to watch the waterhole while Caballo slept. Her leaving awoke me, but I soon drifted back to sleep after I felt Caballo lie down beside me.

Then I had a bad dream in which a great bull with long, sharp horns, the kind owned by the *Indah,* was chasing me across the *llano.* I must have made noise because Caballo Negro shook me awake and held his fingers to his lips with the edge of his hand to signal me to be quiet. I understood and lay there wondering how close to the night the sun's travel was. Sons-ee-ah-ray suddenly appeared, touched Caballo, and silently pointed toward the watching place. He slid out of the shelter, took his bow and arrows, and crept up the hill to see the waterhole. They said nothing to me. I had to see what was happening. Perhaps, Sonsnah and Gah had arrived. I crawled through the weeds to a large creosote bush down the side of the hill and looked out through the branches.

A Mexican cowboy, a *vaquero,* sat on his horse two long bowshots away, and there was a big pistol in his hand. His eyes studied every detail of the ground and brush surrounding the waterhole. Even as young as I was, I understood he was trying to decide if someone was waiting to ambush him if he went to the water.

He looked the waterhole and brush over for a long time. Sons-ee-ah-ray had trained me to be perfectly still when I hid, and I was. I knew Sons-ee-ah-ray watched him too, waiting perfectly still. I wondered what Caballo Negro planned.

At last, the *vaquero* holstered his pistol, rode to a grassy spot near the waterhole, dismounted, and began loosening his saddle cinches. He untied a bedroll from the back of his saddle and tossed it in the grass. Next he pulled the silver-trimmed saddle from his horse and placed it by the bedroll. He pulled handfuls of grass and used them to rub down his horse, a big red one with a white blaze on its face, and then he led it to drink at the waterhole before leading it back to the grass and hobbling it after he removed its bridle.

His big, round bottle with flat sides was like those I'd seen soldiers carry at Bosque Redondo. I had heard the Blue Coats call them canteens. He walked back to the waterhole, knelt on one knee by the water's edge, and looked around, a hand on his pistol in its holster. Satisfied he was alone, he knelt on both knees, pushed his big hat back on his head, and, cupping his hands, dipped the water to his mouth and drank.

The long arrow struck him in the middle of his shoulder blades with a sound like a fist smacking a gloved open palm, and it passed through to his front side. The only sound the *vaquero* made was a gurgling "aghhh," as he fell face forward into the water. It had happened so quickly, I stared in disbelief. It was the first time I'd seen a man killed.

Caballo Negro ran out of the brush, the knife in his hand his only weapon. He stopped momentarily to pull the big pistol from the holster and stuff it in his belt before he sheathed his knife, and, grabbing the *vaquero* by his boots, pulled him away from the waterhole. The body left a bright red trail of blood into the grass, and the water where the man had fallen was red. Caballo Negro walked back and flipped the bloody water away so it did not spoil the rest of the water.

Sons-ee-ah-ray came and began to take the *vaquero*'s boots and clothes. Caballo Negro returned from the waterhole smoothing the sand, and I ran to help them. I remember the metallic smell of blood mixed with the smell of dirt from the man's bowels. I learned that day death from an arrow has an ugly smell, not soon forgotten. Soon, long, dark red streaks filled the sky to the west as the sun disappeared, and I shivered in the cold air while looking at the hairy hide of the naked *vaquero*.

Chapter 4
Cha's Camp

Sons-ee-ah-ray took every piece of cloth and leather from the *vaquero,* and Caballo Negro pulled the arrow all the way through his body and washed it off. A good arrow was hard to make, and one with its power shown was even more valuable. The *vaquero* was a small man, and Caballo Negro picked him up with a little grunt and carried him away on his shoulder to hide in the sand. When I asked why, he said, "It will keep the coyotes and buzzards from finding him until we're gone. The Blue Coats know to look where buzzards circle. Sometimes they show the place of a raid."

Late that night, Sons-nah and his family appeared. They came running in the moonlight from the east, and Gah was riding on her father's back. The horse he had taken had been too weak to run far even without any weight on its back. When it couldn't get up, he had killed it and took slices of meat for them to eat and a large piece of hide to make, repair, and replace moccasins. The other warrior, Klo-sen (Hair Rope), appeared a little later, his woman and two older boys, both near the age of apprentice warriors, running with him downriver.

That night was a time of thanking *Ussen* for helping us leave the place of suffering, protecting us on our separate trails, and bringing us together at this waterhole. Caballo Negro showed the others the good horses he had taken the night before, and when he gave one to each of the men and their women and one to Klo-sen's two boys, they were very happy. Gah and I helped the women and Klo-sen's sons dig a deep fire pit in the arroyo and gather brush to roast some of Sons-nah's horsemeat. After we ate, the men sat near the fire, smoked their cigarettes, and told stories of their escapes across the *llano* from Bosque Redondo.

Klo-sen's sons kept watch while we slept that night. At dawn, the warriors decided no Blue Coats were looking for us and that it was safe to ride by day. Riding in daylight, we didn't have to go slowly to follow the trail, so we traveled far that day. The women and children rode together in a group while the warriors stayed a few hundred yards on either side and behind us for our protection. Riding by day also allowed us to see from a long way off the best way into the mountains.

Near sunset, after riding hard all day, we came to the foothills and mesas of the Guadalupes and found a box canyon where we could make a fire so the women could cook without its light being seen. Gah and I played in the freezing dark while the meat cooked, and the warriors and the sons of Klo-sen watched for *vaquero*s and Blue Coats, but none appeared.

The next day we began the ride up canyons and ridges south into the Guadalupes and along their high ridges to the west. In some places, the trail was very steep, so steep the women and Klo-sen's sons had to get off and lead the animals while the small children rode. I looked many times over my right shoulder on the narrow trails winding along the top of nearly vertical ridges and saw nothing but jagged cliffs and boulders far below in the basin between us and the next range of mountains.

In the high country, the air was cool and junipers and piñons, tall, not like the twisted, stunted brush on the *llano.* In all my life, I had never seen so many kinds of plants or ridden or walked in the high places. The high places and long views far out over the mountains and *llano* sang their song to me. Those things I will never forget.

We rode the high rims covered with tall grass and scattered junipers as they swung south toward the highest peak in the mountains. As we rode, the high peak stayed to the west of our trail. That day we covered many miles and saw no sign of Cha's camp, only patches of snow to go with the cold, hard wind. The shadows grew long. Our trail carried us on the top of a mighty canyon twisting west far below. The canyon turned south and opened out on to the *llano*, stretching as far as I could see in the fading light. We were nearly all the way across the mountains, and still, no sign of Cha.

Straining my eyes, I saw a trail in the shadows that seemed nothing more than a deer path down into a canyon falling off the ridge toward a darkening crack in the earth made by the canyon walls and late shadows. Looking up, I thought I saw men watching us from behind boulders and junipers on the canyon walls. I told my mother, but she only shook her head for me to be quiet.

Caballo Negro stopped and stared down into the canyon, saying nothing. Sons-nah and Klo-sen did the same. We waited, and the horses watched, too, with their ears up. Soon, a man appeared on the little canyon trail, waved us toward him, and then disappeared. He disappeared so quickly and easily, I thought he must be a spirit man. My father led us down a steep winding trail. It grew steadily darker and harder to see, and then we came to a stretch that was so steep we had to get off the horses and lead them, but soon the trail flattened out, and we remounted. At the bottom of the ridge, there was a long flat place covered in long brown grama grass and scattered with tall junipers where a small stream flowed down one side. We smelled smoke and cooking meat and saw through the trees the flickering orange light from cooking fires.

We rode on but soon stopped in the middle of many brush lodges surrounded by warriors, women, and children who said nothing, only stared, their faces masks of indifference. A man with a broad chest, big muscular arms, and a round, flat face with a slash mouth and narrow black eyes stepped before us.

My father said, "*Dánt'e* (Greetings), Cha, brother of Santana, Roman, and Cadete. I am the warrior Caballo Negro." He swung his arm toward Sons-nah and Klo-sen. "These warriors speak for themselves. We ask to join you. We've suffered many seasons at the hands of the *Indah* at the place on the river to the east and north called Bosque Redondo. All Mescaleros at the Bosque left there five suns ago. The Blue Coats do not follow. Cadete goes to Santana.

"The *Indah* took all we owned, treated us like slaves, and said no more raids, even across the great river. Cadete said we should come to you because you're good at raiding *Indah* and *Nakai-yes* along the great river and the wagon roads from the east. He said you wanted more warriors. We will never again be *Indah* slaves. We'll stand, fight, and die, but always we will be men, not slaves. We will take what we need and help make Cha's band become even more feared. Do you want us, or do we move on?"

Cha's eyes looked at all of us, even Gah and me, one by one, his face revealing nothing. At last, he said, "You speak well, Caballo Negro. The sun rides west and hides its face. Care for your ponies, and feed your children. Eat. Rest. We'll talk later. Come to the fires. You're our guests, you are Mescalero, and we welcome you."

Cha's people were generous and offered us warm fires, hot food, places to sleep, and places to make our own fires and set up canvas-covered brush arbors or our ragged tipis in the days that followed. They listened, and they understood the stories of our hard lives at the hands of the Blue Coats. Cadete was right. Cha wanted the Bosque Redondo warriors who were ready to raid, fight, get their wealth back, and make the *Indah* suffer for the wrongs they had inflicted on the Mescaleros at Bosque Redondo. Cha welcomed our families and saw opportunities for more and bigger raids that he had seen only in his dreams.

An older couple, He Watches and his wife, Socorro, sheltered and fed us as if we were invited guests until Sons-ee-ah-ray raised her tipi and fed her family with plants she found and meat from Caballo Negro's hunting. Sons-ee-ah-ray's mother and father and two younger brothers had died at Bosque Redondo. Socorro and He Watches had lost an unmarried daughter during the Blue Coat attack on the *Shis-Indeh* at Canyon del Perro; their three sons, taking women in the band of Espejo in the Davis Mountains south, had left to live with their wives, who, as was the custom, lived near their mothers. Cha's people had given Socorro her name because she knew how to take corn and make the best tiswin, a weak beer, of anyone in the band.

■ ■ ■ ■

A few days after Sons-ee-ah-ray finished her tipi, the warriors from Bosque Redondo followed Cha on a raid along the big river a sun's ride to the west. That day, I played with Gah.

She said, "Let's play family. I am Woman; you are Warrior, and this doll my father carved is our baby. With all this grass and brush, I can build a brush arbor, and we won't have to pretend we have a tipi like we did at Bosque Redondo."

I thought it good fun to have a real brush arbor. I pretended to be a mighty warrior, crossed my arms, and spoke as I had seen Caballo Negro speak to my mother. "Woman, build a brush arbor, and keep our baby safe. I go to hunt and raid. I will bring meat and supplies."

Gah and her friends made little arbors out of bundles of long, yellow grama grass stalks. They built them under junipers within sight of their family fires. From the grass, they also made rough little baskets using weaving tricks their mothers had taught them. These they laid inside the small circles of rocks, which were supposed to be their family fires inside the brush arbors, and, like their mothers, they took care of their babies while they waited for their warriors to return from hunting or war.

I joined the arrow shooting and stone slinging games played by the young boys in Cha's camp. Two boys near my age from Cha's camp were new friends. By the time they reached apprentice warrior age, one would be called Kah (Arrow) and the other, Ko-do (Firefly). Our place for playing raiding, ambush, and war was on the far end of the camp in a broad grassy meadow farther down the canyon where it was easy to hide from pursuers and ambush those who hunted us. I did well, although I lost an arrow. I ambushed three enemies without being hit during their surprise ambush when their slings filled the air with small stones from the little stream of water.

While we waited to ambush our enemies, I found a gourd vine, brown and dried, the only gourds left, too small and bitter tasting for use by the village women, but just right for Gah's shelter. I was careful when I pulled two little pear-shaped gourds off the vine and slid them to the bottom of my bow and arrow sack.

I finally beat my last opponent, wounding him in an ambush, taking the rocks he called supplies. Then I ran through the junipers around the camp until I came to the little dwelling where Gah waited for me.

"Woman, I return from war and bring us meat and supplies."

She picked up the lumpy bow and arrow sack I had tossed on the ground in front of her and, smiling with delight, pulled out the gourds. "My man brings us good meat. I will roast it on the fire."

I nodded and, saying nothing, sat down by the circle of rocks while my woman put the gourds in the fire circle and pretended to stir and add to the stew that cooked there. Soon she took a forked stick and lifted a gourd off the fire. Laying it on a thin flat rock, she passed it to me saying, "Careful, husband, it still holds heat."

I pretended to chew on the gourd as if it were a piece of freshly roasted meat, smacking my lips and wiping my mouth with my hand. I rubbed my fingers, as if they were greasy from the meat, up and down my bare legs as I had seen Caballo Negro do after he ate from Sons-ee-ah-ray's cook pot, and I said, "My woman cooks good. The meat is good. It makes me strong for more raids."

Night was coming fast, ending our day of play. Shadows from the high mountains were falling over the camp, and other children in their little wickiups under the juniper trees began leaving for real meals at their mother's wickiups. Gah broke our pretend spell and said, "I will save this meat for tomorrow's stew. Now it is time to go to our mothers' fires."

I gave her my plate and gourd, and she put them away. She cradled our baby in her arms and nodded at me she was ready. Picking up my bow and arrow sack, I slid the bow in first, and then the arrows, careful not to break them. I hung the sack over my shoulder and, jerking my head toward the camp of our fathers, said, "Come."

She led the way, and I followed, since the back of the line was always the most dangerous place on a march.

CHAPTER 5
THE WARRIOR'S
JOURNEY BEGINS

Two years passed. Our family was changing, growing, and becoming a strong part of Cha's band. At age seven, I looked ten. Caballo Negro still called me Ish-kay-neh (Boy), my true name not yet given by my father, as was the custom in his family. Caballo Negro took many horses and cattle during Cha's raids, which made him admired throughout the camp and a respected voice in Cha's councils. Sons-ee-ah-ray, her belly swollen to the size of a ripe melon, carried my brother, her second child.

He Watches, admiring the strength and skill of Caballo Negro, and Socorro, wanting a daughter's help and the support of a good son-in-law, asked Caballo Negro if they might adopt Sons-ee-ah-ray as their daughter and thereby attach his family to the lodge of Socorro and He Watches. Supporting the old couple was an extra burden for Caballo Negro, but he saw them adding stability to our family's life by becoming my grandparents. Since Sons-ee-ah-ray was not their blood daughter, Caballo Negro wasn't required to observe the custom of never seeing his mother-in-law, an imposition that would require unusual vigilance since their tipis would be moved side by side for the convenience of the women. Even better, Socorro, an even-tempered woman who helped Sons-ee-ah-ray make fine pots and baskets for trade with other women, was not likely to harass Caballo for too much support.

My father knew my mother worked hard and needed help as we recovered from the short supplies and bad water we had endured at Bosque Redondo. He considered for many days taking a *Nakai-yi* or *Indah* woman as a slave to help her. But, slave women often took a lot of beating and time to train well, and they might have to be killed if they couldn't adapt to Apache life. He decided it best to join with the old couple, but kept them waiting a moon for his answer, knowing the longer he waited the more anxious they would become to have us and the less likely he would ever need to tell He Watches that Socorro asked for too much. At last, he told He Watches he agreed to the adoption. Sons-ee-ah-ray moved her tipi next to Socorro's and told me to call He Watches Grandfather.

He Watches had once been a mighty warrior in the camp of Cha until a bullet shattered his right knee during a raid on an hacienda by the great river. The knee didn't heal properly, and the joint stiffened and swelled with arthritis. Only the ball of his foot showed in the track of his right moccasin, and near that track was always the little round hole made by his staff as he hobbled about camp. He often rode a big, red mule, stolen in El Paso, up the steep path to the ridge top where he watched the wagon road for dust plumes in the far, bright distance telling of new supplies coming, ready for Cha's warriors to take, or more Blue Coats coming for his warriors to kill for rifles and ammunition. He Watches always took one of the younger boys with him to watch the road. After he studied a dust plume, sometimes for hours, with a brass telescope he called *Shináá Cho* (Big Eye), he sent the boy running back to camp with word that supplies and booty were coming for the taking. Cha would return with a couple of his lieutenants, study the dust plume with He Watches, decide on what was probably coming, and discuss what to do about it. When Cha was gone from the camp, He Watches built small, nearly smothered fires and sent towering smoke plumes high into the air signaling Cha to come for wagons or Blue Coats on the road.

I was still too young to guard the horses, but I often slipped off to watch them grazing in the mountains' high pastures. I particularly liked the pintos and the way the brown, white, and black patches lay dappled like colored shadows on their hides in golden sunlight. I learned to climb on a gentle pinto mare by grabbing hold of her mane, putting my foot on the elbow of her leg, and swinging up on her back. It was exhilarating, like being on top of the world, to watch the other horses from her back. I was never mean to the mare, and, from those days spent on her back with the grazing herd, she taught me much about the ways of horses.

One day, two suns after returning from a raid during which much booty was taken, Caballo Negro had a life changing talk with me. We had finished an evening meal sitting by the tipi fire. After rubbing the grease from his fingers onto his legs and high moccasins, he waited until I did the same, and then he reached behind himself and held up in the flickering orange firelight a buckskin quiver filled with real arrows and a sheathed, unstrung bow. The arrows were long, perfectly fletched with three feathers, and fixed with fire-hardened hardwood tips. I eyed the quiver with envy and wished I had it rather than my small toy one. At that time, I spent more time defending myself with a sling and small rocks in fighting games than shooting targets with those who had a real bow. When Caballo Negro handed me the quiver of arrows and sheathed bow, I was shocked and delighted.

"My son has passed through seven years," he said. "You have the size and strength of one who has passed through ten. This night I give you a man's bow. He Watches made the arrows. He will teach you how to make more. You have learned much from your child's bow. Now learn from a man's bow. To become a good warrior, you must first learn to hunt. I have watched you shoot at birds and squirrels, but you kill nothing. You shoot good, but you do not know how to hunt.

"Remember, even the smallest animals are not tame. They see you as soon as you come. You must see them first before they run away. You do not run up to birds, squirrels, or rabbits and shoot them. In hunting, you must go very carefully and make no noise with your feet against stones or grass. If you have to crawl to them, if you have to hide and wait a long time to kill them with your bow, then do it. It is the same with deer and antelope. Like the cougar, you must move slyly, carefully, and with much patience. Deer can see you before you see them, can smell you before you smell them, can hear you before you hear them. You must be very cautious."

My father stopped speaking, and I thought he had said all he wanted to say, but just as I started to get up, he said, "Now that you have a man's bow, I'll start training you. In a few years, you'll be as good as any man. Your mind will think good and think fast, and your legs will be strong, so nobody will outrun you. You will be admired for your skill, strength, and courage. You will bring food to the women, and you will not go hungry.

"Rise before tomorrow's sun comes. Run. Do this every day. Begin by running to the bottom of the canyon trail before you return. This running will be hard at first because you still have the legs of a child, still think like a child, and still control yourself like a child. When you're a man, you will run as a man, think as a man, and control yourself as a man. It's best you learn in your own way, but if you don't learn, I'll make you."

I nodded to show I understood, and said, "I will learn to run and think and control myself as a man."

Caballo Negro gave me a sad smile and said, "My son, no one helps you when you are a man. You must be strong. Rise early. Run hard. Make yourself strong. No one is your friend, not even the daughter of Sons-nah who still plays with you, not your mother, your father, or even Grandfather He Watches or Grandmother Socorro are your friends. Your legs are your friends. Your mind is your friend; your eyes are your friends; your hair is your friend; your hands are your friends. Use your friends well. Do something with them. When you are a man, you live with these things, and you think about them.

"Someday you will be in need, or you will be with people who have need. You'll have to get them something. When enemies attack you, disappear. Before they attack you, get them and bring them back dead. When your enemies are great, you be greater, and you kill them. You make our people, the *Shis-Indeh,* proud. Be a man of Power. Then all people will speak your name with respect and honor. Your stories will be told around the fire. This is the reason I speak to you this way: if you stay with the *Shis-Indeh,* they will all be for you, brothers, sisters, uncles. All in Mescalero camps will talk about you. If people speak my name, I want them to say my son is a fine man and does good work. I want all to find pride in you. If you are lazy, the *Shis-Indeh* will despise you. Do you understand, Ish-kay-neh? I speak these things from my heart."

I slowly nodded, feeling like I had just taken all the water from a big jar in one swallow. "Yes, Father, I understand. There is much to learn. I will begin making my body strong tomorrow. I'll run the trail to the lower canyon that leads to the *llano* and back. I will learn hunting and take many animals for mother's cook pot."

Caballo Negro grunted, "*Enjuh.* You'll make many mistakes. Learn from them. You'll make me proud when you learn and grow. He Watches also has something to give you."

He Watches had been drinking his cup of coffee across the fire from us. He lit a cigarette, its tobacco rolled in a corn shuck, Mexican style, and he blew the smoke in the four directions, and then gave it to Caballo Negro, who also smoked to the four directions and gave it back, and then he gave it to me to do the same. It was the first time I had smoked, and even though it burned my throat, I was very proud that these men believed I was ready to begin the work of learning to be a man, not just any man, but one the *Shis-Indeh* one day would be proud to call their own.

He Watches handed me a leather sheath from which protruded the bone handle of a fine, polished steel knife.

"This blade is strong. I took it from a brave man many seasons ago. He fought well and died with courage on the wagon road when I still ran and rode like a warrior. When you sleep, you should keep your weapons by your side. You never know when you will need them in fighting for mothers, brothers, sisters, fathers, and all the *Shis-Indeh*. Carry it when you run, and your legs will not be all that defends you. Carry it hunting, and animals will know its strength. Use it well, my son."

"This I will do, Grandfather," I said, bowing my head to him.

He Watches said, "Caballo Negro and I agree. I am your teacher in many things a man needs to know. Caballo Negro's wishes are my own. I will help you grow strong and grow to be a mighty warrior for *Shis-Indeh,* but it will be a long, hard ride, a warrior's journey. Are you ready?"

I looked in the eyes of old He Watches, saw the firelight flickering in them, and said, "I am ready, Grandfather."

Caballo Negro nodded. "So it begins, Ish-kay-neh. Be strong, and you will become a man. Show weakness and not even the *In-dah Lickoyee* will accept you."

Chapter 6
Shináá Cho

I had a hard time sleeping the night my father gave me that bow and old He Watches gave me the warrior's knife. I lay still and, staring up into the darkness, felt the handle of the long blade in the sheath beside me and wondered what a crippled old man might teach me about a warrior's skills. As I went to sleep, I decided it must be something special, something worth waiting and working for, perhaps even a special gift of Power from *Ussen*.

The dark outline of Caballo Negro pushing aside the tipi blanket door after returning from a visit to the bushes awakened me. Darkness outside the tipi was tinged with dawn's gray light, and a few birds were beginning their calls. *Time to run.* I left my warm blanket like smoke rising into the cold gray air, and tied the blade in its sheath around my waist, the blade so long that, by comparison to my height, it might have been a sword on a grown man. From the drinking jug, I took long, cold swallows of the sweet water I had brought to the tipi for my mother from the stream near the camp. I went outside and lifted my hands to the dawn, thanking *Ussen* for the coming day, singing the prayer my mother taught me.

From his blankets, Caballo Negro said in a low voice, "Run as far as you can today, and a little farther each new day. Learn to pace yourself as a warrior paces his horse. Run the watched trail down toward the *llano*. You are not yet strong enough to defend yourself against the *ndolkah* (cougar) who might try to carry you off for his morning meal. The guards will watch and help you if he comes. I will watch for your return. Now, go."

I ran down the path between the village tipis and along the trail toward the low canyon. At first, I ran too fast, and my breath came hard in gasps and wheezes, but, as dawn pushed the night aside, making it easy to see the path falling away toward the big black mouth of shadows from the low canyon walls opening before me, I found my rhythm and didn't labor as hard as when I started. I reached the steep part of the trail and ran down into the darkness that swallowed me. I ran too fast down the switchbacks into the low canyon. My breathing was fast and struggled to keep up with my racing heart.

At the end of the first switchbacks, I picked a juniper growing by the side of the trail to use as a reference marker for my run to go past the next day. I ran around it and headed back up the trail, feeling shaky and weak. Knowing it would be a hard climb, I took deep breaths and ran on. The distance from Cha's camp to the turnaround juniper was longer than I thought. Returning up the canyon trail, my legs churned as if caught in river mud. I thought, *Maybe I won't have strength to make it back to the camp unless I stop to rest.* The thought of stopping shamed me, and I kept running, no matter how weak I grew.

When the trail reached the higher plateau, a twisting pain began to grow in my side. The air was colder than in the lower canyon; every breath I took felt like fire filling my lungs, and my side cramped and hurt more with each step. I made each foot take one more step as I ran through camp to my mother's fire. Running was not fun as it had been the day before when I was just a little boy. The trail I ran now was hard and long, and it gave me great thirst.

Caballo Negro sat in front of mother's wickiup watching me come up the trail, sweat streaming down my body, very tired and weak. He nodded and said, *"Enjuh!"* as I staggered to the fire. "My son, running to the limit of your strength makes you grow strong."

He motioned me to sit beside him while he finished a bowl of stew made with meat from an *Indah* cow stolen in his last raid. My mother, her belly swollen with the new baby growing inside her, moved slowly. She had made a stew with wild onions, dried mesquite beans, potatoes, and *Nakai-yi* peppers she traded from another woman for one of her baskets. She gave me some water, filled my bowl with stew, and handed it to me, smiling, after I drank. I knew she was proud of me.

Caballo Negro smiled, too, his dark eyes studying me. "Not too much water so soon after a run. It will make you sick. Grow strong, and you will not need as much. Eat, take water again, and then rest a little. He Watches takes you today. He goes to his place on top of the mountain. Take your bow. Be ready when he comes. He waits on no boy."

I was so weak my hands were near to trembling, but I said with a rasping voice,

"I am ready." I slurped gravy from the edge of the bowl my mother had given me. I've never forgotten the hot, spicy tingle of her stew gravy sliding down my throat. Because I ate too fast, gravy ran from the corners of my mouth and down my jaw. I felt strength returning to my bones and joy coming to my heart as I wiped the gravy from my face. I knew I had done well. I had made my father proud.

Finished, I handed the bowl back to Sons-ee-ah-ray and said my thanks. She gave me a cup of strong coffee made from piñon nuts, and I sat with Caballo Negro, who was still drinking his coffee.

I didn't know the place where He Watches sat to watch the *llano.* Children were told to stay away from the high ridge above the camp. My mother had demanded I never go there alone. She said it was too easy for a little boy to fall off the rugged cliffs on the ridge crest. The climb to the top of He Watches' ridge filled me with surprise. Grandfather, crippled and using his staff, moved faster and stronger up the hard-to-see path than I did. I struggled for air when we came to the top of the world. He Watches stopped to let me catch up and see the unending *llano* far below that I had first seen in the dim light of dusk when we had come to Cha's camp two years before.

My eyes grew big. Just to the west, I saw the peaks the *Nakai-yes* called Guadalupe and El Capitán rise above us. To the east, beyond the mountains, water occasionally threw points of bright light at us. He Watches told me they came from the same river that ran by Bosque Redondo, the one the *Indah* called Pecos. At the bottom of the cliffs, ruts of an *Indah* wagon trail twisted through the foothills off to the east and threaded around a few mountains and back again to the *llano* heading for the great white salt beds to the west that the *Nakai-yes* and *Indah* had fought over many times.

He Watches led the way along the top of the ridge to a shelf of rocks on the edge of the cliffs. Rocks circled ashes and charcoal from earlier fires, and dry juniper branches and weed stalks were piled nearby to make more. He Watches climbed down the cliff side of the shelf rocks and disappeared. I climbed to the top of the shelf and looked over its edge expecting to see him on a ledge, but he was not there. Surprised, fear jumped in my guts. I thought he'd fallen, but then he called to me, "Come, Grandson, walk around the edge as I did."

I worked my way around the cliff side shelf

89

and discovered it formed a shallow cave about ten feet down the cliff face, facing due south. It was a shady place, and the air in its shadows cool. Several blankets smelling of smoke and showing a few scorched places lay stacked to one side along with three full water bladders, and toward the back, there was a small fire pit in a natural hollow in the rocks with firewood and an ax beside it. He Watches sat on a blanket in the shade against a big, smooth boulder, his stiff leg crooked out in front of him. He smiled and said, "Take a blanket, Grandson. The rocks are hard, and the day is long."

I opened one fold of a blanket, and spreading it beside him, sat down and pulled my bow and quiver of arrows over my head to lay them on the edge of the blanket. He Watches fished in a big leather pouch slung over his shoulder and brought out a yellow metal tube with a large, clear rock with a shiny, smooth, curved surface on one end and another like it but much smaller in a large, black circle on the other end. I had often heard stories from men sitting around the campfires of the power of his fetish. My heart raced with excitement at seeing it for the first time. He handed it to me.

"Grandson, take care you do not drop it. Do you know what it is?"

"Pesh-klitso (yellow iron)?"

He Watches smiled. "It is strong like pesh and colored like klitso, but it is different. The *Indah* do not dig in the ground like badgers for this pesh-klitso. It is the same pesh-klitso in the shoots-many-times rifles warriors take from the *Indah,* and I took it from a wagon driver on the road down there below us many years ago. He defended his wagon with a long knife when we ambushed it. His long knife wounded several warriors before he went down. I needed four arrows to kill him, the last in his throat. He was a great bear before wolves, a worthy opponent for a warrior, and he died well. I looked for weapons in his wagon, but found none as good as ours, only big, straight sticks of wood. These we burned. His cloth I gave to Socorro, who shared it with the other women in camp. I thought this the only thing worth taking. At first, like you, I thought it pesh-klitso. I learn it is not the same, but stronger, harder, not as easy to scratch with a blade.

"It took awhile to understand this thing. It grows long." He Watches took it back from me and pulled on the end with the small clear rock. The tube grew to the length of my arm. I watched with surprise and asked, "A war club that grows small

91

except for fighting?"

"I, too, thought that for a little while, but I never struck anything with it, for it has not enough weight to be a useful war club. One day I saw light pass through the big end and out the small one. Maybe, I thought, maybe the shiny ends are like the burning glass I saw an *Indah* use once to start a fire with sunlight. I looked in the little end and saw trees on the mountains far, far away. I could not tell there were even any trees there with my own eyes. This thing is big medicine. When I use it, I see things no one else sees. It helps me watch the road for Blue Coats and wagons with supplies. It helps protect the *Shis-Indeh.*" He turned the small end toward me and pointed toward a curve in the road.

"There is a big green bush there. Can you see it?"

I stared at the curve. "Maybe, I cannot tell for certain."

"Look at it through the *Shináá Cho,* and tell me what you see."

I held the small end of the tube to my eye. It took a moment to point *Shináá Cho* toward the right place. I saw a bush as if it were only steps away. I looked at the bend in the road from around the tube and then back through the *Shináá Cho.* I saw things I did not see with my eyes and, nodding, handed it back to He Watches.

"Truly, the *Shináá Cho* is powerful medicine."

"You speak true, Grandson. I use it often. Now you know how to use it if you have need, but take care when you do. The clear rocks on the ends are the sources of its power. If these rocks are broken, it will no longer have medicine. An *Indah,* who measured the land — why he wasted his time doing such a thing I never understood — taught me this. He showed me how to take it apart and make fire with the clear rocks and how when they were gone, it no longer had Power. For this, I let him live."

"Can I use it today?"

He Watches pointed toward a dark spot in the rough foothills far below us.

"Use the *Shináá Cho* and tell me what you see there."

I finally found the spot after squinting alongside the long barrel a few times to be sure it was pointed where I thought.

"I see . . . I see a cliff in shadows, and at its bottom, there is a river or maybe a big arroyo that runs in front of it. The top of the hill is flat, and the arroyo or river winds east and west among the hills, and the east end seems to swing back in this direction.

To the west of the cliff are small hills. They look like stacked circles of dough my mother fries when she makes bread."

He Watches nodded. "You describe the place good. You will be a powerful warrior one day. You have good eyes for important details for one so young. What if a great gaagé (raven) came and took you while you slept and left you on top of that flat top hill? You have never been there, and there is no one to help you. It is half a sun's run away from here. How would you find your way back?"

I looked at Grandfather and started to say I didn't know, but pride choked off the words. *If a question, then an answer. I know I can find it.* I stared at the flat top hill through the *Shináá Cho* and then looked for landmarks along the most direct path I might walk. I tried to imagine what the cliffs where we sat looked like from the flat top hill so far away and thought of what signs to look for that showed where the camp was.

I studied the scene for a long time before I said, "I know the camp sits near a high place. The arroyo by the high cliffs I see makes many great turns but moves toward the mountains here. I would follow it in this direction and save my strength rather than climb many hills. Perhaps I would find green spots where there is water. When close to the cliffs, I would search east and west looking for signs of horses and mules and follow their trails up into the mountains here. If it was night, I could look for signs of fires. I know of no other ways, Grandfather. Teach me."

Grandfather smiled and said, "You cannot walk along the sides of these mountains and expect to find a horse trail. The ground is too rocky, and has too many paths you might follow. If you found a real one after several suns of walking, you would have great luck. Instead, choose a trail or a path to a high place on the cliffs. Climb high. Climb to the top if you can. From there, you would see places you would recognize, and then you would know how to return to the camp. Listen to my words. Someday not far now, one of your manhood tests will come like this. He who cannot find his way home will be a long time becoming a man. Do you understand?"

I nodded. "I understand, Grandfather. It is a good lesson."

"Are you ready to learn something harder? Something that will take a long time to learn?"

"What can possibly take a long time to learn? Teach me, Grandfather. I am ready."

"Your father's name, Caballo Negro, you know that it is a *Nakai-yi* name, meaning Black Horse in their language. Why does your father take a *Nakai-yi* name and not one the Shish-Indeh gave him?"

The question had never entered my mind until He Watches asked it. I had always called my father Caballo Negro. As I thought about it, I realized that all of the best warriors in our camp used *Nakai-yi* names.

"I do not know, Grandfather. Why does he take this name?"

"The *Nakai-yes* fear the great warriors. They know who they are and give them names in their own language. It is a sign of respect, of honor. For Shish-Indeh warriors, it means our enemies fear them and know who they are. A warrior keeps that name because it is an honor, and he is recognized by the people that way. Perhaps someday you will have a *Nakai-yi* name. Do you want this?"

"Yes, Grandfather, I want this."

"*Enjuh.* If you are given such a name, you need to know what it means in the tongue of the *Nakai-yi.* Do you want to learn the words of the *Nakai-yi,* to speak in their tongue? It takes a long time and many lessons to do this."

96

"I am ready, Grandfather."

The old man smiled once more.

"Bueno."

I frowned, and the old man laughed and said, "Your first lesson in the tongue of the *Nakai-yes,* my son. *'Bueno'* means 'good.' "

I laughed and tried the unfamiliar word. "Beyeo . . . bue . . . eno . . . buen . . . *bueno.* Is that correct, Grandfather? *Bueno?"*

"You learn quickly, Ish-kay-neh. Today I will teach you the *Nakai-yi* words for colors. Remember them well."

He pointed at the sky and said, *"Azul."*

Chapter 7
Nah-kah-yen

Caballo Negro, finishing his stew, speared the last chunks of meat out of the gravy with his knife, slid the juice-dripping morsels in his mouth, and then drank the remaining gravy directly from the bowl. Wiping the grease from his mouth and rubbing his hands over his legs and high-top moccasins, he turned to me, now fourteen years old, and nodding toward the wickiup doorway, said, "Come." Outside, the cold night air puckered our skin making it prickle in the light from the falling sun, nearly gone.

We walked to our horses near a tall, ancient juniper. Caballo Negro tightened his saddle cinches and swung into the saddle in a smooth, cat-like leap. He waved his hand up, motioning for me to do the same.

My heart pounded with excitement as I tightened cinches for my black and white pinto and swung into the saddle. I had watched him mount many times and practiced how he did it. I could do a near perfect imitation of Caballo Negro's mount.

Caballo Negro said, "You have your knife and a bladder of water?"

"Yes, Father."

"Enjuh."

Guiding our horses to a spot outside the camp, we joined five mounted men and their sons, all about my age. Caballo Negro, a leading Cha warrior, spoke for the men.

"You who now take this long journey do well learning how to fight, hunt, and make war. You want to go on raids with warriors. You want to become warriors, prove you are men. In this trial, prove your skill and stamina, and you will come with us as apprentices. This run tells the warriors if you have grown strong enough and smart enough to enter manhood. It tells us if you can take care of yourselves if you become separated from a raiding party. The fastest among you might finish this run in four, maybe five, suns. Eat nothing; drink only water for the first two suns. After two suns, eat whatever you can catch or find. Follow your pony's path back to the camp. Every warrior knows the tracks of his own horse, even in a herd of others. Run only at night. Hide and rest in the day. Each warrior knows where to start his son. Be strong. Run hard. Soon Cha's warriors will know you as men. We ride."

We rode down the canyon trail to the *llano* covered in darkness and shadows made by light from myriad stars. Half the night passed before a fingernail moon rose above the Guadalupes to cast thin, sorry light on the mountain passes and *llano* brush.

For two days we rode south, staying out of sight, riding down arroyos, finding water at the hidden places, always avoiding exposure on the horizon, making little or no sound, until approaching the Davis Mountains with the sun fast falling into darkness, we began to separate and were soon lost to each other.

Caballo Negro led me up a small canyon to a natural water tank in a jumble of boulders surrounded by piñons. He directed me to care for my pinto and then to dig a small pit and make a fire in a bare place in the center of the boulders.

We sat by the fire and ate dried meat and fat pounded together with dried berries, mesquite beans, and piñon nuts that Sons-ee-ah-ray made for us. Caballo Negro studied me in the flickering light, and I could tell he felt pride in me. The other boys and I had been running every morning before sunrise, running for long hours in front of switches held by the warriors, who chased us. I had been fighting in sling and arrow battles with other boys without getting badly hurt. I hunted often and brought meat to Sons-ee-ah-ray's cook pot and could follow the tracks of a snake over hot rocks. I was ready for this last test before I became an apprentice warrior. Then after four successful raids as an apprentice, the warriors would accept me as a full-grown man, ready to take a woman when I had enough ponies, ready to make a child, ready for raids and war. The great circle of life, like the seasons returning, was closing ready to begin again.

Caballo Negro said, "My son, I have watched you and taught you through many circles of the seasons. You are ready for this trial. It won't be easy; keep your mind on what you do. Use the lessons you've learned in hard games and long hunts, and you'll do well. It's not important that you are first back to camp, but that you return without marks of foolish mistakes or from those of an enemy. If you can do this, then with another passing of the seasons, you will be a man, a *Shis-Indeh* warrior."

I looked Caballo Negro in the eye and

said, "I'm ready, Father. I will not fail. I'll make you proud. Soon I'll ride with the warriors."

Caballo Negro grunted and said, "*Enjuh.* This we will see. He Watches says you do the best in camp at finding and reading signs of wagons or Blue Coat soldiers on the road from the east. Return from this trial, and your name will become *Nah-kah-yen* (Keen-Sighted)."

I bowed my head in gratitude. I had often wondered how long I must carry my little boy name when many of my friends already had their adult names. "A good name, Father. I will take it with pride."

Caballo Negro nodded, "Use your powerful eyes to follow me and your pony home. Keep quiet as Cougar and smart as Coyote. Run in the night. Rest in the day, but not near water or deep shade. That is where *Nakai-yes* and other enemies will look for you. If you see someone and do not know who it is, stay hidden until they pass. When you are a man, you can build a smoky fire and hide where you can see them when they come to it. If friends, you can come out from hiding. If enemies, you attack them. If you don't know them, stay hidden until they leave."

He pointed out through the boulders

toward a black, ragged outline against the stars. "When the moon rises over those mountains, leave this place. Follow my trail. It will not be the same trail we followed here, but I will not hide the new one, and your pony follows mine. It will be an easy trail to follow. Give our horses their fill of water, and I leave you to your long run home."

I took the pinto and big black, watered them at the tank, and led them to where Caballo Negro waited. Swinging up on the black and taking the lead rope for the pinto, he said, "We'll wait for you in the mountains," and he disappeared back down the canyon.

I trembled inside with excitement at the thought of my new name and the long run. I went to the tank, filled my water bladder, and then sat by the dying fire, sharpening my knife and waiting for the moon to rise above the mountains' far, black edge.

True to his word, Caballo Negro left me an easy-to-follow trail even in the dark, one even an *Indah* or *Nakai-yi* might follow. I followed it across rough country filled with brushy flats, deep arroyos, and rolling hills with flat tops covered with grama grass, mesquite, yucca, and creosote bushes. As

the gray light of dawn drove the stars away,
I ran to the top of a high, flat-topped hill
covered by small thickets of mesquite and
piñon and stopped to rest and take note of
where I might be.

The sun rose, pouring its light like a liquid
gold seam across the horizon. Birds called
in sharp chirps from the brush and flew out
of their night perches in big fluttering flocks
from thickets of light green mesquite,
piñons, and junipers. *I am Nah-kah-yen,* I
thought, resolving to use my childhood
name no more, as I waited for the light to
grow bright enough to see the distant mountains.

I knew I ought to see the tops of mountains to the north and south, but in the gray
horizon haze and, later in the morning,
through shimmering mirages, it was impossible, and few signs, clumps of strong green
bushes or glints, in any direction, showed
any hints of water. High on a thermal,
circling, floating without effort, Buzzard
watched, waiting for me to make a mistake.

The trail of the pinto and big black moved
on through the brush toward the haze hiding the mountains. Even from the top of the
hill, I saw evidence of it out on the flats
swinging around the next hill. I found a
piñon tree in some tall grass, looked care-

fully to ensure it was not the resting place of a snake, and crawled under it to rest.

At midmorning, the shadows were growing shorter, the air growing warmer, when after a short nap, I crawled out from under my piñon to study the northern horizon in the full light of day. I was certain a bump I saw on the horizon had to be the highest mountain in the Guadalupes. I looked to the east of the bump and guessed Cha's camp location, knowing it ought to align with the general direction of Caballo Negro's trail. Even in the brighter light, no green brush stood out on the *llano* to show water, no dust in the shimmering air betrayed the presence of wagons or horses. I was alone. In the deep, reverent stillness, I lay back down under the piñon and slept again.

When the sun was passing halfway from the top of its arc into the edge of night, my eyes snapped open. The air was still and hot. Nothing moved. Except for the shadow positions around me, nothing had changed. Yet, something was not right. There! I heard the faint clink of iron on iron. Slowly, careful to disturb nothing around me, I sat up and surveyed the top of the hill and saw nothing. I rose up on my knees and looked down the hill to the *llano* and the trail north. My heart began to pound.

At the bottom of the hill, two *Indahs* in trader clothes and a Blue Coat soldier sat on their horses studying the trail left by Caballo Negro and talking among themselves. One of the *Indah* led a mule loaded with supplies. Tied across the pack frame along with the supplies was my friend, Kah (Arrow), one of the other boys running home.

Kah had earned his name because, of all the boys in camp, including me, his arrows rarely missed their targets. The day Kah was given his name, he had won a shooting contest by driving his arrow into the center of my arrow, which was already in the center of the target.

As I watched, questions filled my mind. *How did they catch Kah? Who are they? Where are they going? Are there others?* Kah showed no signs of torture even though his left eye was swollen shut and there was a long bruise down the side of his face. I saw raw, red places around Kah's wrists and ankles, which were tied with rawhide ropes.

As the men talked, I studied them carefully. One was ugly, like an animal with a big pile of hair growing at his nose, and wore a big-brimmed, black hat. Tall and lanky, he laughed as he spoke to the Blue

Coat and gestured toward Caballo Negro's trail. The other man rested easily in the saddle and had a narrow pinched face, which reminded me of a rat. His skin dark, probably from an Indian or a Mexican ancestor, he kept turning his head toward Kah to see how he reacted to what was being said. Both *Indah,* heavily armed with rifles and two pistols each, probably scouted for the Blue Coat. He Watches had told me of *Indah* scouts once when we watched a troop of cavalry pass far below us on the road from the east. The scouts rode outside the main Blue Coat column.

I knew Kah understood nothing they said. Although he had let himself get caught by a Blue Coat chief and two of his warriors, I imagined that he was determined to wait for his opportunity to escape and redeem himself by killing those who had taken him. The Blue Coat said something else to one of the scouts and then jerked his head southwest, leading his men, and Kah, along the middle of an arroyo and away from the trail left by Caballo Negro.

CHAPTER 8
FIRST BLOOD

I watched the Blue Coat lead the others down an arroyo meandering west. As they passed, I squatted by the piñon tree and decided what to do. *My father's instructions are to run following his pony's trail, to run it at night, and to find Cha's camp as fast as possible. Kah got himself caught; he must get himself free.* To try freeing Kah would run the risk of being caught or killed, something warriors rarely did except when there was no other choice, as when a friend called his name. I knew I ought to continue my own run north, but sitting in the shade of the piñon, I thought of Kah's family and our good times together when we had raced each other in the mountains, played with Sons-nah's daughter and the other girls, slung rocks and arrows at each other in staged fights, swapped arrows in bow shooting contests, hunted, and learned endless lessons from He Watches. *No, regardless of my own risk, I must not leave my friend a prisoner of the Blue Coat and his scouts.*

As the late afternoon sun began painting the sky, I ran down my hill and toward the arroyo the Blue Coat had taken. I followed their trail, wanting to run fast and catch up, but I paced myself, knowing I needed all my strength to free Kah and disappear from the searching eyes of the Blue Coat scouts.

I ran half the night following the Blue Coat trail until I finally saw a faint glow from a dying fire on the *llano* off toward the great river. I worked my way toward it, careful to keep the night breeze flowing into my face, remembering what Caballo Negro had told me about horses and mules, especially mules, raising alarms better than dogs after smelling or hearing the sounds of an intruder's approach.

I crept close enough to the dying fire to see two bodies wrapped in blankets lying near it and Kah with no blanket, his hands tied behind him, the end of the rope running from his hands, tying his feet together, and then to the tall scout who wrapped it around his wrist. The Blue Coat snored nearby. The quarter moon gave me enough light to see, but it took me awhile to find the rat-faced scout on watch, a rifle in the crook of his arm, and smoking a pipe near the horses and mule a hundred yards away.

Lying in the black, moonlight shadow of a big creosote bush, I studied the little camp and considered how best to retrieve Kah. It was going to be harder than I imagined when running down the arroyo. One mistake, and both of us might either be killed or caught and made slaves.

I crawled through the creosotes and mesquite, careful to avoid rattlesnakes and other night animals that would be hunting, until I was on the horse side of the camp. The mule, used to the Indian smell of Kah, didn't find it strange when I approached, my sharp knife slicing the rawhide hobble like fat on meat fresh off the fire. I slowly maneuvered her away from the other stock, keeping her body between Rat Face and me.

It took awhile for Rat Face to notice the mule had wandered nearly a quarter mile away from camp. I waited on the far side of the grazing mule and heard him swear in short temper and come for the wanderer.

He approached the mule slowly, not wanting to spook her and chase her for miles in the shadow-filled desert. He spoke softly to her. "Whoa, Sally. Where you goin'? There ain't no graze out here," until he grabbed her firmly under the chin to lead her back.

I'm not sure he even saw me rise off the ground like a shadow before I stuck the point of my long blade into his windpipe and slashed to the right. He opened his mouth to scream but only gurgled, drowning in his own blood as he collapsed sitting down, and then falling backwards, his head barely attached to his body.

I felt the drops of warm blood shower my face and body. I had killed my first man. With the night and surprise on my side, it had been easy. However, I felt no joy in killing the scout, rather it was more relief that now I had only two others with whom to deal. The new metallic smell of blood made the mule nervous. She bucked, kicked, and then trotted a few yards away, her eyes showing their whites. She was ready to run at the slightest provocation, but luckily didn't bray. I decided to let her calm down while I stripped the scout's body, taking his leather vest, bullet belt, pants belt, revolver and holster, and shoots-many-times rifle. I was tempted to take his boots, but they looked very old and worn, so I left them. I did collect his campaign hat, which seemed nearly new, a nice prize I could show off every day in the camp of Cha just by wearing it.

Soon, I began maneuvering the mule back

to the horses. They stopped grazing and stood watching, ears up in curiosity. They snorted a couple of times at the blood smell on me and the mule and then returned to finding grass hiding in the brush. Leaving the mule to graze with the horses, I crept back to the edge of the camp.

All that remained of the fire were a few orange coals turning to gray ash. The Blue Coat continued to snore, his right hand resting on his revolver. The scout's blankets were thrown aside; he was nowhere in sight, and his weapons were gone. I froze. I wished I knew how to operate the firearms I had taken from the rat-faced scout, but in Cha's camp only warriors had those. Ammunition was too hard to come by for apprentices to practice with firearms. A few yards away, I heard a cough, and the tall scout hawked phlegm and spat. I saw the scout's dark outline, and then heard his night water splatter against the sand. Like Wind, I was at the Blue Coat's blankets. His eyes fluttered open, but I was too quick for him and quietly cut his throat, moved back behind a greasewood bush, and left him lying as though sleeping on his side with his back to the scout's blanket.

The scout buttoned his canvas pants and made his way back to his blanket. At the fire, he checked the knots on the rope holding Kah before he crawled under his blanket and pulled his big revolver to hold against his chest before he lay back. He looked at where the Blue Coat lay snoring no more. I worried he might check him, for then it would be a hard struggle killing him. But he just smiled and shook his head, supposing, I guess, that no more snoring from the Blue Coat meant a better sleep for him. I waited until the sounds of sleep were on him and crept from behind my bush. Kah was watching him and saw me come. I killed the big scout, as I had the Blue Coat, this time Kah looking on and smiling.

When I cut the ropes holding Kah, he kicked his feet from the entangled ends and sat up rubbing the circulation back into his arms and legs. His wrists, raw from the tight rawhide that bound him, were slick and bleeding. I knew he didn't care; he was free. He found his knife sheathed in the belt of the tall *Indah* and pulled the clothes from the body as I washed the blood splatters from my face, hands, and arms with sand. We needed to get the blood off our bodies because when the sun came up and the blood had warmed, it would stink and call Buzzard to follow us, a sure pointer for prying eyes.

As I washed, I saw Kah ready to use his knife to mutilate the scout's body. I said, "My father is a great warrior, and he says he never cut a dead body. It is not good. There are better ways to make the living suffer and humiliate the dead."

Kah sheathed his knife and frowned. "How?"

I shrugged. "He says it depends on the situation and to always think about what you do and why you're doing it."

"What do you think we should do?"

We finished our sand baths and brushed the dust from our heads and shoulders. Off to the south coyotes were howling. "Take their clothes. Leave them here bare. Soon animals come and have a good meal. Tomorrow the buzzards will circle and fall on them. In days, there will be no trace of them, except maybe a few bones, nothing for their friends or chiefs to find. That will be good for us. You pull their clothes; I'll load the mule and saddle the horses. We'll ride the rest of the night. Find a place to hide for the day when the sun comes."

Kah nodded. "Your words are wise. I'll follow you."

CHAPTER 9
RIDE TO CHA'S CAMP

We rode away from the dead scouts and their Blue Coat chief. We rode in sand-filled and sometimes rocky arroyos, used stars to guide us toward the place of the rising sun, and then drifted north, working toward Cha's camp in the Guadalupes. As long glimmering shafts of light filled the eastern sky, we raced to a far hilltop to look for signs of water and a place to rest.

Soon bright yellow light over the edge of the far mountains came, and birds in the brush began their calls. I saw a dark green spot a short ride out on the *llano* and pointed toward it. Kah squinted, stared hard, and then nodded, smiling.

We rode slowly, careful not to show ourselves to anyone near the dark green brush. We stayed downwind and dismounted to crawl the last bowshot forward to look for enemy tracks, sniff the air for smoke and animals, and listen for the sounds of men

116

coming from sleep. No smell of smoke or horses. No sounds except wind in brush. No man tracks, Indeh or *Indah.* Nobody stood there, no one to challenge, no one to fight. Near the center of the green brush and weeds, water leaked from rocks and disappeared into the sand. We circled the water place looking for man tracks, but found only those of deer, quail, and coyotes. We stopped, sat down by the spring, and ate and let the horses and mule drink and graze before we moved away to sleep.

We looked in the supplies we had taken from the Blue Coat chief's camp and found things I knew the *Indah* call "cans." They had pictures of fruit and beans wrapped around them. We also found hard, tough bread. My mother never made bread this bad. Kah said he saw the *Indah* open the cans with their knives and that the pictures showed what was inside. He took a can with a picture of fruit and showed me how the *Indah* opened it. The fruit inside was good, the juice sweet. We ate fruit from three more cans, drank water, and filled water bladders and the *Indah* canteens we had taken. Giving the animals another drink, we tightened cinches and wiped out our tracks as we left. We went to a nearby hill as the sun began its ride across the sky

We hid the horses and mule in tall brush and crawled to the top of the hill where we rested and watched the watering hole for strangers. I said, "You rest first. I'll wake you when the shadows are short." Kah nodded and made a nest for himself in the tall grass and lay down.

His voice low, he said, "One day, brother, you will be a mighty warrior. Last night you attacked two *Indah* scouts and the Blue Coat chief and killed all. You have not yet ridden on apprentice raids, and you're not yet fifteen Seasons of Green Leaves. Maybe the warriors won't make you ride as an apprentice. Maybe they'll accept you already as one of them. You saved my life and destroyed our enemies. I'm forever in your debt."

A breeze rippled through the grass, and I said, "There is no debt between friends. I cannot leave you to the *Indah Lickoyee.* My father said before I started this run that I'm now called Nah-kah-yen, the Keen-Sighted."

A big grasshopper landed on a grass stem near Kah's head. He reached up and flipped it away. We do not eat grasshoppers.

"Ha!" Kah said. "At last you have a name, and a good one, too. It's past the time you had a man's name. You'll have much honor in the camp when I tell the story of what you did. You'll need your name for the warriors to show you the respect you deserve."

I said, "Yes, I have pride in my new name. The warriors will use it and know who to ask to watch for them. But now let's speak of yesterday. Tell me how the Blue Coat and his scouts caught you."

Kah shook his head. "I'm a fool. I didn't do what my father told me and ran in the daytime. I thought if I returned first, no one would care if I had disobeyed his instructions.

"I was running in a deep arroyo when I saw the Blue Coat and his scouts. We were both surprised. I turned like Rabbit and ran back down the arroyo, but the rat-faced one pulled out his *reata* (rawhide lasso) and caught and tied me before the others came. The other scout pulled his knife to cut my throat, but the Blue Coat chief stopped him. They tied me to the mule's carry frame and rode on west with me tied on that mule in disgrace. I was downwind of the *Indah* the whole day and gagged many times from the smell of them. They stink and are very nasty people. Do they ever bathe? I prayed to *Ussen* to give me Power to kill them and get away. He sent you. I thanked Him."

I looked over my shoulder and smiled at

Kah. "All you say, brother, is true. The *In-dah* and Blue Coat smelled even worse when I killed them. I don't know if *Ussen* used me to free you. We were lucky. Rest. I can see clearly the tallest mountain near where Cha camps. A good ride tonight, and we'll be there with the sun tomorrow."

Kah shrugged his shoulders and made a bad face. "I thought I might go first on apprentice raids. Now I will be lucky to go on any raids at all. Still, I have much luck. You saw me a prisoner and freed me. Perhaps my name ought to be Lucky."

The day was quiet as the sun rode across the sky. No one appeared at the waterhole all day, not even deer or coyotes. As the sun hid behind the far mountains, we ate more *Indah* supplies, fed the horses and mule, and then led them to the waterhole for a last drink before we rode on.

The night was nearly gone when we crossed the *Indah* wagon road from the east and saw the black outline of the tallest peak blotting out the stars behind it. We followed the road toward the rising sun until we found the mountain washout that goes to Cha's canyon camp. Dawn was coming, and the cold air falling down the mountain valleys made us shiver. With our skin like that of plucked birds, we were anxious for the fires and hot food in our mothers' wickiups.

As we approached the camp, I saw trail guards watching us, their faces pushed forward in the low light, their eyes, squinting in frowns, curious. We rode to the ancient juniper near Sons-ee-ah-ray's wickiup and began unsaddling the horses and unloading the mule. Women at their morning fires and children playing turned to watch us, but not for too long, for that was bad manners. Their eyes seemed to ask what we were doing returning with horses and supplies as if we had been on a raid. We had left the camp boys and returned warriors. I knew they must think it a strange sight that had a good story. Then I saw Caballo Negro coming and wondered if he planned to beat me or praise me.

"*Dánt'e,* Father. We return from the long run."

"*Dánt'e.* You are the first to return. You bring horses and supplies. How is this?"

I heard the whisper of anger in Caballo Negro's voice and felt fear for the first time since we left camp for the long run.

Kah spoke up. "I did not listen to my father and ran with the sun. An *Indah* Blue Coat and two scouts caught me, tied me to their mule's carry frame, and rode west.

121

Nah-kah-yen saw them with me and followed. He killed them in their sleep and freed me. We took their clothes, supplies, and horses and mule. We rode for two nights and watched our back trail. No one followed. Nah-kah-yen is a strong warrior. He has much courage."

Caballo Negro stared at us and said, "Hmmph. Hobble the animals and leave what you have taken here. It will be given away later. Kah, go to your mother's wickiup. Nah-kah-yen, come. Your morning meal is on your mother's fire."

I met Kah's eyes and then followed Caballo Negro to my mother's wickiup, not sure what might happen to us for disobeying our instructions.

Caballo Negro motioned for me to sit with him for a meal of meat and acorn bread. He waited until I ate, and we drank piñon nut coffee before he said, "Is this story Kah tells true? Three *Indah,* a Blue Coat and two scouts, you killed with only your knife?"

I said nothing, only nodding that the story was true. I knew the less I said, the fewer reasons for my punishment.

Caballo Negro's face cracked into a smile wider than the horizon. "*Enjuh!* You have much to learn, but you are ready to join the warriors on their next ride. Soon you will be a man. My heart swells with pride that Nah-kah-yen is my son."

CHAPTER 10
FIRST RAID

I sat with He Watches in his place at the top of the ridge above the camp. He used the *Shináá Cho* to study the road far to the east. I saw only a tiny white streak on the eastern road. The old man handed me the telescope and pointed toward it with his nose. I looked and saw the white streak turn into a heavy dust plume. Lines of specks moving through the dust freight said wagons drawn by mules. He Watches smiled.

"Your first raid as a warrior comes, my son. The wagons will be here in two, maybe three suns. Will you ride on this raid? Are you ready?"

I lowered the *Shináá Cho* and smiled with him.

"Grandfather, many seasons I've waited for this day. I gave the People the guns and blankets I took after I killed the *Indah*s and Blue Coat to free Kah. I kept nothing for myself. Caballo Negro said I ought to join the warriors because I gave away all I took and alone killed the *Indah*s and Blue Coat. Still, the warriors said I must go on four war raids as an apprentice as much as luck for them as training for me. This I did. I passed all the apprentice tests that showed I'm worthy of trust in battle and that I always do what I'm told. Now the warriors say I am ready. They've all accepted me to their counsel. I have only my bow and arrows and knife for weapons, but they're enough. You've taught me how to make arrows that fly where I send them. You gave me the knife that has already killed three *Indah*s by my hand. I'm ready."

The old man nodded. "*Enjuh.* Yes, you're ready. Go. Bring Cha and Caballo Negro. They will see these great freight wagons for themselves and make a plan to take them."

Sleep came many times, but did not stay, the night before we left on that raid. I was more nervous than when I went on my first raid as an apprentice. On the apprentice raids, I had guarded and held horses, made fires, found water, cooked, and guarded booty. I had even learned to drive a wagon and *Indah* cattle after a raid on a ranch south of the Davis Mountains, but there was no great danger to boys doing apprentice work.

Now, in two suns, I would fight as a man among warriors, take a share of the loot, kill the hated *Indah*s and *Nakai-yes,* and risk being killed. I wanted to do well and take weapons and loot from the men I killed. Across the wickiup, Caballo Negro slept without moving, breathing easily, breathing deeply, and beside him, Sons-ee-ah-ray rested her hand on my little brother, his mouth open, sleeping gurgles filling his throat. Caballo Negro had decided to call him Little Rabbit until he had a proper name. I smiled. Little Rabbit was already asking Caballo Negro when he could join the warriors on a raid.

I remembered when Little Rabbit was born. Sons-ee-ah-ray was gone from the wickiup most of the day and Socorro with her. When she returned, she carried Little Rabbit in her arms, and Socorro made the evening meal. He was red and wrinkled, his black hair sticking out in all directions, but he held on to the finger I offered him like a river turtle biting a stick. He was strong, learned my mother's lessons quickly, and stayed quiet even when he wanted her breast or the moss catching his dirt needed changing. He was a good baby. I had liked him even then.

Before dawn, our raiding party left the camp by twos and threes and rode out of the mountains and down many scattered trails through the *llano* brush to avoid raising dust plumes that might warn the approaching freighters. They were in no hurry, and took care to reach the appointed spot by the time of shortest shadows.

Years of Apache ambushes on the rising sun road kept the freighters wary and on guard, especially in places like foothill passes or deep arroyos near the mountains. Regardless of how wary the freighters, or the site, quickness and surprise were the most important parts of a good ambush. Cha picked a place where the road crossed two arroyos about four hundred yards apart. About fifty yards downstream, the arroyos turned and ran together to form a single deep arroyo running parallel to the road on its south side. A low, brush-covered hill rose above the road on the east side. On the west side of the road stood a higher hill, its top not more than two hundred yards away from the middle of the road.

Cha made a dry camp in the arroyo running behind the hill on the north side. We worked in the brilliant, searing afternoon

127

sun, digging pits and covering them with brush on both sides of the road near where it crossed the arroyos. Only a man knowing where to look might see us lurking under the brush ready to bring death. Kah and Ko-do, my boyhood friends on their first apprentice raid, watched over the horses and brought water from a distant tank to the camp.

The ambush plan used three bowmen hiding in the brush near each side of the road, and their work was to kill the outriders and wagon drivers before they could escape the trap. I would be among them. At Cha's signal, warriors hiding in the pits were to shoot the lead mules and their drivers in the first and last wagons and trap the other wagons between them. Cha placed marksmen on top of the north and south hills to pick off any freighters who survived the first round of shots and arrows. He sent his least experienced warriors and poorest shots to hide in the brush and seal off the road from those who tried to escape back the way they came. Caballo Negro and his warriors hid in the brush a hundred yards past the second arroyo, ready to take any who tried to escape by running forward.

Near the end of the day, Cha flashed a "ready" mirror signal toward He Watches' lookout. Immediately, He Watches flashed back, "They come. One day more."

That night there were no fires to warm aching muscles and tired backs. The warriors wrapped in blankets and ate what their women had sent with them. Men guarded the camp from the top of the north hill. Kah and Ko-do took turns watching the horses.

The warriors had made Kah wait until I finished my apprenticeship before he started his, the price he paid for disobeying his father by running in the day and being caught by enemies. Kah said he didn't mind starting his apprenticeship late and was thankful I rescued him from the *Indah*s and Blue Coat, thankful for the opportunity to be an apprentice and eventually become a warrior.

Caballo Negro sat with me, smoked a cigarette to the four directions, and said, "You'll do well tomorrow killing the *Indah* and *Nakai-yes* on the wagons."

"I'll make you proud, Father."

"I know it will be so. Don't fear meeting the enemy face to face, but be sly like Coyote in the fight. Do nothing foolish."

I nodded, wondering how to be brave and smart at the same time. I finished my meal and went to check my pony. He was a fine painted one, steady around gunfire, and, if need be, willing to run all day until its heart burst. I swapped breath with it and felt my courage grow.

The camp stayed quiet and the men smoked, alone with their thoughts, alone with *Ussen.* I watered some brush down in the arroyo, found a spot near a big creosote bush, and rolled up into my blanket. There was excitement in my guts but no fear. Soon I slept.

Many of the warriors already sat by the fire eating when my eyes crept open in the cold light of a pink sky in early dawn. I shivered as I shook out and rolled my blanket before eating what I had left from the night before.

Caballo Negro and Cha sat together, eating, talking, and drawing maps in the sand with pieces of dry yucca stalk. When the morning grew to full light, Cha ordered Kah and Ko-do to take the horses far up an adjoining arroyo, so the freighters wouldn't hear them, and the team mules wouldn't smell them. He planned to direct the attack from the north side hill, so he told the warriors to take the places he'd assigned the day before while he watched the distant road using an old pair of Army binoculars.

Near the south side of the road, I found a

little shade under a creosote bush and, motionless, waited for Cha's signal. The air grew hot; the day, blindingly bright. Caballo Negro had taught me to put stripes of black charcoal powder mixed with a little fat under my eyes and across the bridge of my nose to lessen the glare, and this lesson, like so many others, had become second nature, ingrained as part of the ritual preparation for a raid. It was quiet; even the birds made no noise. The only thing moving was the sun following its arc across the sky.

Though now accepted as a man, I still often thought as a boy. I thought of the plunder I might take and wondered when to begin looking for a woman. Sons-nah's daughter, my childhood friend I called Gah, had had her Haheh, her puberty ceremony, already. She was marriageable. I liked her, and though we had spoken often and played together before her Haheh, after her Haheh, she had not spoken to me at all. Two warriors ready for a wife had already left horses in front of her mother's lodge. I smiled at the memory. She had not taken either pony to water, signaling her rejection of her suitors and that she still waited for the one she wanted or the one her mother would make her take. I thought, *Maybe she waits for me. If this raid and two or three oth-*

ers provide many presents for the band and increase my own fortune, I might yet have her. Only Ussen knows. Only Ussen, the great creator God of the Apaches, knows the lives of men.

I saw a flash of light from the top on the northern hill. My wandering thoughts ended. Down the road, in the shimmering distance, dust, the kind wagons made, rose high in the still, shimmering air. I dimly saw riders on either side of a single wagon outlined against the brown cloud.

My heart thumping, I pulled my bow from its sheath, and rising to my knees, strung it. I pulled four arrows tipped with iron points from my quiver, checked each point, laid one arrow across the bow, and held the others under the fingers of my left hand gripping the bow's handle.

Through the roiling air, shapes of the outriders and wagons grew clearer. A faint tinkle from harness chains and the creaks of the wagon frames broke the stillness as the mules pulling the wagons strained forward up the slight grade toward the arroyo.

The south side outrider, his rifle across the pommel of his saddle, rode up to the edge of the first arroyo and looked up and down it, as if it were an *Indah* road, and then rose in his stirrups to look over to the second one.

I froze like a hunted rabbit and willed myself to be invisible to the outrider.

He rode over to the second arroyo and looked at it. A second outrider came and looked over the arroyos as the first rider had. He studied the north and south hills on either side of the road.

The first outrider returned to join the second one and they spoke together in the *Indah* tongue, too low for me to understand, as they pointed to boulders and cactus on the hills and looked at the sand and bushes on the sides of the arroyos where Apaches might hide.

The second outrider waved his rifle forward down the road for the wagons to continue. The outriders crossed the first arroyo, one on each side of the road, and stopped near where the road began dipping into the second arroyo. They turned their horses, and cocking their rifles, watched the other riders and the wagons advance across the dip in the road made by the first arroyo.

The wagons struggled forward. The dust in the road was deep, making the going slow, and the mules strained against their harnesses to move the heavy wagons. I was so close I could smell the nasty, sweating bodies of the drivers and the good clean sweat of the mules. There were ten wagons in all, big freight wagons, their sides high, their front wheels tall as a man's shoulders, the back wheels even higher. Six mules pulled each wagon, and six heavily armed outriders, three to each side of the wagon train, served as guards.

I remember my mouth was very dry, and as the breeze changed, the smell of gourd flowers was strong in my nose. I studied the *Indah* I intended to kill, a heavyset man broad across the shoulders, a big black flat-brimmed hat shading his eyes. His boots were the kind the Blue Coat who had taken Kah had worn, jet black, their shafts reaching above his knee. A lever rifle lay across the pommel of his saddle, and he carried two holstered revolvers, a heavy hunting knife pushed under a belt around his waist, and a bandolier of bullets across his left shoulder. Surveying the area around the road slowly, he stared directly at the bush where I stood unmoving, bow ready, frozen in place, willing myself invisible. He looked directly at other warriors and did not see them either. He waved the wagons on and began turning his horse around to cross the second arroyo. A man of experience, but not enough, he made the fatal mistake of not seeing us hidden in front of his eyes.

Waiting for Cha's signal, I thought, *Indahs abused me, abused all Mescaleros at Bosque Redondo when I was a little child. Now in less than a season, I've killed three, and you're next. Many more Indahs will die before I'm finished. Now Cha, let's spill blood.*

A flash of bright light from Cha's signaling mirror hit the outrider in the face. He reflexively looked toward it, turning his attention away from the direction of the road, and raised his rifle to his shoulder. Light also hit the other outriders' faces, and they, too, turned toward the sources.

I bent my bow to my arm's full length, the sinew bindings around the arrowhead rough, rubbing the top of my forefinger. I made a small step to the right for a clear shot, paused to steady my body, and released the arrow, the whispering bowstring slapping my wrist protector with a solid snapping sound. The arrow streaked forward straight and true striking the outrider with a solid thump a little below his armpit, slicing through his chest and punching through to his other side, the arrowhead pinning his arm to his side. Making no sound, limp and empty like a drained water bladder, the rider slumped off his horse, dead before he hit the sand.

Time slowed, flowing like wild honey from

a clay jar. I saw arrows hit the other two outriders, their faces filled with a look of startled surprise as they, too, making no sound, fell from their horses. Instantly, the quiet day changed to the roar and noise of attack as the forward drivers were popping their whips and whistling for their mules to charge forward. Men on the seats beside the drivers raised their rifles and fired wildly into the brush on the south side of the road. I felt the air next to my head swirl my hair as one of the wild shots from the wagons nearly ended my warrior's life before it began.

Warriors sprang out of the pits next to the road firing rifles and bows. They killed the lead mules starting to race forward, and then turned their fire on the wagon drivers who were frantically trying to make the mules run forward. But the mules were balking, smelling the blood of their brothers, confused by the roar and smoke of rifles and screams of the Apaches running for them. I sent arrows into two of the drivers. Bullets fired from the north and south hills were like sharp knives slicing through new green grass as they cut down outriders and drivers.

Deadly fire poured into the wagons, leaving big, splinter-filled holes from bullets passing through wagon boxes where a few surviving drivers and their passengers took shelter before they died hiding behind the wood. Only one man left the wagons. He desperately tried to run back down the road until he collapsed on the arroyo bank against its light brown sand, bloody wounds scattered across his back.

The firing stopped. Warriors under Caballo Negro, waiting across the second arroyo, ran forward to cut the dead mules loose from their harnesses and unchain the surviving teams to bring them forward to the dry camp behind the north hill. Dead men hung over the sides of the wagons, all shot several times, a few carrying multicolored arrows buried in their throats, chests, or backs.

Caballo Negro and his warriors cleared the top of the arroyo bank and charged the wagons. A few survivors hidden in the wagons managed an occasional shot. I saw an *Indah* rise from the third wagon, sight his rifle, and fire at Caballo Negro. A bright red streak appeared as if by magic on the upper arm of Caballo Negro. Continuing to sight the rifle in place, the shooter, in the space of half of a breath, levered another round, but before he pulled the trigger, my arrow struck him in the side of his head.

His eyes bulged as life left him like a startled bird taking wing. His hands froze around his rifle, and he fell backwards across the wagon seat. Caballo Negro shook his rifle toward me in thanks. The warriors walked among the *Indah*s, ready to cut throats of those still alive.

It was a great victory — all the *Indah* dead, and no Mescalero with more than minor flesh wounds. The air smelled of death, smelled of men killed violently, the pungent smell of blood mixed with the stench of loose bowels. I looked up into the deep, blue, afternoon sky and saw the great black buzzards already sailing high, growing in number, and waiting for their turn at the dead *Indah* bodies.

The wagon train had been hauling supplies such as I had seen in trading posts and stores in the land of the *Nakai-yes*. There were bolts of cloth, canned goods, sweet candy, tobacco, grain, and many heavy pieces of iron tools used to scratch in gardens made in this hard, dusty land. Two of the wagons were nearly empty, holding only a few tools. I thought, *Probably for digging a load of salt in the great salt flats another sun west.* The warriors loaded the mules with all the supplies they could carry.

Cha and Caballo Negro looked over

weapons carried by the *Indah,* picking out guns they wanted for themselves, and leaving the rest for the other warriors to choose. Caballo Negro took a holster holding a revolver with a long barrel and a lever rifle, old, but well cared for. The rifle's barrel was long and black with no fore stock, and its lever fit into yellow metal like the *Shináá Cho* used. I remembered that a Comanche visiting Cha's camp had carried such a rifle and, in English he had learned from a trader, had fondly called it "Yellow Boy."

Caballo Negro levered a round into the rifle's chamber and sighted at a distant target before lowering it and easing the hammer down to a safe position. I felt a strong affection for the rifle, though I had not even touched it, and I wished I had found and kept it. Still, I knew that, after a few more raids, it would be my turn to choose before the less experienced warriors. As it was, I got canned goods, blankets, cloth, and knives for my mother and a box of long, skinny, rolled tobacco sticks for myself.

Caballo Negro searched among the wagons until he found a small, very heavy wooden box. He gave it to me and said, "Keep this with your other trophies. I'll show you what is in it when the time comes."

The sun was racing for the night when we finished loading the mules and set fire to the wagons, sending tall columns of greasy, black smoke high into the still, late afternoon air.

We left the dead *Indah* naked and smeared with blood where they fell. After taunts by Cha and a few other warriors that they didn't have stomachs to be warriors, Kah and Ko-do mutilated several bodies. Caballo Negro watched, shook his head, and said to me, "Never do that unless there is a useful purpose. Men enter the land of the grandfathers carrying only the marks of their death, not the way their bodies are butchered after their ghosts leave. Only weak men do such things to please themselves. They are afraid of the living and taunt the dead. Ghosts of the dead repay disrespect. It is an evil thing to suffer the dead's revenge. Cha makes a mistake teaching Kah and Ko-do to do this. Remember what I tell you."

The warriors divided the pack mules between them and rode away fanning out in all directions, leaving too many trails to follow. We met later in the night at the trail to the canyon camp. Cha sent a rider to tell the camp of our great victory and to have the women prepare for a feast. The next night, there would be many gifts for everyone and much dancing. I hoped the eligible girls would show their interest and choose to dance with me for a small gift.

CHAPTER 11
JUANITA

As moonlight began spilling over the mountains, we came near our camp, where women holding torches formed lines on each side of the trail. When the first warrior, leading a pair of mules loaded with booty, appeared, they broke into songs and calls welcoming the "mighty warriors returning, the men bringing us gifts." When the singing began, He Watches lighted a big fire in the wood and brush the women and children had gathered for the victory dance, and old men on its west side began a slow drumming thump on a big, stiff buffalo hide and sang victory songs.

The warriors rode to their wickiups where their women, sons, daughters, and slaves unloaded their booty and cared for their horses and mules. The women greeted the men modestly and let them wash and eat while they looked through the loot, picked out what they needed or wanted to keep,

143

and left the rest to be given away. The big fire grew as the old ones and young children heaped more brush on it, driving the aging night's chill away, making the circle of light larger. As flames leapt toward the stars, the drumming grew more intense and the songs louder.

The Fierce Dance began. First four men, one for north, south, east, and west, circled the fire, then together formed a line, a wheel spoke, that circled the fire. Then four more men joined them in a repetition of the first pattern, and then four more. Soon all the men who had been on the raid were in the spokes of the wheel turning about the fire.

Someone called a man's name, one especially brave in the raid, then another was called, and with each new name, the men gave a great shout of *"Enjuh!"* as the women ululated in high warbles while the warrior's deeds were sung. When a man's name was called, he left the group of dancers, moved into the open space closer to the fire, and danced alone, reenacting his bravery in the raid. Then, before returning to the warriors in the dance, he left the circle of light, and returned with what he would give away. He put the gifts on the east side of the fire opposite the drummers and singers and told the People to help themselves.

To my surprise, I heard my name, a deep rumbling voice singing:

"Nah-kah-yen I know what you did.
"You did a great thing.
"With a bow, you faced a man with a many
   shoots rifle.
"With a bow, you killed him.
"With a bow, you killed another man.
"With a bow, you stopped his shot at
   Caballo Negro.
"Nah-kah-yen, you did a great thing.
"Nah-kah-yen, I know what you did."

I left the men in the outer circle of warriors to dance next to the fire in its brightest orange and yellow light, my feet pounding the dust, and pulling an imaginary bow and making my worst war face as I released my arrows. Each time I shot an arrow, the men and surrounding crowd shouted, "Ho!" After four times around the fire, I slipped out of the ring of dancers to bring back an ax, a shovel, and some blankets for the People.

When all the warriors whose names were sung had danced, the women formed a circle, rotating east to west outside the circle of the men, who stayed close to the fire circling east to west also and facing them.

They sang songs of war and loss and of sharing wealth taken from enemies.

As a new shift of drummers took up the beat, the men left the circle and sat down, and a new dance began, the Wheel Dance. Single women formed in pairs and made a spoke wheel rotating east to west around the fire. Once the wheel was turning, each pair of women took turns leaving the fire to tap the men they wanted for dancing partners. Then the women and their partners returned to the wheel, faced each other about a yard apart, and danced an easy timed step a few forward and less back so the wheel turned slowly around the fire.

Although I was weary to the point of exhaustion, I sat on the west side of the fire with other young men who wanted to dance. This was my first opportunity to dance in a partner dance and learn if Sons-nah's daughter had any interest in me. I saw her pair with Juanita, a girl I knew from the Bosque Redondo days who was a year younger than I was. She and Sons-nah's daughter, who was now called Deer Woman because of her speed afoot and her large doe-like eyes, had shared the same Haheh ceremony two years earlier. Before the Bosque Redondo days, Juanita's mother, who was a tall, beautiful *Nakai-yi* woman named Maria Valesquez, had been taken by Juanita's father, Porico (White Horse), during a raid across the great river in Chihuahua. It took over a year for the *Nakai-yes* to find her, and they had offered to ransom her back, but she wouldn't go. She had chosen to live with Porico as his wife.

Juanita was born after the first Ghost Face Season at Bosque Redondo. She had been too young to play with me much back then. I liked Juanita, though. She had matured into a good-looking woman with a ripe body made for having and nourishing children, but she didn't stir me like Deer Woman.

The turn came for Deer Woman and Juanita to choose partners, and they left the wheel of women and men and moved in my direction. I felt weary no more, and my heart fluttered in anticipation as I saw Deer Woman smile at me. My muscles tensed, ready to stand when she tapped my shoulder, but she slipped past me and tapped an older boy, tall and slender, one with many horses, one who had even taken a scalp, one who already had a *Nakai-yi* name, Delgadito.

I bowed my head, stared at the ground, and swallowed back the bile of disappointment filling my throat. Deer Woman had no interest in me after all. Then I felt a solid tap on my shoulder, and raising my eyes, I looked into the dancing eyes and bright, white smile of Juanita. I smiled back, genuinely glad she had chosen me, and sprang up to join her. *Who knows women's thoughts about men?*

The wheel turned slowly. Three steps forward, two steps back, three steps forward, two steps back. I kept my eyes on Juanita's, and she locked her eyes on mine. I tried to remember all I knew about her and wondered why she had picked me. However, it was impolite to ask a woman that question, and besides, one dance meant nothing.

Juanita and I danced until the sun's coming light set fire to the edges of the high, dark ridges of the canyon walls. I studied her brown, smooth skin, square jaw, long crow's wing hair that rippled and flashed in the firelight, and most of all, her brown eyes that never left me. The longer we danced, the more I felt a strong attraction for her and wondered how I had missed noticing her sooner.

When the Wheel Dance ended, we stood awkwardly for a moment as I frantically thought of something meaningful I might say to her.

"Juanita, you are a good dancer. It is good that you tapped me. I hope you do it again.

I see Porico and Maria by the drummers. Will you wait with them while I bring you a present?"

She shyly looked down and murmured, "Yes, I'll wait. I'll wait a long time for a good dancer and a brave man for whom there are songs."

I smiled and felt my chest grow large with her words, then nodded and said, "Soon I come."

I turned from her and strode toward Sons-ee-ah-ray's wickiup. In my loot, I found one of the hunting knives I had kept for myself and started to leave when I thought, *All the women have knives. What can I give her that is special?* I looked back and saw a heavy, wool blanket, blue with fancy geometric designs in red and green. The nights were cold, and it would keep her warm. I left the knife and took the blanket, folding it over my arm.

I found Juanita with Maria and Porico, standing near the drummers who had stopped for a while, and lifted the blanket to offer Juanita. I nodded at Maria and Porico, who stood with crossed arms watching me, as I placed the blanket in Juanita's hands.

"I'm proud to give you this blanket. It will keep you warm in the cold Ghost Face nights and cool nights of New Green Leaves."

She smiled and, glancing at Porico and Maria, said, "You are generous and thoughtful with your gift, Nah-kah-yen. I accept it with a happy heart."

I held her brown eyes for a moment, then nodded, and turning away, walked toward my mother's wickiup, more weary, but more exhilarated than I could ever remember.

I slept all day and into the night without even getting up to visit the bushes. My eyes finally opened, and, staring at the stars through the wickiup smoke hole, I realized the night approached dawn. I listened to the sleeping sounds of my family for a moment, and then my near-to-overflowing bladder demanded relief, so I walked out into the cold air.

When I returned, I tied my hair back, drank deeply from the water jar gourd, slipped on my high shaft moccasins, tied my knife around my waist, and slipped outside for my prayer to *Ussen* and then to run. Five days had passed since my last run, and I felt a need, a compulsion, to feel the rhythm of my body in motion on the winding canyon trails.

The sun cast long shadows down the

canyon walls, calling the birds to sing and my mind to thought. I reveled in the feel and pull of my youth and the strength in my lungs and legs as I ran. I thought of the dance with Juanita and what it might mean and smiled. I thought of the destruction of the wagon train and the men I had killed with my arrows and strong bow. As Caballo Negro had instructed me, I had disfigured no corpse as Kah and Ko-do had done. Kah had made a bad start on the trail to becoming a man, and Cha had shown himself a poor chief teaching him to do it.

The memory of Deer Woman smiling and walking past me to choose Delgadito made me feel angry at first, but then I relaxed and shook my head. Delgadito was a successful warrior ready to take a wife, and that made him someone she ought to consider. Still, Delgadito was not reluctant to tell stories about the *Nakai-yi* women he took, often brutally, after raids across the great river. I thought, *Deer Woman had better take care in her choices of suitors. Delgadito has no honor when it comes to women. A man of honor doesn't force women who are taken in raids. Still, what do I care?* I had danced with Juanita, and she had said we would dance again. She was a fine woman who signaled her interest in me in a good and proper way.

Perhaps . . . but then, who knew of the future of such things?

The sun was well above the mountains, and the air warming when I returned, tired but relaxed, to Sons-ee-ah-ray's fire. The smell of fry bread from her big iron skillet was intoxicating. Caballo Negro, eating a big piece wrapped around a strip of meat, waved to me.

His cheeks full, Caballo Negro said, "Sit. Eat. You do well to run. Young warriors become lazy after a raid. That is a good way to die in the next raid."

I took the large piece of fry bread and meat my mother handed me. "I had a good run. I don't feel right unless I run every day I can."

"You danced long and well with Porico's daughter. Does she interest you?"

"Yes, she's a good woman. I like her. I liked dancing with her."

"*Enjuh.* She is built to make strong children, her eyes are kind, and I see she works hard with her little sister, Moon on the Water, to help Maria. Porico is a great warrior who has killed many *Indah* and *Nakai-yes.* Her children will have his power in their blood as well as yours and mine. Wait two Seasons of Many Leaves before you take a pony to Maria's wickiup. You'll have many more raids by then and will be able to afford a good bride price. Tell Juanita your intention in a season. If she wants you, she'll wait. If it is for you, Maria will let her wait. This I know. In the time between now and your asking, stay out of the bushes with her. I don't want Porico ready to kill you. Be a man of honor with the woman you want. Don't be like Delgadito and steal the bride price of every woman who has eyes for you."

"What has Delgadito done?"

"He talked your friend from your boyhood days, Deer Woman, into the bushes the other night after they danced. Sons-nah and his wife drank too much tiswin to watch her. She was eager like a mare in heat and didn't take much convincing. I hear Delgadito laughs with his friends and says Deer Woman expects he will marry her now because she wore him out in the bushes. Maybe wife number two, but not the first, ever, he says. If Sons-nah finds out what happened, Delgadito will be a gelding and will not need a wife."

I slowly chewed my bread and meat as I listened to Caballo Negro. I felt bad that Deer Woman had made a bad mistake with Delgadito. She expected what he wouldn't deliver and would be disappointed at her life. On the other hand, it sounded like Caballo Negro had already talked to Porico and Maria about Juanita. One Wheel Dance did not make a couple ready to marry. Still, I knew my father's words were wise, if not premature. I thought, *I would never take a woman to the bushes, even if I planned to keep her. Taking a woman without marriage first shows disrespect for her and lowers the bride price due her family. Besides, a good woman never does that anyway.*

From deep in my thoughts, I heard Caballo Negro speaking words that slowly penetrated my consciousness.

". . . driver might have killed me if your arrow had not filled his skull. Already a strong warrior, one who will be wanted on raids and in wars against the *Indah* and *Nakai-yes,* you shoot well; your bow, strong, powerful. But a warrior needs a weapon with long reach. I have presents for you to increase your power."

I looked up in surprise and my heart raced as if I were still running when Caballo Negro handed me the Yellow Boy rifle and the long-barreled revolver, still in its holster, that he had taken from the wagon train.

CHAPTER 12
FIRST SHOTS

Caballo Negro and He Watches took me to a canyon west of the low canyon trail to teach me how to load and fire the Yellow Boy rifle and the pistol taken in the wagon train raid. They had me bring the small, heavy wooden box Caballo Negro had given me during that raid.

We stopped in a canyon with nearly vertical walls winding north. Juniper, scattered across the bottom of the canyon, offered shade, so we made a camp there in its cool, dark shadows. He Watches showed us a small burbling spring nearby, its cold water springing from the rocks with a life of its own but leaving only a damp spot when it disappeared in its sandy wash.

We spread a blanket in the shade and sat down. Caballo Negro, his muscles bulging with the weight, heaved the small box into place in front of us. He slid his knife blade into the tight, narrow crack where the top joined the sides, carefully prying the top up, its long straight nails looking like a demon's crooked teeth as it slowly raised up, the nails against the wood squeaking and groaning. Inside, we found small, brightly colored boxes made of the stuff the *Indah* call cardboard, each box fitting together perfectly to fill the much larger wooden box. I stared with interest, wondering what the boxes held.

His fingers like an eagle's talons gripping the edges of a box, Caballo Negro pulled it straight up and out of the wooden box. He gave it to me, took another, gave it to He Watches, and then took one for himself.

I hefted the box, surprised at its weight, more like a rock of the same size than a block of wood. Caballo Negro showed me how to lift off its top. Inside, four neatly aligned rows contained shiny, short pesh-klitso tubes. Lifting one out, I saw it had a short gray tip on one end. It looked like the bullets Caballo Negro put in his shoots-many-times rifle.

Caballo Negro said, "The *Indah* who make this type pesh-e-gar call it a rifle, and they make these pesh-klitso tubes with the gray heads. The *Indah* call them cartridges or bullets. Guns shoot them. Learn these and other *Indah* words used with this weapon. Some day you may have to trade for them and ask for them in the *Indah* tongue. Do you understand what I tell you?"

I nodded. "Yes, Father, I understand." I turned to He Watches and asked, "What are the *Nakai-yi* words for them? You have not told me."

He Watches grinned. "The *Nakai-yi* say rifle, same as the *Indah,* but for cartridges, they say *cartuchos.*"

Caballo Negro took a cartridge and held it end-to-end between his thumb and fore-finger. "These give the rifle its power. The gray heads are the bullets it shoots. Without them, this rifle is only good for a club. Even if the rifle has a belly full of these, it cannot shoot them if it is broken or dirty.

"Warriors risk their lives on raids to get cartridges, and some die. But, we cannot fight the *Indah,* cannot raid effectively, and cannot win wars without them. Don't waste them. Be sure the cartridges you use are the right length and circle size. Be sure they are made for your rifle. They must not be too small or too big or your rifle will not work. If you don't use the right kind of cartridge, the rifle can explode in your hands and send you to the grandfathers. These boxes of cartridges I know are the right ones. They have the same *Indah* symbol on the box that is on the barrel of the rifle. See, the symbol looks like two forked twigs side-by-side, and there is the same symbol here on the barrel of the rifle. The *Indah* call the two forked twigs side-by-side forty-four. You will be wise to learn these symbols. Remember this forty-four cartridge when you raid against or bargain with the *Indah.* There are other parts and words you must learn. Take care of your rifle. Clean and oil it often. I'll show you how to do this. If it breaks and will not shoot, you'll have to find another. This is all I have to say. Do you understand my words?"

"I hear you and understand your words. I will remember them." The words were hard to learn at first, but I held them fast in my memory. I knew my life might one day depend on them.

I had held the rifle since it had been given to me that morning. The feel of it in my hands gave me as much pleasure as a man might have for the feel of his woman or holding his baby child. Its shiny golden receiver gave me pleasure, shiny enough to see my reflection as I saw it in a bowl of still water. Its long black barrels gave me pleasure, one on top of the other, the bottom one having a long slit cut in it until the slit was within a hand's width of the end of the barrel. I even enjoyed the smell of its gun oil and the bits of unseen gunpowder clinging to it. I carried it in the crook of my left arm as I rode. That day, as I sat on a blanket, legs crossed, with Caballo Negro and He Watches, it rested across the top of my thighs.

Caballo Negro curled his fingers toward the palm of his hand, motioning for me to give him the rifle. I handed it to him butt first. Caballo Negro took the rifle, saying, "Now I'll show you how to load and shoot it."

He held the rifle erect, resting the stock butt on the blanket, and pulled the lever up until it stopped and was parallel to the ground. He turned the rifle so I saw how pulling the lever down pushed the hammer back and how pulling the lever up raised the loading elevator, carrying a cartridge in the receiver until it aligned with the open breech of the barrel. He pulled the lever down again and carefully laid the cartridge he took out of the box on the loading elevator. When he pulled the lever back up, the elevator went up and at the same time a rod pushed the cartridge into the top barrel, and the end of the rod covered the barrel breech.

Caballo Negro sighted the rifle toward a

rock on a cliff wall on the far side. He squeezed the trigger and the hammer snapped forward. I flinched at the unexpected, overpowering boom that hurt my ears when the rifle fired. Caballo Negro and He Watches laughed. They said they had done the same thing the first time they were shown how a many-shots-rifle works. He Watches held out two small balls of piñon gum in his open palm to me.

"When you shoot many times, use these in your ears. If you do not, you will not be able to hear like you should for a time, and an enemy may come without you hearing him."

Without moving the lever, Caballo Negro pulled the hammer back with his thumb until it clicked about halfway back. He stopped at the click and released the hammer. It didn't move. He squeezed on the trigger, but it didn't move. He explained that, even fully loaded, the rifle did not fire until the hammer was pulled back all the way until it clicked a second time. He pulled it back to the second click and squeezed the trigger again, and the hammer snapped forward as before.

Next, he put his thumb on a flat piece of yellow iron just above the yellow receiver at the end of the second barrel with the slit cut in it. I saw there was a coil of iron inside the second barrel and that the spaces between the coils began to vanish as Caballo Negro pushed the flat piece of yellow iron up toward the end of the slit. The coils completely disappeared when the yellow iron reached the end of the slit. Caballo Negro held the yellow iron tight and turned the end of the barrel in a west to east motion, and the end of the barrel rotated open to expose the opening of the barrel on the bottom. He let go of the twisted end piece and it stayed in place.

"Now we'll fill the belly of the rifle with cartridges."

He tilted the rifle so it made a shallow angle to the ground and began sliding cartridges, their brass first, down the empty tube with the slit. He counted as bullets slid down the tube until he reached fourteen, and having filled the tube, stopped. Then he twisted the barrel end back into place and slowly lowered the end of the yellow iron down on the cartridges, which held it within a knuckle-joint length of the where the barrel twisted to open. The stack of cartridges, easy to see in the tube slit, looked like a golden arrow, the gray bullets making identifying bands down its length.

"Now the rifle's belly is filled with cartridges. You have only to move the lever out and back to take a bullet from the belly barrel and put it in the shooting barrel to make it ready to fire."

Caballo Negro pointed at the hammer, fully cocked, and then at the closed barrel breech where the cartridge had disappeared from the loading elevator. He held the hammer under the web between his forefinger and thumb, and squeezing the trigger slowly, eased the hammer down, then pulled it back to half cock, and stopped so the rifle could not be fired.

"Do you understand what I have shown you?"

I nodded. Caballo Negro, careful to keep his finger off the trigger, cycled the lever fourteen times and let the ejected cartridges fall on the blanket. He motioned me to pick them all up.

"How many cartridges came out of the rifle?"

"Fourteen."

"Good. That is what I loaded. Always count your cartridges. One day it might save your life." Caballo Negro handed the rifle to me. "Now you do all the things I did, and always keep the barrel pointed away from anyone else unless you intend to kill them. Sometimes a cartridge can hide from you, and the rifle will fire when you are not ready. You must be careful. But first, look along the barrel top."

A hand's width down the length of the barrel from the loading gate opening squatted a small rectangular piece of black iron with a notch cut above the center of the barrel. At the end of the barrel was a short, vertical blade.

"The rifle will shoot a bullet where you point it when your eye on what you wish to shoot makes the blade on the end of the barrel lie in the middle of the notch and the blade's top is at the top of the top of the notch. Do you understand what I have told you?"

I nodded, not entirely certain I was telling Caballo Negro the truth. I then went through all the motions of loading and unloading the rifle while Caballo Negro and He Watches rested their eyes in the shade under the high canyon wall. The precise feel of the weapon was a joy, a pleasure I'd never known before, as I let the cartridges slide down the loading barrel and then ejected them by cycling the lever up and down. As my father had instructed, I was careful to count the bullets as I loaded and picked them up, always counting, so I didn't lose any.

■ ■ ■ ■

Disappointment filled my soul when I fired my first shot at a target and saw a little geyser of dust scatter more than the length of a forearm away from the stone for which I'd aimed.

Caballo Negro, watching with his arms crossed, grunted, "Hmmph. Lever another cartridge and try again. Do not squeeze the trigger unless the v-notch and front blade hold on the rock."

Another shot, another miss, this one struck even farther from the rock and high. I levered another round and shot, then another and another, faster and faster until the barrel filled with cartridges was empty, and the rifle barrel burned my hand. I hadn't hit the target rock a single time. I felt sick and angry. This beautiful weapon was of no use to me. I was far more accurate and deadly with my bow than this *Indah* rifle. I wanted to throw it on the ground, walk away, and never see it again. But it was Caballo Negro's gift, and I would never dishonor my father that way.

Caballo Negro nodded toward the blanket. "Put the rifle on the blanket and buckle the revolver belt and holster around your waist. I will show you how to use the revolver, and then we will return to camp."

I saw the disappointment in Caballo Negro's eyes and swallowed the ball of cactus thorns in my throat as I strapped on the revolver.

CHAPTER 13
RUFUS PIKE

When I returned from my morning run the next day, Caballo Negro and He Watches sat by the fire eating. Our ponies were tied under the tall juniper near Sons-ee-ah-ray's wickiup.

Caballo Negro nodded toward the cook pot and said, "After you eat, we'll go. Bring your rifle, pistol, and the box filled with cartridges. I have trail food ready."

Puzzled, since Caballo Negro had not said anything earlier about a trip, I asked, "Where are we going?"

"To a man of honor, who teaches you how to shoot good, who teaches you how to deal with the *Indah* in days coming."

"Where is this man? What is his name?"

"His ranch is four days west and north. He is called Roofoos Peek. Eat. Soon we go. Soon your rifle misses no more. Soon you know the ways of the *Indah* and can bargain with them for cartridges and help your

People deal with them."

We rode the canyon trail out of the mountains until we crossed the *Indah* east-west wagon road. To keep out of sight from anyone on the wagon road, we stayed in the brush just to the south and followed the road west around the southern end of the Guadalupes, across the fiery salt flats and then across the spare, thin desert toward the great river. Circling around villages and Blue Coat forts, we took nothing, and passed unseen and silent through the land. After two days, we came to the great river, and staying on the east side, rode north around the greatest village I had ever seen. The *Indah* and *Nakai-yes* called it El Paso. It spread out on both sides of the river, and many *Nakai-yes* and *Indah*s camped there.

Camping for the night in the mountains above the village, we used a small fire in a deeper than usual fire pit hidden in the rocks to drive away the cold night. I didn't like the camp. I had a hard time seeing the stars, and scattered across the mountains were big bright fires in the camps of men Caballo Negro called miners, men who scratched holes in the ground like Badger, foolish men looking for pesh-klitso, looking for the metal they called gold, metal *Ussen*

168

says we can take only without digging.

Before the sun, we rode out of the mountains the *Indah* called Franklin and stayed north in the trees and brush along the great river. When the sun was halfway to the time of shortest shadows, we left the great river and rode east through tall, dark green creosote bushes toward the jagged mountains the *Indah* called the Organs. As the sun swung past the time of shortest shadows, we rode up a rocky wagon trail toward a canyon running back into the mountains. The canyon's entrance, guarded by a house the color of old salt weed and two other gray buildings, looked out over the valley from at least a third of the way up the mountains. Looking west, back over my shoulder, I saw a line of mountains breaking above the horizon maybe two days' ride away.

Near the house was a large, gray iron holding tank half the height of a man and nearly as wide as two tall men across. Water, carried in a wooden trough that snaked back up the canyon, pooled there. I followed its form with my eyes toward a pile of rocks across a wash against the south side cliffs. Caballo Negro rode up to the holding tank and we let the horses drink. He studied the house and outbuildings with arms crossed, leaning back a little in his saddle while his pinto sipped the fine, clear water.

He Watches' eyes darted from one shadow to the next, the fingers of his right hand passing through the lever loop of his rifle, his index finger near the trigger guard, and his thumb on the hammer. I saw Caballo Negro relaxing as if he sat next to Sons-ee-ah-ray's wickiup, so I relaxed. My eyes roamed over the canyon walls, the house, and the two outbuildings, one a place of shade for horses and mules, and one a small house with its door hanging open barely big enough for one man to sit inside. Cattle up the canyon were bawling, and there was a young gray mule in the corral, her ears up, watching us as if we carried socorro for her next meal.

Soon the house door opened, and an *Indah* stepped out onto the shaded porch. He carried the biggest rifle I had ever seen. Its barrel was maybe two hand-widths longer than the one for my rifle, its receiver, wider. It had no lever and no barrel to hold cartridges. The *Indah* chewed on something in his cheek, and with his friendly, alert eyes taking in every detail, he rested the big rifle in the crook of his left arm. Wisps of hair sticking out from under his campaign hat had streaks of gray, and his black and gray speckled beard had streaks of brown flowing on his chin like tiny rivers escaping from the dam of his lower lip, and he wore a thing balanced on his nose holding small clear rocks like the ones on the end of the *Shináá Cho*. I had learned the *Indah* called the thing "glasses" and suddenly I recalled seeing it on the noses of a few Blue Coats when I was a child at Bosque Redondo.

The *Indah* stared at Caballo Negro for a few moments and then broke into a big grin, saying in the *Indah* language, "Well, I'll be damned. You Caballo Negro? Ain't seen ya in years. Ain't seen ya since ya was a pup. Come back to finish what ya started? I'm still here, aye God, jess like I tol' ye I'd be. You wanna have a go at 'er, I'm a ready."

Caballo Negro smiled and held up his hand, palm out, and, although I knew he understood the *Indah* words, he replied in Spanish, which he knew much better and which He Watches spoke well. "No fight today, Roofoos Peek." He swung his arm toward He Watches and me. "These *hombres* are my son, Nah-kah-yen, and his grandfather, He Watches. Speak in the words of the *Nakai-yes* so they'll understand you."

Rufus Pike nodded toward us and said in Spanish something like, "Howdy, boys. Git off them stolen ponies and sit a spell. I'll whip us up somethin' to eat here in a bit."

We slid off our ponies, tied the reins to the fence near the holding tank, and, following Caballo Negro, walked to Rufus' porch and sat down in its shade. Rufus spat a long stream of brown juice into the yard, swiped the back of his hand across his beard, and sat down in the porch shade with his back against the house wall, facing us with the butt of his long rifle planted squarely between his feet, the barrel resting on his shoulder. He Watches and Caballo Negro kept their rifles in the crooks of their arms, but when I saw the way Rufus Pike held his rifle, I tried to hold mine the same way.

We sat for a long time not saying anything as the sun lighted the distant clouds with many colors and slowly disappeared for the night.

Rufus broke the long silence. "Can I get you fellers something to drink? Got some coffee in the pot on the stove, it's a little strong now, but you'll probably like it."

Caballo Negro said, "Whiskey?"

"Now you know I ain't got no whiskey for no Apaches. You boys is used to drinkin' tiswin. It ain't too strong. Whiskey is too much for you to handle the way you swallower it down so fast."

"Hmmph. Then I drink your coffee."

"Good. I'll get ya some. These boys want any?"

"Hmmph. We'll all drink coffee. Then we'll talk. You agree, Roofoos?"

Rufus stood, using his rifle to push himself up, groaning under stiff joints slow to unbend, and said as he opened the door, "Yes, sir, I agree. Back in minute with some cups and the coffee pot."

He brought four blue-speckled, enameled cups and poured hot, syrupy brew into each. We all slurped the coffee, sounding like horses at water after a hard run. Caballo Negro and He Watches looked toward the far mountains to the west at the last blaze of colored glory. I studied this *Indah* and wondered how Caballo Negro knew him and why he was so special in teaching a man to shoot a rifle. I was puzzled. My People killed *Indah* where we found them. I knew I had a lot to learn about *Indah* and rifles.

Crickets and peepers down by the tank and wash had already begun tuning up when Caballo Negro turned from watching the far horizon disappear in the dusk and said, "Now we talk, Roofoos Pike?"

"Since you ain't aimin' to rip me a new

one this visit, reckon we can. What's on yore mind, amigo?"

Caballo Negro nodded toward me.

"My son is young, but a strong and powerful warrior. I gave him his first rifle and showed him how to load and shoot. After I said, 'You shoot,' he shot and missed many times. He never hits targets up close and never hits ones far. I bring him to Roofoos Peek before he learns bad ways to shoot and never shoots straight. You never miss with your rifle. You know how to shoot from far away. You shoot today, kill tomorrow. You can kill a man so far away he never sees you, never hears the gun that kills him. Teach Nah-kah-yen to shoot, to send bullets straight up close, to send bullets true from far away. You make him always shoot good. You do this, Roofoos Peek?"

Rufus slowly chewed his wad of tobacco, and then turned his eyes from Caballo Negro to me and the Yellow Boy Henry rifle leaning against my chest. Rufus thought awhile, chewed some, spat again in the yard, and turned his gaze again to Caballo Negro.

"What's in it fer me?"

Caballo Negro nodded. I knew he liked the way Rufus looked him in the eye and spoke straight to the point.

"You do this, Roofoos Peek, you teach

Nah-kah-yen to shoot the Yellow Boy rifle fast and straight, close and far, and I'll never come for you. I'll no longer claim rights of trial with you. The Apaches will never raid or attack Roofoos Peek if you give water for horses and meat for the trail."

Rufus spat again in the yard as the evening light grew dim and the cold air rolled off the mountaintops and down into the flats and canyons. He wiped his mouth with the back of his hand and groomed his big moustache with his thumb and forefinger, and said, "Aw right. I think that there is a fair bargain. I'll do 'er, but it's gonna take at least another case of cartridges and about three moons of time. Ya want me to teach him 'bout that pistola he's packin', too?"

"Hmmm. You show how to shoot rifle. No pistolero unless he teaches himself. You understand, Roofoos Peek?"

"I do. My feedbag's 'bout empty. They's plenty of eats on the stove. You boys camp where it's comfortable for ya. Come back here an' I'll give ya supper. Good spot to camp is up the canyon there where the spring water is dammed up and you'n take a little swim to git the trail dust off if you want. When you're ready, come on back, and we'll eat and talk a spell."

Caballo Negro nodded at me and He

Watches, and we all stood up as if pulled by the same string.

"We return *pronto,* Roofoos Peek."

CHAPTER 14
FIRST LESSON

Rufus fed us steak and beans. We sat on the porch's rough-cut lumber, our legs crossed, eating out of battered pie pans with our knives and big soupspoons. We were hungry. The steak filled our mouths, and the juices from the meat ran down our chins as we grunted in pleasure and slowly chewed the remains of a tough old bull that had tried to gore Rufus once too often.

Rufus watched us eat and appeared to study me as I sat back in the shadows made by the rising moon. I wondered if he was impressed with my jet-black hair, woven in a long braid that reached my waist. Since he was to be my teacher, I tried to project strength and self-control and returned his gaze without fear.

When we finished supper with good belches of appreciation all around, Rufus poured another round of coffee in the blue-speckled cups and carried the ancient, dented pot back inside. He soon returned from the shack's dim interior to sit on the porch edge with us, cut a chew, and watch the lights twinkling in the villages and ranch houses along the Rio Grande valley.

When Rufus pulled his twist of tobacco, Caballo Negro and He Watches pulled corn shuck wrappers and bags of tobacco out of their vest pockets to roll cigarettes. Caballo Negro snapped a big red head phosphorous match to life with his thumbnail and lighted the cigarettes.

Rufus watched with raised brows and with a grin and said, "I ain't never seen an Indian strike a match like that before. Where'd you learn that trick?"

Caballo blew smoke to the four directions and then blew a long draw straight up into the still night air. He said, "Hmmph. I found a *vaquero* at his camp one night. He made fire with his thumb at the end of the little stick. I watched close. The little sticks make fire for cooking, fire for four maybe five cigarillos. I killed him when sun came and took guns, saddle, pony, good boots, good sombrero, and the little fire sticks. The *vaquero* makes fire no more."

Rufus puffed his cheeks, blew, and shook his head. "Shore glad I ain't got nothin' you're a watchin' . . . Have I?"

Caballo Negro grinned, took another long draw from his cigarette, blew the smoke out through his nose, and shook his head. At the far end of the porch, I produced an ugly, short, black cigar, about a hand-span long, narrow and slim, but tapered, shaped like a baseball bat. I said in my best Spanish, "Will you bring fire for this *tobaho* also, *Padre*?"

Rufus grinned at the surprise on Caballo Negro's face as he reached in his pocket and pulled another match, snapped it with his thumbnail, and lit my *tobaho*. I puffed on it hard until it had a good coal and blew the smoke to the four directions. The cigar smelled acrid and harsh, not smooth like the cigarettes, and Rufus' nose wrinkled. The other two ignored the smell of my cigar, as if by doing so, its stink might go away. It was my first real smoke, and I thought it left an ugly taste in my mouth, but I would rather have been tortured than to admit I didn't like it.

Rufus asked, "Where'd you get that nasty ceegar, Nah-kah-yen?"

They all looked at me as I puffed on it, even though I felt a little sick and woozy. "I found a box of many on a wagon train."

Rufus nodded. "Well, don't smoke too many of them things. They stink and'll ruin your wind."

I looked at Caballo Negro and He Watches, who shrugged their shoulders. I, a man, made smoking my choice.

We sat with Rufus and told stories of fights and raids, and Rufus gave us the latest gossip of what had gone on between Santana and the *Indah,* Doc Blazer, who ran La Máquina (The Machine), a sawmill on the Tularosa River in the heart of the Mescalero reservation. Santana had died from pneumonia that winter in the Ghost Face Season after Doc Blazer had nursed him back to life from smallpox. He told us Cadete had died in a canyon not far from the reservation four years earlier, murdered by *Nakai-yes* after he gave evidence in a trial against them for selling whiskey to the Indians. On hearing this, I remembered that when my father and Cha had first learned of this over three years earlier, they had led a long murder raid against the *Nakai-yes* in the land across the great river. Cha was Cadete's half brother, and although they didn't get along, blood was blood, and vengeance unpaid was vengeance due.

As the moon swung toward the west and the time between stories grew long, we left our porch seats without a word to return to our camp by the cattle pool. Rufus raised his right hand, fingers spread, and said, "Caballo Negro, we speak together?"

Caballo Negro nodded for He Watches and me to go on, and he turned to face Rufus. I walked away, but not far, before turning into some shadows to watch them by moonlight and listen. He Watches knew this and did nothing to stop me.

Rufus spat off the porch, leaned his shoulder against a post, crossed his arms, and squinted at the face of Caballo Negro, who stared back at him unblinking.

"Tell me why you want me to teach that boy to shoot. You're a purty fair shot. You don't need me to teach him — oh, I'm glad to do it — but what else is he supposed to get from me?"

Caballo Negro said, "Roofoos Peek, you have eyes that see more than the day. You're an *Indah* who speaks truth. You keep your word. Nah-kah-yen must learn not only how to make his bullets go where he wants, he must also learn *Indah* ways, ways of the thing the Blue Coats call *Indah* law, and he must know *Indah*s he can trust to keep their word. Three moons with you, and he will shoot good, have an *Indah* amigo, and will have learned many *Indah* ways from a man who speaks straight and does what he says he will do.

"Cha is a skillful war chief, but does not use good judgment. He wants only to kill and fight. He loses warriors with almost every raid, every fight. Those who remain take more wives, the women of the warriors who die. Cha must stop his foolish raids, or all his warriors will live in the land of the grandfathers. In a few years, only women and children will be left. Without warriors, they'll go hungry and live in rags. The *Nakai-yes* will make 'em slaves.

"*Indahs* increase every day. We never kill enough to make them leave. Soon I'll take my family and live in peace on the reservation Santana started with this *Indah,* Blazer. I'll make no more raids, no more war. It fills my mouth with ashes to say this, but my only other choice is to die like a fool in some Blue Coat ambush or from a stray *In-dah* bullet in a raid and leave my woman and little son to starve and crawl in the dust before my enemies. This I will not do. I will not die except face-to-face by the hand of my enemy or if *Ussen* takes me."

Rufus nodded and took a couple of thoughtful chews and spat off the porch. "It's a honor to teach Nah-kah-yen and to hear what you say about me. You gotta right to know how to defend yore self against the

Indah. They's a bunch that deserves killin';
I ain't got much use fer most *Indahs* either.
Come back in three moons, and he'll be
shootin' good as he can, and he'll know
enough to live with the *Indahs.* Leave him
longer and I'll teach him more. I know I
don't need to tell you to watch out for the
Blue Coats when you go back to the mountains. They're all over the place just waitin'
fer Indian trouble."

"You speak true words, Roofoos Peek." I
quietly started for our camp, sensing their
talk was almost over and not wanting Caballo Negro to catch me eavesdropping.

Dawn's gray light was driving away the
night when I heard Rufus stirring in the
house. When he stepped out on the porch,
he jumped back, apparently startled at seeing me wrapped in a blanket with my back
to a porch post and my rifle posted up
against my shoulder. I fastened my eyes on
Rufus' face.

"Haw! Didn't expect to see you this early.
Where's Caballo Negro and He Watches?"

"They left before the moon found the far
mountains. I stayed. Caballo Negro said
you'd teach me many things."

Rufus jerked his head toward the door.
"Go on inside. I got to visit that little house

yonder, and then I'll make us somethin' to eat before we start your lessons. Does that suit you?"

I stood and nodded. Evidently in a hurry, Rufus stepped off the porch and took long, fast strides toward the little house with the door hanging open.

Sunlight flooded the valley, but the canyon was still in deep shadows, the air cool and dry, and a slight breeze from the top of the Organs whispered past the shack. Sitting on a blanket at the porch edge, Rufus asked me to show him how I loaded the Henry, levered the cartridges, and aimed along the top of the barrel using the sights.

Rufus said nothing as he watched me repeat the lever and sighting actions until the rifle was empty and all the scattered ejected cartridges collected. I compressed the loading spring and twisted open the bottom barrel to reload, but Rufus held up his hand for me to stop and said, "That's good. You're fine handling that Henry. We're ready to start shootin'. Let me get my thunder stick and a few tools, and we'll go. Put them cartridges in your vest pocket and reload when we get up to the end of the canyon."

We walked to the face of a high cliff that

leaned back toward the tops of the Organ spires. I saw a string of foot notches that someone, probably cliff people and used by Apaches many years before, had made to help climb the steep cliff face. There was a crack, twenty yards wide in the south canyon wall opposite Rufus and me. The crack ran perpendicular to the south wall and was more than four hundred yards deep before it became impassable. Sunlight only penetrated the little side canyon near the middle of the day, but there was enough light for me to see the glittering mounds of dirt about twenty-five yards apart that stretched from where they stood at the north canyon wall to the south side and disappeared into the little south side canyon.

Rufus sat down in the shadow of a juniper, set his rifle across his knees, and said, "This here is where I come to shoot. Ain't nobody gonna bother us back here. Go on and load your rifle."

He pointed to the second mound fifty yards away. "When you're ready, take a shot at that piece of glass halfway down the side of the number two mound yonder. Before ya start shootin' put these here things in your ears." He put two small rolls of wax in my hand, then took two more out of his pocket and worked them into his ears.

"Keeps ya from goin' deaf from too much shootin'. Comprende?"

I smiled and said, "Caballo Negro already showed me this."

Rufus grinned and nodded. "Shoulda knowed he showed you proper."

I used the wax to stop my ears, filled the Henry's cartridge barrel, faced the target mound, and levered a cartridge into the firing chamber while Rufus watched every move I made. Then I sighted on the broken glass and fired. The bullet missed the second mound and raised dust ten yards in front of the third. I turned to Rufus and frowned.

Rufus extended his hand and said, "Lemme have a look."

I handed the rifle to Rufus and stepped back, waiting. Rufus rested his elbows on his knees and sighted on the glass. When he fired, a small geyser of dust flew up about eight inches to the right of the bottle. He looked at me and grinned. "Thought so. Sights need adjustin', and you ain't breathin' and squeezin' the trigger right. We'll git them fixed, and you'll be bustin' targets pronto."

I didn't understand all of what Rufus meant, but I nodded to show I'd heard what he said. Rufus opened the small canvas bag he'd brought with him and pulled out a small double-headed hammer with a piece of rawhide laced over one head. He stared at the rear sight for a few moments, then gently tapped the right side, looked again, tapped once more, looked again, nodded, and tossed the hammer back in the bag. "Now let's see how she shoots."

I nodded, uncertain of what I had just witnessed.

Rufus levered another round into the firing chamber and, again resting his elbows on his knees, sighted and fired. The piece of glass exploded into a sparkling shower that rained glass bits out of the accompanying dust cloud. Almost faster than my eyes could follow, Rufus smoothly levered round after round, the full cartridge barrel load, into the same spot, creating a large puff of dust around the mound as the cacophony of shots filled the air with a continuous rumble of thunder and echoes back and forth between the canyon walls. It sounded like the hail of gunfire poured into the wagon train where Caballo Negro had found the rifle. I could hardly believe it.

Rufus grinned and nodded as he handed the rifle back to me. "That there is a powerful weapon. When you git good with it, you'll be a deadly man. Wouldn't want to shoot more than a barrel load with it at one time, though; that piece o' iron gits hot. It'll burn your hand if you ain't careful. Load her up again and let's see how you do sittin' down like I was."

Ignoring the hot steel in my hands, I carefully filled the loading barrel again. Rufus pulled a whiskey bottle from a sack under the juniper and stood it in the place where the bits of glass from the last target were scattered.

When Rufus returned, he showed me how to sit and rest my elbows on my knees while I sighted the rifle on the bottle. He squatted to one side and told me to shoot when I was ready.

The Henry roared and a small dust plume jumped about six inches high and to the right of the middle of the bottle. Rufus, nodding, said, "Again." This time the shot landed a little lower but further to the right.

Rufus rested his hand on my shoulder and held up one finger on the other hand to signal me to wait.

"Couple thangs I see right away you need to learn. First, take a deep breath, and then let it about half out just before ya fire. That'll make yore sights steady on the target." To demonstrate what he meant, Rufus took the rifle, sighted the target, took a deep breath, puffed away part of it, and sighting down the rifle said, "Pow!"

He handed the rifle back to me and nodded for me to try it. I imitated Rufus perfectly even to the point of saying, "Pow!" I grinned because I had seen how steady the sight picture became just before I said "Pow."

"Another thang I noticed, you're jerkin' the trigger instead of squeezin'. Try pushin' the trigger straight back and try to hold steady a bit after she fires. Try 'em and let's see how you do."

I sighted once more, controlled my breathing, and thought of pulling back a bow string with my trigger finger. The shot barely missed the bottle.

Rufus said, "Again. Keep shooting at the same spot, doin' what you're doin' now."

The next shot shattered the bottle and those that followed were within two or three inches of the shot that broke the bottle. When the cartridge barrel was empty, I turned to Rufus and nodded.

Rufus grinned. "You still got a lot a practicin' to do, but you got the idee."

Chapter 15
Rufus' Story

When I consistently hit my targets on a berm, Rufus increased the range to the next berm. As the range increased, I saw my bullets consistently fall lower than my aim point. Rufus taught me to aim a little above the target to compensate for the increased range until, at about two hundred yards, the rifle's aim point was well above the target. At that point, Rufus showed me how to flip the adjustable rear sight up and raise the sight notch to compensate for the longer ranges and still have a sight picture on the target. Since I didn't understand the meaning of the tracks of the numerals on the adjustable sight, Rufus demonstrated the setting for three hundred yards and showed me that the aim point through the sights was now back on target and how adding four more berms of distance required raising the sight notch to the next big mark.

My respect for my rifle increased as I

learned to shoot and hit targets at distances even Caballo Negro did not attempt. As Rufus had told me I would on our first day of shooting, I began to think of the rifle as part of myself and the bullet hitting the target where I looked. It was like shooting a bow without consciously sighting the arrow, a skill I'd learned as a boy, only using the rifle was easier.

In the evenings when the sun was falling below the Florida Mountains far to the west, the light in the valley slowly fading, Rufus and I sat on the shack porch. Rufus helped me speak more of the strange tongue of the *Indah* I had heard at Bosque Redondo. I cleaned and oiled my weapon as I listened and attempted to make my tongue form the awkward, clipped *Indah* sounds Rufus made me repeat over and over until they sounded like the ones the *Indah* spoke, including Rufus' name. Before long, Rufus was insisting I try to speak to him in English.

One evening as my first moon with Rufus approached, I lay my cleaned and oiled rifle across my knees and said, as well as I could in English, "Why Rufus Pike and Caballo Negro amigos? I think after we go from Bosque Redondo, Caballo Negro and me, we kill every *Indah,* every Blue Coat we see. Why he no kill you, Rufus Pike? Why he want us amigos?"

Rufus grimaced and stared down the valley at the twinkling lights and the low glow of El Paso lights behind the black outline of distant mountains to the south.

"Well, son, we ain't exactly friends, but we ain't enemies, either. I owe Caballo Negro a debt. He saved my life one time."

I was surprised, as I had not heard this story before.

"How? Why?"

" 'Bout twenty-five year ago, I's scoutin' fer Cap'n Ewell tryin' to keep the Apaches off the San Antonio road, the road your People call the *Indah* Road from the Rising Sun. We's in winter camp in the great river *bosque* one night when they stole 'bout half our mounts. Cap'n Ewell, he's real mad and tells me to try and find 'em so's he'n come take 'em back an' make them Apaches pay fer disturbin' his winter camp. I saluted and took off jes like he ordered.

"I's like a ol' dog a chasin' his tail roun' and roun' follerin' them Apaches. They led me all over the country an' I never would've found 'em 'cept I made a mistake and went to sleep when I should've stayed awake. When I woke up, they's this sharp blade across my throat. The biggest, ugliest Apache I ever seen before or since held it. He had this young man, this kid, Caballo Negro, with him. Reckon he's about your age, and the feller with the knife was tryin' to show the kid how to cut me and make me suffer a long time 'fore I died.

"I give my soul to God that very minute and was a prayin' I didn't scream too loud when they started cuttin'. But the kid says, naw, he ain't gonna cut no *Indah* so weak he gets caught sleepin'. Ain't no Power in that, ain't what his medicine told him, he says. Kid says if I git strong, he'll come around again so's we'n have us a fight worthy of his time. The warrior stared at the kid a long time before he nodded and said he respected the kid's medicine.

"I told the kid I was gonna ranch in the Organs, and any time he's ready, we'd have a go at 'er. He nodded and said if I'n survive in the desert without clothes and weapons I might be worth killin'. So they took 'em and run me off in the desert but didn't kill me. Brother, let me tell you, it was cold. I had to run just to keep from freezin' to death. I run fer 'bout half a day 'fore some peons on a little spread north o' El Paso took me in. My feet was tore all to hell, but I made it just the same.

"After I got this here ol' ranch started, a few years went by, and Caballo Negro and a few warriors from Cha's band stopped by for water. I's glad to give it to 'em and never made no fuss 'bout it. We knowed each other, but he ain't never said nothin' about increasin' his Power by killin' me."

I pursed my lips and frowned. "You show me how to shoot so Caballo Negro and Rufus Pike no fight?"

"Yes, sir, I reckon that's about the size of it — at least that's the reason it started that way — but you learn pronto, and I'm glad to show you my shootin' tricks."

I thought for a while over what Rufus told me. Despite the idea that Caballo Negro was just calling my training the payment of a debt Rufus owed, I believed they were friends, and so I, too, was Rufus' friend. Here was an *Indah* who could tell me the truth about the *Indah*s. Now I understood why my father had brought me to Rufus.

"Rufus Pike, another question?"

"Shore. Ask it."

"This reservation the *Indahs* make for Mescaleros, why must we go there?"

Rufus spat off the side of the porch and frowned with clenched teeth.

"You need to go fer yore own pertection. They's too many *Indah*s for you to fight.

Fer ever hundert *Indah*s you kill, they's ten thousand to take their place. Fer ever' Apache the *Indah*s kill, there might be one to take his place — if yore lucky. I know it ain't right fer us Americanos to come here and just claim the land, but we did, and before that, the Spaniards did, too. By rights, the *Indah*s and *Nakai-yes* oughter be on a reservation rather than your people, but it ain't never gonna happen. You want your people to live through more'n one or two generations without yore tribe disappearin' fer ever, that's the life you gotta accept, life on the reservation and the end of war and raidin'. That there is what I think."

I knew Rufus spoke the truth, but his words were like sour mare's milk to me.

"All warriors get shoot-many-times guns like this one. Make each Apache like ten. Drive *Indah*s and Blue Coats away?"

Rufus shook his head.

"Still ain't enough to fight off the great flood of *Indah*s a comin' to this here land, and you need to understand they'll have big guns that can kill many *Indeh* with one shot from far away."

I stared off in the darkness and said nothing for a long time before turning to Rufus. "What Mescaleros do on reservation, Rufus Pike? When I small boy, *Indah* told *Shis-*

Indeh they must dig in ground and grow plants to eat. Woman's work! Caballo Negro says *Shis-Indeh* try to grow plants four seasons of Many Leaves. Navajo come. Frost come. Grasshoppers come. Sickness come. Plants turn black and die, worms everywhere. No food to save for Ghost Face time. Many babies cry hungry. What Mescaleros do?"

Rufus spat off the porch again, wiped his moustache, leaned against the side of the shack, and sighed a long, weary sigh.

"It ain't gonna be easy. Them idjits in Washin'ton, they's sendin' Indian agents either crooked as snakes or dumber'n rocks. If'n you can git past 'em, I'd figure maybe you might raise cattle and cut a few trees fer ol' Doc Blazer to run through the sawmill, and cut you some planks and beams fer buildin' and sellin'. Wood fer buildings is hard to come by in this here country an' it costs a lot of money. Your women, they's experts at makin' baskets and such. Trade 'em at the tradin' post fer food. The *Indah* women can't make such things. You understandin' my words? Comprende?"

"Sí, comprendo. But, Rufus Pike, what is this thing, money?"

Rufus explained how the *Indah* used money to capture the value of things without trading one thing for another. When Rufus finished explaining money, I nodded that I understood, but I wasn't really sure I did.

When I finished cleaning the Yellow Boy, I saw Rufus deep in thought, his jaw moving slow over his chew as he stared at the lights down the valley.

Rufus said, "We're gittin' low on cartridges for the Yellow Boy. You're a purty fair shot now at two hundert yards. Caballo Negro said he'd bring some more cartridges. He probably didn't think you'd use 'em up as fast as you have a shootin' with me. If he ain't come with some more 'fore we run out, I'll just go buy some more and swap out with you when yours gits here. What cha think about that?"

I nodded and asked, "Where this place with cartridges?"

"Aw, it's over to Las Cruces. Ol' Marty Amador took over his mama's store and runs it along with his freight business. He's got stuff comin' in there all the time. I ain't never been there when there weren't a wagon or two out back a waitin' to be unloaded. Don't worry. Ol' Marty tol' me last time I's in town he's expectin' cartridges in a shipment in a couple o' weeks, and that'd be 'bout now. We'll git 'em if Caballo

Negro ain't brought 'em by the time they's needed."

I stared off into the night and smiled like Coyote.

Chapter 16
The Apache Way

When Rufus Pike told me of the *Indah* place where cartridges were traded for this thing he called money, I thought, *Why not raid this place or the wagons bringing supplies and take what I need? I'm as powerful as any man with a rifle. If I'm quiet enough, I won't have to use the rifle when I take the cartridges. I'll find this place and take what I want. This is the way of the Apache.*

The moon floated high when I left the canyon ranch and rode down the trail toward the village Rufus Pike called Las Cruces. I came to its lodges near dawn and rode my pony in a big circle around them until I saw five freight wagons and mules in a corral behind an *Indah* big house that looked like a trading post. I hid my pony in an arroyo north of the trading post and worked my way back to the wagons, thinking, *Maybe what I need is still in a wagon,* but nothing was there. Dawn came. A door to the big house opened and a man walked plenty fast for the little house like the one Rufus Pike goes to behind his house. I hid, watched, and waited to see what these *Indah* would do.

When the sun came, the *Indah* and *Nakai-yes* loaded wagons and harnessed mules. The feet of many men stirred dust in the corral. They made much noise, bringing plenty of water to their faces and shirts. I saw a cartridge box like one Caballo Negro took for the Yellow Boy. It had the symbol of two broken twigs side-by-side. The driver came, a young man like me, but tall, with yellow hair and a big hat that made shade on his face. He hitched six mules to the wagon. Then the outrider came, his face covered with hair. He had a bad eye and many lines on his forehead. He was much ugly and carried a rifle across his saddle. When the driver called to the mules and slapped the reins down their backs, they strained in the harness, pulled the wagon out of the corral, and turned east toward mountains where Rufus Pike had his canyon ranch. I slipped back to the arroyo, mounted my pony, and followed the wagon, making sure the driver and outrider didn't see me. The wagon road pointed to the place in mountains where Rufus Pike said the *Indah* dig holes in ground for pesh-klitso (gold). The dust and sand were deep where wheels followed the road, so the mules worked hard pulling the load. I thought, *Ambush this wagon. Shoot straight. Shoot like Rufus Pike teaches you. Be a mighty warrior. Take the box with cartridges and maybe more loot. No need for more cartridges from Caballo Negro.*

I followed the wagon while the sun climbed high and waited for a place to make an ambush.

When the sun had risen to the time of shortest shadows, the wagon stopped at a place of water next to a high wheel that turned, creaking in the wind and sitting on four long legs. I had heard Rufus Pike talk about this thing. He called it a windmill and the *Indah* used it to pull water from the earth where there was none. The driver unhitched the mules and took them to drink while the outrider stayed on his pony, rifle cocked, ready, watching the wagon.

I left my pony in the arroyo so the outrider wouldn't see it and crawled through bushes toward the wagon and outrider. Soon, the mules finished drinking. When the driver led them back to the wagon, birds flew out of a bush when I passed. The outrider saw the birds and pointed his rifle toward me. I stayed still, did not move or breathe, willing myself to disappear, and he didn't see me. He yelled to the driver, "Hurry up! We gotta git outta here."

I waited until the outrider looked away, then I stepped to one side of a mesquite bush, and aimed at his chest, but he saw me and swung his rifle toward me, too late. My Yellow Boy rifle thundered, and the outrider's rifle answered. A red place came in the middle of the outrider's chest, and he fell off his horse backwards, and the horse ran. The driver, his eyes big, dropped the mule harness and ran up the wagon road after the outrider's horse.

I worked the rifle's lever to load a new cartridge, then started toward the wagon. My leg felt on fire. Glancing down, I saw blood from a cut a hand span above my left knee. The outrider bullet could have killed me. I thanked *Ussen* that I'd lived to fight again. I knew I must ask *Ussen* for my Power if I was to be a mighty warrior.

I went to the water and washed the blood off my leg, thinking, *Ussen protected me. The cut is not deep, not much blood.*

"Yore damned lucky that ol' boy you killed didn't drill you between the eyes. What in hell did you kill him for?"

I turned, surprised to hear the old man's

voice. Rufus' face was a thundercloud of anger, teeth clenched, eyes wide. The butt of his big buffalo gun stood against his thigh, its barrel pointed up, his thumb on the hammer ready for action.

"A boy waits on his father for cartridges," I said. "A warrior doesn't wait. A warrior takes what he needs." I pointed with my nose toward the outrider lying face up, the dark hole in his chest leaking blood into a big, dark patch on the front of his shirt. "The outrider rode like a warrior, died like a warrior. I killed him like a warrior. How'd you find me, Rufus Pike?"

"Never mind how I found you. We got to git outta here 'fore anybody finds this and we're both hung. Where's yore pony?"

I pointed toward the arroyo a few hundred yards away.

"Git him and wait for me on the road."

"What will you do, Rufus Pike?"

"I'm gonna run these here mules and horse off in different directions and hope them that comes along next ain't smart enough to figure out what happened. Maybe they'll think it was some kind of fight between two old enemies and not an Apache raid. Did th' driver see you?"

I shrugged my shoulders. "I'll take cartridges from the wagon and then git pony."

Rufus shook his head. "No. Go now. We gotta git back down the road so we don't leave a easy trail for the law to foller to my door."

I raised my jaw and narrowed my eyes. "I take cartridges from the wagon and then git pony."

"Oh, hell! Be quick about it. Don't tear up that wagin any more'n you have to. If they's just cartridges missin' they'll start thinkin' maybe Apaches done it 'cause they're always after cartridges. They's liable to be trouble over on the reservation if they think that. Can't help it though."

Rufus unharnessed the mules and drove them out into the desert. I had watched the case of ammunition slide under the wagon seat, and was able to pull the heavy box out without disturbing the rest of the load. Ignoring the pain in my creased leg, I ran to my pony with the case of cartridges, struggled to mount with the awkward, heavy box and rifle, and rode to the windmill to let my pony drink before riding back down the road to join Rufus.

Rufus led me in the jumble of tracks down the road away from the mountains, and then in a stretch of rust red and volcanic black-colored gravel, we turned south toward the road that ran along in front of the Organs and eventually to his ranch. We stopped in the shade of a mesquite thicket to rest the horses, and Rufus used his old cavalry binoculars to scan our back trail but saw nothing.

The first stars were appearing when we rode up to the cabin porch. We had said nothing since starting back for the ranch. Rufus dismounted and said, "Leave them cartridges here, and go take care of my horse and yore pony. I'll make us some supper and start a poultice a cookin' for that crease in your leg, and then we're gonna talk."

I nodded, handed the cartridge box into Rufus' waiting hands, and slid off my pony. I took his mule's reins and those for my pony and limped away toward the corral.

CHAPTER 17
THE *INDAH* WAY

Rufus and I sat on the edge of the shack porch wiping the last of the beans and meat out of our pie pan plates with tortillas. We had not spoken since our supper began, and with the moon slow to rise, deep darkness filled the canyon. Our only light came from a kerosene lantern sitting on the rough-cut table near the stove, its flame pouring a yellow glow through the open window and door.

Rufus set his pie pan down, patted his swollen belly, and said, "That there ain't half bad, even if I do say so myself."

I finished my pie pan plate, and, setting it aside, nodded. "Uhmmph, good, Rufus Pike."

Rufus leaned over in the light's glow to look at the poultice he had fixed for me. Made of a mixture of boiled herbs known for their healing powers and a medicinal mud, it stank and made Rufus grimace as he pushed his round wireframe glasses back up the bridge of his nose.

"Yore scratch don't seem to be doin' too bad. Th' poultice making it feel any better?"

I nodded. "Better. Good battle scar. Good story for winter fire."

I pulled a thin, black *cigarro* from a vest pocket and popped a red head match with my thumbnail to light it. Rufus, wrinkling his nose like it stank, watched me put fire to the tobacco. When the end of the cigar was a nice orange coal, I puffed and blew smoke in the four cardinal directions before handing the smoke to Rufus to do the same. Rufus puffed and blew smoke in the four directions as I had done and handed the *cigarro* back to me before cutting himself a chew of tobacco off a twist he kept in his scratched and worn vest pocket.

I smoked most of the *cigarro,* dropped it in the sand by the porch, and crushed it out with my heel. Then I looked directly into Rufus' eyes and asked, "Why you angry with me, Rufus Pike? I raided a wagon to get cartridges. I no burn wagon or kill driver. The outrider died well fighting for wagon. Now I have plenty cartridges. When Caballo Negro comes, maybe you have more cartridges, or maybe you have less, but I'm ready. Why you angry?"

Rufus leaned against the wall and spat into the darkness. "Son, by your people's code, you done a good thang. But I'm here to tell you, it was mighty dangerous. That little wound on yore laig proves it. And, maybe we ain't seen the last of that raid. If the *Indah* ever figure out I'm hidin' the Apache who killed that outrider — and make no mistake, that teamster is gonna say it was an Apache done it whether he seen one or not — they'll probably stretch my neck 'fore they stretch yore's. I know raidin' is the way you been raised. Take what you need when you need it and share with the People, but it ain't the *Indah* way."

"What is *Indah* way, Rufus Pike?"

Rufus blinked, his chew unmoving in his jaw. I could tell this was a question he'd not thought about much.

"When the *Indah* take the land from the *Shis-Indeh,* their chiefs gives folks a piece of that land and makes tracks on a paper sayin' it belongs to them. They make their livin' from the land growing crops or cattle or doin' anything else comes to mind. They trade for what they need usin' money they earned off o' their land. They don't go out an' take what they want or need from some other feller less'n they pay or trade for it. Them that take what they want without

209

payin', and they's *Indah* like that, is called outlaws. Outlaws is run down and captured by the sheriff an' made to work as a punishment for a time, dependin' on how much they took. If an outlaw kills somebody an' the sheriff catches him, then that outlaw's likely to be hung by the neck till he quits kickin'. That there keeps the family of the man the outlaw killed from comin' after the outlaw's family. I guess you'n say in the *Indah* way, everbody keeps score an' it's all supposed to come out even, 'cept some *Indah*s play better an' wins more'n others."

I listened to Rufus' words fill the cool night air and smiled. "You say *Indah* first take land from Indeh. That no raid? *Indah* think I am outlaw when I no take land, only take supplies, take cartridges? *Indah* foolish men. I no outlaw. I warrior."

Rufus spat a long stream into the yard in front of the porch and grinned. "Yes, sir. I ain't gonna argue with you on that one. But, whiles we finish up yore trainin' you gotta stay outta sight o' the *Indah* that might come around, or they's gonna be trouble. Can you do that?"

I looked him in the eye and said, "I do that, Rufus Pike."

"Good. An' don't say nuthin' to nobody 'bout what happened today, either. Now, let's git some sleep. I'm tarred; it's been a long day. I'll change yore poultice first light 'fore breakfast, and we'll start shootin' tomorrow when the light is good enough back in the canyon. That there suit you?"

I pumped my arm holding the Yellow Boy and grinned. *"Enjuh!"*

Rufus opened the shack door and breathed deep in the cool morning air. I was at my usual place by the corner porch post, and he gave me a nod as he stepped out on the porch headed for his usual morning visit to his little house. I was grinning. Next to my knee was the new box of ammunition with "1000 Cartridges US Army .44 Caliber Ball" inked on the sides.

Stopping in mid-stride, Rufus said, "I'll be danged, where in the devil did you find that?"

"Caballo Negro came when moon was high. Left cartridge box. Disappeared in night. He thought I slept, but I saw him. He comes again in two moons. You'll see, Rufus Pike."

"They ain't a doubt in my mind that's gonna happen, boy. We better git you shootin' real good by then, or he ain't gonna be happy."

■ ■ ■ ■

The sun's glare was unmercifully bright. The shadows in the canyon crack Rufus used for a shooting range had disappeared to reveal high, rock walls narrowing to a final mound of earth supporting an ancient, five-gallon galvanized water bucket. I sat five hundred yards away holding the Yellow Boy rifle and supporting my elbows against my knees in the shade of a juniper tree against the north wall of Rufus' box canyon. The rifle's rear sight was flipped up, and the notched crosspiece was raised to the five hundred yard mark. I sighted the bucket, looking not much more than a gray dot in the light scattered off the canyon's smooth, high walls. The rifle was fully loaded, its hammer back, and my finger curled around the trigger.

Nearby, Rufus sat with sweat streaming down his face in the hot, still air and spoke in a low, calm voice. "Just relax now, son. Remember to breathe deep and let half of it go. Think about pullin' the trigger straight back. Don't jerk it. Nice and easy. Think that bullet all the way to the bucket. Easy does it."

I focused on keeping the gray dot aligned

with his sights. The hammer fell, and the Yellow Boy jumped, breathing flame, roaring thunder and a light puff of smoke. Rufus and I remained frozen in place as the cloud of gun smoke drifted out of our field of vision and the echoes of the shot died away. The gray dot had disappeared.

Rufus shouted, "Yes, sir! That's the way to do 'er! Six times out of six at five hundred yards! Ain't nobody gonna do better, includin' me with the Sharps or Caballo Negro with his Winchester. You done good, son; you done real good. Yore daddy's gonna be mighty proud of you."

I smiled. "I shoot good, Rufus."

"You shore do. Come on. Let's git some beans. This afternoon, after it cools off some, I'll start you on movin' targets. They ain't too hard once you git the hang of it."

We retrieved the bucket, which looked like a sieve, filled with dents and bullet holes, and strolled back to the shack.

CHAPTER 18
NAH-KAH-YEN'S DREAM

It was dark. I was running, running hard, running for a long time. My lungs strained to pull in more air, and I heard the breath of the Giant behind me. I looked over my shoulder and saw only two great eyes glowing in the darkness chasing me. I made my legs pound the sand harder, my strength failing, the eyes coming closer. From a long way off appeared a point of brilliant, golden light. Thunder spoke, and lightning flashed, and the point of light stretched into a slowly tumbling bar with a golden center until it formed the Yellow Boy. Wind moaned in a roaring rush, and a voice said, "In two days, go to the top of the first mountain above Rufus Pike's canyon. Take no food. Take no water. Take only the Yellow Boy. Go, and you will save yourself and protect your people."

I jerked awake in my blanket and sat up, sweating and panting as if I had run a long way. I raised my eyes to the heavens and saw only the many stars in the night sky. I looked around the canyon walls and saw only the smooth darkness of the night, heard my pinto snort, the shift and snuffing of cattle picking grass among the cactus and creosote bushes, the trembling flow of water into the little catch basin nearby. Above these sounds, the voice in the roaring wind burned in my mind. I lay back down and slipped into a deep and dreamless sleep.

We sat with full bellies and watched dust devils play touch and go on the desert floor and the shadows of clouds sail down the valley toward El Paso. The air was hot and still under the shack porch roof. Rufus, ready for an afternoon siesta, closed his eyes. I leaned against the wall by the window, the Yellow Boy rifle barrel leaning against my chest, and said, "Rufus Pike, I have dream. I see giant eyes. They chase me. I hear voices of Thunder People and Wind."

"Hmmm, I'm glad to hear that. Have dreams all the time my own self. Just don't remember 'em."

"They told me to go to mountain. I think *Ussen* calls me. I go."

Rufus turned his head and, with one eye

open, squinted at me. "When did you have this dream?"

"Night before this day."

"Well, you come to the right place fer mountains. Did the dream say where you were supposed to go?"

"Wind say go to the top of first mountain above Rufus Pike's canyon. Say no take water. No take food. Take Yellow Boy. Wait. They come. They speak to me."

Rufus blinked and opened his eyes wide. "When did they tell you to go?"

"They say two days. I go day after next with rising sun."

"You ain't gonna be up there in no storm are ya? Lightnin'll come right for ya when you're up high like that."

"Dream say go in two days. I go. Thunder People and Wind, they come."

"That there is a mighty long climb without no water and somethin' to eat and packin' ten pound o' rifle and expectin' to hear thunder and wind, mighty dangerous. You ain't likely to come back. Sure that's what you heard?"

"No water. No food. Bring rifle. Listen to Wind. I hear. I go."

Rufus closed his eyes. "I'd shore hate to tell yore daddy that a dream killed ya up on that mountain."

"Power takes me. Power brings me back. No worry. I come back. You see."

Rufus mumbled, "Yes, sir, I reckon I will."

Rufus walked with me to the back canyon wall to begin my climb. He had tied a strip of rawhide to the rifle so I could strap it across my back and have my hands free for climbing. Before I put my moccasin on the first foothold on the canyon wall, I paused to look in Rufus' eyes. I saw much worry there. I turned to go. Rufus said, "Come back when you've had your talk with the Thunder People and Wind. I'll be waitin'."

I nodded. "I come."

When the footholds ran out at the top of the canyon, I came to a rough, boulder-strewn plateau. After crossing it, I climbed vertically another fifty feet up a drainage tube before I reached a canyon lined with junipers along its bottom that climbed gently and steadily toward the south, making swings between two ridges before it was split by a third ridge from the east.

The most direct path to the first mountaintop above Rufus' canyon was to my left on the north side of the ridge. It led directly toward the ridgeline near the top of the mountain, but the path crawled over five giant steps made by cliffs, perhaps fifty yards high, that climbed to the next plateau before finally reaching the ridgeline leading to the mountaintop.

The path to my right on the south side of the dividing ridge was steep, but had only one shallow, gently sloping cliff to climb, and after that, a relatively easy climb before reaching a ridgeline that could be followed up to the top of the mountain.

Sweat ran in little arroyo floods down my chest and belly, and I breathed harder than normal in the high, thin air. I studied both paths and took the easier south side one to save my strength. The trail up the south side of the ridge was steeper than any of the others I had climbed that day, but I easily scrambled up and stopped briefly to rest when it crested in the ridgeline saddle. Far below to the south, I saw the trail I had just climbed and the shadows in the little notch made by Rufus' box canyon. To the north, mountains dropped way toward the browns and scattered greens of the desert, and in the distant west, more mountains shimmered gray in the midday haze.

The ridgeline was narrow, but easy to walk, and from the notch where I rested, I was about six hundred feet below the mountaintop in my dream. I found a small, smooth pebble and popped it in my mouth to ease my thirst, and then I began the climb along the ridgeline toward the top of the mountain. The climb was steep, but not hard, the path relatively wide, but with heart-pounding drop-offs on either side. I moved slowly, taking care where I placed my feet and watching for snakes, especially around the windswept junipers that tended to grow in the middle of the ridgeline, making me edge closer to the precipice than I wanted, where loose rocks, with a small shift, might send me headlong down the steep cliffs into the forever land of the grandfathers.

The climb up the ridgeline ended on a bald knob in the middle of a ridgeline that ran northeast to southwest, almost perpendicular to the ridge I had been climbing. The highest mountaintop on the ridgeline was to the east. The one to the west was slightly lower, but it was the first mountain overlooking Rufus' canyon, and it was the one to which I turned. To reach it, I had to climb around the knob, which meant climbing down a short, boulder-strewn draw to another draw filled with junipers and then climbing back up to the ridgeline that led to the western peak.

The last climb was no more than a hundred yards high, but it was steep and required much stretching between boulders and ledges to get to the top. Halfway up, my hand slipped, and I nearly rolled off the edge, but I managed to stop in time when my hand caught a crack in the smooth rock and held on.

The late afternoon shadows on the eastern side of the mountains merged into the coming dusk, but the light was still brilliant on the mountaintop when I finally reached it, panting for air, my upper body covered in sweat, thirst burning in my throat. Wearily, I stood and looked out across the world and was stunned by the many days of pony riding distances and areas below my feet, as I slowly turned toward the four directions and felt a cool breeze sweep over my body.

Far to the west were the mountains Rufus called the Floridas. From this height, no longer able to hide behind the horizon, they appeared much higher than they looked from Rufus' porch. The great river in the near distance made a bold, green slash running north and south across the yellows and browns and scattered greens of the desert, and scattered in clusters along the green slash were smeared points of light around white adobe buildings on the ranches and in the villages.

A large boulder, smooth and long, lay like

a giant egg tilted in a nest of much smaller boulders. After looking for snakes and other poisonous demons, I pulled the Yellow Boy off my back and sat down against the boulder's warmth to watch the sun in a distant glory of red and orange clouds fall below the horizon just behind the midsection of the Floridas. Tired and thirsty, I relaxed and lit a *cigarro*. I blew smoke in the four directions, thanked the Mountain Spirits for a safe journey, and prayed that Wind might come soon.

Then I leaned back and watched the sun slip away in a golden glow as the clouds slowly disappeared. The stars came out, shining bright and steady. Their light was steady in the high places, not blinking as it did when I watched it from the villages far below.

I watched the stars turn slowly about the North Star and wondered why Wind had called me to this place high above the plains and deserts. After a while, I got up, walked to the edge of the south cliffs, and relieved myself. When I returned, I lay down with my feet to the east and head to the west, held the Yellow Boy across my chest, and looked into the deep dark forever before my eyes. I had little time to think of the unblinking white points of light in the velvety blackness, before sleep, in the warm robes of fatigue, took me.

Chapter 19
Power Comes

My eyes fluttered open in the early morning light and stared straight up into the dark sky turning light blue turquoise on the horizon. The high stars were still bright, and the high places, scattered up and down the valley and mountains catching the sunlight peeping over the horizon, formed lakes of yellow in the darkness still covering the ground and the western side of the mountains. I stretched like a cat stretches after a long nap, stood, and leaned the rifle I had held all night against a boulder. Facing the sun, I raised my hands to sing my morning prayer, the same prayer my mother had taught me, and the one I had sung every day since I was a small boy at Bosque Redondo.

"Come Sun of the morning
"Bright light of *Ussen*
"*Ussen* give us its Power
"Give us the Sun of the morning"

Standing high on a point above the desert floor surrounded by light and darkness, I felt I was in a holy place and sang the prayer three times more, facing the other cardinal directions.

The night air had been warm, not cold like it was in the desert below. The rock on which I lay kept its heat, and I had slept comfortably all night. I cradled the rifle in the crook of my left arm and walked from my resting place to where cliffs fell away from the rounded top of my mountain to the wreckage of boulders far below. I saw a thin, white pillar of smoke rising from Rufus' shack, and many more like it from the barely visible villages and ranch houses up and down the great river. The smoke rose straight up until at a particular height it bent parallel to the brown desert to drift and break up in a light intermittent breeze that carried it for miles before it finally disappeared.

On high cliffs in the Guadalupes with He Watches, I had many times watched the sun rise over the road from the east and cast its light over the *llano* south toward the Davis Mountains. The height didn't bother me in the Guadalupes, and it didn't here. In the Guadalupes, when the Thunder People and Wind came, He Watches and I had left and gotten out of their way. But this mountain, where my dream sent me, was nearly a thousand feet higher than He Watches' place in the Guadalupes, and there was nowhere to hide. Either I left this place with my Power, or storm spirits would take me, never to be seen again, that I knew for certain.

I sat down in the cool shadows, leaned the rifle against a boulder, crossed my legs, folded my hands in my lap, and tried to focus my mind on the gifts of Power I might be given and whether I ought to accept or reject them. As the sun climbed higher, no images or thoughts passed through my mind, which was strangely empty and blocked — something I had never before experienced.

The sun was hot against my skin, my deepening thirst burning on my lips and in my throat. He Watches had once told me about finding Power by letting go of body needs. Until my Power came, I focused on letting go of what bound me to life, the sun's searing heat, thirst, hunger, and the sense of my spirit floating above me tethered to my body.

The passing day brought the sun to hide behind far mountains and the sky on the horizon to fill with the color of fresh, dark red blood. I dimly saw gray, billowing clouds building to the southwest and smiled, my dry lips cracking. I thought, *At last they come.* Darkness came slowly and with it the recognition of dim flashes of light within the clouds far away, as they strolled toward my mountain on slim, dark legs of falling rain.

Directly above me, the stars appeared in the night sky. A cool, moist breeze washed over me, bringing relief from the heat of the day, giving me strength. The flashes in the clouds grew brighter as they came closer, and the slim legs of rain grew to giant black stubs striding across the waiting, thirsty desert. The stars above me disappeared, and the weak, cool breeze became a gentle wind growing in power as the dark, stumpy legs brought the flashing clouds ever closer. The Thunder People and Wind were coming to take me or bless me with my Power. Holding the rifle, I pushed myself erect and walked to the top of the mountain a few paces away from the boulders that had sheltered me with their shadows during the day. I faced the coming storm and waited. It arrived with flashing lightning arrows and rumbling thunder and moaning from the strengthening wind as it swept over the place where I stood.

I raised my arms, holding the rifle high, and began to sing, over and over, in a loud clear voice.

"*Ussen* has the Power
"Over all the world
"*Ussen* has the Power
"Over the Storm Spirits
"*Ussen* brings the Thunder People and
    Wind
"For *Ussen,* they will take me or leave me
"For *Ussen,* they will leave me with a gift
"A gift for the benefit of the People"

The clouds rolled toward me like great running horses; the storm spirits riding them came shouting and shooting their brilliant, blinding arrows into the ground and between clouds. The voice of Wind came in a thousand whispers, came in myriad shrieks, filling my ears and pushing me backwards, trying to push me off my mountain, trying to kill me. I stood leaning against the Wind and saw a long, crooked arrow of lightning strike a low mountain far below me near the little *Indah* village on the great river. Wind slowed and was still. The whole world seemed to pause as if suspended in the night, waiting, like I waited, for Power.

I sat down, lay the lightly oiled rifle across my knees, and stroked the long, smooth barrel and beautifully finished stock before laying my left hand on the brass. Sliding the web of my thumb to just behind the hammer, I pulled it to safety. Then, locking the trigger and wrapping my fingers into the trigger guard and loading lever, I held it erect before me. I stared at the weapon against the distant flashes of light, and my thoughts condensed from thin, vaporous feelings to a towering white anvil cloud in which flashed the lightning of a single idea. I thought, *This rifle is Yellow Boy, an extension of myself, its power part of me. Its power strikes wherever I look. It is part of my Power.* I waited, wrapped in this new thought, wondering what it meant for my life, for my gift.

The black rolling clouds drew closer and Wind grew strong and powerful. A brilliant, white lightning arrow flew across the night sky, blinding me for a few seconds. Instinctively, I grasped and squeezed the rifle with both hands to avoid losing it in my blindness, and recognition, like an electric current, flowed from the rifle up my arms and settled in the middle of my chest. My arms shook with the power of the current. I gasped, pulling into my lungs the moaning wind, my reflexes attempting to relax my fingers, which were locked around the rifle, but I sat paralyzed and trembling in the growing wind until the current went away, and I felt my arms and body relax, and still holding the weapon before me, I collapsed slowly backward until I lay flat and still on the rusty, red rock of the mountain, the rifle resting on my chest.

My mind suddenly active, thoughts moving at blinding speeds, filled with fluttering images and words from prayers, raced to stay even with the mad pounding of my heart. The only thing I remembered seeing just before the current passed through me were the two great eyes I had seen in my dream. They were gone. I wondered if I was in a dream, but I knew better.

A male rain came sweeping over me, washing me clean, filling my mouth and taking away the fire of thirst. Another lightning arrow, bright as the sun, blinded me and seared the air, ripping the sky like a woman tearing cloth. A crack of thunder followed so loud it hurt my ears. Another arrow, greater than the one before, lighted the entire sky and struck the mountaintop above me, struck the mountain where I had been warned not to go. Wind came and rushed over me, howling and shrieking like demons caught under the earth. It pulled at me but did not move me, then left at last and pulled no more.

And despite the passing fury, there was stillness in my being, and in the stillness, a voice spoke clearly to me but not in my ears. It said, *The Yellow Boy protects the People. Wherever you point it, there its power will go. It is your Power. You will shoot and not miss. Remember Evil is a witch. It wants to kill you. It always speaks lies. It wants your spirit. The Yellow Boy protects you, protects the People, and will destroy Evil. It is a killer of witches.*

Witches will be blind in the Happy Land, in the land of the grandfathers. When you confront a witch, shoot out its eyes, and it will become a blind ghost. Ghosts of blind witches cannot see you, cannot kill you, cannot harm you. You are Yellow Boy. You are Killer of Witches, their destroyer. Ghosts cannot harm you. Do not be afraid of them. Live free and be strong for the People. Ussen leaves you this gift. Do you accept it?

From the center of my being, I cried into the storm, "Yes, I accept it! Give me this gift. I will have it." And the voice was no more.

The storm broke over the eastern side of the mountains and, rumbling in distant thunder and lightning arrows between clouds, passed on. I lay unmoving, lay where Wind bathed me, lay with thoughts of my gift and my new name entwined in my spirit. I knew *Ussen* wanted my shooting ability to benefit the People. I needed to listen to *Ussen* and use the Yellow Boy in a good way, for *Ussen* had chosen me and the rifle to be his tools. Steam rose off the boulders and mountaintop and surrounded me in a cloud in which I slept the rest of the night.

Morning came in light and shadow, bringing me back from the world of visions. I stood and sang my morning prayer to *Ussen* and then drank cool, sweet water left in the hollows of the rocks for me when the Thunder People and Wind passed by.

As the sun lifted above the far horizon, I began my way back down the mountain, back to the house of Rufus Pike, back to my friend and mentor.

CHAPTER 20
POWER

At midday Rufus returned to the shack from repairing the cattle pool catch basin. His jaw dropped and his face broke into a wide grin when he saw me stretched out relaxing in the porch shade, my hair and breechcloth still wet from jumping in the corral watering tank.

Rufus spat on a nearby creosote bush and said, "Well, I'll be. Th' lightnin' in that there storm last night didn't kill you after all, did it? I's right worried it mighta wiped you out after I seen that big lightnin' strike up on old Baldy, and the rain come down so hard 'bout washed us away down here. You all right? You find what you were a lookin' fer?"

I sat up and nodded. "I not hurt. Wind brings me gift of Power."

Rufus slowly chewed and waited, but I said no more. At last, he asked, "Are ya hungry? I's just about to eat a little dinner."

"No eat in three days, Rufus Pike. I have

hunger. I wait when I return to eat with you."

"Well, I'm proud you did. Come on in the shack. I got beans and corn, chilies, and a little strip of beef on the stove. That an' some tortillas oughta fill ya up."

I ate two pie pans full of Rufus' cooking before putting down my spoon and knife and patting my uncomfortably full belly. "Good food, Rufus Pike. You cook better than woman. After siesta, we shoot?" I hadn't said anything, but I was anxious to show off my new Power. I had not yet seen it work, but I knew it was there. The spirits told me it was. I believed them.

"Why shore, we'n shoot after we rest our eyes and it cools off a bit. Light won't be all that good, but it'll be okay for just shootin' across the canyon."

I walked out on the porch and lay down in a shadow next to the door, my hand never leaving my rifle. I'd even kept it close while we ate. Rufus came out and stretched in the shade on the other side of the door.

The back of the canyon was catching oblique shadows cast off the western wall, but the eastern wall was aglow with fading golden light. Light would remain before dusk for a while, but shadows made it impossible to see a target at any useful distance. Rufus leaned his Sharps against a ragged ancient juniper and began pulling target bottles out of a nearby sun-bleached, gray packing box. He wrinkled his nose and made a face. "Dang if these old whiskey bottles don't stink of cheap licker after a hot day."

I picked up a rock half the size of my fist and handed it to Rufus.

"Throw far, throw hard, any direction."

Rufus grinned and shook his head. "Yore gittin' purty good at hittin' movin' targets. But this'n here? I doubt you can see 'er more'n ten or twenty yards in this light. You ain't gonna hit this rock when I throw 'er. Might as well wait till I set some bottles up."

"Throw rock, Rufus Pike."

"Okay. Just hate to see you waste a bullet."

Rufus cocked his arm and threw the stone hard and fast toward the dark shadows on the far canyon wall. I moved the lever on the rifle as his arm came forward and had the rifle's butt plate against my shoulder just as the rock curved into the sunlight above us and began to disappear into the shadows on the far wall. When the rifle thundered and the rock exploded into a brown puff of dust, catching the falling light in golden twinkles, Rufus yelled, "Damn!"

I smiled, feeling strangely warmed, and said, "Throw again, Rufus Pike."

Ten times Rufus threw stones, big and small, low and high, slow and fast, and ten times the stones turned to dust and a shower of fine gravel from my rifle bullet. In the near darkness, Rufus stared at me and said, "Yore shootin' is way beyond what you could do before you went up on the mountain. Is it your gift that you'n shoot like that?"

"It is part of gift. I tell all when Caballo Negro comes."

"Well, I shore hope he comes soon. Watchin' you hit them rocks ever time you pulled the trigger has got me more'n a little curious how ya did it."

Later, Rufus said that in all his years of shooting, he had never seen a marksman go from a tolerable shot to one that was deadly accurate in three days. He said this sort of marksmanship usually required many years to accomplish, and that, with constant practice.

I waited outside his shack for Rufus to awake. My pony snorted, and soon the old man was on the porch with his revolver. I had heard him cock the gun when he climbed out of bed and open the shack's door, but I sat motionless on my pinto watching him. When he saw me, Rufus lowered the hammer on his revolver and asked, "Where you goin', boy? It ain't even dawn yet."

"Have dream. Witch attacks my People. I go. I stop him."

"You mean you gotta go now? Caballo Negro and He Watches oughta be here in a few days. I know yore people thinks them things is real and has lots o' power, but if a witch is after 'em, what makes you think you can stop it?"

I stared at Rufus, who was shivering in his long johns, the heavy pistol dangling in his right hand as the night peepers resumed their songs.

"My Power. Vision says this rifle and me, we one. It shoots where I look. No miss. Yellow Boy shoots out witches' eyes. They no more in land of living. They blind in the land of the grandfathers. They no do harm there and suffer in the long time night. My Power says I am Yellow Boy, Killer of Witches. My name is Yellow Boy."

Rufus sat down on the porch step and smoothed his hair, which looked like prairie

237

grass after a hard wind. "That there sounds like a mighty powerful vision. So you're no longer called Nah-kah-yen; you're Yellow Boy now, and that there rifle shoots where you look? Is that why you didn't miss yesterday evenin'?"

"It is so. I go now. You good friend to Yellow Boy, Rufus Pike. I not forget. Adios."

Rufus stood and gave a salute, touching his pistol barrel to his brow as I swung my pony toward the valley. "Use yore head, and be careful. Tell ol' Caballo Negro and He Watches I'll be expectin' 'em one o' these days. Kill them witches that's a hauntin' yore mind. Make 'em pay if they's after yore People. Adios, Yellow Boy."

I rode into the darkness, proud to be chosen by *Ussen,* proud to have the Power of the Yellow Boy.

CHAPTER 21
THE MASSACRE

I like riding at night. Most of my People won't ride or move around at night unless they have to. They think their horse will take a bad step or a deadly snake or centipede will bite them when they cannot see all. But riding at night hides me from enemy eyes, and cool night air helps horses go farther with less water. These are good things worth the danger.

When I rode away from Rufus Pike's ranch toward Tortugas Mountain, and beyond to the great river, a thin moon gave only a little light, but enough. I turned southeast across the desert before I reached Tortugas Mountain, I rode alongside the eastern mountains until I found the low pass I had seen when I sat on the mountain-top waiting for Power. From there, I rode my pony hard all night, east across the *llano*. As the sun rose just above the horizon, we stopped to rest in the little mountains at the

239

big, natural tanks the *Nakai-yes* called Hueco, which were filled with water from the season of rains just past. The tank's cool, sweet water was the treasure we had hungered for in our long, dark ride, and we drank long, good swallows, filling our bellies and grateful to *Ussen* we had found it before the sun came.

I rested my pony, rubbing him down and hobbling him in some grama grass growing behind a juniper thicket next to a high canyon wall. Nearby, I crawled under a piñon for shade. It was a good place to sleep, the pine needles soft, and the crisp, pungent smell of pine sap filling the air. I kept my rifle on safety and slept easily. I remember no dreams there.

Before the sun came to the top of the day, I was riding east toward the great salt flats and the high peak in the Guadalupes called El Capitán by the *Nakai-yes*. From the Hueco Tanks, I followed nearly the same trail east Caballo Negro had used riding west to the ranch of Rufus Pike. I rode my pony fast as I dared, first walking, then a jog, and a lope that ate up the miles. I wanted to ride faster, but I knew if I pushed him too hard, he might drop and slow me down even more. The sun was hot and dry, but the season of rains was passing, and all the waterholes were full wherever I stopped.

I saw no other riders on or near the *Indah* road from the east. The fear of what I might find at Cha's camp was like a ghost haunting me, driving me. I feared I might not come in time to catch the Witch and kill him before he destroyed the People. I kept asking myself, what happens if the Witch comes and I'm not there to kill him?

My pony and I crossed the great salt flats close by the Guadalupes after the sun was gone and the stars were out. I rode around great sparkling stretches of shallow water that collected there for a short time in the season of rains. The outline of the mountains with the one the *Nakai-yes* call El Capitán, the most south, ragged and black, blotting out the eastern stars on the horizon, told me I was so near, yet so far away from Cha's camp. Studying the stars as I crossed the salt flats, I decided I ought to reach Cha's camp a little after dawn.

I rode up the wash and into the big canyon as golden light in the east lighted the top of the mountains. Even in the low light, I saw the trail sand churned up and tracks from many ponies running down the wash heading for the *llano.* Birds in the junipers lining the low reaches of the canyon walls began to call.

241

I smelled smoke. I had never smelled smoke before this far from the camp. Fear of what my dream told me sent my heart racing. My pony, almost home, wanted to run for the camp. I let him go.

I passed the horse herd meadow, but there were no horses, not even mules, and the boys who watched them, too, were gone. I checked the rifle's cartridges, cocked the Yellow Boy's hammer to safety, and rode on. Up the trail climbing to the camp's meadow, the trail I had run up so many times as a boy and beginning warrior, I saw thin plumes of smoke twisting and curling above the treetops at the camp.

I wished my eyes lied as I stared at what was left of the camp and felt the sour water from my gut rise in my throat. Ashes still smoking lay where once the People had lived in their tipis, slept and kept warm in their blankets, used pots and baskets in their work, and made weapons. Bodies of children, women, warriors, and old ones lay scattered around the camp meadow and under the trees, some shot, some trampled, some with their throats cut, and all scalped. I slid off my pony and desperately ran from one body to the next, hoping I would not find my family, but I found my father and never felt more helpless and in so dark a place in my life.

Dragged through brush and fire, his body was so torn and scraped, I barely recognized him. His body showed many bullet wounds. I counted five in his front torso, one in the back, and one in his temple. The scalpers had included his ears, from which had hung a silver wire loop with carved turquoise horses in the left ear, when they scalped him, and they had cut off his genitals and stuffed them in his mouth and ripped open his belly so his guts spilled out. Without his scalp, his face sagged into a nearly shapeless mass. Staring at the man who made me and taught me nearly everything I knew about the land, about hunting, about weapons, and about life, I swore in a cold, focused fury that settled in my chest and burned there that the Witch who did this to my father and our People would take many days to die, cursing the day of his birth, and enter the land of the grandfathers blind forever.

I looked at the remains of every body in the camp, but my mother, little brother, Socorro, He Watches, and a few others, I did not find. I prayed to *Ussen* that somewhere they were still among the living. I swore to find them, swore to *Ussen* to avenge this evil. Then I sat down by the remains of my father, buried my head in my hands, and prayed a long time to *Ussen* that my father would go to the Happy Land. Water comes to *Indah* eyes when their hearts burn with the fever of sorrow, but my eyes stayed dry. I am an Apache, a son of Caballo Negro and a son of *Ussen.*

I put my father back together as best I could, pulling his face back straight, tying his guts back together, and laying his genitals back where they belonged. I lay him on my horse blanket and wrapped and tied him in it. I strained to lift him, and the memory of how he had looked when I found him filled my throat with mesquite thorns. I carried him to a spot in the talus along the west side canyon wall and, laying his body there in a crack in the canyon wall, covered it with stones. The rest of the day, I spent burying the other bodies under rocks in the talus.

I covered the last body, a girl child, as the shadows grew long. Finished, I fell to the ground weak and hungry, almost out of my mind. A bleeding wound bathed my soul in grief and rage for the deaths of my father and our People. I tried to think clearly on how to find the living in my family, but images of vengeance for this day made all my thoughts dark.

I lay there in the grass and growing darkness, my body smeared with the blood of my father and my people, my mind drifting from one thought to another as the stars appeared. My growling stomach reminded me I hadn't eaten in over two days and nights, and I had worked hard all that day. I drank from the spring-fed creek that ran by the camp and washed a little before I stumbled along the trail to the cave hidden in the east canyon wall where the women stored food for the winter. I pulled back the junipers in front of the entrance, lighted a match, and had enough light to see our winter supplies hadn't been touched. A parfleche case on top of the first layer of grass and sticks that separated other layers of parfleches held dried beef. Another, not nearly as heavy, had dried berries and nuts, another dried mescal, and another dried prickly pear fruit.

I didn't want to risk revealing myself with a fire, but carried a few food parfleches back to the creek and ate some dried beef, cutting off small pieces and letting them soften in my mouth for a while before I chewed them. A few handfuls of dried berries mixed with acorns and the beef made my hunger go away.

In the deep twilight, I pulled off my moccasins and lay down in the cold creek water, its flow full and fresh from the season of rains, its rushing water surrounding me and washing away the heat of the day and the grime of my labor and the blood of my father and the people I'd buried. I had often played in this stream as a boy, and for a moment, I was a child again hunting monsters in the water before the memory of the day returned to me. I rested there, not moving, until the full night came with a chorus of crickets and frogs and tree peepers. I scrubbed my body with sand from the slow pools and crawled up on a rock shelf next to the stream to dry.

Somewhere down the canyon, a coyote howled the grief I had not spoken. I took my blanket and found a place under a juniper to sleep. I wanted my mind clear and rested before I decided what to do next. I remembered what the People said about ghost sickness coming from handling dead bodies not of your own family and other things they made and touched, but I didn't care. I remembered *Ussen* told me not to fear ghosts. If ghost sickness didn't take me now, I had heard the voice in my vision correctly and would know for certain that I had the blessing of *Ussen.* Perhaps *Ussen* meant for ghost sickness to stay away from a killer of witches because its power brought death

I was not meant to have.

At dawn, I crawled from under the juniper and ate more meat and berries. The sorrow and burning need to avenge my People and family were hot, heavy stones pressing on my heart. Many questions fluttered through my mind. *Who did this evil thing? Did a witch truly come, or just a great enemy? Why didn't Cha and other warriors drive them off? Why were the People all scalped? Why murder children and women when they can be made slaves and sold to the Nakai-yes? How had the* Witch *surprised the camp when guards watched the trail? Had the guards escaped or been taken for slaves? Where is my family?*

I decided to look for my family beginning first at the place He Watches used on the high ridge. Perhaps, if I were very lucky, I might see a dust or smoke plume that showed where they were on the *llano.* Maybe they went south to the Apache camps in the Davis Mountains. Maybe that was where Cha and his scouts were. I had to find them. I had to learn who did this and take the full measure of vengeance against them using the Power *Ussen* gave me.

CHAPTER 22
FINDING HE WATCHES

I stood on the big flat rock a long time where He Watches had built his fires for signal smokes and thought of the times I sat with him under the overhung shelf below the rim and used the *Shináá Cho* to look along the road from the east and across the *llano* disappearing into the gray haze to the south. Now alone, staring at the *llano,* the taste of bitter disappointment was strong in my mouth for not killing the Witch before he spread his evil on the People. Many thoughts came. Many thoughts left. I knew only that I had to find what was left of my family and pour burning coals on the head of the Witch.

Maybe, I thought, *I'll see some trace of our enemies or my family if the spirit of He Watches helps me.* I climbed down the path through the big rocks to He Watches' place. When I stepped around the boulder that hid the place from above, a cocked rifle was pointed at me and two bright eyes stared at me from the gloom. My surprise and joy made me jump and nearly carried me backwards to the rocks far below. I ran forward, held his shoulders, and looked in his face.

"He Watches! Grandfather, is it truly you or a spirit from the Happy Land?"

Relief flooded He Watches' face, and he croaked, "I am here. You return. *Enjuh!*"

"Are you hurt?"

"Shot through the meat in my good leg, but the bullet hit no bone. Socorro made medicine from her herbs. It heals."

"Where are the others? Tell me what happened."

He Watches lay against his favorite boulder, bowed his head, and sighed. He motioned toward a water bladder. "I need water before I can speak of these things. I thought I might die of thirst unless I saved enough to keep me alive until I am strong enough to crawl down to the creek. But, I'm not healing fast enough to crawl to water before I run out of it here. You've saved my life."

I handed him the bladder, and he pulled on it slowly for a time before giving it back to me. He licked his cracked lips and said, "The day we were attacked, Socorro, Sons-ee-ah-ray, and your little brother left the camp at dawn with some of the other women and their children to gather plants and nuts to keep us fed in the Ghost Face Season.

"Caballo Negro planned to come here with me, make arrows, and watch for Cha when there was enough light to ride his pony and my mule up the trail. We ate from Sons-ee-ah-ray's stew pot and decided in two or three suns we must go for you at Roofoos Peek ranch. We had just finished the last of the stew when we heard shots from down the canyon in the horse herd meadow. Caballo Negro grabbed his rifle, and, with a few other warriors still in the camp, ran for the horse meadow. He didn't get far, just beyond the biggest circle of lodges, when Comanches and *Nakai-yes* came charging up the trail shooting anyone in front of them — warriors, children, women, old men — everyone they saw. I fired my rifle from the tipi, but I don't think I killed any of them.

"I saw Caballo Negro go down, and then rise to one knee and shoot a *Nakai-yi* and two Comanches off their ponies before many bullets killed him. They roped him around his feet, and a giant with no hair, his body painted black and his head painted to look like a skull, dragged him back and forth through the camp, across fires, stones, and cactus, while shooting into the tipis, killing many.

"One of their bullets hit my good leg. I tied it off to stop the bleeding and crawled off to the brush from where I shot when I could. I hid there and watched what they did. I have never seen such evil. They were worse than the Comanches in the old days when we fought them. They killed everyone and cut up your father, expecting to disgrace him in the Happy Land, but they were too late. He was long dead when the giant started dragging him. He was the one who led them, the big, ugly giant with no hair and the painted body and head, probably a *Nakai-yi* — Comanche mongrel. He sat on his pony laughing and shooting anyone still living while he watched the Comanches disgrace your father. When he saw no one still alive, he told his men to take every scalp. Across the great river, *Nakai-yes* pay much for Apache scalps. I have never seen so many bodies mutilated, so many disgraced. Those men were not human beings. They handled the dead with no fear. They even took Caballo Negro's hair with his ears and gave the scalp to the giant, who, I have no doubt, is a witch. He held Caballo

Negro's scalp high and shook it whooping in victory. No doubt they were all witches come to kill us. Our People cannot fight this great evil so much stronger than us."

I hung my head, remembering my vision. "Because of me, this happened."

Grandfather squeezed my shoulder and shouted, "No! Not so!" He looked in my eyes and said, "Those who lived prayed to *Ussen* that you'd return. They need you now. Cha and the other warriors are nowhere to be seen. If you were here at the attack, that witch would have killed you, too."

I shook my head. "You don't understand. My vision came in a high place near the ranch of Rufus Pike." I told him of the gift *Ussen* had given me to help the People and that my name was to be Yellow Boy. "Three suns later, a dream that this would happen visited me and said I must return to the People, but I didn't come in time. My Power is strong enough to kill this witch and those with him. All this death and destruction came because I was slow to return."

He Watches stared off into the haze over the far *llano,* slowly shaking his head, his eyes narrowed, brow wrinkled. At last, he said, "Your vision and Power from *Ussen* comes when the People need them. Your enemies will call you Yellow Boy. It is a great name for a great warrior with a strong weapon. *Enjuh!* Your dream told you to come to this place. One day you will kill the Witch and leave him blind and cursed in the land of the grandfathers. This I know. Do not look back. Do what you can each today. Each new rising sun is another chance to make past days right."

We sat together saying nothing for a while. His words gave me comfort and hope to put the past day's attack in balance and make the murders of my People and my father right. I started to wonder if the others were alive, maybe slaves. "Grandfather, what of the women and children not in camp? Where are they? What happened to them?"

"When they heard the shooting, they ran back to camp but kept their heads and stayed out of sight until our enemies left. Socorro and Sons-ee-ah-ray found me passed out in the brush. Socorro made medicine for my wound, and they helped me up to the watching place. They hid a fire here, fed the children, and ate with me. We talked of what must be done. The old camp is now a place of the dead. We cannot stay. Many ghosts and much sickness will be there. Even if we could stay, the enemies who found it might come back. Some wanted to wait for Cha to return and ask him what to do, but that might be many days, and new food supplies have to be gathered. All the food they put aside is now in a place of the dead and cannot be touched without danger of ghost sickness."

I stared at the ground. I had handled dead bodies to bury them. I had eaten food that might give me ghost sickness. Again, I prayed to *Ussen* that my Power made me safe from ghosts and ghost sickness. I cannot become sick, if that is part of my Power.

He Watches said, "Some of the women wailed. Gathering new food supplies takes time. No time left, not much food to gather. The little ones and women will starve in the Ghost Face Season. One said not to worry, that Cha could raid the *Nakai-yi* villages across the great river for food. Another said that with many of his warriors gone to the Happy Place, he might steal a little, but there could be no big, quick raids. Then Juanita spoke."

My ears stood up like those of a listening wolf when He Watches spoke of Juanita. I liked her and was happy I had not found her scalped and mutilated like her father, whom I had buried with the others.

"She said her father spoke often of the Mescalero Reservation six or seven days' ride to the northwest where, if you go in and give up to the agent, the *Indah* will give you food and protect you from the other *Indah* who want to kill you. 'Let's us go there,' she said. 'We can walk there in maybe ten or fifteen suns, less if we find horses. We have knives, blankets, and a little food. We can do it. Why not go there?'

"The women were quiet a long time as they thought about Juanita's words. I stood, leaning on my stick, and said, 'Go. Do as Juanita says. She speaks wise words. You won't starve. I'll stay here until Cha returns and tell him what happened and where you have gone. When the sun comes, go. Stay on the eastern side of the mountains. There's more water on that side, and it's easier to find than on the west side. I'll follow you with Cha and his warriors.'

"The women looked at each other and nodded. With one voice they said, *'Enjuh!'* When the sun came, they left for the reservation. Socorro wanted to stay with me. I told her the young women and little ones needed her wisdom and skills, so she must go with them. She didn't like it, but she went. They left yesterday. You must go and help them. They need a warrior with them."

I said, "I'll find the women and help them to the reservation before I find and kill the

Witch, but you must come with me, Grandfather. We all need you and your wise words. When Cha comes, he'll follow our trail. Now, we go."

He Watches looked in my eyes and nodded. "Now we go . . . Yellow Boy."

Chapter 23
Finding Survivors

I tied He Watches and his supplies on my pony, and leading it, followed the women's twisting trail out of the mountains. It was the same trail through the dark green junipers and mountain brush that Caballo Negro had followed into the mountains when we had run from the Blue Coats nearly ten years earlier.

The women left a trail that was easy for an Apache to follow but impossible for an *Indah* to see. They walked some, ran some, stayed on rocky ground, and hid well where they made water. Down from the mountains in the rough, brown foothills, where scattered mesquites, creosotes, and yuccas grew, they turned northwest but stayed in foothill arroyos where they couldn't be seen on the horizon.

Before the sun fell the first day, we found campfire charcoal buried in the sand at the bottom of an arroyo, and at the top of the arroyo bank bent grass in the brush where they had slept. From their tracks and stopping places, I believed there were ten women and five children, two girls and three boys. He Watches didn't know for certain how many had survived the attack. We expected to find them before the next sunset.

The next day, in the middle of the afternoon, we stopped to water the ponies and rest in the shade of a small juniper foolishly growing in a wide, deep arroyo, junipers lining its top edges like feathers in a war bonnet. The arroyo, certain one day to be a roaring, rushing river made from male rain in the mountains and taking everything before it, wound around billowing foothills and the ends of smaller arroyos, and even an occasional canyon wash emptied into it. As we rested there, my pony pricked up his ears and stared down the arroyo to the point where it turned a curve and disappeared. I tapped the shoulder of He Watches and threw my thumb toward the top of the arroyo. He nodded, and I climbed to the top of the steep sandy bank and crawled into the junipers.

I crept through the weeds and brush until I saw the other side of the bend where my pony stared. Two women, Juanita and her mother, Maria, knives in hand, squatted behind a big boulder in the bottom of the arroyo. Staring at the bend beyond which He Watches and I had stopped, they no doubt were planning to find out who followed them and why. I found a couple of pebbles and tossed one that bounced off the boulder in front of Juanita with an unexpected click in the sleepy, hot silence. She recoiled back from the sound, landing on her rear, looked at her mother, who was frowning, and then toward the top of the arroyo where she saw me hold up my hand, fingers spread, and wave to them. Juanita's throaty, girlish giggle filled me with relief. She was all right, and it made my heart happy to see her.

I ran down the side of the arroyo toward them and said, "*Dánt'e,* Maria and Juanita. He Watches and I have come to help those who go to the reservation. At last, we've found you. All is well?"

They sheathed their knives in scabbards behind their backs and Maria, a smile under her full, sad eyes, answered. "*Dánt'e,* Nah-kah-yen. Never has a mother been so glad to find a young man chase after her daughter. All is well. The others wait hidden further down the arroyo. Where is He Watches?"

"Around the bend with my pony and the

supplies you left him. Stay here. I'll go for him."

She nodded. "We'll stay. Bring him."

Maria and Juanita led us to a small canyon out of the mountains that emptied into the arroyo. There, Maria stood in the middle of the wash and, cupping her hands, called like a Gambel quail, "chiii-caaago . . . chiii-caaago."

From up the canyon, five children appeared from the brush as if they were quail. Eight haggard women followed them: Socorro; my mother, Sons-ee-ah-ray; Sonsnah's woman and Deer Woman, her daughter; an old woman and her grown daughter; and two grown women with children whose men I had buried two days earlier. The children included my little brother; Juanita's sister, Moon on the Water, not more than three or four years old; another little girl no more than six or seven years; her little brother, maybe four years; and a young boy, maybe ten years.

All the women carried water bladders, small bags of food, and a blanket, but the bladders were becoming flat, and their moccasins were torn and falling apart. I was the only warrior to protect them, and we had no horses except for my pinto. Having the

261

responsibility of protecting them and getting them safely to the reservation made me feel I had the weight of huge stones settling on my shoulders. They all stared and waited for their newfound warrior to speak.

I stood straight and said, "My vision came. *Ussen* gave me Power two days before a dream called me back to the camp of Cha. My name is no more Nah-kah-yen, but Yellow Boy."

I saw Juanita nod, a faint smile brushing her lips. Deer Woman folded her arms and stared at me, her eyes dark, probing mine. My mother and Socorro smiled and nodded, and my little brother's jaw dropped, his eyes big.

"The one who attacked and destroyed our camp and killed our men, women, and children is a witch. Someday I'll kill him and send him blind into the land of the grandfathers. First, we go to the reservation. The agency will give us food when we need it, and we can hunt. You've made a wise choice.

"When we find a place with ponies, I'll take them for you so we can ride to the agency and get there before the Ghost Face Season comes with snow and ice. For now, the four littlest ones ride with He Watches, two in front of the saddle, two in back.

Make two sacks with your blankets to carry the supplies. We will carry them on my pony. This will help you run or walk faster while saving your strength until I find ponies. We go."

They shook their fists and said with one voice, *"Enjuh!"*

With the children mounted, we ran far on the hard sand and gravel in the arroyo beds and didn't stop until nearly dark. The women built a small fire, making little smoke under an arroyo bank overhang. The night grew cold and they all sat close to the fire to keep themselves warm and eat a little.

I sat nearby with Sons-ee-ah-ray and my little brother, and He Watches sat with Socorro. I had never seen such pain in my mother's face, but she held her head up and held my little brother close to her. I wished my tongue was smart enough to comfort her then, but I knew in time her sorrow must heal. I was thankful my little brother never saw the torn body of our father. One day *Ussen* would deliver the Witch into my hand and make things right again.

The women asked to hear about my time with Rufus Pike and my vision. When I finished my story, they said nothing for a long time until my mother said, "Uhmmm, a very powerful vision. You were favored to live through it. *Ussen* told the Thunder People and Wind to spare you. I am glad for you, but I have a heavy heart. Your father goes to the Happy Land, his hair stolen by a witch. Promise me, Yellow Boy, one day you will avenge your father."

The coals of vengeance burning in my chest and head burst into flame. "My mother, by all the spirits, I swear it so. Avenging my father is never far from my thoughts. One day, I'll put out the eyes of the Witch, and my father's spirit will know peace in the Happy Land. Today, my duty makes me protect and feed those who escaped the Witch and lived. I'll guard the camp tonight from the top of the arroyo. When you are ready, take the others to the brush and sleep there. I'll come to you with the dawn, and we'll go."

"Avenge your father and your people. You, Yellow Boy, be a killer of many witches, a mighty warrior." She seemed to taste the words of my new name on her tongue and smiled. "Yellow Boy . . . we'll sleep in the brush apart from you, ready to run when you tell us."

I climbed to the top of the arroyo and, in the black night filled with stars, heard

Coyote call his brothers. A light twinkled far out on the *llano,* and I kept my eyes on it as I spread my blanket, afraid to gaze away my eyes, afraid it might disappear into nothing more than hope. I sat on the blanket and pulled open the *Shináá Cho.* He Watches had placed it in my hands before we left his watching place in the Guadalupes. He said I might need it. I had learned over the years to listen to my grandfather. He was right again.

I looked through the *Shináá Cho* at the far glow of twinkling yellow light, a star fallen to the ground, and saw it was a fire, an *Indah* fire with men around it, men with big hats and big guns in their arms, *Indah vaquero*s watching cattle. I smiled. *Indah* always had horses and mules for the taking. Traveling by myself, I might have gone after them that night, but, to protect the women and children, I waited for the sun before leaving to scout the *Indah* camp.

By the middle of the night, the light from the fire had died from a few orange and gray coals, and the women and children slept in the brush a bowshot from me. I worked hard to keep my eyes from closing when I heard a foot crunch on dry grass and a soft whisper, "Yellow Boy?"

I whispered, "Here."

Deer Woman appeared out of the night and sat down beside me in the dark shadows from the moon.

"Is there trouble?"

"No. I cannot sleep. I came to keep you company. My mother already snores. We are alone together in this dark place. No one sees I am with you in the night."

I felt her warm arm across my shoulders and the push of her breast against my arm. She was offering herself to me like some Comanche girl taking any man she chose. I thought how good it must be to lie with her, but since my father had told me about Deer Woman night crawling with Delgadito, she no longer stirred my dreams. I felt no desire for her. Only Juanita filled my heart.

"You must go."

She smiled and said, "Yellow Boy is afraid to take a woman? Don't you want me? I will show you what to do."

She stood and dropped her skirt and pulled her shirt off over her head and knelt beside me once more, naked and unafraid. She knew she had power to stir any man's passion and asked again as she draped an arm over my shoulders, "Don't you want me?"

"I have wanted you since your Haheh, even since before your Haheh. You must go."

"Why?"

"Your father was killed by the Witch. Your mother has no man. Her wealth is gone. If it becomes widely known you've lain with a man before you are married, she will get nothing for you, and only men of little worth will want you and will be of little support to her. Many of the People knew you night crawled with Delgadito and, like me, said nothing. Already your mother may die poor because you'll bring a small bride price. I will not make that certain. You must go."

Her eyes narrowed and even in the dark, I saw her face darken.

She hissed in a whisper, "Delgadito wanted me. He has taken me every time I offered myself to him since my Haheh. He'll make me his wife, give my mother four horses, and keep us well. You're weak, Yellow Boy."

"If you were my woman, I'd beat you for your insults. Delgadito takes many women and brags. He is a man of no Power except to make *Nakai-yi* women cry out in pain. Life will be different on the reservation. You'll never have a life with me. Maybe Delgadito will take you for a wife, or maybe he'll want one with virtue and leave you to an old man who cannot mount you. Go!"

She stood, snatched up her shirt and skirt, and said, "You're a fool, Yellow Boy. No woman wants you. You're weak and a fool." She disappeared into the darkness, pulling her blouse over her head. I heard her stop and step into her skirt, and her steps fade away.

CHAPTER 24
ANGRY WOMEN

The desire for sleep left me after Deer Woman's visit, and I thought about her the rest of the night. My father taught me always to do the right thing. He said a man does not take scalps, mutilate dead bodies, or take a woman who is not yet married, even a captive. An unmarried woman's virtue is her father's property. If she loses her virtue before marriage, then her father loses her value. Deer Woman said Delgadito took her many times, and I knew my father saw them at least once, but he had turned away and said nothing because it wasn't his business to tell Sons-nah. She had no more value to her mother than a woman divorced or widowed. She did not command, nor deserve, a high bride price.

I thought Deer Woman and Delgadito should be beaten and made to marry. Delgadito had no honor with women. He had forced many captive *Nakai-yi* women before he killed them. What he did to those women was shameful. He didn't act like a true Apache man, and I believed Deer Woman would never be his wife. He had no interest in a woman like her carrying and raising his children. What would she teach them? He could not trust her around other men. How would he know for certain she carried his child? He would not know. He would not take her for a first wife, but only for pleasure and maybe as a second wife. I hoped the old man she deceived into a marriage had good ears and eyes to catch them. He would cut off her nose and maybe shoot Delgadito.

I knew speaking the truth made Deer Woman very angry, but I didn't care. Perhaps this night I had made an enemy for life. I knew I must watch her. A woman with no virtue can cause much trouble in a camp, even get undeserving men killed and start long blood feuds between families. The wisdom of my father grew in my mind as I thought about these things. I was glad I did not take Deer Woman and had endured her insults.

Dawn came. I sang to *Ussen* and then looked northwest in the direction I remembered for the *vaquero* fire and saw a thin plume of smoke rising straight into the sky.

I used the *Shináá Cho* and saw men saddling horses by a wagon, its top covered in white cloth. Some of the *vaquero*s sat on the ground, their legs crossed, eating as the *Indah* do.

Although I watched from a far distance, I saw *Nakai-yes* walking around with rifles in the crooks of their arms and the ones sitting down, keeping their rifles across their knees, and eating from pie pans like those Rufus used. They were nervous, scratching their dirty, wooly faces, and straining their necks out of their shirts to look east across the desert toward the river called Pecos by the *Indah.* Their ponies were in a corral next to an *Indah* windmill. The *vaquero*s expected someone, maybe someone coming to attack them. I watched them and studied the ground around the corral, and thought about how to best make a raid for horses there. The *vaquero*s, alert, expecting something or someone, meant I must take great care when I took their ponies or risk being killed.

I spoke with He Watches and told him my plan for taking the *vaquero* ponies. With his head bowed and cocked to one side, he listened to every word. When I finished, he nodded and said, "Pick your helper well.

When bullets fly, so does a plan. Your helper must be someone you know will do exactly as you say. Raiding belongs to men, but the women here can take care of themselves and help if you have need. I only wish I could help you."

"Your wisdom is enough, Grandfather. We will have horses before the sun rises again."

As the sun floated big and red above the far mountains, I sat with He Watches and the women and children. I told them how I had seen a *vaquero* camp out on the *llano,* a camp with many horses. As I spoke, Juanita kept her eyes from me. Deer Woman, smiling like a woman who knew a secret, never took her eyes away.

I said, "I have a plan to take their horses, but I need a helper."

The boy with ten years said, "I'll go. Take me, Yellow Boy."

"How many seasons have you worked the horses, Ish-kay-neh?"

"Almost one."

"Hmmph. How many arrows do you have from shooting contests with your friends?"

The boy thought a moment and said, "I have five new arrows I won the day before the *Indah* and *Nakai-yes* came."

"Hmmph. You are a good shot with a bow."

I raked my fingers through the coarse sand and gravel to find five easy-to-throw pebbles, smooth, shaped like quail eggs. I pointed my nose toward a yucca and its tall, dry stem growing from a broad base of many leaves. "Can you hit that yucca with these rocks and your sling?"

He squinted toward the yucca and said, "I can try."

"Then, try."

He used his sling with the three pebbles I gave him. He had good style and threw hard, but he missed even the wide base of the yucca. Three times, the pebble flew high and to the right. He bowed his head and murmured, "I still have much to learn."

I felt no sympathy for him. When I was his age, I could hit the yucca base three times out of three with a sling at that distance. "Yes, you have much work to do, Ish-kay-neh. You must —"

Juanita stood and went to stand by the boy.

"Give me your sling, Ish-kay-neh, and you, Yellow Boy, give me three more stones for it."

I started to tell her to sit down, but the fire in her eyes said to hold my words and let her make a fool of herself rather than have her disobey me. I saw my mother smile and Socorro nod, grinning.

She took the pebbles I gave her and the sling from Ish-kay-neh. The easy, self-assured way she handled the sling straps and dropped the stones in a pouch tied to her belt told me she was no child learning a sling. She stood with her feet turned a little off the line between her and the yucca and paused a moment staring at it. With a motion so fast it was hard to follow, she placed a stone in the sling pouch, whirled the sling with a fast whip, and sent the stone blazing forward to break the yucca stem a hand width below its seedpod. Within the space of a breath, she clipped off two more pieces of the stem about the length of my forearm. I had never seen such skill with a sling and was about to say so when she handed the sling back to Ish-kay-neh and, looking at me with the fire still in her eyes, said, "Women must be able to take care of themselves. Shall I show what I can do with a bow?"

I shook my head.

"No? Then I will help you get the horses. My father taught me much about ponies and how to ride."

She sat down and turned her face from

me to look with a faraway stare at Deer Woman. Deer Woman smiled no more and kept her eyes off me.

I said to Ish-kay-neh, "Go with the women and children. Stay in arroyos and behind them as you move. Behind is the most dangerous place. Protect them from attack. Help He Watches and the little ones with him. Do not go fast and raise dust that can be seen. We will find you and bring horses before the next dawn.

"Juanita, bring the rope He Watches carries. Now go."

He Watches shook his fist. *"Enjuh!"*

Before we left, Juanita's mother spoke to me out of sight of the others. Her dark eyes full, on the edge of water, she said, "Muchacho Amarillo, I know you are a good man, and one day will be a leader of warriors. Bring back my daughter. She is all I have left. Give me your promise not to take her, even if she desires you. I need her true value so a warrior of means will want her for a first wife, give me a good bride price, and take care of both of us. Will you do this for a woman who no more has a man?"

I stared at her. *Why do these women and their mothers suddenly think I have forgotten all my father taught me?*

"Juanita will bring you a full bride price and marry a good man. This I promise, Maria."

"You will not take her when you are together alone in the desert? You promise this?"

"I will not take her. I vow it so before *Ussen.* Go and help the others. The day is long and you all will suffer in the heat with little water. Go."

She smiled, turned to go, and said over her shoulder, "Ka dish day (goodbye) Yellow Boy. You have the spirit of a true warrior."

Juanita and I crept down small winding arroyos toward the fast disappearing smoke column from the *vaquero* fire. I carried my rifle and pistol, knife, a pouch of bullets, and a bladder of water. She ran with Ishkay-neh's sling tied to her belt, smooth stones she found in the arroyo in a pouch, and my bow and quiver of arrows. Before we began, she went behind some creosote bushes, loosened her shirt, and tied it so her breasts were better supported, for she was large but knew how to take care of herself, a companion to be respected and depended upon.

We ran for a time without stopping, the

sun rising, and the air growing warm. Halfway to the *vaquero* fire, we looked at each other, and I still saw the anger and fury in her eyes. I wanted this to stop and attacked her look with calm words.

"Why are you angry with me? I'm doing the right things."

She clenched her teeth, stared down the arroyo, and said, "Did you do the right thing lying with Deer Woman last night? You took her mother's best chance to live easy in her grandmother years. Was Deer Woman's body that fine? Did you enjoy it that much? I don't believe you'll take her for a wife after you used her. No good man will want her now. I thought you a better man than that."

Her words stung like the switches men had used on us as boys to make us run faster when we trained. Hot blood filled my mind. "Who told you this? Did you see us with your eyes or was this a dream?"

"Deer Woman said she went to thank you for helping us and you took her. She said she didn't resist because we need you and was afraid you would leave us if she did not. Now you've ruined her chances for a strong warrior husband. Will you take me, too, now that we are alone? She said she had to show you what to do. I'll resist. I will not help

277

you. You'll regret it if you try to take me. Stay away. I'm not afraid of you."

I knew Deer Woman was angry with me, but these were bad lies, and I had to speak. My fury blew like Wind against her. *Someday, Deer Woman,* I thought, *I'll cut off the end of your nose and show the people what a liar and whore you are. Your husband will want to beat you every day. I cannot believe she was my friend when we were children. She has changed much.*

I spoke slowly, not letting my fury betray me.

"I took an oath, swore to *Ussen* and your mother that I would not touch you. I will not. Ask Maria if I did this. You're safe with me. Deer Woman is Coyote. She lies. It's true she came to me last night. She offered herself and said she wanted me to lie with her. I said no. I said she must go. I said I would not take her and destroy the price her mother can ask from a warrior who wants a virtuous first wife. Deer Woman grew angry. She said Delgadito had been with her many times. It's true. My father saw them night crawling in the bushes. She said someday Delgadito would take her as first wife. I told her Delgadito would never take a used first wife. She didn't believe me. She lied to you because she knows I watch

278

you with happy eyes. She tells lies about me among the other women? This cannot stand. I will not have it."

Juanita's eyes narrowed, studying my face for the truth. She said nothing and looked away.

CHAPTER 25
HORSE RAID

We reached the place of the *vaquero* fire well before the shadows grew short. Many horses stirred dust in the corral, and a *Nakai-yi vaquero*, his sombrero pulled low over his eyes and a rifle in the crook of his arm, sat on the gate scanning the *llano* to the north. Five other *Nakai-yes*, four napping, and one sitting cross-legged on a blanket smoking a *cigarro* and cleaning a pistol, were in the shade made by the dirty white cloth pulled off the top of the wagon. Another man, using his skinning knife and a piece of plank for a cutting board, cut pieces of meat he tossed in a big pot on the fire. This was about half the number of men I believed I had seen by the fire the last night. I wondered where the others had disappeared and considered wiping out all the *vaquero*s left in their camp and taking all the horses rather than running off with a few after sending the *vaquero*s chasing a decoy as I originally planned.

Off in the brush and weeds surrounding the corral, a roadrunner clicked and a small flock of desert wrens fluttered from bush to bush. The big windmill by the corral creaked and groaned, catching little occasional puffs of breeze to pull more water into the big iron tank half in the corral and half out. I was sure the *vaquero*s thought little of possible danger in the peaceful late morning around them.

I studied the horses using the *Shináá Cho.* Some had no brands at all. Others were marked with the symbol "US" the Blue Coats used. Several different marks branded the rest, and many carried no iron on their hooves. I realized many of the horses in the corral must be Indian ponies stolen from the reservation. If we returned them, I knew the reservation People would be happier to see us than if we came poor with empty hands, and all the women and children could ride the rest of the way to the reservation. The *Nakai-yi* guard looked like he waited and watched for other *vaquero*s, maybe those I had seen around the fire. More ponies might be coming, but with more *vaquero*s. More *vaquero*s made our chances of taking some ponies and getting away without a fight small. I decided to wipe

281

out those in front of me and take all the ponies.

We moved down the narrow arroyo that passed by the camp. It was maybe a man's arm span wide, and chest high deep. I motioned Juanita to work her way to the corral fence on the side opposite the guard. At my signal, she was to use her sling to brain the guard and then stay near the gate until I took the others.

I planned to take the *cigarro* smoker and the man cutting meat for the pot first. Awake and alert, they acted as guards for the whole camp and would raise the alarm when I attacked.

I believed my bow best to use against the *vaquero*s rather than my rifle. The *vaquero*s not in camp might hear the sound of gunshots, and at a distance of less than thirty long strides, a bow could be as fast and as deadly as a rifle.

Juanita went to her place by the corral fence. I made a circling motion with my hand and wrist, signing her to begin. Her stone struck the *vaquero* in the back of his head just below his sombrero brim. He slumped off the corral gate and fell like a sack of rocks, raising a puff of dust at the bottom rail of the corral gate when he landed. Juanita was quick over the corral bars and through the milling horses to re-appear like a ghostly shadow at the rails near the gate.

The *cigarro* smoker heard the guard hit the ground, and looking toward the corral gate, frowned to see the guard gone and a puff of dust at the gate. He stretched up for a better look. My aim with the bow was good but the smoker was turning his head to say something to the meat cutter when the arrow hit him low and in the neck rather than in his throat where I had aimed. He grabbed the shaft and opened his mouth to yell when a stone struck his forehead and he fell back, silent and still. The meat cutter looked up, saw the smoker lying with an arrow in his neck, and opened his mouth to bellow an alarm when my arrow hit his windpipe. Clutching its shaft and gurgling blood, he began to stand up from his stool but pitched forward into the fire. Hitting the bucket of cut meat made enough noise to rouse the napping *vaquero*s. Too late; a stone struck one man behind his right ear and he fell over hard, his revolver clutched in a death grip, his eyes wide and frozen. The other three caught arrows in their hearts and fell back, their hands on the shafts and their bodies trembling in death. I ran forward, my knife drawn, ready to finish off any *vaquero* still living, but there was no need.

Juanita ran from the gate and joined me. We took guns and bullets from the bodies, pulled down the white cloth providing shade, and emptied the wagon of food supplies, mostly cured meat and sacks of cornmeal and beans. While Juanita made piles of supplies and weapons to load on ponies and filled canteens, I tied brush to the tails of five ponies and setting fire to it sent them running south raising dust and laying a smoke stream for anyone to see. I used the *vaquero* saddles on the ponies and loaded them with blankets packed with supplies Juanita had organized. We drank our fill from the great iron tank and there I dumped the bodies and gutted one to poison the water enough to delay their returning amigos from following us.

I tied the ponies carrying our loot head-to-tail and we mounted two that I pulled for us to ride. We followed the tracks of the ponies I sent running south until we turned off west on hard ground, leaving little sign of our tracks. Unless an Apache rode with the *vaquero*s tracking us, they would never see where we turned toward the mountains.

Shadows were growing long when we

stopped to rest the horses in the same arroyo the women and children were following. I climbed up a hill, used the *Shináá Cho* to look for them through the wavering heat against the far gray haze, and looked back over our back trail to ensure no one followed us, but saw nothing in either direction. When I returned to Juanita, she looked at me, her brow wrinkled with questions, but I shook my head and took the canteen of water she offered. We sat in the hot shade of the arroyo's west bank and listened to the occasional buzzing of insects and the ponies stamping against flies attacking them.

Juanita spoke in a low questioning voice.

"It is true? What you told me earlier in the cool of the day? What Deer Woman said and did? What my mother asked of you and you swore to?"

I snorted, looked in her eyes, and nodded. "I did not lie."

She held my eyes. "I believe you. I was wrong to speak to you with an evil tongue. I have much regret for those words. Deer Woman and me, we were friends since leaving the cradleboard. We had the same Haheh. The lies she told me I didn't want to believe, but I knew you were with her. I saw her go to you. I believed her when she said you'd asked her to come. I didn't like it. I expected you to be a better man, not a one to steal a widow's chance for her daughter's bride price, not one to deny a woman a powerful warrior, one who is rich, for a husband. I had my own hopes for you. Now, I know my hopes are gone. What I wanted, you are, but my friendship with her blinded me to the truth."

I looked away and stared at the bright mountains against the dark, blue sky and felt my heart open like a morning glory at the coming of the sun.

"This day you showed you are a worthy warrior, one I always ride with. You're better than I am with a sling, and you have great courage. I'm proud you came with me. Four moons ago, I expected Deer Woman to tap me for the victory dance. She chose Delgadito instead. Now I know why. At that dance, you chose me. Our dancing was good. I felt like a man who had found a piece of turquoise he never knew he had in his treasures.

"I spoke of you to my father who now has gone away. He told me to wait two years before I tied my pony in front of your mother's lodge. By that time, he felt I would have much to offer Maria and Porico for you. He said to tell you my heart because many warriors would bring a pony to your mother's lodge, but if you knew my heart and wanted me, you would wait for mine.

"Much has changed in the time since we danced. My father walks in the happy land of the grandfathers. Many in Cha's camp have been wiped out. I have a new name, and *Ussen* has given me Power. Now we'll go to the reservation and submit to the *Indah*. Our warriors can no longer raid and make war. There are no more ponies to take except these we have here. I speak to you now what is in my heart. Will you wait for a husband until I bring my pony to your mother's lodge?"

I looked in her eyes. She had never stopped looking at me since she began speaking. Streams of water on her cheeks, a smile on her mouth, she said, "I'll wait. Bring your pony soon, Yellow Boy."

I laughed, filled with a pleasure I had never known.

"I'll come in the next season of Many Leaves. But know this, woman. After you are my wife, if you speak to me as you did this morning, I will beat you."

She looked at her hands folded in her lap and said, "I know. I will deserve it."

CHAPTER 26
RESERVATION

Near nightfall, we found the women and children. As the sun slipped behind the mountains in a glory of oranges and lavender tinting high, thin clouds, I spotted the little group with the *Shináá Cho*. Their faces filled with smiles of relief, as they squatted silently below the ragged edge of a low, grassy hill and watched us come. At the foot of the hill, dusk turning to black sky pierced with burning white stars, I told them to come down, eat, and rest.

To avoid confrontation with *vaquero*s, Blue Coats, and marauding Indeh, I decided we ought to travel at night, and He Watches agreed with me. The younger children rode with their mothers, and the women without little children and the boy, Ish-key-nay, led the ponies in groups of three or four to avoid losing them all in one fell swoop if we were attacked. The ponies, prizes sure to earn us many friends and supporters on the reservation and gifts of food, clothing, and hides or canvas for shelters, carried us far and fast.

At this distance, the Sacramentos, where the reservation nestled, appeared as dark bumps on the northwest horizon. He Watches told me what he knew about the trail to the reservation, and I led my little band along dry arroyos and across foothills lying like giant lumps of bread dough on the *llano*. It was mid-September by *Indah* reckoning, the Season of Large Fruit as the Mescaleros count time, and some arroyos still held shallow, life-saving pools of water from the Season of Large Fruit rains. The easy access to water and cool nights made the long ride a ride we would all remember with pleasure in later years.

After reaching the light-splotched shade and shadows of deep tree cover and cool water in the lush green valleys leading into the Sacramentos, I decided the risk was small enough to ride during daylight. After a few days of crossing ridges and following long narrow valleys, we rode to the top of a high ridge and looked down on a wide, green valley where a small village nested along the sides of a fast-flowing creek.

With He Watches beside me, I pulled out

the *Shináá Cho.* I saw *Indah* working a pile of logs next to a building set on the edge of the creek. The building looked like an adobe house with its sides open to the creek and some of the creek flowing under the house.

The village had several small adobe and rough-frame buildings scattered up and down a road that ran past a large, two-story building with a place for a lookout on its roof peak. A large two-story house, surrounded by wood and adobe outbuildings, and behind it, corrals for horses and cattle beside a large barn, sat across the road from the open-sided adobe on the creek. Near the open adobe on the same side of the road stood a building with horses, some hitched to wagons tied to a hitching rail near the door. Indeh went in empty-handed and came out with bulging sacks.

Up and down the valley, I saw a few tipis, usually in canyons leading off the road. I heard the ring of steel on steel from one of the houses close by the house on the creek, and from the house on the creek came squeaking metallic sounds and a rhythmic chuffing sound like a bear running through mountain brush.

I handed the *Shináá Cho* to He Watches, who stared at the open-sided adobe house and whispered, "La Máquina (The Machine). I've heard many stories about it. The *Indah* medicine man, Blazer, owns it. When the reservation began, Santana asked Blazer, his good amigo, to stay after the other *Indah* were made to leave the reservation."

I frowned and asked, "La Máquina? What is this máquina? An *Indah* medicine man spirit?"

He Watches shook his head as he studied the building and then the rest of the village. "La Máquina uses a big knife with teeth to cut logs into pieces of wood the *Indah* use to build their lodges. The *Indah* call it a *sow-meal.*" I looked at him, waiting for him to explain more about it, and though I'd heard Rufus call La Máquina a sawmill, I did not correct him, as that would be disrespectful.

He said, "The blade that cuts the logs is taller than you and has teeth the size of your thumb. The creek is made to run through a box under it that makes the blade go up and down and causes the creaks and groans we hear. Mules pull the logs on to a pesh (iron) wagon that carries them to the blade."

He twisted in his saddle, and stared at the two-story house. "Ho! I see Indeh at the big lodge and several waiting. It must be the place for the *Indah* reservation chief. Let's go down to that building and surrender to him. He'll help us find a place to winter and shelter and food."

The agent, Fred Godfroy, smiling and nodding and with his arms spread, welcomed our little group through an interpreter, although I understood nearly everything he said. He told us the great father in Washington wanted to help us, that we also should learn to help ourselves, and that we must swear never again to raid or take the warpath against the *Indah.*

When Godfroy saw the ponies Juanita and I had taken back from the *vaquero*s and heard our story, he sent riders to the camps scattered in the canyons across the reservation saying ponies had been returned by a group coming into the agency from the Guadalupes and for the people to come and see. For ten days thereafter, they did, whether they had lost any ponies or not. Half the ponies were claimed, and the grateful owners gave us presents from the little they had. It was enough to get us through the Ghost Face Season in a nearby canyon, which Godfroy had suggested we use to shelter us from the hard winds and deep snows.

However, regardless of how glad to see us the agent seemed to be, I didn't trust him. There always seemed to be a lie lurking behind his eyes.

On the other hand, I was fascinated by the sawmill and went often to watch slabs and planks being cut from logs in the pile near the rails for the pesh wagon. One day, just before the snows came, I watched the great knife with many teeth take a plank from a log. A tall, white-haired man with a black beard approached me, stuck out his hand, and said, "I'm Joseph Blazer. Glad to know ya."

Rufus Pike had taught me that the *Indah* shook hands for introductions to show they were friendly, so I gave Blazer's hand two solid pumps and replied, "I'm Yellow Boy. Máquina yours? I like to watch it."

Blazer nodded and smiled. "Yes, it's my sawmill. I like to watch it, too. From where does your name come?"

"My rifle shoots where I point it. My rifle and me, we're one."

"Ah, I see you have a Henry rifle with one of those shiny brass receivers. I've heard Comanches call them Yellow Boys, and I think Santana even called his a Yellow Boy. When you tire of watching La Máquina, come to the store there." He pointed toward a small building next to the mill house where we stood and said, "We can sit by the fire, drink coffee, and speak together."

■ ■ ■ ■

Throughout the winter, I had several long conversations with Joseph Blazer. When not sitting by the fire, I learned the dangerous art of snow-trapping elk from the old hunter Kah Tensakes (Crooked Arrow), who showed me and the other young men how to herd the animals onto ice-crusted snow just strong enough to support a man but too weak to support a thousand-pound elk. It was dangerous business to hunt this way, for if the hunter misjudged the strength of the ice, he might fall through into deep snow, or a charging elk in the same fix might trample him.

I also joined hunts for the whitetail deer that followed the elk, whose passage cleared snow, so it was easy for them to find places to graze. The whitetails are more timid than blacktail deer, and the sight or scent of a hunter sends them running over distances impossible to follow. They tended to return to the mountains with signs of warming weather and often got caught in storms in the higher elevations. Then, they took shelter from howling blizzard winds under the drooping branches of snow-laden pine trees where circular drifts built by snow sliding off the branches sometimes reached the height of the branches dumping the snow. Finding such a tree, it was not unusual to find whole herds crowded together under the branches and hunters made short work of them. I used my bow to save bullets, but I rarely returned without an elk or a deer and gave the meat and some of the hides to those living in the camp.

My mother, Sons-ee-ah-ray, was an expert in tanning hides and used the tough, water-repellant leather of old bull elks to make soles for fine, long-lasting moccasins. One night as the warm winds from the west melted the deep snows in the valleys and brought the Season of Little Eagles, she worked by the fire, while my brother slept and I stared at the twists and turns of the dancing flames.

"What does my son see in the fire?"

I looked at her and shrugged. "I wonder about Cha and the men with him. They ought to have found us by now. I burn for the blood of those who slaughtered our People. Cha knows how to find these enemies. I know how to kill them. Cha needs to come before the season of Little Eagles, so we can catch and kill the Witch who nearly wiped us out."

Sons-ee-ah-ray said, "Cha may never come here. When his brother, the one who was chief here, lived, only two years ago, he warned him never to come here or blood would be spilled between them. Wherever Cha goes, trouble always brings Blue Coats or *Indah* ready to kill us. Your father knew this, but still he raided and went on revenge wars with him. You will find the witches with or without the help of Cha. This I know." She smiled, the wrinkles of hard life and age crinkling around her eyes. "What I do not know is when you will tie your pony in front of Maria's tipi and leave mine."

I frowned and continued to stare at the fire. "What makes you think I want to take a wife? What makes you think I will tie my pony at Maria's tipi or that Juanita will take it to water? I have not spoken to her since we came to the reservation. I will not leave you without meat and shelter."

She shook her head. "Your brother and I will be taken care of. Of this you must not worry."

"Has someone already spoken with you?"

"Ogo (He Fell In) lost his wives to the pox last winter. He works for your friend Blazer at the sawmill. He wants to come to my tipi. I told him I would think on it. But I will not accept him. He likes to gamble too much. We might wind up poorer than we are now. Others want me and have spoken to He Watches, but have not yet spoken to me.

"But you, you've avoided even looking at Juanita since you took the *vaquero* ponies. I see the look in your eyes when she's near. I see hers when you pass by. You have ten ponies in this canyon now. You can afford her. Maria will accept four ponies and smile. This I know."

I stared in the fire and listened to her awl make little squeaks as she pushed holes in the tough elk hide. After a while I said, "In the Season of Many Leaves, when the plants with yellow flowers bloom, I will ask for her."

Sons-ee-ah-ray looked at me and smiled.

CHAPTER 27
THE WARRIORS RETURN

The Season of Little Eagles came, patches of snow remaining only in a few deep, shady spots in the valleys and on the high ridges of the great mountain, Sierra Blanca, and the creeks in runoff were still high but passable. He Watches and I sat near our tipis on a blanket watching the women work. I oiled and cleaned my rifle and was rubbing off the excess with a rag to put a golden sheen on the brass receiver. He Watches sharpened his skinning knife, slowly stroking its edge back and forth against a black volcanic stone the boy Ish-kay-neh had found and given him on the ride to the reservation. Enjoying the sun's warmth after a long winter, we spoke of Agent Godfroy.

He Watches frowned and shook his head. "Each time Socorro goes to the agency, Godfroy gives us less. The meat is gone after four days when it should last seven; the blankets and cloth they gave her last time were no good. I know Sons-ee-ah-ray and Maria and all the other women also complain that he withholds what's due us. I think Godfroy steals the food out of our mouths. Many of the young men on the reservation want to go out on a raid in Mexico for supplies, but none of the old, skilled warriors will lead them. What do you say we ought to do, my son?"

"True, Godfroy steals from us and gives us less. My friend Blazer says even the *In-dah* know this and fear it will cause us to raid because of cold and hunger. Blazer says the Mescaleros must think clearly and be clever like Coyote. Soon another agent will come, and our part will get better. The *In-dah* squatters want our land. If the young men go out, the Blue Coats will come and shoot the women, children, and old ones. The *Indah* will say to their great chief that he ought to take back the land they have returned to us. My friend Blazer says we must earn our own money, like the *Indah,* and trade it for things we need and not depend on the agency to give to us. Blazer says we should use the agency school so the children can learn *Indah* ways. This is not a bad thing, but the children must also learn the *Shis-Indeh* ways. They must know who they are. They must not become pets of the

Indah and turn against their own people. They must learn how the true Indeh live also. This is all I have to say."

"Uhmmm. You and Blazer talk much. Blazer, a good friend, speaks true. We'll see if he speaks true of Godfroy leaving and of sending our little ones to the school to learn *Indah* ways."

He Watches laid the knife down and pulled from his vest pocket a beaded leather pouch of tobacco and a piece of cornhusk for a cigarette. He rolled the tobacco, lighted it with a match, and offered smoke to the four directions. He handed it to me, and I also offered smoke to the four directions before handing the cigarette back to He Watches, who smoked the rest of it. We sat listening to the women chopping wood back in the pines or working with their stew pots and the sounds of children playing and imitating their elders.

He Watches crushed the butt of the cigarette by the blanket and said, "The women say you'll marry soon. How will you find this *Indah* money Blazer says you need for your woman and sons?"

"I've not yet decided. I must find a way to leave the reservation and return so I can kill the Witch who murdered our People. I —"

I sensed them before I saw them ride out

300

of the tree shadows, nothing on their saddles or their riders to jingle or make noise, the horses stepping quietly on the long pine needles and into a big pool of sunlight. Ten warriors had left the Guadalupes with Cha. Now five sat their horses, Cha not among them. Their horses thin, heads hanging, had been ridden hard for a long time. Two of the warriors, Kah and Ko-do, had wounds covered with poultices tied in place with bandanas. Delgadito had a long, ugly, red welt from a knife or saber slash across the top of his chest. Klo-sen and Beela-chezzi, two of the more experienced warriors who rode with Cha, I had known as warriors since Bosque Redondo times. Their faces thin and haggard, they showed no signs of wounds. The entire camp grew silent, all eyes questioning every detail about them.

I stared at the warriors for a moment and then stood and waved them forward, saying, "*Dánt'e,* brothers! We have watched for your return for many moons. Come, let the women bring you something to eat while we share news and speak of your return to us."

Klo-sen grinned as he slid from his pony. "*Dánt'e,* Nah-kah-yen. We have ridden far to find you on the reservation where the great chief Santana warned his brother Cha and his people never to enter. Now, they both walk in the land of the grandfathers, and you live here safe and in peace. Maybe peace for us here, too?"

"Yes, our place of refuge, our land as long as we stay. Come. The women will bring blankets and a cooking pot, and the boys will take care of your horses."

Socorro brought her bubbling pot of stew meat and sat it on a circle of rocks so it wouldn't cool too quickly, and blankets appeared as if by magic for us to sit on. When the men were seated about the pot, the women and children sat down behind and around them. Klo-sen and Beela-chezzi looked at the faces of the women and frowned. I saw Delgadito look at Deer Woman, who was smiling, and make the faintest of nods. Kah and Ko-do were interested only in the cooking pot. The warriors ate like starving dogs, the gravy from the stew pot running down their chins and onto their ragged shirts as they speared chunks of beef with their knives and filled their cheeks with meat and fry bread.

When they finished, I pulled a cigar from my vest pocket, lighted it, smoked a puff to each of the four directions, and passed it to Klo-sen sitting on my right, who smoked a puff to the four directions and passed it on. When the cigar returned to me, I put it out and waited for Klo-sen, as the eldest, to speak first.

"When we left on our raid, ten warriors rode out of the mountains of our People. Five warriors returned, and our leader walked in the Happy Land. The raid started good and ended bad. We rode south past the mountains the *Indah* call Davis before we turned west and crossed the great river just below two small villages across the great river from each other, each village not too large for us to raid. Many fine horses stirred in the east village corral. We rode into the country of the *Nakai-yes* west of the great river to raid villages there before we returned to take the two on the river. The *Nakai-yi* villages we raided had nothing of value; most were abandoned. We rode many miles west and north and south and found little to take except a few cattle and horses from well-guarded ranchos. We saw *Nakai-yi* soldiers raising dust in the distance, but they never came in our direction; always they went west and north. We lost no warriors in our empty raids.

"We rode back to the two villages on each side of the great river. There were still many good ponies in the corrals on the east side of the great river and few in the corrals on the west side. We decided to take those on the east side. We were fools. The good ponies on the east side belonged to Tejanos with many big guns. I think they waited for us to come. Many bullets filled the air the night we tried to take the horses. The Tejanos know how to shoot good, and they have big knives. Ask Delgadito. We fought them a long time. Two of us died early trying to get the ponies out of the corral. When our bullets were few, Cha told us to ride away, saying we can always come back. He rode hard toward the rising sun. We rode not far behind him when he fell from his pony, and then we heard powerful thunder from a Tejano rifle. I have never seen such a long shot. It began yesterday and hit today. Our rifles cannot reach that far. There were other shots and two more fell when we stopped to pick him up. The Tejanos followed us, but we lost them in the Davis Mountains.

"We waited five suns in the Davis Mountains for the Tejanos to go away. We did not want to return to our camp without our chief and with nothing from our raid, but we had been gone a long time. When we rode up the canyon creek, we found nothing but the burned places where wickiups and tipis had been and graves in the talus by the canyon wall. Even the place of He Watches on the high ridge was empty. With the Ghost Face Season coming and all the food supplies contaminated by Ghost Sickness from the graves nearby, we went back to the Davis Mountains and stayed with the band of Nicholas. As you see, three of us had wounds, and they cared for us. Nicholas heard that a group of Indeh from the Guadalupes went to the Mescalero Reservation in the Season When the Earth is Dark Reddish Brown. He said only two warriors were with a few women and children. We waited to ride until the Season of Little Eagles to come look for you. The first camp we found on the reservation told us where you camped. Here we are. This is all I have to say."

I looked at He Watches, who nodded for me to speak.

"I'll tell you my story. Those who sit behind you have theirs and will speak when they're asked and ready. My father and grandfather wanted me to learn to shoot good. My father gave me this Yellow Boy rifle and took me to his *Indah* amigo, Rufus Pike. He lives in a box canyon in the mountains the *Indah* call Organ. He has a ranch there with good water, and he taught me much about the rifle. He has a rifle that shoots far like the one the Tejanos used to kill Cha. After two moons, I had a dream. It said I must go to the tallest peak next to the canyon of Rufus Pike and wait for my Power. This I did. The Thunder People and Wind came, bringing me a vision and lightning arrows. I heard a voice say my name is Yellow Boy and that the rifle given me by my father and I are one. The voice said I must kill *Witch*es who do evil to the People by shooting out their eyes and that ghosts have no power over me. Witches I shoot will be blind in the land of the grandfathers.

"After I returned from my vision to Rufus Pike, I never missed with my rifle. Any target he challenged me with, I did not miss. Soon another dream told me to return to the Guadalupes pronto. This I did and found our camp burned and still smoking and bodies everywhere, all scalped, and He Watches and some of the women and children gone. I hoped they lived. I buried those killed, including my father and other warriors and ate from the food stores we had in the caves nearby —"

Klo-sen frowning, held up his hand, palm out. "You did not get the Ghost Sickness when you did this?"

"I did not."

Klo-sen slowly shook his head. "You have great gifts from *Ussen*. The ghosts do not bother you, and you can blind witches, sending them to the land of the grandfathers. Tell us the rest of your story."

I told the warriors of finding He Watches and the women and children, of my raid with Juanita to get horses, and how we came to the reservation, made our camp, and lived through the Ghost Face Season. When I spoke of Juanita, I saw the eyes of Delgadito and Kah and Ko-do turn to her and then to Maria. Lastly, I told them life on the reservation was hard, about how the *Indah* stole our horses in Nogal Canyon, and about how the weak agent cheated us of our due, though the Blue Coats still protected us and the agent gave us a little food and let us hunt. Then I said, "Blazer, the *Indah* who owns the store and sawmill, is our friend and helps us all he can." I looked down for a moment and finished with, "I'm not a chief. Wise He Watches leads us. You're welcome here. Choose to stay, for there are widows who need men to support them. Show yourselves to the agent for food and blankets. Come and join us. That is all I have to say."

Klo-sen and Beela-chezzi and the others

nodded. Klo-sen replied, "We hear you, Yellow Boy. We will think on what you have told us and camp here if He Watches permits it."

He Watches nodded. "Camp with us. Do what you think you must."

The returning warriors stayed with our camp three days and then rode to the agency. When they came back, they said they had spoken with Chief San Juan of the Mescaleros and Agent Godfroy and had decided to stay on the reservation.

CHAPTER 28
COURTSHIP

The Season of Little Eagles warmed to the Season of Many Leaves. The camp women made the returning warriors wickiup shelters, and the warriors gave them most of their allotment supplies for the opportunity to have meals at their cooking pots. Klo-sen went more often to the fire of Sons-ee-ah-ray than to that of the other women. I noticed that her meals had greater variety and more spice when Klo-sen came, and she seemed glad to see him at her fire. He often sat and smoked with He Watches and me after a meal. One evening as we sat and talked of the old days, Klo-sen asked me if Sons-ee-ah-ray might consider another husband and if so, did I object? I smiled and said, "Her choice, not mine."

During the Season of Many Leaves, I often sat back in the dark shadows of the tall pine trees, smoked, and watched the moon rise over the mountains as the tipi fires burned low and the camp grew still, the rustle in the brush from the passage of small animals, and an occasional bird call the only sounds. Three times that season, late in the evening, I saw the flap on the tipi of Son-nah's widow open slowly and carefully like it was about to float away. Then Deer Woman would step out, pause to look for prying eyes, and, when satisfied none watched her, move quietly toward the line of trees above the camp where a tall, slender figure pulled her into the shadows. I shook my head and thought about the proclivities of Delgadito and what lay in store for foolish Deer Woman.

A moon after Cha's surviving warriors joined the camp, He Watches and I sat by the fire outside Sons-ee-ah-ray's tipi finishing our evening meal when we saw the boy Ish-key-nay lead Delgadito's pony to Maria's tipi and tie it there. I reached for my knife in its sheath behind my back. Smiling, He Watches put his hand on my arm and said, "Wait. Wait and watch. This will be good." I stared at the horse beside the tipi for a few moments, and then relaxed, glanced at He Watches, and nodded.

It wasn't long before Deer Woman stepped out of her mother's tipi and, turning toward their woodpile, stared at the pony, and then stretched to look where Delgadito's lodge stood. He Watches nodded and smiled and I did too. This was good to watch. Of course, Delgadito was nowhere in sight. Deer Woman disappeared back into the tipi not to be seen at all the following day.

Juanita appeared the next morning and did her normal chores helping Maria, but she ignored the pony tied by the tipi. Used to being offered water during the day, the pony, black and shiny and hot in the bright sunlight, hung its head with thirst. Still, Juanita ignored it. Dusk began to settle on the second night, and still the pony had not been watered. It still stood thirsty on the sunrise of the second day.

As the setting sun cast long shafts of light through the trees on the second day, the horizon streaked with purple and orange clouds, I watched Ish-kay-neh retrieve Delgadito's pony and take it to the creek to drink in long thirsty swallows before leading it back to Delgadito's wickiup.

The third evening, Ish-kay-neh led another pony, this time belonging to Kah, to Maria's tipi and left it tied there. Ignored by Juanita, this pony also suffered through two days and nights without water before Ish-kay-neh retrieved it and took it to the creek.

The sixth evening, Ish-kay-neh led Ko-do's best pony, a roan with glistening coat, and tied it at Maria's tipi. It met the same fate as the ponies of Delgadito and Kah. He Watches and I sat on our blanket and smoked, enjoying our evening, and watching Ish-kay-neh lead Ko-do's horse to water.

He Watches said, "See? I told you it would be good. Those fools never asked one of the old ones to speak with Maria to learn who had her favor, and Delgadito cannot go night crawling with Deer Woman again. At least he won't if he doesn't want his head broken with a rock by a woman he has deceived."

I nodded. "Uhmmm. What will Maria want for her? The best bride price on the reservation, four ponies, I want to offer."

"Four ponies for Juanita? She already knows you're a good hunter and a powerful warrior. She already knows you're respectful toward widows and a man of your word. Maria knows who she wants for a son-in-law; she knows who Juanita will accept. No, don't offer four ponies. Offer Maria five ponies and at least two saddles."

"Five ponies? I never heard of such a bride price on the reservation. Why five?"

"Maria wants you. Juanita wants you. She already knows you and your Power. Show her you're generous. Show her how much you value her. She's built to have many strong sons, and you know her courage and her skill with a sling as well as a cook pot and baskets, none better on the reservation, maybe in this territory. Offer Maria more than expected for Juanita, and she'll fill your days with happy times."

I smiled. "Your wisdom shows bright and clear, Grandfather."

Three days after the rejection of Ko-do, I rode my paint pony into the creek and washed it, curried burrs out of its mane and tail, and brushed it until its coat glistened in the sun. I tied it in front of Socorro's tipi and gave it water as often as it would drink. As the sun began to cast long shadows, I called Ish-kay-neh, put the paint's bridle in his hand, and said, "Take my pony to Maria's tipi. Let the reins fall to the ground, no need to tie him. He will not leave unless she picks up the reins. Go!"

I watched the boy lead the paint to Maria's tipi, drop the reins, and walk away. I glanced toward the warrior wickiups and saw Delgadito, who was sitting with Beelachezzi and cleaning his revolver, stretch to see what pony Ish-kay-neh now led. He looked away frowning.

The stars had made a quarter of a circle around the pole star when I lay down in Sons-ee-ah-ray's tipi. My pony, a black and white pinto, still stood without water outside Maria's dark tipi. The pony stood there all the next day, thirsty, but, unlike the ponies from Delgadito, Kah, and Ko-do, it didn't snuffle and beg when the women walked by, but held its head high. When shadows from the falling sun filled the canyon and brilliant reds and oranges and purples covered the western sky, He Watches and I sat on our blanket smoking and drinking coffee, discussing Blazer's wisdom for the People. We spoke of Blazer's idea that the People should make this thing called money to trade for supplies and not face the failed promises of *Indah* support.

Although I kept feelings from my face and tried to appear relaxed, I kept glancing toward Maria's tipi. He Watches smoked his cigarette and blew the smoke toward the tree limbs in the still, cool air. I saw Juanita's little sister, Moon on the Water, playing hiding games in the falling light with the other children in the camp, but Juanita stayed out of sight. He Watches and I spoke until the night settled on us like a blanket on a child, until conversation went to sleep, and we slipped through the doors of the tipis of

314

Socorro and Sons-ee-ah-ray for our sleeping pallets.

After a while, I rolled to my stomach and silently slid under the edge of the tipi, and, taking a *cigarro* to chew on unlit, moved to a stand of tall pines where, under their towering darkness, I could clearly see the fronts of Maria's and Sons-ee-ah-ray's tipis.

I watched the stars advance around the pole star until I grew tired of chewing the *cigarro,* threw it away, and made a big yawn to keep my brain clear. I saw the flap on Maria's tipi rise slowly in the waning moonlight, and a figure step through the door with a large bundle. The moon was still low over the east side ridge of the canyon, but it didn't take much light for me to recognize Juanita from the way she carried herself and to see the bundle was long sweet grass found in the high meadows. I smiled and wondered, *How did she cut and hide the grass without me seeing her with it? Clever woman you are, Juanita.*

Holding the grass bundle under one arm, she picked up the paint's reins, held its nostrils to hers, and breathed in its breath and he hers. Its skin shuddered when she rubbed it with an understanding hand. She led it to the creek and invited it to drink. It drank in great long gulps, raising its head several times to look down the creek toward the tall pines where I sat. Juanita let it drink enough to satisfy its thirst but didn't let it drink enough to founder. She led it to stand near Sons-ee-ah-ray's tipi, where, after looking around the camp, she dropped its reins and opened the bundle to spread the grass before the nose of the pony. As it ate, she smoothed its mane and forelock. Near its withers, she platted a tight little rope in its mane. She finished, sliding her hand in a final rub down its back, and disappeared into Maria's tipi.

Socorro told me her story and the story Maria told her of the day He Watches had negotiated Juanita's bride price with Maria. These stories made my heart proud I had chosen Juanita and made me glad Maria was my mother-in-law.

Socorro said it was barely dawn when He Watches sat up on his blankets and yawned. She had already cooked a morning meal of baked mescal, one-seeded juniper bread, and locust tree flower soup. She said, "Get up, Old Man. You have work today. She chooses."

He rubbed his palms against his eyes and asked, "Who chooses? What are you talking about, Old Woman?"

"The girl, Juanita, brought Yellow Boy's pony back to Sons-ee-ah-ray's tipi after she took him to water and then fed him. Now you must talk presents with Maria and learn what she wants for the girl. Pretty soon now, our grandson will know the pleasure a good woman brings to the fire when her man sleeps by it. You make Maria happy, and Yellow Boy will be happy."

He Watches said, "Hmmm. I've spoken with Maria already. I know her price for Juanita, and Yellow Boy has agreed to give her more than what she wants. That boy is smart and generous. You'll see."

"*Enjuh.* Come eat this meal I fix for you, then put on your best clothes and go visit Maria."

He replied, "Stop nagging, Old Woman. I know what I'm doing."

Maria told Socorro she'd seen the dark outline of the figure leaning on a long, straight stick before her tipi door. She smiled, feeling pride and happiness for Juanita, and said, "Daughter, go outside to work and look after Moon on the Water playing down by the creek. A man has come. I have business to discuss with him." Juanita stepped out the tipi door, nearly ran into old He Watches, and Maria heard her say, "I'm sorry, Grandfather. I didn't expect you standing there."

He replied, "Perhaps that's so, my daughter. But, you hoped I might be."

Maria said she waited a respectable time before saying, "Who stands at my door? What is your business?"

He said, "I come to speak for the man, Yellow Boy, my grandson, who asks for your daughter and offers presents to you."

"Come. I have coffee with *Indah* sugar for us while we speak of this man and my daughter."

Maria told Socorro He Watches drank two cups before they spoke of the business of joining me to her daughter. She said she knew a bride with a high price made a husband realize he had a woman of value and had decided to ask for four ponies, but to accept only two or three if He Watches and I had lost many of their ponies to *vaquero* raiders.

He Watches rolled a cigarette, lighted it with the bright yellow flame on a splinter pulled from wood in the fire, and blew smoke to the four directions before handing it to Maria, who also smoked to the four directions.

After the smoke curled out the top of the tipi, He Watches said, "My grandson is anxious to offer the mother of Juanita good presents to show the respect he has for her. What will her mother accept as a good present?"

Maria stared at the little fire beside them, stirred the coals with a little green stick, and thought for a while. She lifted her dark eyes to He Watches, who sipped another cup of coffee and watched her with a faraway stare as though he were watching from his perch high in the Guadalupes in happier years.

Seeing this, Maria decided to back off her original decision to ask for four ponies and said, "I'm happy to give my oldest daughter to your grandson for three ponies and a saddle."

He Watches lowered his eyes and stared into the little orange and red flames in the fire pit.

"Hmmm, three ponies and a saddle? That is an expensive present for a bride."

At that, she said her heart fell. She thought, a widow without three horses lives poorly. But, if she takes less, at least, her daughter will be nearby, and she and Moon on the Water would have a man to hunt for them.

Then He Watches said, "Mother of Juanita, I offer you a different present. Will you consider it?"

Maria nodded. "I'll consider it."

"My grandson's gift to you is five ponies, two saddles, and cloth for their first tipi."

Maria told Socorro she remembered covering her mouth as though to keep her spirit from flying away. She stared in his eyes a few moments to be sure she'd heard him correctly.

He Watches laughed and asked, "Has the mother of Juanita lost her voice?"

"No, Grandfather, my voice is still with me. I'm astonished that my daughter has chosen this man. I want him in our family even if he is too poor to offer a gift of one pony. Bring the cloth for their tipi today, and it will stand ready for them in two days. Now go, *mi amigo.* I and the other women in camp have much to tell my daughter about the care of husbands before she enters her tipi with your grandson."

He said, "Yes, I'll go. I have a glad heart for you, and you have much to do. I'll bring the cloth soon and leave it by your door and send men up the canyon to cut lodge poles for Juanita's tipi."

"Enjuh!"

She followed him out the door and motioned for Juanita and Moon on the Water to come to her. Maria told Socorro she laughed when she heard a loud, *"Enjuh!"* after He Watches entered Socorro's tipi. Despite all the losses and hard times of the past year, the great circle of life was beginning again.

CHAPTER 29
THE TIME OF NEW BEGINNING

Long shadows from tall pines fell across the canyon floor. The empty spaces between the branches let through bright yellow beams filled with myriad fluttering insects looking like specks of gold as they drifted through the fading sunlight into pallid darkness. From Maria's tipi my adoptive grandmother walked with Juanita, quietly passing through golden beams and still shadows to the tipi of Sons-ee-ah-ray, where I stood straight and proud with He Watches at my side. Juanita's crow's-wing shiny-black hair glistened in the light and lay on her shoulders in long, full braids down the front of a fine, white-finished, beaded buckskin robe, soft as lamb's wool and trimmed in long, thin fringe, each string ending with a little tin bell. Her moccasins had long, supple shafts, the curled toes distinctive of the Chiricahua People, and the beadwork on the toes and shafts were symbols of life and rain. Holding my rifle, the symbol of my Power, its brass receiver oiled and shiny in the crook of my left arm, I awaited her in a new white shirt and a black dress vest Joe Blazer had given me.

Socorro stopped before me, Juanita standing a respectful distance behind her.

"My grandson, I bring you your new wife. Treat her well. May your lives be filled with many children and lived in harmony with each other and with *Ussen.*" She took Juanita's hand and placed it in mine.

Sons-ee-ah-ray laid a fine Pendleton blanket woven in black and red designs over our shoulders and led us to the place of honor for a feast for the entire camp and where later a long night of dancing would begin.

Before the moon began dropping into the western mountains, Juanita and I no longer sat among the others, but walked together with the black and red blanket around our shoulders toward our new tipi, which was back in the trees near Maria's tipi. Custom dictated that Juanita live near her mother and that I must never see or be seen by Maria, even though I was now the only man in a family of two women and a little girl.

The moonlight falling through the trees splashed in little pools of light we silently passed through, hand-in-hand, to the chorus of fiddling crickets and smell of cedars and pines. In a whispery, throaty voice Juanita said, "I waited so long for you that I thought you had forgotten me."

"I could never forget you, Fine Woman. I wanted to wait a little longer until I was certain I could support you, but Delgadito and the others forced my hand. I knew Delgadito never had a chance with you, but I wasn't so sure about Kah or Ko-do. I'm happy you chose me."

She giggled. "I wanted a man. Kah and Ko-do are still boys. I have what I wanted. I hope you do, too."

I stopped in the shadows, looked into her eyes, and took her gently by the shoulders. "I have wanted you since the night you chose me to dance with you. I wanted you even more after you showed me your courage and skill when we raided the *vaquero* camp. My heart has burned for you since I told you I wanted you and you said not to take a long time." I embraced her and kissed her, feeling the desire I had long held for her rise from my heart like the morning mists in a high meadow against the morning sun.

She kissed me back, and I felt the cool night grow warm. I had kissed no one since my childhood days, and the shock of her warm lips pressing against mine lit a spark below my belly that became a hot fire. I loved the feel of her strong nubile body in my arms, the smell of her sweat mixed with that of cactus flowers and the pines around us, the warmth of her skin, the flow of her breath on my cheek, and strength of her arms around me. That first kiss lasted a long time, but it felt all too short.

When she pulled back from me and looked into my eyes, her face flushed and warm, she said, "Someone may see us. Let's go in the tipi."

I started to follow her inside, but she made me wait in the darkness for a few moments. I could hear her movements from outside, and I envisioned her in my mind as she sat down on the pallet by the unlit fire pit, pulled off her moccasins, carefully folding them and laying them to one side, and rising to her knees to lift her robe over her head, folding it so the fringe was inside and the beadwork designs unbroken by a fold. I knew the chill of the night air would make her nipples hard and that stirred me more. After she slid under the blanket on our pallet, she called softly to me, "Come."

I lifted the entry cover, slid under it, and

stepped inside. It was so dark I could not even see my rifle barrel a few inches in front of my nose. I eased to my knees on top of the blanket, and sensing her form to my left under the blanket, I laid the rifle down. I sat down and pulled off my moccasins, unbuttoned my vest and folded it, and then my shirt, and then lay down beside her, but I stayed on top of the blanket.

She asked, "What are you doing, you-whom-I-have-chosen? A blanket separates us on our first night together?"

"I'll wait on top of the blanket until you tell me you're ready. You know what will happen then. If you want to wait a night or many days until you are used to me, I'll understand."

"I've waited for you too long already. Come to me that we can truly know each other."

I finished undressing and slid under the blanket. I caressed her cheek and whispered, "Woman, your man lies beside you."

"Husband, kiss me as you did under the trees and feel my body next to yours. Come to me as a stallion to his mares, as a buck to his does, for I'm your woman and long to give you sons and daughters."

Kissing her, I felt the fire in my middle grow hot again as she pulled me to her, and

I caressed her with gentle hands gliding smoothly over her skin, exploring the curves of her body.

All night, with the barest of breezes off the tall mountains to whisper through the trees over us, I found Maria's daughter beyond my imaginings of the pleasures of having a wife. I marveled in her great hunger and eagerness for me, the way she gave herself with joy and pleasure, taking me as I needed, and when she wanted, so many times that we lost count of how often she received me that night.

Chapter 30
Al Sieber

Juanita worked hard with Maria and the other women to collect and save food for the hard, hungry times coming in the Ghost Face Season. For reasons only *Ussen* knew, she had not conceived with me, though we joined our bodies with unbridled desire through the moons of the seasons of Large Leaves and Large Fruit.

As the seasons changed, I worried over what I needed to support my wife independently of what the reservation agent gave us and tried different jobs in the sawmill, worked as a drover of Fort Stanton cattle used to feed the reservation, helped cut timber in the high mountain forests and drag it to the mill, and took a wagon on two trips to Tularosa loaded with lumber and returned with supplies for Blazer's mercantile store. I liked none of this work enough to stay on any job more than a few weeks.

The work I wanted was that of tribal

policeman, but I didn't like the *Indah* in charge who made the officers wear pants, and there was even talk the officers might have to cut their hair short. Caballo Negro once told me that foolish leaders killed more warriors than all the bullets the *Indah* ever shot or might shoot, and I never asked to be considered for tribal policeman. I thought the business of wearing pants and the possibility of cutting my hair for a job to settle quarrels and catch thieves was foolish, and it showed the tribal policeman *Indah* chief a fool.

One day early in the Season of Earth is Reddish Brown (late fall), Juanita and I rode the trail from our camp across the high ridges and through the tall pines and junipers sprinkled with bits of color from oaks and aspens in crisp, brilliant air to Blazer's store. We planned to buy winter supplies with the few dollars I had earned trying different jobs.

I waited outside the store with the horses and sat on the porch edge listening to the whirring, chuffing sounds of the sawmill next door while Juanita decided on a new cooking pot, chose an ax, and selected a few yards of cloth to make shirts for me and shifts for her mother, sister, and herself.

Behind me, the sound of boots clomping

out the store doorway stopped, and then I heard them moving in my direction. Ever vigilant, I pulled the hammer back on the rifle and waited. Fingers touched my shoulder, and Joe Blazer said, "Yellow Boy, there's a feller here wants to meet you. Name's Al Sieber."

I let the hammer down on the rifle before I stood and the movement along with the associated metallic clicks didn't appear to be lost on Al Sieber, whose eyes and ears seemed to collect every detail around him. I faced them, the rifle resting easy in the crook of my left arm.

Al Sieber, at six foot, three inches, and 175 pounds of trail-tough muscle, was five inches taller than me and thirty pounds heavier. His big, soft, gray hat tilted back on his head, and a heavy black moustache covered his upper lip. Sieber smiled, stuck out his hand, and said words I had not heard an *Indah* say before, "*Dánt'e,* Yellow Boy."

I took his hand, felt the power in its strong, callused fingers, pumped it twice, and said, "Nish'ii' (I see you), Al Sieber. Why you speak to me?"

Before Sieber could reply, Blazer said, "Al was Chief of Scouts for General Crook over in Arizona. He's always looking for Apaches who have nerve, can shoot and track, and are willing to end Apache raiding for the good of the People in Arizona and New Mexico. I told him I thought you were probably a good shot, even if I haven't seen you shoot, that you're plenty smart, and you might be interested in being a scout to keep the Blue Coats from attacking peaceful people, so he wanted to meet you."

Sieber nodded at the rifle resting in the crook of my left arm. "Can yah hit anything with that ol' Henry? Where'd yah get it anyway?"

"My father gave it to me. Rufus Pike showed me how to shoot. My Power is in this rifle. I always carry it. You know Rufus Pike?"

He sounded like he was jerking air back in his chest when he said, "Yah. Rufus Pike I know. We're friends a long time. I asked 'im to come back to th' Army and help lead scouts. He said no. Said he had a personal treaty with the Apaches — they leave him alone, and he don't bother them. If ol' Rufus taught yah to shoot, then yah must be a good shot. Let's walk over across th' road to the doc's corral. Show me ya shoot good, and maybe we talk about scouting sometime for th' Blue Coats. Yah?"

I nodded and followed Sieber and Blazer

across the road to the barn and corral behind Blazer's house. No livestock were in the corral, and junipers and pines growing up the side of a ridge in front of us formed a dark green wall. Sieber leaned against the corral rails, studied the trees at the edge of the ridge, and pointed toward a pine about two hand spans in diameter and about a hundred and fifty yards away. "See that tree yonder? Think maybe yah can hit that tree with your ol' Henry rifle?"

I smiled. "Where do you want the tree shot?"

Sieber shook his head and smiled. "Yah got the smart pants. They on, eh? Okay. We'll see. Shoot where the stub of a limb that's been cut off sticks out about a man's height on the right side. I can see where it is with my binoculars, and just barely with my eye. Yah see it?"

I lifted the rifle, flipped up the rear sight, raised the sight bar a notch, and then butted the stock to my shoulder. I sighted the tree for the space of a long breath and fired. As the thin smoke cleared and the echoes from the old rifle's thunder died away, we could see a piece of white against the dark brown bark where the bullet hit just under the limb stub.

The sound of gunfire brought folks in the

store and agency out on their porches. Blazer raised his arms and yelled, "Just a little target shooting! Nothing to worry about!" The *Indah* nodded and most went back inside.

Sieber squinted in his binoculars and mumbled, "Damn! I don't think I could have hit that. Maybe it was a lucky shot. Shoot again."

I smiled, again raised the rifle to my shoulder, and effortlessly put three more rounds within the size of my palm around the first shot.

Sieber shook his head. "I'm a good shot, but I ain't sure I coulda done that. Best shooting I've seen in many moons. Can yah hit movin' targets?"

I squatted down by a corral post, swept my hand across the sandy soil, and picked up three rocks the size of small green apples. I held them out to Sieber, who took them and said, "How many at once, and how far you want 'em?"

I shrugged. "You throw. I shoot."

The rocks all fit easily in Sieber's big hand. He cocked his arm and threw them hard. I shouldered the rifle in a smooth motion, tracking the three rocks flying a few feet apart and falling together like a flock of birds. My first shot turned the middle rock into a puff of dust. I levered a second round, the rifle never leaving my shoulder, and fired with virtually no pause to sight on the other two rocks. The Henry thundered, and the second rock exploded. The third rock was just a few feet off the ground when my third bullet blew it to pieces.

Sieber turned to Blazer, who was grinning and scratching his beard. "Blazer, why ain't yah told me 'bout this man before?"

Laughing, Blazer said, "Because this is the first time I've seen him shoot. He told me that rifle was part of his Power. I didn't doubt it then, and I sure don't doubt it now."

Sieber, shaking his head, shook my hand again. "You're best shooter I've ever seen. You're better'n me. Let's go over to th' store and drink some of Blazer's coffee and talk about yah scouting for the Blue Coats one of these days if there's a need for it. Ain't much goin' on right now, to tell the truth. Hell, I was gonna run for sheriff over to Arizona and decided I'd be better off ramblin' an' lookin' for places to mine."

I nodded and followed the two *Indah* back to Blazer's store.

That night, Juanita served me a fine meal of beef and corn, fry bread made with acorn flour, and piñon nut coffee. I grunted in satisfaction as I ate it and nodded, "Good, good," when she looked at me and raised her brows to ask. When I sat my cooking pan plate down, she filled a plate for Maria and left to carry it to her. Soon she returned, served her plate, and sat down by the fire, her feet folded under her. I finished my coffee, lit one of my thin, black cigars, and blew smoke to the four directions. I nodded at her, grinned, and said, "Ask, and I will answer."

"What said the *Indah* Sieber?"

"Sieber said I'm the best with a rifle he's seen. Better even than him. He thinks I'd make a good scout for the Blue Coats, but things are quiet now. When the time comes, he wants me to scout for him."

"Will you do this?"

"Maybe so. The Blue Coats give their scouts bullets, clothes, food, and as much money as Blue Coat soldiers to help the Blue Coats catch those who leave the reservation and raid the *Indah* stores and ranches. He says when trouble comes and I scout for the Blue Coats, I probably must stay at San Carlos Reservation or one of the forts on the Tonto Rim. I saw San Carlos during Cha's last long raid across the great river. Not a fit place to live. It's a land of snakes, spiders, and centipedes. Many people get sick. Many die. Bands that hate each other are forced to live together. Many fights among the People. Not much food. The agent steals and sells like Godfroy at this place. It's like Bosque Redondo when we were little. I won't live there. Maybe it will change someday, but it's no good now."

"When you go, I'll go."

"No. You'll stay here. Your mother lives here. She'll help you with our children. We'll live good with money the Blue Coats give me. I'll come plenty of times. But I don't go now even though Sieber said if I wanted to start soon he would ask the Blue Coats to take me. That is all I have to say."

Juanita bowed her head acknowledging she understood.

CHAPTER 31
NANA

Deep in the night, my guardian spirit woke me up. I listened but heard nothing except the rainwater gently dripping off the pine tree needles onto our tipi from the middle night rain. The dim skylight I saw against dark, lumpy clouds through the tree limbs above the smoke vent showed dawn was close. Juanita, deep in sleep, her warm, naked body beside me, made me smile. She was a good woman. Already an expert in husbandry, she knew well how to please me. The thought came to me that perhaps she might please me again at the edge of the morning light as she had earlier in the night before we collapsed safe and peaceful in lovers' sleep.

As the thought filled my mind and body, I heard a horse snort, a horse far too close to be ours. I sat up, my fingers closing around the cold, steel barrel of my rifle. The sudden change from warm blanket to cold air woke Juanita, and she instinctively reached for her shift. I touched my fingers to my lips for silence, and she nodded. Then I slid on my moccasins and listened for other sounds, but there were none. By the time Juanita reached for her moccasins, I was under the edge of the tipi and moving silently through the trees.

I stayed low in the shadows to keep from being outlined in the soft dawn light. Soon, I saw a horse tied at the edge of the trees but no shadowy outlines that shouldn't be there. I waited for more light, unmoving, barely breathing.

Behind me, an old man's thin, whispery voice said, "Nish'ii' (I see you), my son. My horse and I mean you no harm."

Only through years of disciplined training was I able to control my reflexes and not jerk in surprise. "Idiits'ag (I hear you), Grandfather. Who are you, and why are you in our camp?"

"I am Nana, leader of a band of Mimbreños who no longer camp with Victorio. I bring my people to find shelter in the Ghost Face Season with the Mescaleros. The women and children and old warriors wait down the wagon road near the village (Tularosa) on the Rio Tularosa; my young men have already crossed the high western ridge and wait in the Rinconada. I come to talk with Yellow Boy, learn what to expect on this reservation from a warrior not long here who sees with his head and is wise."

"What you ask I will answer, but how do you know me to come to our camp?"

"I will tell you, but first, can we get out of the rain and sit by your fire? I carry many years, and the cold and rain make my bones ache. They make me move slowly in rain times."

"My woman makes her fire as we speak. Come."

The old man said the fire was a gift from *Ussen* and nodded his thanks when Juanita poured him coffee and then filled my cup. Nana took a long swallow, smacked his lips in satisfaction, and said, "*Enjuh!* It makes my belly warm and helps me move my arms and legs. Daughter, you do good for this old man." Juanita smiled, nodded, and continued preparing a meal. Through the steam rising off his coffee, Nana looked across his cup at me and said, "You are the warrior called Yellow Boy?"

I nodded and waited.

"Chief of Scouts, the *Indah,* Sieber, told his chief he saw you shoot. He said you're the best shot he ever sees, and the man who runs the mill at the agency here, Blazer, whom the Mescaleros call friend, said you carry bright light in your head. He said Sieber wanted you for his scouts." I frowned, wondering, *How does the old man know this?*

Nana grinned and nodded.

"One of the scouts who heard this is married to a Mimbreño woman whose cousin is in my band. Ha! Apache news travels faster than that on the *Indah* telegraph . . . Sorry, I talk too much. I come to the Mescaleros because the *Indah* cannot decide what to do with my people. First, they sent us to Ojo Caliente where we wanted to stay. Then they changed their minds and said, 'No, the Mimbreños must go to San Carlos.' Victorio is my chief. He knows San Carlos is a place of death, and he won't go, won't let his people go. He and warriors go to Mexico. I'm too old and have too many women and children to go to Mexico in the Ghost Face Season. We ask to come here and live with the Mescaleros after Victorio refused San Carlos. The *Indah* chief said, *'Enjuh,'* and the Mescalero Chiefs, San Juan and Roman Chiquito, agreed to share the Mescalero Reservation with us, but said we must promise not to do anything on the reservation that would bring trouble, bringing the Blue Coats down on the Mescaleros. I have given my word, and it will be so.

"I came to you because I believed you would speak straight about the way of things on this reservation. I don't trust this Agent Godfroy. I don't trust any agent. My young men, I will not bring in. They will be free to come and go as they please, and as I send them, but they will do nothing to bring the Blue Coats down on the Mescaleros."

He drained his cup and sat it down. Juanita poured him more coffee and said, "Grandfather, I have sugar. Do you want some for your coffee?"

"Daughter, you're generous to an old man. Sugar in the coffee brings a good taste to the morning and strength to my bones."

I blew across the top of my steaming hot cup and smiled as I watched Juanita charm the old man. After we finished our second cup of coffee, I spoke.

"It's very cold in the mountains in the Ghost Face Season. In the canyons, out of the wind, a good tipi or covered wickiup with a fire will keep you from suffering. As you see, here there is plenty of wood for fires. The Rinconada touches good canyons. Camp there to stay away from prying eyes. Yes, Godfroy is a thief, but I can't prove it. He keeps part of our rations and only gives us enough to go three or four days. We can draw more every seven days. But, there's plenty of game to fill the empty days, and no one goes hungry."

When he heard this, Nana grinned and said, "We must stop this thief."

I nodded. "Blazer speaks straight and is a friend to the Apaches. He offers them work for the same pay he gives the *Indah*. When he gives advice, the listener does well to follow it. Beware his temper. He does not suffer fools with a smiling face."

Juanita finished her preparations and gave us a morning meal of slices of baked mescal, roasted venison, and acorn bread. When we finished eating, Nana smoked with me, thanked me for my hospitality, and promised to visit again when his band was settled.

The next day Nana brought sixty-three women, children, and old men to the agency. Godfroy registered them, gave them their brass identification tags, an initial offering of meat, flour, sugar, corn, and green coffee beans, and left them alone to find a place to camp. Later, Nana told me that Godfroy assumed what he saw was what he got. He didn't ask about the whereabouts of the young men, and Nana didn't tell him.

The Ghost Face Season fell on us with a

fury and filled the canyons and passes with deep snow, making travel to the agency for supplies long and hard and visits between camps few. Many of the Mescaleros moved their tipis closer to the agency to avoid the long weekly walks to the agency, but others, including my little band and Nana's band, chose to stay in our canyons and supplement what little we managed to take from the agency by hunting.

Soon, a moon had passed since Nana visited me in the early light, and clear weather came, bringing crackling cold that split pines, air brilliantly clear, and snow cover frozen deep and solid, just right for hunting elk. Juanita and I decided it was a good time to visit the Rinconada.

We found the Mimbreño wickiups set deeply back in the trees of a little box canyon, many covered with fresh deer hides and other animal skins to keep the lodges warm and hard to see, looking to untrained eyes like piles of snow. Most times the Mimbreños lived in the desert below the snow line and rarely went east as far as the prairie, and so had not adopted the tipi like the Mescaleros, who had often rubbed shoulders with and fought bloody wars with the Comanche and Kiowa. Wickiups were colder in winter than tipis, but could be made warm enough by covering the tops and sides with hides or canvas and keeping a hot fire in the middle.

We found Nana's wickiup, and the old man bade us share his fire with him, his young grandson, a fine looking boy he called Torres, and his old wife, who sat in her part of the wickiup preparing a meal, a ragged robe around her shoulders, sharing the latest camp gossip with Juanita.

Nana and I shared a cigarette, blowing the smoke to the four directions. The old man said, "As you told me, it is cold in these mountains. We were much warmer in the land of our fathers around Ojo Caliente. But here there is a little food, wood for fires, and plenty of game for the young men to hunt and keep us fed through the cold time. The agent steals from us, this I can tell, but he leaves us alone. When the Season of Little Eagles comes, I will take back some of what he steals. This reservation is a good place to rest. You must like it here. You're not riding with Sieber as a scout. Maybe you'd want to ride with a war chief like Victorio instead?"

Sitting cross-legged and leaning on my rifle as if it were a staff, I shrugged. "I still try to make our first child with my woman. There's my family for which I must hunt and protect when the *Nakai-yes* and *Indah* try to take our ponies. Maybe one day I'll ride with Sieber's scouts if Indians still fight other *Shis-Indeh*. Maybe one day I'll ride with Victorio. Maybe one day you'll stop Godfroy from stealing from us. Who knows?

"I heard you say your band was once part of Victorio's. Now I hear he is in Mexico with Juh and Geronimo while you sit by your fire in the mountains. I can tell you're still a strong warrior with light behind your eyes. Why are you here?"

Nana looked away and stared in the fire crackling beside them. At last, he looked back into my eyes and said, "Victorio leads his people."

CHAPTER 32
VICTORIO

In the time of the Ghost Face Season the *Indah* call February, Victorio, who had disappeared into Mexico with eighty men in the Season of Large Fruit, reappeared at Ojo Caliente. During his visit, he spoke of how much better off those warriors were who went to Mescalero with Nana and said that maybe he ought to go there, too. The *Indah* in charge agreed with him and asked their chiefs to let them send him there. However, when the order came to take him to Mescalero, fearing the *Indah* were trying to trick him and take him to San Carlos, he disappeared again. Of course, I didn't know all of this at that time.

Nana knew of Victorio's words in Ojo Caliente through riders who came to the reservation over the western edge of the mountains to avoid being seen in Mescalero, and he shared them with me. During his visits with me in the Season of Little

Eagles, Nana hinted to me that the great Chief Victorio had decided to settle in Mescalero and live in peace with the *Indah* as long as they kept their word, but maybe not until late in the Season of Large Leaves. While the Mescaleros waited for the famous Mimbreño war chief to make up his mind, Nana decided to settle accounts with Agent Godfroy.

Late one afternoon as I sat cleaning my guns on a blanket by an open side of the tipi, Nana with his grandson Torres rode up, leading a heavily loaded packhorse, and stopped to visit. He left the boy in charge of the ponies and walked into the shade where I motioned him to come and sit with me. Juanita brought him a jug of cool water for which he expressed much thanks. Then he pulled corn shuck cigarette makings from a vest pocket, carefully rolled one, and had a smoke with me, signaling that he wanted to talk some serious business. I waited until he spoke.

"You know the Agent Godfroy steals from us. I learned he sends part of our rations by wagon to a man in the *Indah* village across the mountains, Las Cruces. The man sells and trades it and shares money he makes with Godfroy. I took back our rations."

I frowned. "How did you do this? Have

you caused trouble for the Mescaleros doing the right thing?"

The old man laughed.

"I caused no trouble. Near the village of
La Luz, the wagon road from Tularosa
winds through a long thicket of big greasewood bushes and twisted mesquite. The
wagon carrying the rations Agent Godfroy
stole from us came through the thicket
pulled by a team of mules and driven by
two Mescaleros Godfroy had ordered to
drive the wagon to Las Cruces.

"When the Mescaleros drove the wagon
far enough into the thicket so it had to stay
on the road, my warriors rode out of brush
and stopped three in front and three behind
wagon. Their cocked rifles rode butt first
against their thighs. The middle warrior held
up his hand palm out for the wagon to stop,
and it did. The Mescalero holding the reins
asked, 'What do you want?'

"My warrior said, 'We want the wagon.
Those supplies belong to people on the
reservation, not the thieving agent who
steals food from our hungry bellies. You go
back to the reservation and forget the names
of any you know here when you tell Agent
Godfroy what happened.' The drivers nodded, climbed off the wagon, and ran for the
reservation. They never looked back."

I continued cleaning my gun, rubbing my hands up and down the barrel, leaving a thin layer of gun oil on the rifle. Finished, I set the rifle across my knees and said, "What did you do with the supplies?"

Nana grinned. "A part is cached in the Rinconada for when my people need them, and the rest was given to the Mescaleros." He shrugged. "Why not? The supplies are yours. The supplies there on my packhorse belong to your camp."

I nodded. "*Enjuh!* If Godfroy tries stealing from us again, I'll help you take it back."

Nana's face broke into a smile. *"Enjuh!"*

Early in the Season of Large Leaves (late June), Victorio rode into the Mescalero Agency with thirteen of his warriors. He had learned that the Mimbreños held at San Carlos were coming to Mescalero, and he told the new agent, Samuel A. Russell, who had replaced Godfroy, if that was so, he agreed to live on the reservation and stay peaceful. Russell assured him that he had heard correctly, and the move included giving his people protection from the *Indah* and food for their bellies. Victorio camped near the agency in order to know immediately when his people came in, but he often visited Nana and his people in their

Rinconada canyon.

During Victorio's visits, Nana sometimes brought him to my camp. The men around the fire, the women behind them in the shadows, sat and listened to his stories of how the *Indah* lied to him, the miserable life at San Carlos, how he had stayed with Juh on his flat, mountaintop fortress deep in the Blue Mountains (Sierra Madre), which protected them against soldier raids, and how he had raided the *Nakai-yes,* most of whom had nothing of value left and starved in the winter because raiding Apaches destroyed or took nearly everything they owned. He shrugged his shoulders at that and said to nodding heads around the fire, "The strong live; the weak die. Apaches aren't weak."

Victorio's charisma pulled fighting men to him like iron to a magnet. Delgadito, Kah, and Ko-do listened to his stories with rapt attention, often smiling, even laughing aloud, and nodding they understood.

I liked Victorio, too, but I listened, as Caballo Negro had taught me, with a critical ear, a small inner voice asking if what Victorio said made sense. Some of what Victorio said made a lot of sense, the lesson being the *Indah* were untrustworthy and often betrayed the *Shis-Indeh*. But his pronouncements that the Blue Coats could never defeat the Apaches if they fought true warriors rather than women and children made me think of Bosque Redondo, and I knew it was not true. The way Victorio irrationally bounced between the extremes of wanting all-out war with the *Indah* and wanting to live on the reservation in peace made me decide to do nothing with him. In his own way, Victorio was dangerous to both the *Indah,* murdering and raiding across the *Apachería* that covered New Mexico, Arizona, and most of northern Mexico; and the *Shis-Indeh,* who followed him into lethal clashes with Blue Coats and *Indah* fighters like Sieber, experienced killers, expecting no mercy and giving none.

At the end of his last visit, Victorio and Nana spoke with Delgadito, Kah, and Ko-do in the night shadows for a long time. When Victorio and Nana rode off to Nana's Rinconada canyon, I knew for certain Delgadito, Kah, and Ko-do planned to join Victorio if he left the reservation.

In the Season of Large Fruit (late August), Victorio learned that the Grant County authorities had issued indictments against him for horse stealing and murder and might come for him. Victorio didn't believe

Agent Russell had the brains and courage to protect him and wavered between running and staying on the reservation. A few days after Victorio heard about the Grant County indictments, he saw Judge Warren Bristol, Albert Fountain, and several others he recognized cross the reservation on a hunting and fishing trip. The sight convinced him they were coming to arrest him. Despite pleas from the Mescalero chiefs and Doctor Blazer, with whom he had become friends, Victorio and his people, including Nana's band and several Mescalero warriors, Delgadito, Kah, and Ko-do among them, jumped the reservation in early September to leave a trail of blood and murder across southern New Mexico.

In the months after his return, Delgadito often disappeared alone with Deer Woman into the pines and junipers. Still, he did not approach Deer Woman's mother to ask for her. Deer Woman was even more haughty and rude than on the trek to Mescalero as if saying with her actions, *See, he wants me after all, but he doesn't have the horses yet to offer for a bride. You fools were wrong about Delgadito and me.* After he jumped the reservation with Victorio, she let it be known in a voice filled with triumph that he was after horses to offer her mother a suitable bride price. He was coming back to take her to be his wife. Juanita and I kept our counsel.

As the days drifted through the Seasons of Brown Earth and Ghost Face, stories reached the reservation about the raids and killings Victorio had inflicted on ranchers, sheepherders, and any other *Indah* or *Nakai-yi* living in southern New Mexico who happened to be in his path. I heard that four troops of Indian scouts from San Carlos and the Warm Springs had joined the long lines of Blue Coats and mule pack trains carrying their supplies following his depredations. But luck and skill were with Victorio and his fighting men, and they moved into the Blue Mountains in Mexico with few casualties, there to join Juh and other camps to sit by the fire through the Ghost Face Season and make plans for again raiding north in the Season of Little Eagles.

On an achingly cold, clear day filled with bright sunlight and ice blue sky, I rode to Blazer's store to buy cartridges. Blazer sat in the circle of men around the big pot-bellied stove listening to the latest gossip and stories, and he waved for me to join them when I came through the door. I knew all the men, had even worked with some, and they all knew of my accuracy with my rifle. They nodded hello or waved a hand at me and kept talking. I raised my hand, palm out flat, and going to the counter said, "Rifle need .44 caliber bullets." I held up my right forefinger. "One box it need."

The clerk pulled a box of cartridges off the shelf behind him.

"Doin' some huntin,' Yeller Boy?"

"Soon big snow come, deer stay under trees. Make much meat when snow stop."

I handed the clerk my money pouch, and the clerk counted out the cost of the cartridges, and returned it.

"Good luck with them deer. They's good eatin' sure 'nuf."

I nodded and quietly moved around the circle until I came to a large barrel filled with apples and sat down to lean my back against it and smoke while I listened to the men talk. Before long, they apparently forgot I was there, and the subject changed to Victorio and what the Army might do when he came north in the spring.

A man with close-clipped hair, whose missing front teeth made him hard to understand, said, "I's over to Fort Stanton not long ago talkin' to a sergeant friend o' mine. He's claimin' that the Army thinks ol' Victorio is gittin' men, guns, and horses from the Indians on the res here, and they gonna put a stop to it by takin' their horses and guns away. Can you believe it? Why, the Rio Tularosa will run red with blood. The Mescaleros need their guns and horses to hunt and defend themselves. They ain't gonna part with their guns." He rose up a little, looked around his shoulder, saw me sitting there, and added, "Is they, Yellow Boy? They need 'em to hunt. Thievin' agent'll starve 'em to death if they don't."

I nodded. "Need to hunt. They no take Yellow Boy's rifle."

CHAPTER 33
THE DISARMING

The long lines of distant Blue Coats with their troops of Indian Apache scouts and mule pack trains converged on the Mescalero Agency from trails in every direction during the Season of Little Eagles at nearly the same time of day on the day the *Indah* called 12 April 1880. High on a ridge above the agency, I held the *Shináá Cho* tightly in my hands without using it, astonished at the size of the army descending on the peaceful reservation now looking from the heights like a kicked-over anthill.

A company of dark-skinned troopers passed within a couple of hundred yards of where I had disappeared into the brush. An *Indah* Blue Coat officer led them, accompanied by a civilian scout leading about twenty Apache scouts I recognized as Chiricahuas, hard-looking men armed with pistols, knives, and long-range, rolling block rifles normally given to Blue Coat soldiers who fought standing on the ground rather than shooting or swinging long knives from their horses. Their trail drifted down the side of the ridge, making them pause often as the horses and mules picked their way along the rocky, twisting switchbacks down to the agency where a big, newly erected officer's tent sat across the road from Blazer's store.

From my peephole in the junipers, I studied the soldiers passing me and saw them well armed, their animals not worn down from a long trek fighting through the wilderness. I caught my breath and felt my heart pounding in my chest. At the end of the column, surrounded by six Chiricahuas, walked the women from my camp — Juanita, Maria, Socorro, Sons-ee-ah-ray, Sons-nah's widow, and Deer Woman, two other old ones, and the young children. I didn't see He Watches, Klo-sen, Beela-chezzi, or Ish-kay-neh, and I prayed to *Ussen* they still lived. Besides being the only men left to our little band, I needed them to help free the women.

Confusion and questions fluttered through my mind like startled cactus wrens fleeing brush. *Why did the Blue Coats take women and children when, if the man at Blazer's store spoke true, they wanted Mescalero guns and ponies? If I rescue the women, how will we get away, and where will we go?* I shook my head. *Didn't the Blue Coats and Indah agents ever speak the truth?*

I looked through the *Shináá Cho* and first studied Juanita, then Sons-ee-ah-ray, and later Socorro. They showed no ugly blue bruises or other signs of beatings. The Chiricahuas seemed respectful and didn't hurry them along. In less than an hour, they were down the ridge, and reaching the store, the Chiricahuas made them sit in a group of other women and children who had voluntarily come in to the agency at Russell's invitation.

Swinging the *Shináá Cho* to Blazer's store, I saw Agent Russell leave the commander's tent, throwing up his arms in disgust and anger while his lips formed words I recognized as curses, for I had heard them when I worked at the sawmill.

I had not brought in our little band as Agent Russell requested, but had decided to wait and watch what happened at the agency for a few days before I risked it. I knew Russell had acted like a fool for refusing to bend the rules in last year's Season of Large Fruit to give Victorio rations without written approval from Washington. His fear of doing something for which Washington bureaucrats might criticize him had enraged Victorio and started a war that left southern New Mexico burning, and many ranchers, miners, and sheepherders slaughtered. The Army had spent much money for soldiers to find Victorio and punish him, but they always came up, as Rufus would say, "A day late and a dollar short."

Fury burned in my heart. Russell had betrayed the Mescaleros. He had asked Mescaleros to come to the agency where, the following day, Blue Coats from all directions surrounded them, took their weapons and horses and a large number of treasured personal items, and killed the men who tried to slip away. If my rifle had had a chance of reaching Russell at that moment, I might have killed him, but I focused instead on how to retrieve the women and children and escape the Blue Coats, especially the Chiricahua scouts, who would be able to track us even if we floated away in the air.

I watched Russell and a Blue Coat officer lead a group of soldiers, rifles ready, out to the families who had come in, saw the massive number of Blue Coats converging on the agency, and, uncertain what to do, stayed close to tree cover. Russell and the officer rode over to them and appeared to urge the band to come on in close to the agency. The officer made a short speech, and a few men handed over their rifles. Others began to drift away. Soldiers raised their rifles but didn't fire, waiting for the women and children to separate from the warriors, who were beginning to run. The Blue Coat with Russell raised his revolver and fired three signal shots, making those drifting away break into a mad dash for the trees. Suddenly a group of soldiers, their rifles up, appeared out of the line of tall pines toward which they ran. Swerving, the warriors ran toward another tree line. With women and children separated from the runners, the soldiers began to shoot. They killed fourteen men, but twenty-five made it into the trees. They took the rest prisoner and marched them back to the group of women and children sitting in front of the agency.

The sun was falling in the west, and it was growing cold. The chiefs in the group before the agency directed the bands make fires, and Russell brought supplies out of his store to feed them. The group was eerily quiet. Adults didn't speak, and babies didn't cry. Most sat unmoving wrapped in their robes, staring at the black and white soldiers going about their business. After a long last look at the women and children, I slipped out of my cover and back off the ridge to run for my camp.

Late dusk lay on the land when I approached the spring in a hidden box canyon, the air cold enough for me to see my breath, but little else. I reached the spring, saw no signs of recent use, smelled nothing on the air, and cupping my hands in the cold water, raised them to drink long swallows I had wished for all day. I moved back down the trickling stream a few feet, squatting by a boulder a little taller than my rifle to wait for enough light from the rising moon to search for a path up the canyon wall and to think through the ideas flying in my mind for freeing the captives. *If I have to kill every soldier and risk being killed, those women and children must go free.*

A young voice whispered from behind me, "Brother, what took you so long?"

Turning slowly, embarrassed to be caught by a boy, I said, "You hide well, Ish-kay-neh. Where hide the others?"

"They wait for you in a cave on the other side of this ridge."

"Horses and guns are safe?"

"Yes."

"*Enjuh!* Go!"

"So the women and children distracted the

scouts while you got away with your horses and guns?" I asked.

He Watches nodded and stared into the fire. "Ish-kay-neh ran into the camp and said he saw a line of soldiers and scouts coming from the Rinconada. We didn't know if the scouts who rode off to the sides of the trail might find us. At first, we decided to all come here, but your woman has a warrior's mind, Yellow Boy. She said, 'If we all go, the scouts will find our trail and take us. Let the men stay hidden and free us when they can. Then we'll all run from this place together.' From what you heard at Blazer's Mill, she knew the Blue Coats came to take our horses and rifles. She said the women and children must get between the scouts and our tipis and act as if they gathered food and did not know the Blue Coats would soon come down the trail. Then the scouts would see them and stop before they reached the tipis. She was right; it happened that way. Juanita led the women toward the trail with their baskets. I guess a scout found them, and the *Indah* scout chief told the scouts to take them on with the soldiers to the agency. Of course, he will send them back to catch us.

"Yellow Boy, tell us what we do to get our women and children back from the Blue

Coats before the scouts find us."

I slurped coffee Ish-kay-neh poured for me and thought while the men and boy across the fire stared at me. Finishing the cup and throwing the last few drops on the little blaze, I said, "Who rides with me?"

There were grunts and nods from each man and the boy.

"*Enjuh!* When the sun comes, we'll go back to the ridge where I hid today and watch what happens until, like Coyote, we learn how to trick the Blue Coats into giving us back our women and children so we can leave this place."

I watched them nod, and asked, "Where can we go to get away from the *Indah*? They cover the land."

He Watches replied, "Victorio spoke of living with Juh in the Blue Mountains before he returned to Ojo Caliente. We could ask Juh to shelter us in his camp. With Juh's help, we could go west of the great river, ride into the land of the *Nakai-yes,* the land of the Witch who kills and scalps our people. Maybe then we'll find and kill this witch while Juh gives us a place to camp. I've waited a long time to find and kill him."

Klo-sen nodded and spoke up. "I know the way to Juh's mountain."

"Klo-sen leads us to Juh," He Watches said.

"Enjuh!" Shaken fists went up around the fire.

CHAPTER 34
THE STONE CORRAL

From a high northern ridge above the agency, I stood with the others and stared from behind the branches of piñon and pine, my eyes narrowed and teeth clenched at the scene far below us. Up and down the valley swarmed Blue Coats, their Apache scouts, and pack train muleskinners. Soldier tents stood along Tularosa Creek, forming long orderly rows, the soldiers' horses and mules tied to picket lines, with other much larger tents sheltering supplies brought in by the pack trains. The scattered white from so many tents up and down the valley made it look like early March with patches of snow still on the ground. A haze hung in the crisp, cold air from cooking fires and the dust raised in the big stone corral where more than two hundred Mescalero horses milled.

Using *Shináá Cho,* I eventually found Juanita and the other women huddled by a fire near the creek's southeast side where the People had been herded. Juanita's little sister sat between Juanita and Maria, the three sharing a blanket. Studying every nook and cranny in the area with the *Shináá Cho,* I began to form a plan for stealing our women and children back by entering the creek above the Army camp after dark, moving downstream to the camp, getting the women to come to the creek, and leading them down to a place where the men could meet them with horses for a long, hard ride into Mexico. Beside the fury burning in my chest, hope for taking back the women grew, making my heart pound with anticipation.

I motioned the others to huddle with me.

"I see our women close to the creek near high banks. Before the moon rises, I'll wade into the creek above the soldier camp and follow it down to them. The women will come with me. We'll go down the creek and meet you with the horses and supplies from camp. We'll ride to join Juh in Mexico. Ride west. Go around Tularosa village. Maybe camp and rest in Jarilla Mountains before riding to Mexico using night for cover."

Beela-chezzi said, "Strong way you offer. How will the women know to come to you in the creek?"

I nodded toward Ish-kay-neh. "Little

Brother will wander into the camp of the Blue Coats and say he's separated from his family. The Blue Coats will put him with the others. He'll find the women and tell them to listen for three calls of a *googé* (whip-poor-will) before moonrise. Because there are many women in camp, the guards let them go to bushes along the creek to do their business, going back and forth all night. Our women will go to do their business, but won't go back. Instead, they'll come into the creek with me. No one will miss them until sunrise. Will you do this thing, Ish-kay-neh?"

Ish-kay-neh was smiling. "I'll do this. I'll show I'm ready to be a warrior."

I nodded. "It's a dangerous thing you do. What say the warriors?"

They nodded, and Klo-sen spoke for them, "Ish-kay-neh goes. He'll soon be a warrior."

From the agency came the sound of low thunder, whistles, and yells. Looking back through the piñon and pines, we saw mounted Blue Coats driving the Mescalero ponies out of the stone corral standing across the creek from the agency house. They were headed up the valley road toward Fort Stanton. The warriors looked at each other and shook their heads in disgust. The

Mescalero ponies would never be seen again, despite what Agent Russell had said.

The ponies gone and the dust beginning to settle, Ish-kay-neh turned to me and said, "Should I go now?"

I slowly nodded, despairing at the risks the unproven boy took. "Take no chances. Do as the Blue Coats tell you. If nothing changes, I'll come tonight. If I don't come, listen every night for three calls of the *googé* from the creek before the moon rises. We'll never leave you and the women. Be strong. Let no fool shoot you, especially the scouts. They'll shoot first and then ask why you're there. The Blue Coats are slower to shoot. Use them when you can.

"Follow the ridge trail east; don't go down to the agency on the same ridge trail the Blue Coats used who took our women because the scouts might backtrack and find us. In the valley off the ridge, move south down the trail going to the creek. The soldiers will find you soon."

Ish-kay-neh swung his flat palm in an arc parallel to the ground and said, "I hear and understand. We'll wait for the call of the *googé.*" He jogged up to the trail a few hundred yards and disappeared into the brush and junipers.

Just past the middle of the morning, the

guards surrounding the People began herding them with their blankets and cooking pots into the now empty stone corral, which had a high stone wall and only one gate. The *Shináá Cho* showed me nothing as I tried to understand why they herded the People like livestock into a corral everywhere covered with fresh and dried horse manure to at least a hand width depth. My anger grew, fanned by my helplessness to do anything.

A little after the sun passed the top of its arc, using the *Shináá Cho,* I was able to spot Ish-kay-neh, who had wandered onto the agency grounds unnoticed. Soon a Blue Coat guard grabbed him and led him to the stone corral where words were said with the guards on the gate who thumbed Ish-kay-neh inside and motioned the Blue Coat away. Crowded into the corral, most of the People sat stoic in their misery.

After a while, the *Shináá Cho* showed a Mescalero go to the gate, making signs he needed to do personal business. The guard laughed and pointed toward the corral's back wall. Later, a chief, tall and straight, that I recognized as Nautzile, went to the gate guards and was led to the agency house. Soon Russell and Nautzile went to the commander's tent. After a while, Nautzile returned to the corral, and soldiers appeared with picks and shovels and gave them to men near the gate to dig trenches in the brush a few yards away from the corral gate. Others came with buckets of water and poured them in the horse trough that the People had drunk dry. By late afternoon, a steady stream of two or three Mescaleros at a time left the gate for the trenches to return looking sick and exhausted.

Before nightfall, Blue Coats appeared driving a wagon loaded with wood and let the women build a fire in the middle of the corral. Soldiers brought big cooking pots used in their mess to feed them, but many of the captives refused to eat.

Before the moon rose, we crept away to our camp, wondering if fighting and dying with Victorio was the only way to end Blue Coat outrages.

Three days passed. Four. The original trickle of Mescaleros passing back and forth to the trenches had become a flood. After two days, they covered the stinking and full original trenches and dug more. By the fourth day, they covered the second set of trenches and dug more. Russell and Doctor Blazer made repeated visits to the commander's tent. High on the ridge above them, we watched with increasing and helpless fury. Klo-sen and Beela-chezzi talked about committing suicide by attacking the guards on the corral gates so some might get free, but I fixed my eyes on getting the women and children out of the grasp of the Blue Coats and talked them out of their foolish ideas.

On the morning of the sixth day, the commander came out of his tent accompanied by Russell, Doctor Blazer, and the command surgeon. They stopped at the gate and talked to the guards, watched the sick Mescaleros stagger to and from the trenches, and then walked among them in the corral, the commander nervously slapping his gloves against his free hand. Soon they retreated to the commander's tent. By the afternoon of the sixth day, the Blue Coats herded the People out of the corral and sent them back to the place where Russell had told them to camp near the creek in the first place.

We watched the new camp and waited. Juanita and the other women again spread their blankets and made their fire near the creek. Ish-kay-neh kept to himself, but stayed near them and spoke with Juanita or Socorro every day. In seven more days, nearly all the sick Mescaleros were steady on their feet.

That night around our campfire I said, "Tomorrow night there is a little moon and the *googé* calls from the creek."

CHAPTER 35
RESCUE

G-prrip-prEE . . . g-prrip-prEE . . . g-prrip-prEE . . . I waited, straining to hear above the chorus of frogs and peepers. There! A faint splash upstream, I looked to my left and stared into the darkness. And then she was beside me, her chin up, standing straight, her little sister in her arms, the faces of the others appearing faintly in the darkness behind her. My first impulse was to reach for her, but, fearful of being caught by the guards or seen by others, I only smiled, beat my fist against my heart, and jerked my head for her to follow. She smiled and nodded as she hugged Moon to keep her still and motioned those behind her forward.

We stayed in the icy creek, slowly feeling our way downstream for a couple of hours, until it began to widen into a swampy place, its frog chorus deafening. I led them out of the creek and up onto the road where our men with the horses came out of the juniper shadows. Last out of the creek was Ish-kay-neh. I watched him and made the sign for "good," my palm moving in an arc parallel to the ground. Ish-kay-neh nodded, smiling, obviously pleased he had been recognized for his courage and loyalty.

There were enough ponies for us all except for the little ones who rode with their mothers. I led them down the road toward Tularosa strung out in a line at a fast trot that became a lope and then eased back into a fast walk, a rhythm I kept up all night. In the distance, even with only a quarter moon, we could see the brilliant white sands in the black outline of the San Andres Mountains blocking out the horizon stars.

I stopped to water and rest the horses when we crossed Tularosa Creek. Juanita and I moved off to stand alone in the dark shadows of a cottonwood tree. She threw her arms around me, and I held her as we stood together silently sharing our joy in each other.

I said to her, "Wife, you're a warrior. You make my heart soar. We must hurry. When the sun comes, the Chiricahua wolves will come tracking us. *Indah* chiefs will be eager to kill us all for getting away. Wolves do what chiefs say."

"What will you do? Where will we go?"

"Two, maybe three, bowshots beyond this stream stands the village of Tularosa. We'll ride around it and go to a hiding place in the Jarilla Mountains that He Watches knows. We'll rest there and watch. When the wolves come, we'll wipe them out. Soon, we'll hide in the Blue Mountains in land of the *Nakai-yes*. In the Blue Mountains, you'll live with me again. Maybe Juh can tell me of the Witch who attacked our people."

She nodded. "I'm always your wife where we go, where we live."

I said, "You're my woman until the grandfathers take me."

We crossed Tularosa Creek and turned west along the south edge of the great, billowing ocean-like waves of the white sands. When we rounded the monolithic cliffs of the Sacramento Mountains, we turned south across a great sea of newly green grama grass, and set a steady lope beside the high eastern cliffs rising a thousand feet above the basin still black in the shadows of the brightening dawn.

When the sun came, burnished, glowing gold above the mountains, we saw the gray and rusty red Jarilla Mountains off to our right, midgets compared to the giant, high cliffs on our left. As the day brightened, He Watches rode up beside me to take the lead into the Jarillas. He swung west around their northern end and rode south in their shadows until he came to a large thicket of ocotillo covered in brilliant red flowers growing next to a high vertical wall. He disappeared behind them, following a faint trail. In a hundred yards, dodging their sharp, ugly thorns, we turned into a crack in the cliff wall and rode deep into a narrow canyon that gradually widened and ended at a small natural tank fed by a spring dribbling out of the vertical southern wall.

We and our ponies drank long and deep. The women scraped sticks of ocotillo under low ledges on the canyon walls to drive out any snakes, scorpions, and centipedes before spreading their blankets to sleep in their shadows with the children. The men rubbed down the horses with handfuls of grass from small patches that grew near the tank overflow and then hobbled them to graze.

Then we ate a mixture of dried meat, mescal, herbs, and nuts the women had made before the Ghost Face Season. Ish-kay-neh and I were the first to climb to a ledge thirty feet up on the back wall to keep watch for the scouts sure to follow.

Ish-kay-neh, thrilled to be treated and

respected like a man by the others, climbed to the high ledge and found a place to sit in the shadows and gaze across the sea of thin green grass dotted with dark green creosote bushes and light green mesquites, their leaves waving gently in the slow morning breeze. Thousands of yellow *Nakai-yi* poppy flowers and yellow and blue gourd flowers bloomed below with distant gray mountains surrounding them. Handing my rifle to Ish-kay-neh, I pulled myself up on the ledge and sat down to let my legs dangle off the edge as I looked across the scene.

Ish-kay-neh said, "Are the scouts coming?"

"They're coming. But maybe we'll leave before they find this place. They won't come before dark to catch us. They won't hunt for us in the dark, but we'll ride far in the dark. He Watches knows this land."

"How will we go?"

I pulled the *Shináá Cho* out, put it to my eye, and scanned the distant mountains to the west. I started my scan from the high mountains north and swung to the ragged peaks south before realization hit me, and I abruptly swung back a few degrees for a second look.

"What you see?"

I continued to stare at the mountains for

a moment before slowly lowering the *Shináá Cho,* smiling.

"I remember I know those mountains. I recognize two close together that Rufus Pike calls Rabbit Ears. I saw these mountains from the mountain where *Ussen* visited me. Tonight, we'll ride to those mountains and find Rufus Pike. We'll rest the horses, take care of the scouts there if they don't come today, and then go to the land of the *Nakai-yes* in three, maybe four, suns. *Ussen* is good to us."

"Who is Roofoos Peek?"

"An *Indah,* a friend of my father and me, the one who taught me to shoot. He lives alone and has cattle. He rides a mule and is a good shot. He will help us."

"*Enjuh.* I'll watch first. Yellow Boy rests."

I nodded and pointed my rifle toward the sun's position halfway to the top of its midday arc. "When the sun is there, I'll watch, and you sleep."

Ish-kay-neh nodded and moved into the shade of a boulder to watch.

When I sat with He Watches to discuss my idea about going to Rufus Pike, the old man asked, "What will we do there?"

"We'll wait for the scouts and then ambush and kill them. I know a place where we can do this. You'll see." He Watches broke into a broad grin and nodded.

By deep twilight, we'd seen no sign of the scouts, not even dust streamers on far trails. We watered and saddled the horses and ate again as the night blanketed us with safety. At full dark, we mounted and filed out past the ocotillo, its red blossoms closed until the sun came again.

CHAPTER 36
CHIRICAHUA WOLVES

We waited by Rufus' porch in the light of dawn until he emerged from his outhouse. When he saw me with my rifle, he yelled "*Dánt'e,* Yellow Boy!" as he pulled his suspenders over his shoulders and broke into a long, hurried stride toward me. My companions looked at each other frowning, but I grinned, swung my arm toward the others, and said, "Nish'ii', Rufus Pike. We have come. We stay three, maybe four, days?"

Rufus shouted as though I were a mile away, "Why, hell, son, stay as long as ya need." He swung his palm parallel to the ground and added, "I'm shore glad to see ya. I see ol' He Watches and his walkin' stick." He held up his palm toward He Watches, who nodded and palmed him back. Then Rufus glanced over our group, raised his brows, and asked. "Where's Caballo Negro?"

"Land of the grandfathers."

A look of sorrow came over Rufus, who said, "I purely hate to hear that. He was a mighty good man." He looked out over the valley below for a moment, then turned and said, "Go on an' make yoreselves to home. Yellow Boy, ya know the best places to camp and the little mine where I keep my supplies. Take what ya need when ya need it. I'll make some coffee and heat up some steak, beans, and tortillas. You'n tell me what's happened while we eat."

I led our group up the trickling wash on the south side of the canyon, and we made a comfortable camp by the cattle tank dam, close enough for an easy walk to the shack, but far enough to keep ourselves out of sight of Rufus' visitors. The women made small cooking fires and cooked a hot meal while we checked our weapons and rubbed down the horses before turning them loose to graze. The children gathered brush and dried cow patties to feed the fires.

At the shack, Rufus and I sat on the porch finishing our steaks and beans and wiping our pans clean with tortillas. I belched my appreciation and said, "Rufus Pike cooks better than many women. I'll take you to land of *Nakai-yes*."

Rufus grinned and shook his head. "No thank ya, amigo. Only place in Mexico I'd be interested in goin' is them houses filled with women down to Ciudad Juárez on the other side of the river from El Paso. Whoooeee, now that there is a good-time visit.

"I figured you mighta left the Guadalupes an' put yore tipis over to the reservation. Ain't heard from you in a couple years. How come ya're out galavantin' 'round the countryside with them women and children? Th' way ol' Victorio is raisin' hell, ya run into cavalry an' they'll shoot first an' ask questions later. Long as they kill any Indeh they see, they'll figure they're doin' the right thing."

"Hmmph, Rufus Pike speaks true words. Blue Coats come to reservation. Kill many Mescaleros who run, no fight. Blue Coats take Mescalero rifles and ponies. Mescalero no longer hunt. No longer ride ponies. We leave."

We watched the morning light spread over the Mesilla Valley making long shadows from the Organs disappear. Unlike the cloudless, bright, blue morning sky, a thundercloud filled Rufus' face as he spat tobacco juice on a scorpion in the shadow of a nearby rock and shook his head.

"That there is about the dum'est thang the army ever done, and they done a passel. What can Colonel Hatch be thinkin'? A few Mescaleros mighta joined Victorio, maybe even give him some cartridges, but that don't come close to justifin' what Hatch done. Chiricahua Blue Coat scouts is after ya? Ya know they'll be out to kill ya. It'll make 'em look good to their *Indah* Blue Coat officers an' it'll make ol' Hatch think he's got the reservation sewed up tighter'n Maud's purse. It's gonna be you or them. Ya gotta take care of business with them wolves now an' then git on down to Mexico where the army ain't got no callin' card."

"How we do this, Rufus Pike?"

Rufus slowly chewed on the wad of tobacco in his cheek, rested his elbows on his knees, and, staring out across the valley, said, "You say ol' He Watches brought you here from the Jarillas? Did he stop at the springs on th' other side of th' mountain? *Indah* calls 'em Aguirre Springs. They's below a steep pass on the south side of the Rabbit Ears. I spec he went to the springs first and then follered the trail 'bout a mile north over the Baylor Pass. Rabbit Ears Pass is pushin' it hard fer horses an' San Agustín Pass is outta the way."

I nodded and said, "We water at this place you call Aguirre Springs. Go across pass you call Baylor."

Rufus spat and said, "Them scouts is gonna stay on top of yore trail. They'll come by th' springs 'cause that's where yore trail leads, an' it's the first water outta th' Jarillas. Ya got two growed warriors with ya, ol' He Watches, who ain't much on his feet but can ride an' shoots good from an ambush spot, an' ya got me. That's five rifles 'gainst 'em. Oughta be enough fer that pack of wolves. We'n wait fer 'em at the springs and take 'em out with an ambush. What 'cha think?"

I pulled a cigar from my vest, lit it, blew smoke to the four directions, and gave it to Rufus to do the same. When Rufus handed it back, I said, "*Enjuh.* Rufus Pike great war chief. We go now. Wolves come soon. Ishkay-neh comes with warriors and holds horses. First time he makes war. My woman, Juanita, she good warrior with sling, protects women and children."

Rufus groaned, his arthritic joints slow to move, as he pushed up from the porch floor. "Uhhhh. Gittin' old, Yellow Boy, gittin' mighty old. I'm gonna git my gear and rifle and saddle Lulu. When you're ready, we'll go."

■ ■ ■ ■

The old Salt Trail over Baylor Pass had not been used often since the wagon road from Las Cruces went over San Agustin Pass, which was a little lower in altitude and more accessible to mines on the north side. The Baylor trail our band followed the night before was faint but still easy to see. Topping the pass, we looked out over the great Tularosa Basin we had come across the night before. Off to the south in front of us, the Jarilla Mountains appeared to crawl out of the sands like some long forgotten animal. Directly behind the Jarillas were the Sacramentos standing tall in the blue, hazy distance. Rufus pointed south toward the springs and said, "That there is where we're headed. Stayin' outta sight, we'n make it by midafternoon. They ain't but a handful of ranches between here and Tularosa, so we ain't likely to run across any *Indah*s. We got to be careful at the springs. The scouts might already be there. Comprende?"

I nodded and, telling my warriors what Rufus had said, waved them forward. They rode down the steep, winding trail out of the Organs, letting their animals pick their way and guiding them behind junipers to stay out of lines of sight from the basin and the springs.

Rufus rode Lulu up to the springs while the Apaches stayed hidden back in the brush and boulders. He wanted to look around first and ensure no one was already taking water or an afternoon siesta in the shade among the boulders. When he found no one around the springs, he waved us in. We came forward, dismounted, and let the thirsty ponies drink at the natural tank filled by a burbling spring's trickle. I sent Ish-kay-neh with the horses up the trail toward Rabbit Ears Pass and then down into a juniper lined arroyo where the ponies wouldn't be seen or heard by approaching riders.

The springs, high enough to see smoke plumes all across the basin, marked the kitchens of ranch houses or a few cowboys eating their dinner by their herds. The roof of the San Augustine ranch house, owned then by Ben Davies, almost three miles away, shimmered in the distance. Patches of white, flocks of sheep grazing on the ranch, lay scattered across the newly green range-land.

Our warriors hid behind boulders, most, higher than a man's head. Their positions roughly made the shape of a horseshoe with the springs in the center. Klo-sen, Beela-chezzi, and He Watches hid behind boulders forming the horseshoe's top arc. Rufus and I stayed close to the spring's entrance to close the circle of fire and stop the scouts from charging out of the trap.

Warm breezes filled the air up from the basin. I kept the *Shináá Cho* to my eye throughout the brilliant afternoon, scanning every uncertain detail. I saw nothing, not even dust plumes from riders. If the scouts had followed our trail, then it seemed we ought to see them by the time for long shadows off the mountains. A sense of impending disaster began to settle in my guts. I crept over to Rufus, who had also spent the hours scanning the basin with his old cavalry glasses while he chewed and spat tobacco juice on any insect within range.

"See 'em, Rufus Pike?"

"Naw. I ain't seen nuthin. Don't believe they's there. You seen 'em?"

"No see. Maybe scouts no follow us. Maybe scouts fool us. Maybe they wait on other side of pass to ambush us. Know where we go. We ride now."

"You got the right idee, amigo. Let's saddle up."

■ ■ ■ ■

The horses were rested from the long afternoon wait, and we made good time on our ride over Baylor Pass and down the western side. Rufus and I talked through our strategy of what to do if the scouts had somehow known where we were headed, got around us, and took the women and children prisoners.

The moon barely floated above the Organs when we led our horses up the trail to the shack. No one met us. Looking up the canyon, we saw the glow from several fires near the dam tank. Klo-sen crept up the trail to the camp. When he returned he nodded and said, "Blue Coat Chiricahuas."

We left Ish-kay-neh and He Watches with the horses at the shack porch to stop escapes out the front of the canyon. Rufus moved up the north side of the canyon to block any escapes up the back of the canyon's west cliff face. I moved up the canyon's south side, staying in the shadows of the wash. Klo-sen and Beela-chezzi worked their way to the camp through the brush and grass in the middle of the canyon.

I took care to avoid stepping on loose stones in the gurgling wash and to stay in the black shadows cast by the rising moon. I reached the dam and, crawling on my belly to a boulder looking like a man's head half-buried in the ground, found a place in the shadows where I could see the fires.

There were six Chiricahuas, three wearing blue cavalry jackets. They carried pistols and knives and a full bandolier of cartridges across their chests. No *Indah* cavalry officer was with them, but one Chiricahua was obviously in charge — his coat off, at least five inches taller than the rest, muscles rippling under his shirtsleeves, black eyes in a dark, pox-scarred face scanning the darkness beyond the fires. He wore a red bandana tied around his head and carried his Winchester in the crook of his arm as he paced in front of the fire looking down the canyon. The others called him Soldado Fiero (Fierce Soldier), and from the way the others cowered before him, he carried the right name.

Our women and children sat together in the shadows at the edge of the camp, a scout sitting on either side of their group, eating what Juanita and Deer Woman brought them from the pots on the fire. The three remaining scouts sat back in the shadows eating and furtively glancing down the canyon toward the shack.

Back in the canyon cows bellowed, at times drowning out the myriad frogs in chorus around the cattle pool and the crackle of the fires. I studied the camp and scouts, taking in every detail, deciding what to do. Shooting into the camp from many directions was likely to kill or injure the women and children as well as the scouts and was not an option. It was better to wait for another opening.

Soldado Fiero paced before the nearest fire and stared into the dark, looking from one side of the canyon to the other, cocking his head to catch any unusual sound. It was apparent that he didn't like their situation. I imagine he knew the Mescaleros, growing tired of waiting at the springs, would soon return to their women and children, believing they had escaped the Blue Coats.

He looked over his left shoulder toward the cattle tank, sweeping the dark side of the wash past my position and carried down the wash, but then he stopped and turned back to stare at the black shadows where I lay barely breathing, my legs protruding from behind the boulder.

My heart pounded in my chest as I saw Soldado Fiero's eyes narrow into a squint and his arms slowly raise his Winchester.

His rifle was nearly to his shoulder. The

finger on his rifle trigger was poised to kill anything that moved as he stepped toward the shadows. The other Chiricahuas saw him looking at a particular spot below the cattle tank and stood up to watch the spot, bringing their cocked rifles to their shoulders.

Before Soldado Fiero seated his rifle butt against his shoulder, I shouted, "Hold or die!" He slowly lowered his rifle and looking over his shoulder nodded back to the other scouts to do the same.

"I speak true. Lay down your rifles and pistols, and no harm comes. We'll talk. Choose to fight, and you'll die. Choose now!"

He laid down his rifle, drew his long-barreled Colt from its holster, and laid it down, too. The other scouts followed his example.

I said, "You wear Blue Coats. You've come to kill us because the Blue Coat chief wars with Victorio. We don't ride with Victorio. We don't war against *Indah.* We're going to the far Blue Mountains and won't come back. Go back to Blue Coat chief and say you didn't find us. Leave, and you'll live. Stay, you'll die. Give us your word to track us no more. You lie? You'll die. What will you do?"

Soldado Fiero crossed his arms and stared into the dark.

I yelled, "What will you do? Speak!"

He said through clenched teeth, "We'll go! We won't track you to the Blue Mountains! Why do you hide in the dark? Let us see the great warrior who defeats us."

"You go? *Enjuh!* Remember my words when night comes. You'll think maybe I'm there. I'll kill you if you come back . . . How did you know we were here?"

"The *Indah* sawmill chief said the woman of Yellow Boy was with the Mescaleros who ran. He said you wouldn't join Victorio and told the Blue Coat chief not to chase you because you do no harm. The Blue Coat chief said all Mescaleros must stay in front of his eyes. He sent us to take you back. Al Sieber said Yellow Boy never misses with a rifle; said Roofoos Peek showed you how to shoot. This is the place of Roofoos Peek lodge. We saw you ride for Jarilla Mountains and knew you'd find Roofoos Peek. We took an easier, faster road for ambush here. We didn't go by the springs."

Soldado Fiero told this with a self-satisfied sneer that seemed to say to those around him, *See how smart I am. You don't have a chance if I decide to take you.*

"Get your ponies and guns. Go. If you

come back, you'll die."

Two scouts went for the horses hobbled in the dark pasture behind the women and children. I stared at Soldado Fiero, waiting for him to make a move, expecting to kill him, but the Chiricahua with folded arms calmly waited.

I glanced at Juanita, who sat near the fire in front of the women and children, her head bowed, her long black hair falling in front of her face. She played in the dirt, running her fingers through the soft sandy soil, catching handfuls, and then letting it fall through her fingers. I squinted to see her better, but I couldn't tell what she was doing except entertaining herself. I hoped the scout in front of me hadn't knocked her senseless when he took her.

The scouts, leading their horses, stopped to pick up their guns and swung into their saddles without using their stirrups. Soldado Fiero, continuing to stare into the dark where I waited, stood his ground and didn't move.

I said, "Go now."

The other scouts began walking their mounts down the trail out of the canyon.

Soldado Fiero smiled slightly, shrugged, and took a step back, and then, glancing toward Juanita, turned in slow motion, to reach for his guns, which were lying by his moccasins.

A soft slapping sound like a fist striking an open palm broke the stillness. He grunted, collapsed to his knees, and fell face forward into the sand without another sound.

Juanita ran to him, pulled his knife, stabbed it into the ground beside her, then rolled him on his back and stared at his face. In seconds, I was across the tank dam, kneeling beside her, and looking at him. His eyes were rolled back in his head, seeing nothing, but he was breathing. Juanita raised his bandana and pulled up the hair above his right temple where there was a rapidly swelling bump about the size of a chicken egg. The skin, unbroken, was beginning to turn to a blue-black color and spread across his face. By morning his right eye, maybe even his left, would be swollen shut.

I whispered to her, "You probably saved us. I was thinking maybe I'd kill him when he shoots. You're magnificent with that sling. I barely saw your arm move."

She whispered, "My father taught me well, and I have a wise and mighty husband who depends on me. We'll send this one back to his Blue Coat masters alive. His head will hurt for one or two moons."

Leading his pony, Soldado Fiero tied across the saddle, I walked out of the dark from behind the corral shed down to where He Watches was waiting. I handed the reins to the scout in the lead, who cocked his head to see Soldado better. Frowning, he asked, "Dead or alive?"

I said, "Alive. He's lucky. He decided to shoot, but a sling stone stopped him before my rifle killed him. When the sun comes, he'll wake up, eyes swollen shut and head hurting. Take him. Go back to the Blue Coats, and follow us no more. We'll raid and war only in Mexico. Go!"

The scout grabbed hold of his saddle horn and swung into the saddle. He looked at me, nodded, and said, *"Enjuh!"* before riding down the trail into the night, leading Soldado's pony.

CHAPTER 37
JUH

At the corral, Ish-kay-neh and Rufus met me and He Watches, and one look at Rufus told me he was on fire with curiosity. I said, "Scouts go, no come back. Mescalero camp here, and women make feast."

Half grinning, half scowling, Rufus looked at me. "What the devil did you do? Cut the throats of them Chiricahuas?"

"Come, we eat, tell story at fire. In two suns, Mescaleros ride for Blue Mountains."

Rufus grinned and nodded. "Okay, *Aashco* (friend), lead the way."

Filling his growling belly with steak, acorn bread, and mesquite bean flour cakes, Rufus listened and laughed aloud, crumbs of acorn bread falling from his lips and collecting across his shirt, when we told him the story of how Juanita had given Soldado Fiero a bad headache before his fury had killed anyone. The story and meal finished, smoke made to the four directions, I relaxed around the fire with the other men. In the fire's flickering orange and yellow light, Rufus turned to me and whispered just loud enough to be heard above the frog and cricket chorus, "Son, that there woman of yore's is a danged good un. I hope she gives ya many sons and daughters. Even if she can't, keep her."

I looked into Rufus' earnest face and said with certainty, "Maybe another woman will make my children." Then I laid my fist over my heart and said, "I keep Juanita always here."

Our little band of Mescaleros rode down the rocky, washed-out trail leading from Rufus' canyon. To ensure our ride to the far Blue Mountains was unseen and unknown, Rufus gave us enough provisions to make certain we wouldn't have to raid for supplies.

We rode south along the east side of the great river, staying in the shadows of the bosque until we waded a cattle crossing and passed west of the village at the great pass of the north, the place the Mexicans and *Indahs* call El Paso.

For two nights, we pushed at a steady pace across the Chihuahua *llano,* saving our horses, using little of the water we carried except for the children and horses. We stopped during the first day near a water tank our warriors knew from their raiding days and slept where we could see the tank but not be seen by others coming to slake their thirsts. The other warriors and I, vigilant and ready to defend the women and children, took turns watching over the sleepers and studying the Blue Mountains, which were slowly emerging from the haze, for landmarks pointing the way to Juh's camp. Klo-sen was the only one in our band who had been to the fortress, and that, years ago in his very early warrior days. He said he knew it was on top of a great flat-topped mountain south of the little village of Janos and that he would know Juh's mountain when he saw it framed by the mountains surrounding it.

On the second day, we slept hidden in brush on the south side of a small stream fast disappearing under the hot, early summer sun and passing a little south of Janos. Beela-chezzi, on watch that afternoon, reported that he saw a Chihenne Apache, no doubt one who rode with Victorio, creeping toward the north side bank like a big cat approaching a deer. He then signaled for Klo-sen, watching on the other side of the camp, to awaken me and He Watches and have us get ready to ride.

We watched as the Chihenne looked up and down the stream, slid down the bank to the edge of the water, and kneeled, while still looking up and down stream, to drink with a cupped hand while his pony, a tawny buckskin lathered from a hard ride, drank deep, long swallows. The scout didn't let the pony drink too long before jerking him away from the water, and, leading him up the bank, rode back the way he came.

Soon he returned, leading a small band of warriors. Every gun we had was pointed where the scout had stopped to drink. I studied the face of each warrior who followed the scout and rode single file down the bank to drink. I recognized none of them until the last one rode into view. It was Ko-do. It was startling how much my young friend's face had changed from adolescent boy to hard, flinty-eyed man, ready to kill or be killed. I started to signal him, but changed my mind, thinking it better no one knew we hid there.

The scout kept watch while the others drank and watered their horses. Each rider led spare mounts, some two, some three, and after drinking, each man changed to a fresh mount. After watering, the band gathered on the south bank. The leader pointed toward the mountains in the gray haze to the southwest, said a few words that we couldn't hear, and then, pushing his pony to a distance-eating lope, headed in the direction he had pointed. We watched them disappear in a streamer of dust, and He Watches turned to me and said, "We'll follow their trail and find Juh's camp."

"How do you know this, Grandfather?"

"They're leading many spare horses and riding south. These are Victorio's warriors, looking for supplies. Victorio and Juh's wives are related, so Juh gives him supplies."

Klo-sen nodded and said, "He Watches speaks true. They're riding in the direction of Juh's fortress."

"Grandfather's wisdom brings us light. We'll follow their path, but now the women and children need to sleep."

The warrior's trail, not hard to follow in the bright moonlight, headed straight for the black outline of the mountains blocking out the stars on the horizon. As the outline filled more of the night sky, the trail led into an arroyo winding between increasingly steep hills until it became a small, burbling creek running down the middle of a wide canyon between high ridges that lay like fingers growing out of a mountain-sized hand. The sun was a bright glow still behind the southeastern mountains, but it lighted the eastern sides of ridges that ran to the top of the mountains and scattered pools of golden light across *llano* hilltops.

I sat studying the warrior's trail out of the creek when Klo-sen rode up beside me and, pointing to a hulking mountain's black outline in front of us, said, "That mountain-top, big and flat, is Juh's stronghold. Soon we'll find a trail out of the creek that goes up the ridge and follows many switchbacks. It looks like the spine of a snake. Wait here. When more light comes, Juh will see us. He will welcome us in good way."

I nodded. "*Enjuh.* We'll wait."

Sliding off my pony, I led the band into the shadows of a large, dense grove of junipers. The women moved deep into the junipers, wrapped the children in blankets, gave them bits of warrior trail food to eat, and wrapping themselves in blankets, lay down with them. The men, melting into the brush and shadows close to the creek, becoming part of the scene, waited.

I studied the top of the mountain and the trail up the canyon with the *Shináá Cho,* but saw nothing move anywhere and wondered if Klo-sen was right about the top of the pine-covered mountain being Juh's stronghold. When the sun had made a quarter of its arc across the brilliant, effervescent sky, I crept into the junipers, found Juanita, and told her to bring the women and children, and be ready to ride.

Just as Klo-sen had said, the trail up the canyon soon appeared, leading out of the creek toward the top. It was steep and used often, showing the tracks of many horses and cattle, and it used many switchbacks as it approached the top. As the elder of our band, He Watches led the way up out of the trees lining the trail and on to the mountaintop that spread out before us covered in groves of tall pines and long, grass-covered meadows. It was a relief to see groups of wickiups scattered over the top of the mountain and spaced apart for privacy, all facing east, beginning only a few hundred yards from where the trail topped out on the mountain. I guessed that the wickiups in the middle group, which were the largest, belonged to each of Juh's wives.

Before us in the middle of the trail stood a tall, heavyset, Nednhi Apache, his hair in one long braid reaching almost to his knees, his arms, rippling with muscles, crossed, and his round face set in a not unfriendly frown of curiosity. Behind him stood the rest of the camp: warriors first, then the women, and behind them, the children, all studying us, taking in every detail. The only sound was the occasional snort from a horse and the wind whispering through the tall green pines.

The Nednhi said, "Mescaleros, welcome to Juh's camp. Why are you here?"

He Watches rode forward, slid off his pony, and, with the help of his staff, hobbled the last few yards to stand straight before the man who towered over him. He waved his staff toward our little band and said, "Juh speaks true. We are Mescaleros. Once we lived in the camp of Cha in the mountains the *Indah* call Guadalupe. A witch and his warriors wiped most of us out over fifteen moons ago. They took scalps. We believe they came from the land of the *Nakai-yes*. The Witch is powerful and knows much about the Indeh. He came and destroyed our camp when many of our warriors were raiding south, and our lookouts were killed before they could warn us.

"Our warriors here, and three who ride with Victorio, are all who remain. We moved to live on the Mescalero Reservation to help the women and children the Witch missed survive the Ghost Face Season. It was a hard life, but I was told, much easier than

404

San Carlos. The agents at Mescalero stole from us and were fools. But we kept to ourselves and took little from the *Indah.* A moon ago, Blue Coats came from many directions on the same day when the shadows were shortest and demanded we give up our rifles and ponies. Some Mescaleros did what the Blue Coats said. We did not. We hid from the Blue Coats and their Chiricahua scouts and kept our rifles and ponies, but they caught and penned up our children and women. We took them back and rode for the Blue Mountains to find the camp of Juh.

"We ask Juh to let us camp in his stronghold until the Blue Coats grow tired and leave the Mescalero Reservation. We will hunt and help support the stronghold while we are here."

As He Watches finished speaking, Juh, his face a thundercloud of anger, said, "The Mescaleros are our brothers. They have suffered much from the *Nakai-yi* Witch and Blue Coats, which all ought to be wiped out. There are too many to drive away, but many will die from our rifles and arrows. Stay with us. You're guests in my lodge. Put your tipis near us. There is plenty of wood and water. Come to my lodge when the evening star rises. We will smoke and talk of vengeance against the Blue Coats and the Witch."

He Watches said, "We thank Juh for his generous offer."

Well before the sun sank below the western mountains, our women, with the help of the Nednhi women, had our tipis up and our stew pots bubbling. He Watches and I found a place to sit on the mountaintop cliffs and study the eastern *llano* with the *Shináá Cho.* We saw dust streamers on the roads, and on the *llano,* smoke from hacienda kitchens and small villages, herds of cattle, outlines of distant mountains in gray haze, and the occasional shadows of clouds sailing east.

Staring through the *Shináá Cho,* I said, "This is my memory from when we watched the *llano* and the sunrise road from the top of the Guadalupes, Grandfather."

He Watches grunted. "It was not so long ago as men count seasons, my son. Study the *llano* and the mountains here with care. Someday your life may depend on it."

He Watches sat in the place of honor to Juh's left. I sat to his right, and Klo-sen and Beela-chezzi sat next to He Watches and me. Five of Juh's most respected warriors completed the circle around Juh's tipi fire. He rolled a cigarette using an oak leaf and tobacco he had traded for from a mercantile store in Casas Grandes. He lit it using a small stick from the fire, blew smoke to the four directions, and passed it to He Watches, who smoked and passed it on around the circle.

With the smoke complete, Juh, fire in his eyes, dispensed with the normal small talk preliminaries and said, "How can I help my Mescalero brothers?"

He Watches glanced at me, Klo-sen, and Beela-chezzi, and we all nodded for him to speak. "Fifteen moons ago, our camp in a Guadalupe canyon was raided. Many of our warriors, including these two men, Klo-sen and Beela-chezzi, and the three who ride with Victorio, were on a raid to the south with Cha. The raiders bewitched our look-outs, killed them, and wiped out our camp, warriors, women, and children. They scalped everyone, some scalps taken with the ears still attached. Tracks showed *Indah* and Indeh ponies were there. Some women and children who had left the camp early to gather food to save for the Ghost Face Season hid, and the *Witch* did not find them. I saw a giant *Nakai-yi*-Comanche lead the raid. His hair gone, he painted his head like a skull and laughed as he shot children and warriors. Other *Nakai-yes* were with him, and Indeh I believe were Comanches. My grandson here beside you, Yellow Boy, was north learning to shoot with an old *In-dah* scout his father knew. That day, the giant killed Yellow Boy's father. There in those mountains, Yellow Boy had his vision, learned his name, and *Ussen* gave him a gift. His gift? *Ussen* tells him to kill witches and send them blind to the land of the grandfathers. Two days before we were wiped out, *Ussen* sent him a dream. It said he must return to the Guadalupe camp. He saw a witch in his dream. Our burned wickiups still smoked when he returned. A killer of witches, he does not fear ghost sickness, and he buried the bodies left in the camp before he found me. He ate from contaminated food supplies, and did not get ghost sickness. He swears to avenge his father and the others killed in our camp. Because the *Nakai-yes* trade pesh-klitso for Apache scalps, we believe the Witch is here in the land of the *Nakai-yes*. Juh knows all in the land of the *Nakai-yes*. Help us. Tell us where we can find this witch and kill him."

Juh looked at me, frowned, and, ignoring me, said to He Watches, "Why do you think this grandson who has few years as a warrior can kill this powerful witch? It wiped out nearly all of your people."

I looked in the insulting, taunting eyes of Juh and said in an even voice, "*Ussen* told me I would be a killer of witches and send them blind to the land of the grandfathers. His gift of Power speaks in my name." I held up the Henry rifle and explained, "This rifle is called Yellow Boy. We are as one. It does not miss. *Ussen* has given me this as a gift of Power. I will kill witches. I will shoot out their eyes. I do not miss."

Juh's warriors, their eyes glittering, looked at each other and then at me. Juh stared into the fire for a moment and then looked back at me. "*Ussen* has given you a great gift. If it is as you say, then you can kill the Witch who killed your father and wiped out your camp. Perhaps you will show us how well this weapon from *Ussen* shoots when the light comes. Perhaps then I will remember where I have seen the *Nakai-yi* you describe."

I smiled. "When the sun is on this mountain, I'll shoot. I'll show Juh *Ussen*'s Power, and Juh will show me the way to the Witch. This is all I have to say."

Juh nodded. *"Enjuh!"*

CHAPTER 38
JUH'S TRIAL

The morning sky was a brilliant, wildflower blue, the stronghold lighted by a sun of golden fire not yet high enough to burn away the failing dawn mists far out on the *llano.* The air was cool enough to see steam from the mouths of men gathering at the side of a meadow covered with bushes and grama grass. An ancient oak that had been struck by lightning stood alone in that meadow, a twisted, gray specter lifting its arms to the blue above us. With my rifle cradled in the crook of my left arm, I stood to one side of the gathering, relaxed, waiting. As if by magic, standing by my side, Juh appeared, big, intimidating, a slight smile wavering on his thin, brown lips.

"Young warrior, are you ready to show us the Power *Ussen* gives you?"

"I am ready. Choose the trial that can convince you my gift is from *Ussen* and that I have the power to put out the eyes of witches."

Juh made a come-forward motion with the flat of his hand. A woman came out of the trees on the far edge of the meadow leading a *Nakai-yi* child by a rope around her neck. The little one was not more than five or six years old. The woman had tight hold of the rope with her right hand and carried a green, fist-sized gourd in her left. The whimpering child, her short legs churning, ran behind her pulling on the rope with both hands to keep from being choked. Reaching the men, the woman gave the rope to Juh while the child cried and jerked on the rope to be free.

Juh said, "I took this slave a moon ago on my last raid against the *Nakai-yes.* I thought maybe, if she lived, one day she will become one of us and give a man sons, which we need. But she will not stop her noise. Now, I think, soon I'll have to cut her throat. She'll never be an Apache if she can't be silent. You come with your gift from *Ussen.* Now we'll see if *Ussen* wants her to live. My woman will tie a gourd in her hair. She'll free the slave near the lightning tree. The slave will run for the tree." Juh held up his forefinger. "Shoot the gourd off the child without a scratch from your bullet before she reaches the tree, and I will agree that

Ussen has given you Power to kill witches and leave them blind in the land of the grandfathers. Then I'll try to remember where I think the Witch you seek lives, and you will own the slave. Do you agree to this trial?"

I looked at the lightning tree over a hundred yards away and then at the squirming, whining child. I looked at the grinning warriors around me and then at Juh. Lastly, I looked inside myself, found peace, and saw no blood on the child. I looked back at Juh and nodded.

Juh handed the rope to the woman and said, "Make the slave ready."

The woman dropped the gourd, and took the rope. She kicked the child's legs out from under her, knocking her on her back. The wind knocked out of her lungs, the child tried to yell, but, choking for air, made nothing but a sucking, wheezing sound. Like a cowboy tying a calf off for branding, the woman roped the child in an eye's blink so she couldn't move, as scraping sounds in her throat signaled the return of air to her lungs. The woman pulled the child's hair up off the sides of her head and used hair and string to tie the gourd in place on top of her head. She pointed at the gourd and then at her head, which she shook. As the gasping child began to cry, she repeated her signal and raised her brows as if to ask, "Do you understand?" The child continued to cry. The woman slapped her hard to get her attention and repeated her hand motions. This time the child nodded when the woman raised her brows.

She untied the rope from the child, roughly jerked her up, and led her wailing toward the scarred, twisted gray tree. When the woman was fifty yards away from the tree, she looked over her shoulder at Juh, who raised his hand. She stopped, pulled the rope off the child's neck, and held her by a shoulder.

Juh turned to Yellow Boy. "Hit the gourd before the slave reaches the tree, and I'll tell you of the Witch you hunt."

He Watches clenched his teeth and said, "What Juh asks is impossible. He'll kill the slave at that range."

I shook my head. "I'll shoot."

Juh threw the edge of his hand forward. The woman said something in the child's ear and pushed her forward. Stumbling and falling to her knees, the child got up and ran toward the tree in an awkward wobbling gait that made her path crooked and unpredictable. The gourd tied in her hair was an impossible target, difficult to see, bouncing and jiggling, swaying back and forth as she ran.

I pulled the Henry's hammer back from safety to full cock in the smooth, fluid motion Rufus taught me, brought the rifle's butt plate to my shoulder, sighted, and without hesitating, fired. The child was within ten yards of the tree when the gourd exploded, showering chunks of gourd pulp and seeds all over her. An instant later, a burned piece on the tree near the base of its trunk suddenly turned white. The roar from the Henry rippled through the trees and rolled off the stronghold cliffs down into the valleys below. In the group of men watching, there was stunned silence as the child, screaming in terror and covered in gourd pieces and juice, continued to run.

The woman arose from the grass and ran to catch her. She caught her by her shirt, said something to quiet her, and holding her by the shoulders, brushed pieces of gourd out of her hair and looked carefully at her scalp. When she finished, she looked toward Juh, pointed two fingers toward her eyes, and then waved her palm parallel to the ground. The men who watched grunted in wonder and shook their heads in disbelief.

Juh turned to me. "Truly *Ussen* has given

you a powerful gift. I'll go to the sweat lodge and pray he won't punish me for doubting him. The slave is yours. Come to my lodge when the shadows are shortest. Then I'll say to you what I know of the Witch you hunt."

As our warriors sat with Juh on blankets in the shade of tall pines near his wives' tipis, I lit one of my thin, black *cigarro*s, smoked to the four directions, and passed it to Juh, who smoked and passed it to the others.

The smoke complete, Juh said, "This witch you hunt is big, maybe a mongrel *Nakai-yi* and Comanche. His head has no hair. He takes many scalps and sells them to the *Nakai-yes* for silver. Indians and *vaquero*s ride with him, and the Indians may be Comanches. These Indians find pleasure in taking scalps, and in doing so, they prove they have no interest in being clean and purified. Are these the men you hunt?"

I glanced from Juh to He Watches, who nodded. Then I said, "Until He Watches sees them, I cannot know, but these sound much like the ones He Watches told me of when I discovered our people killed and scalped and our camp burned."

Juh grunted, crossed his arms, and stared into the distance.

At last he said, "A few years ago, I learned that a *Nakai-yi,* maybe part Comanche, called Sangre del Diablo (Blood of the Devil), was a brujo, a witch, and a scalp hunter. He had come across the great river with Comanches, and a few banditos had joined them to raid and scalp in this country. He took over an abandoned rancho and acted like a *Nakai-yi* of wealth while he took cattle and slaves, *Nakai-yi* and Indian, from villages out on the *llano* and in the Blue Mountains. I planned to raid his rancho and kill this witch who took scalps and sold them to the *Nakai-yi,* but after reflection, I decided to wait until I knew more about him before I started a war that might make my warriors sick or even die.

"The merchants in Casas Grandes had a trick they liked to use on Apaches. They offered us many gifts when they asked us to come in to Casas Grandes for peace discussions and presents so we'd leave them alone in our raids. At the meetings, they gave us whiskey from a barrel that had no bottom to make us too drunk to defend ourselves, and then they killed as many of us as possible before the rest ran away. We loved the powerful whiskey of the *Nakai-yes* so much that we took the bait twice in the span of fifteen years and saw the slaughter of many warriors. Then a new alcalde (mayor) was selected in Casas Grandes. He let it be known he wanted to live in peace with Apaches, even to the point of giving them bigger and finer gifts if they didn't raid around Casas Grandes. The call was made again for peace discussions, and we came.

"I had learned my lesson from the last massacre. When I took my band in for the peace talks, I camped away from town on the river, and I made sure no more than half of my warriors went into Casas Grandes at one time. For every drunken Apache in Casas Grandes, there was one deadly sober one waiting for revenge just outside the village. None of my people were murdered at those meetings. After a few days, we returned to my stronghold with our presents. I straggled behind the others, still drunk, barely able to sit in my saddle, almost falling in the river getting across.

"The trail back to my stronghold wound through tall mesquite and creosote thickets. I rounded a turn through one of them and there, with sun's glow behind him, stood a giant, naked man, his arms up, a human skull in each hand, strange swirling signs tattooed on his torso, tattoos that looked like fire around his wrists and up his arms, his legs painted red, his face black with touches of white to make it look like a skull, and an owl, death in the flesh, its wings spread in hover ready to fly, perched on his shoulder.

"At first I thought I was having a bad whiskey dream and snapped my head to dispel it, but the figure remained. We stared at each other for a long moment before the figure said, 'I am Sangre del Diablo. I hold in my hands the spirits of death. If I curse you, you'll get sick and die. Your people will disappear, for the owl will come often and take them. Your stronghold will no longer keep out *Nakai-yes* who come to burn it. Stay far from me, and you and your Nednhi will live. Come to my land, and you and all your Nednhi will surely die.' "

Juh paused for a moment and looked at us solemnly, squinting at eternity as he called up his memory of the Witch. "There was a bright flash and puff of smoke. My pony reared and twisted in fright, but I had sobered up enough to grab its mane and managed to stay mounted while calming him. When the pony settled, Sangre del Diablo had disappeared. In the gathering gloom, I looked for moving bushes and listened for sounds or horses and movement. I saw and heard nothing.

"My head began to throb, and I felt sick from all the whiskey I'd drunk and the vision I'd just seen. I knew those who claimed to be witches and shamans had their tricks. Perhaps I had just witnessed one, perhaps not. I decided not to risk assuming what I had seen was a trick and to leave Sangre del Diablo alone.

"I believe the witch you seek keeps his band in a big hacienda half a day's ride from the *Nakai-yi* village of Casas Grandes. I've seen his magic and know it's powerful. As much as I want to kill him, I keep my warriors away from his hacienda. Who can fight against magic, Killer of Witches? Perhaps, even you can't kill him. Perhaps he'll take your hair after he kills you, and you'll have an ugly, sagging face in the land of the grandfathers. But perhaps you can take him if *Ussen* guides your rifle. I don't know. I'll show you the way to his hacienda. We'll leave when the sun comes tomorrow. I'll not risk my warriors against him. You alone, you Mescaleros, have to kill and blind him and destroy his band. If you do, I'll be in your debt. This is all I have to say."

Juh stared at me waiting for an answer.

Sticking out my chin, I said through

clenched teeth, "Show the way."

He Watches and I said nothing, lost in our clouds of thoughts as we walked back to the Mescalero tipis.

Juanita, on her knees in the shade beside the tipi, was grinding corn and acorns with mano and metate stones. She stood and waited for us to reach her tipi. When we were near, she said, "My man shot well today. Juh sent a slave. She is young, cries often, and stinks of gourd. I'll keep her and teach her to work for me and show her our ways."

He Watches smiled and nodded as he turned for Socorro's tipi. I smiled and said, "A slave to help is a good thing. Woman, tomorrow I ride to kill the Witch. I must clean my rifle, sharpen my knife, and straighten my arrows. Bring me a blanket to sit on and my supplies."

Deep in the night, under the shadows of the moon, beneath the glowing white of her tipi, I satisfied Juanita's powerful, insatiable urges for lovemaking. She whispered her need for me and begged me to come back to her as I held her and arched my body against her as a bow with arrow drawn, its release leaving her weak and trembling, praying to *Ussen* that she would become pregnant. She seemed desperate to have some physical part of me growing inside her before I risked my life facing the Witch.

That night, we were one spirit entwined with that of *Ussen,* and we finally slept content in knowing each other and in life lived fully. The time had come to set things right for the remnant of Mescaleros who had survived the Witch's attack, made the long trips across the *llano,* lived life on the reservation, and followed me to this great mountaintop fortress with faith in my vision.

Far out on the *llano* with the Blue Mountains to our backs and the sun high overhead, we rode until Juh stopped his horse on a high hill several miles away from a long winding stretch of green along a small stream that wound its way out of the dry foothills of the Blue Mountains. Juh pointed his rifle toward a white smoke plume rising straight up from a cluster of tiny far buildings nested near the end of the green.

"I never turn from a fight with another man," Juh said. "From witches, I stay far. They are ghosts I cannot kill. There stands the hacienda of the *Nakai-yi* witch. The Nednhi go no farther. We ask *Ussen* for the

Mescalero warriors' safe return to my stronghold after they send the *Nakai-yi* witch to the grandfathers. Your women and children will always stay safe with my band. Go! Kill the Witch. Help us. We wait for you."

Juh and his warriors turned and disappeared down the trail back toward the Blue Mountains.

I pulled open the *Shináá Cho* and studied the emerald green trees and brush east and west along the waterway and the high adobe walls of the hacienda partially hidden by the shade from the trees. West of the walls, I saw a large splash of green and glints sparkling off a lake. I pointed with my nose in that direction as I handed the telescope to He Watches, who stared through it and then passed it to Klo-sen and Beela-chezzi. When they returned it to my hand, I took a final look and said, "Let's ride there. Maybe we'll find a place to hide while we learn more of this witch, this brujo and his hacienda."

CHAPTER 39
SANGRE DEL DIABLO

When we reached the lake, we crawled through the bushes surrounding it, and tasting the water, found no alkali. We watered and hobbled our ponies, screening them in brush from the hacienda, and then rested, waiting for the light to dim.

Lying in the shade of a small cottonwood, Klo-sen said, "The *Nakai-yes* who first built the hacienda feared raids by the Apaches. Do you see the stone watchtower there on top of the hill to the south? There are no signs, paths or cut brush, of anyone being near it in a long time. This witch fears no raiders. His hacienda is easy to approach unseen, and he doesn't even use the watchtower. Why do you think this is so, He Watches?"

"The Witch has great power. Maybe he already knows we're here, but he doesn't care because he thinks he can kill us when he wants. Maybe he thinks we're afraid to raid his hacienda."

Klo-sen raised his brows and looked at me as if to say, "What do you think?"

After taking a puff from a *cigarro,* I stretched out nearby and said, "I think *Ussen* gives me Power. I'll kill the Witch even if he has great power, even if Juh fears him."

Beela-chezzi grunted and said, "I believe this. We'll help you. Tell us how."

I nodded. "You're true warriors and good amigos. Together we'll take revenge on this witch who steals the lives and scalps of our people and many others."

When the thin edge of night came, the setting sun just lighting the tops of the far eastern mountains, we left our resting place and began running parallel to the stream that passed by the Witch's hacienda. As we had agreed, Beela-chezzi ran east a couple of miles before turning into the stream bosque and working his way back west to learn the features of the streambed as he moved back toward the hacienda. Klo-sen did the same thing, except he started a couple of miles upstream, west of the hacienda, and learned the stream east. I ran directly for the hacienda to study its buildings, walls, and fences.

In the darkness, before the moon rose

above the eastern mountains, I crawled through the trees and brush along the little stream until I saw yellow and orange light flickering from a fire of burning wood piled higher than a man's head in front of the compound's gates. Guitars played; fiddles squealed. Hollow log drums pounded a steady thumping rhythm that made it easy to lose all sense of time and space. Around the flames, tall and graceful with long, shiny, black hair in braids that often reached below their waists, danced Indians of a tribe I had never seen before. I knew they must be the Comanches Juh said rode with the Witch. Scattered among the circle of Comanches were drunken *Nakai-yi vaquero*s, probably banditos, who laughed and cursed as they staggered around the fire poorly imitating the smooth Comanche dance steps and gyrations. All the dancers held their right hands high in the firelight and shook scalps of shiny black hair. Other *vaquero*s and Comanches sat with women, keeping time with their feet to the drum's rhythm as they watched the dancers and passed around bottles of whiskey.

Standing in front of an ornately carved chair painted in yellow and black, arms crossed, and watching the dancers, was the tallest, biggest *Nakai-yi* or perhaps *Nakai-yi-*

Indio mix I had ever seen. For a while, he kept time with the dancers and then sat down, still keeping time by pounding the big chair's arms with his fists. His face, with smooth and delicate features, which might have been a woman's, was painted black and touched with white to give it a ghostly, skull-like look, and his hair, looking strange for reasons I sensed rather than saw, was long and black and hung over his shoulders in long braids.

The drums stopped, and the men grew quiet and stood to face the giant. He rose out of the chair, and, raising his arms, said in a deep voice they could all hear, "I, Sangre del Diablo, call the Witch's ghost for my Power. The ghost will fill me and guide us. Soon, we'll go! Be ready! We'll take many scalps, slaves, cattle, and horses! Take your pleasures now. The trail leads far."

The men raised their arms and howled like wolves. The women made long yodeling screams like hunting mountain lions. All that noise made the hair on the back of my neck tingle. The howling and screaming soon died out, but one woman continued to scream in a loud wail. Sangre del Diablo waved for her to be brought forward, and a Comanche dragged her, screaming, to the Witch. When they stood before the Witch, she screamed even louder, her eyes wide, filled with fear. The Comanche drew back a fist to silence her, but the Witch held up his hand and shook his head. He took her under the shoulders and lifted her as easily as a child might lift a small doll, looked in her face, and said something I could not hear above her screams. She stopped her screaming in the space of a breath and seemed to go limp in his hands. He set her on her feet and there she stood perfectly at ease, staring into the night with vacant eyes.

The giant in a soft voice said to the Comanche, "You know how to handle horses but not a woman? Watch, I'll show you."

The Witch sat down in his chair and held her with his eyes. He reached his fingers in a leather bag hung on the chair and blew a light dust over her from his fingertips. He waited, the only sounds the crackling of the fire and tree peepers and frogs, while she stood trance-like, slightly rocking from side to side. He spoke to her, and she took off all that covered her. I wanted to look away, but like the Comanches and the women around the chair, I did not. He motioned her to come to the chair and there he used gentle hands on her body and pleasured her.

A drum began to beat and the giant softly

slapped her face. It was as though she had just awakened, and seeing herself naked before the crowd, without a sound, turned, grabbed her clothes, and ran into the compound, the man who had brought her to the giant following her, and the giant roaring in laughter. The Comanches and their women whooped and shook their fists at the demonstration of the Witch's power over one of them.

I have never before or since seen any woman treated that way. I wanted to run away but willed myself to stay and watch, knowing that soon *Ussen* would use me to kill the Witch.

I pulled open the *Shináá Cho* and stared at the giant's face for a long time. I noticed a thin black line lay between the hair and his forehead. *Why does he paint himself that way?* The longer I studied the face, the more hot anger grew in my gut, a fire almost more than I could control as I lowered the *Shináá Cho.* I felt the cold steel of my rifle barrel and desperately wanted to use it. I hesitated. A cold, steady focus began to settle over me and guide my thoughts.

What is the significance of the hair and paint? What did he mean when he said the Witch's ghost would fill him? Isn't he already a witch? I could easily shoot him from here, but I'd never escape, and Klo-sen and Beela-chezzi wouldn't have a chance when the Comanches and vaqueros swarmed after me like angry hornets. No, it's better to wait, take a full measure of vengeance, and live a long time after we send this evil to the land of the grandfathers.

I watched the scene through the night as the drunken *vaqueros* and Comanches passed out or took a woman, often carrying a blanket, and disappeared into the dark brush along the stream beyond the fire.

Near dawn when the fire was growing low, the giant, bleary-eyed from drinking too much, pointed at a woman and yelled for her to bring him his sack. She disappeared, running toward the big house in the north-western corner of the compound, and soon returned with a black-splotched, greasy bag held out in front of her, her nose wrinkled as if she smelled something bad. When she reached his chair, he snatched the bag from her outstretched hand and waved her away. Grinning, he untied the top and ran his arm down into the bag and retrieved a scalp, long dried, perhaps even specially cured. Its black hair was long, and it filled his fist as he held it up and howled like a wolf and shook it. Staring at the scene through the *Shináá Cho,* I felt sick. The scalp still had the ears attached, and from the left ear, hung pieces of turquoise on a silver wire like Caballo Negro wore.

I collapsed the *Shináá Cho* and left the trees like a ghost passing in the dawn and ran in the dim light and cool morning air back to the lake, glad to be away from a place of such evil.

As I neared our resting place, He Watches, Klo-sen, and Beela-chezzi rode out to me, leading my horse already saddled. Fear filled their faces, and He Watches said, "Come; we must leave this place. The Witch knows we're here. He already plans to kill me."

I swung into the saddle and led them toward the hill with the stone watchtower rising above a thick stand of juniper. From that tower, a guard might sit and see for miles watching for approaching Apaches or other raiders. We found a hollow dip near the top of the hill on the backside facing away from the adobe compound where we could hobble our horses to graze and rest without being seen. After eating a few hand-fuls of cured meat mixed with dried berries and nuts and chewing dried mescal our women had made, we sat close together facing each other. I pulled a *cigarro,* lit it, smoked to the four directions, and passed it to He Watches and then Klo-sen and Beela-chezzi.

I said, "He Watches, tell us how the Witch knows we're here and plans to attack us."

He Watches, pale, his skin gray in the early morning shade, said, "When the moon was high, shining straight down on the lake, I heard an owl call my name. Three times, it called. It was the Witch. Death called, and I heard it. Later, when I crawled to the lake to fill a canteen with water, I saw a fat, ugly snake coiled, waiting to strike me, waiting to make me sick with its poison. The Witch is trying to kill me. I struck the snake with my staff, and it slid away and disappeared. I waited for it to come back, but it did not. That witch knows we're here. He'll kill us in a bad way. I say we go away, and, like Juh, leave him alone."

Klo-sen and Beela-chezzi frowned and nodded at He Watches' words, and then sighed and looked at me. I looked in the eyes of each man and saw fear, so I started speaking. "I found the Witch and watched him all night. His men include Comanches. They danced, making ready for a new raid. They all held fresh scalps. They did this also after they took the hair of our people. The Witch is a giant *Nakai-yi*-Comanche mongrel, very strong, and very tall. He sat on a chair of black and gold, pounded rhythms with his fists, drank the strong water of the *Nakai-yes,* and did nasty things with the women around him, things only a witch dares do to a woman.

"Near dawn, when the fire was low and his Comanches snored in the bushes with the women they took, he sent one of his women for a sack. When she returned, her face told me it stank. He opened the sack, reached in, and pulled out a scalp with long, black hair. He held it up laughing and howling like a wolf. Ears were on the scalp, and from the left ear hung the same blue stones strung on a silver loop like my father wore.

"This is the Witch who killed our People! I don't care if he knows we're here and sends owls calling for our deaths or snakes to strike us. I'll kill him." I thumped the butt of my rifle to emphasize each word as I said, "His . . . evil . . . will . . . not . . . stand! Go or stay. You don't have less heart in my eyes if you go. Here I stay and kill the Witch or die. That is all I have to say."

He Watches stared at the ground, slowly shaking his head. Klo-sen and Beela-chezzi crossed their arms and studied the horizon, and the only sounds came from the wind caressing the grass and junipers and carrying the pungent smell of juniper sap from bushes around the stone tower. I finished my *cigarro,* crushed its last embers in the sand, and buried it, wondering if I were strong enough to face the Witch alone and telling myself I didn't care as long as I had the opportunity to kill him.

He Watches looked in my eyes and said, "I'm the one who heard the owl. My life in this land is nearly gone. The giant *Nakai-yi* Comanche must pay for the evil he did to our People. I will fight this witch with you, Grandson."

Beela-chezzi looked at Klo-sen, who nodded, and then at me. "The Witch must die. If we fight him together and with the Power of *Ussen,* he will die. We're with you."

I nodded, shook my fist, and said, "We'll kill this witch for *Ussen* and our People."

CHAPTER 40
DECEPTION

Beela-chezzi said, "Tell us how we'll kill this witch. The Witch has ten Comanches, maybe more, and seven or eight *vaqueros*, all fighting men. Also, the Witch has demon power. Only three of us can fight the Witch's band from ponies or hand-to-hand. Only you have Power to kill the Witch and shoot out his eyes. He Watches is brave and shoots good, but he can't move fast as warriors do. How can we beat this enemy?"

I pointed with my rifle toward the rutted road passing the hacienda. "The trail southeast goes to Casas Grandes; the trail west turns north and goes to Janos. Juh says the Witch sells scalps for silver in Casas Grandes and trades silver for supplies, whiskey, guns, and bullets. Last night, I saw Comanches and *vaqueros* dance with scalps. The Witch made big talk, saying soon they'd go raid for scalps, cattle, horses, and slaves. He gave his band much whiskey and

435

plenty of time with slave women. He'll send a wagon with scalps to Casas Grandes for supplies. The next day, the wagon will come back."

Beela-chezzi smiled, and I nodded and explained in detail, "We'll ambush them and take the wagon. The wagon that goes to Casas Grandes will come back early and empty with a dead driver. That way, we'll separate the Witch from supplies and whiskey. Without them, the *vaqueros* and Comanches won't stay with the Witch. They'll run, find and ride with other banditos, and go back to their people. We'll make 'em afraid to stay. We'll kill them in the bushes where they take women, make 'em die in a hard way, make 'em think bad enemies have come like the wind. *Ussen* will make them think we are ghosts when we are not. He will keep us men. We'll make right what the Witch did to our People. I'll kill the Witch." I tapped my right index finger against my temple and asked, "What you think?"

The other three, who had leaned forward to listen, sat back, crossed their arms, and as one man nodded agreement.

Klo-sen said, "This we'll do. We'll wipe out all the Comanches and *vaqueros* he leads. These evil ones who murdered our People and took their scalps, we'll make ugly in the land of the grandfathers. They must die." He paused a moment and asked, "Will you kill the Witch in his own hacienda?"

I nodded. "This I'll do. *Ussen* gives me Power. I'll kill the Witch. We'll wipe out his band. They're under his power, so they'll die."

We took turns watching the hacienda the rest of the day, but saw little activity except by a few women and small children working gardens by the stream or *vaqueros* and Comanches working livestock in nearby corrals. Darkness fell under high, overcast skies turned blood red by the falling sun, portending coming rain.

We saddled our horses, rode off the backside of the low hill, and swung around the two adjoining taller hills to ride north across the *llano* until we reached the rutted road from the hacienda running east toward Rio Casas Grandes. In the low light, we rode parallel to the road ruts to avoid leaving tracks the sharp-eyed Comanches might see. Within three miles, we found a good place for an ambush. There the ruts crossed a long stretch of flat *llano,* and nothing but short grass, knee-high bushes, and occasional ocotillo were visible for several miles. I thought, *Perfect, the last place to expect an ambush.*

We spent the rest of the night looking for the best places by the road to hide and talking about what to do when the wagon riders fought back or tried to get away. We marked the places for Klo-sen and Beela-chezzi to hide, using blankets covered with a thin layer of dirt and sand and made to look like innocuous little ripples in the *llano* stretching away into the distance.

A golden glow on the edge of the world defined by the eastern black mountains appeared as we watered our thirsty ponies at the big green lake and then retreated to the stone watchtower where we again took turns watching the hacienda compound and resting in the shade of the junipers around the tower.

It rained in the mountains, but stayed dry on the *llano.* Two days under a fiery sun and two cool nights under a quarter moon passed. During the days, we watched the hacienda and the women and children working in green, fertile gardens and Comanches and *vaquero*s coming and going through the big double doors in the compound walls.

Each night Klo-sen, Beela-chezzi, and I

crept into the tree shadows along the south side of the stream by the hacienda compound and watched the Comanches and *vaquero*s, standing or sitting around fires eating, drinking, playing Monte, and swapping stories before calling it a night and disappearing through the gates toward the bunkhouse inside the walls. Each night a Comanche called Segundo, who appeared to be the Witch's second in command, gave a few men, singled out for a special reward, their choice of women, slave or free, who drank and laughed with them while sitting on their laps. As the moon began falling toward the west, and the inky black shadows from its white light lengthened, the women, carrying blankets, led the men off into the darkness under the trees to places, they, no doubt, had visited many times before.

Sangre del Diablo, towering above them all, visited with his men at their fires, discussing the day's business, telling stories, and listening to their jokes. He watched them gamble, and acting like he was one of the boys, played with the women, laughing as he fondled their breasts, made nasty comments about their need to ride a big horse like him, and slapped their behinds. But for all the good humor, I noticed he only sipped his whiskey and stayed alert before returning to the hacienda with two or three women he had chosen trailing behind him.

On the third night, we crossed the stream to the north side and waited for the men and their women to leave the fires in front of the hacienda compound gates. First one, then a short time later another, and then another couple sauntered away into the dark shadows under the trees and brush where there came laughter, shouts of excitement, and moans of ecstasy. We crept closer to the couples in their brush and grass beds.

In the shadow's dim light, I watched a drunk Comanche, his long, shiny black braid hung over his left shoulder, leave the gates and stagger after a young *Nakai-yi* woman, probably not yet married when she was taken, carrying a blanket. She went to a place by a big cottonwood tree on the edge of the stream where grass and bushes were still bent from previous visits, and I was hiding in the brush across from the place, close enough to reach out and touch the blanket. The Comanche, laughing, stumbled in the dark and flopped down beside her.

I heard her say, "What pleasures does mi hombre want from me tonight? The last time we were together, you wanted me to be the mare to your stallion. You were a big, strong stallion. You pleased *mi* much. I tell the other girls about you. They want to be your mare, too."

The Comanche grunted his pleasure at her words. "Ha! Bring them on. I'll show them what a true stallion is. Here in the dark I can see nothing. Let us play Witch."

"Witch? Do I know this game, Señor?"

"You know, let me do to you what Sangre del Diablo did to that woman in front of us all the other night."

"Ah, yes, I remember it well. She still wants to hide her face from the rest of us. Did the Witch make her sleep so he could pleasure her? Can you do that for me, but not in front of everybody?"

"Yes, yes, I can do that for you and not in front of everybody. I cannot even see my moccasins in this darkness. Soon the moon comes, and then it will be better. Take off your skirt and top and lie close beside me and I'll pleasure you as Sangre del Diablo did that woman, but when the moon comes we'll do other things, eh?"

"Sí, mi hombre. Let me feel how good you are with your hands. I know how good you are with other parts of you."

They laughed and I heard them pull off their clothes and lie back on the blanket. I heard a few moans of pleasure from her and

441

after a while the Comanche snore and the deep breathing of the woman while I waited for a little moonlight through the trees to show me just how they lay.

I cut the Comanche's throat and planned to leave the woman sleeping, but her eyes snapped open when his blood spilled across her chest. She opened her mouth to scream but fear of discovery made the slash of my razor-sharp blade across her windpipe lightning fast, leaving only gurgles and dying wheezes. The last sound she probably heard was the Comanche's scalp with that long braid tearing free from his skull. I crawled into the brush toward another couple I'd heard wrestling around on a blanket. I hoped Beela-chezzi and Klo-sen had it as easy as I had in taking my first scalp.

None of the four couples disappearing into the shadows of the trees that night returned. We hadn't scalped the women. We washed the blood from the scalps we had taken and the blood splatters from our bodies downstream from the hacienda before disappearing to the watchtower hill.

I hung the bloody scalps of the Comanches on a stone in the watchtower next to those Klo-sen and Beela-chezzi had taken and sat down to stare at them. My disgust with what I had done made me want to vomit. I shook my head. *Ussen* played the jokester. The ironies that my father had told me not to take scalps, unless for good reason, and the killing and scalping of men who probably scalped my father, were not lost on me. It was eye-for-an-eye justice. I hoped killing these men and their women was enough to spread fear through the compound, making the band bolt for Casas Grandes, leaving the Witch behind. But, I knew in my heart the taking of scalps was not the Apache way.

After nearly two years, my patience finally felt rewarded, and I knew I had to think and act like a patient hunter, waiting to take an animal with only one shot, all a hunter expected to have, a valuable lesson I'd learned years ago when I'd begun training under He Watches and my father. Now I understood the value of that training. I had one chance to face the Witch, one chance to send him blind, naked, and without hair to the land of the grandfathers. One chance was all I wanted or needed.

He Watches and I used the *Shináá Cho* to watch the groves of trees between the hacienda gate and the stream. The women used by the Comanches and *vaquero*s usually returned to the compound before dawn, leaving the men snoring and passed out on the blankets in the brush until the heat, flies, and other insects finally bit and crawled over their faces and bodies enough to awaken them. Then they'd make their way to the stream, drink the tepid water, wash their faces, have a smoke, and then wander back to the compound for frijoles and tortillas cooked by an old crone on an ancient black and charred cook stove in the big hacienda kitchen. The sun was well above the eastern mountains when we heard screams and wails from the women who had been sent to find the late sleepers.

Soon blankets wrapped around bodies and tied off with rope were placed side-by-side on a high pile of wood in a bare spot by the stream. A bell on a tower in the hacienda rang solemn tones calling men to the hacienda courtyard. Using *Shináá Cho,* I watched Sangre del Diablo, who stood with crossed arms and his face twisted by a scowl. His men listened to him, and after Segundo handed him a torch, he led them to the bodies and put the torch on the wood. Flames instantly reached skyward. The Witch raised his arms and sang as he threw powder on the fire, making it flare brightly. A great, greasy, black column of smoke rose high and then bent toward the east. The Witch turned and walked back to the compound gates as his men then poured into the trees, rifles at the ready. We looked at each other and smiled.

Comanches passed out of the trees on the south side of the stream, their rifles cocked and ready, hunched over, looking for ground signs, motioning others to come look when they found a disturbed stone, a piece of broken grass, or a scrape in the dirt that perhaps shouldn't be there. *Vaquero*s followed them, smoking corn shuck cigarettes, their eyes nervously darting in all directions, their hands on the dark wooden handles of their holstered revolvers ready for instant use. We knew the trackers would soon find signs that pointed them toward the top of our watchtower hill.

I pointed toward our waiting horses tied behind the hill, each saddled and carrying a small juniper tied to a length of rope. Mounting, He Watches, Klo-sen, and Beela-chezzi rode down the backside of the hill staying out of sight of the hacienda and the trackers. I waited, picking targets in case I had to shoot before the trackers were distracted.

They rode out on the rutted road across the *llano* not more than a mile away from the hacienda, dropped the junipers, and galloped east down the Rio Casas Grandes road. The brush bouncing and dragging across dusty *llano* raised a streaming dust plume like that made by many riders. The Comanches and *vaquero*s saw it immediately. They turned from their path up the hill and ran for the hacienda.

The *Shináá Cho* showed Sangre del Diablo, arms crossed, waiting for them at the gate. He listened while they told him with many howls and yells of anger what they saw and pointed where they had seen the dust streamer. He called out four Comanches from the group, made chopping motions with the flat of his hand as he spoke, and then with a feminine flick of his wrist sent them to chase the dust streamer. I thought I saw strange designs, perhaps tattoos on the hands of the Witch. I shook my head as the Comanches mounted their ponies and thundered out of the corral, riding east to follow and perhaps catch the source of the dust plume they had seen. *The Witch is smart. He still has half his fighting men while he tries to learn how many enemies made the dust streamer.*

Sangre del Diablo pointed at three *vaquero*s and spoke. One of them ran inside the hacienda, and the other two caught two horses in the corral, put them in a wagon harness, and hitched them to a buckboard sitting next to a corral. The *vaquero* who ran into the hacienda returned holding a lumpy flour sack in front of him, his nose wrinkled, and threw it in the back of the wagon. One man drove the wagon. The other two saddled horses and rode behind him down the rutted road. I nodded and smiled. *The Witch is cashing in his scalps.*

As we had planned, three miles from the hacienda, Klo-sen and Beela-chezzi slowed their mounts to a walk and gave their reins to He Watches. They pulled themselves up to stand on their saddles and jumped to boulders on a small hill to leave no tracks dismounting. He Watches then raced on toward Rio Casas Grandes, the junipers bumping, rolling, and pounding the *llano* dust to keep the plume in play.

I have thought many times about He Watches and how the Comanches must have caught him. Our plan was for him to get to the river and lose those who Sangre del Diablo sent after him. I can see his pony covered in lather and heaving, He Watches barely hanging on, when it splashed into the Rio Casas Grandes and its cool cottonwood shade on the slow-moving water. He would have cut the ropes tying the junipers to the saddles and let them drift away down-river while the horses took a few short swallows of water. Looking back through the trees, he must have seen a growing dust plume from his pursuers in the distance. He would have led the ponies at a walk upstream toward Casas Grandes until he found the wagon road coming in from the west and rode up on it so the tracks of his ponies mixed in with those already there before he turned to ride for the watchtower. Somewhere along the road, those four Comanches, their rifles cocked and ready, would have appeared out of the hot, fiery afternoon glare, surrounded him, and knocked him off his pony before they tied him across the saddle and brought him back to the hacienda for Sangre del Diablo to enjoy killing. My grandfather was right. He had heard the owl, and his time was not long in this land. When I saw him later, I knew he had not been easy to take.

CHAPTER 41
DISASTER

Klo-sen and Beela-chezzi ran for the ambush spot they had identified three nights before and less than two miles from where He Watches rode off with their horses. I know the sweat must have already covered their bodies after running in that hot, brilliant sunlight, when they crawled under the blankets covered with dirt and sand and waited. We believed that the Witch was certain to cash in his scalps at Casas Grandes to ensure he didn't lose his valuable scalps in an overpowering raid where they might run low on bullets and men in the case of a long siege from Apaches or *Nakai-yes* seeking vengeance for his past raids.

They said the heat under the blankets was mightier than that in a sweat lodge. Klo-sen and Beela-chezzi, pointing their heads toward the road so they saw anyone coming from either direction, must have had to lie in a thin mud gruel formed from their sweat and sand. Their rifles cocked, they waited, barely breathing, ignoring the thick, fiery air scorching their throats and filling their lungs. Beela-chezzi kept his ear pressed to the ground listening for approaching horses. Soon the faint, unmistakable tremor . . . jogging horses . . . four of them, and with them, the steady crunching sound of wagon wheels. He later said he looked across the road and saw Klo-sen watching him from under the edge of his blanket. Klo-sen held up four fingers to indicate four horses and made the sign for a wagon. Beela-chezzi raised the edge of his blanket and looked down the road toward the wagon before becoming just a ripple in the sand. Klo-sen grunted with satisfaction and lowered the edge of his blanket so that he, too, disappeared, leaving only a small wrinkle for a peephole to watch Beela-chezzi and follow his lead.

They described something I've seen happen in other ambushes. When the wagon and the mounted *vaquero*s passed Beela-chezzi, he rolled back his blanket without making a sound and kneeled to sight his rifle on the nearest *vaquero*. Klo-sen, too, rose from his cover and sighted on the wagon driver. They said the shots, barely distinguishable, they were so close together, knocked the *vaquero* off his horse and the wagon driver off his seat. The driver fell in front of and scotched, for a moment, the wagon's right, front wheel. The startled team jerked forward determined to run, but the driver's body slowed forward motion and twisted the wagon's direction to the right, giving Klo-sen time to dash forward and jump on the wagon. Scrambling across the seat and onto the wagon tongue, he grabbed the reins and stopped the team before it ran more than a hundred yards.

Beela-chezzi told me how the third *vaquero* momentarily froze, looking at them over his shoulder with round eyes filled with surprise and fear. Then his spurs' big rowels slashed into his pony to make it run. Instead, it reared up, and the *vaquero* had to lean forward, rising in his stirrups, to stay on his saddle. Beela-chezzi's shot shattered his spine and made his heart explode. He slumped forward and fell, dead before he hit the ground, his reins clutched in a death grip that left his pony dancing in place, its eyes white, filled with fear.

The first rider's horse had charged after the team, but, seeing it stop, it stopped, too, and waited in the middle of the ruts. Klo-sen spoke gentle, soothing words to it and walked up to take its reins to tie to the wagon.

Klo-sen returned with the wagon so that it was headed back toward the hacienda. He and Beela-chezzi tied two *vaquero*s upright on the wagon seat, even tying the foot of the driver to the top edge of the wagon box so they looked from a distance like two men sitting side-by-side on the wagon. They laid the third *vaquero*'s body in the wagon bed, then scalped all three and sent the team walking back down the road toward the hacienda, but keeping the saddled horses to ride themselves. Disgusted, they used sand to clean blood off their arms, hands, and bellies. Later, Beela-chezzi told me, "I took those scalps only for revenge and to help you kill the *Witch*. If I never take another, it will be too soon."

I said, "You speak for both of us, my good friend."

From the tower, I watched the three men in the wagon disappear on the *llano* road toward Casas Grandes. The once sleepy hacienda became an armed camp as slaves filled water barrels and guards were posted on the top of the walls at the corners of the compound. Livestock were driven into a corral inside the compound, and women and children carried firewood from near the corral barn into the compound courtyard. The slaves carrying the wood appeared to beg their Comanche overseer for water, but he beat them in a fury with a quirt hung on his wrist. I thought, *You dung heap Comanche, you'll not beat children or scalp Apaches much longer, but will spend eternity wandering blind in the land of the grandfathers where I'll send you.*

Watching every move around the hacienda, I waited for the rush of men to the supply wagon when it came into view much sooner than they would expect it, which would be my opportunity to kill them in the open without cover. I reasoned that, if we had counted correctly, only eight or nine of the Witch's band now walked the compound, and if I killed four or five as they rode for the wagon, the odds would become about even between us and allow us to breach the compound and kill the Witch before the others chasing He Watches returned.

Then, a brilliant burst of light exploded in my brain, and then darkness, and I was falling, falling, falling like a dry leaf, spiraling into a bottomless hole in the earth until I came to rest on hard, smooth tile.

■ ■ ■ ■

A dull pain thumped like a pounding dried buffalo skin drum on the right side of my head. I touched it above my right ear and felt sticky ooze. Thirsty, I ran my tongue over my lips to find only the salty taste of my own blood.

When I opened my eyes, I was in dark gloom surrounded by windowless adobe walls lighted by a weak, flickering flame from a small oil lamp. I recognized Segundo, the Comanche I'd often seen through the *Shináá Cho,* staring at me. He squatted against the walls in the opposite corner and held a Winchester by its barrel like a staff.

When he saw my eyes flutter open, his lips twisted into a malevolent grin. "So, Apache, you return from the dark place. Soon you'll go again and never come back. I worried I swung my rifle a little too hard against your soft head. Sangre del Diablo told me not to kill you. He wants to see you before he sends you, cursed and hairless, to the place of no return. I hope he gives me a chance to use my knife on you for the life of my brother you killed in the brush last night. If he gives me that pleasure, you will suffer a long time before you leave us. Tell me, dog, why did you want to kill yourself like this?"

As my wandering consciousness returned and focused, I grew furious at myself for being taken. I stared at the Comanche and said nothing, my numb mind already grasping at thoughts of escape while keeping my face a mask of oblivion. *How could this have happened? How could we be so stupid and blind to let them take us?*

"Ah, yes. You will be glad to know we also found your crooked-leg elder. He led four warriors on a good chase until they understood his dust cloud was only one man and a few juniper bushes. He waits nearby like you, except I think maybe he broke a rib or two when he fell from his horse. He should learn to ride faster with his crooked leg and walk upright without limping. Perhaps Sangre del Diablo will use his power to make the leg straight before he sends him to the Happy Land. Even if he is old and has no Power, his hair will bring a good price.

"Whoever you are, Apache, your hair and Yellow Boy rifle will bring a good price in Casas Grandes. Maybe I will even sell that old eyepiece you use, but I'd like it for a trophy to remind me of how one little sparkle from it in the sunlight gave you away. We thank you for bringing these things to us."

A door opened, and a *vaquero* stuck his head inside and motioned for the Comanche to come. "El jefe calls you and says to bring the lamp. The Apache is awake?"

The Comanche picked up the lamp and moved out the door with an easy fluid motion and into the dim light behind the *vaquero.* "Adios, Indio. Soon I see you again, eh?" I heard a key turn against the latch and a lock bolt slide into place.

Total darkness filled the room. I heard the occasional clink of spur rowels and thumps from passing *vaquero* boots and the soft padding of moccasins and bare feet shuffling past the door but no voices of any kind. I sat up, leaned my back against the smooth, cool wall, and tried to think but only wandered through the jumbled clutter of my mind.

So the Witch has taken He Watches but not Klo-sen and Beela-chezzi. Where are they? Does he know about them, too? Does he know how many we are? Is he keeping us alive for what we know or for Witch tricks to impress his Comanches? He must want to find out more . . . Where's my rifle? Where's my pony? I must see Juanita again . . . I must see Sons-ee-ah-ray. Ussen, give me Power to kill this Witch . . . Help me in this place of evil . . . I'm so weary. I need to sleep.

I squeezed and poked all over my body and found no broken bones, and though I was bruised and sore, my muscles felt strong and firm. The pounding in my head slowed, and I slid slowly into a dream.

The dream came as it had at Rufus Pike's ranch. In darkness, I ran, ran hard, ran for a long time. My lungs strained to pull in more air, and I heard the pounding feet of the giant behind me. I looked over my shoulder and saw only two great eyes glowing in the darkness chasing me. I ran harder, my strength failing, the eyes coming closer. Thunder spoke, and lightning arrows flashed, and Wind moaned in a wild, roaring rush, and a voice said, "You hold the Witch in your hand. Choose your way." And then the giant and its two great eyes disappeared. Rest, sweet rest, came, and my spirit lay wrapped in my body, as if my body were a warm blanket in the cool nights of the Season of Little Eagles.

How long I slept, I could not measure. The deep ba-boom, ba-boom pounding of a distant drum filling my ears brought me back to the land of the living. I opened my eyes and, seeing only darkness, pushed up straight from where I had slumped in a corner formed by wall and floor. My mind, clear as a pool formed by mountain springs, whirred with ideas about how to kill the Witch, leave with He Watches, and find Klosen and Beela-chezzi.

Voices began chanting with the drum. They seemed at first far away but grew louder and came closer. I saw flickering images of light and shadow pour under the door. Pushing against the wall, I drew my legs under me and, pushing with my hands, slid my back up against the wall and tried to stand up straight, wobbling on weak knees before becoming stable. I faced the wall with the door, crossed my arms, held my elbows with my hands, and waited.

The drum came closer, the chanting much louder, using unintelligible sounds and words, and there were women randomly ululating through high and low shrieks like bats swooping after insects in the low light before a rising moon. Suddenly the drum and chanting stopped. In the eerie silence, I heard a door latch raise and then a creaking whine as the door opened. For a long moment, a silent pause, and then low, unintelligible words and cadences sounding like Spanish followed by whoops and ululating as the drum began again and moved toward the room where I was being held.

The sounds grew louder until they were in front of the door and stopped again. I squared my shoulders and waited on the clanking of a key thrust in the lock, the sliding back of the bolt lock, and the scrape of the door latch lifting. Creaking on its hinges the door swung open to reveal Segundo. A crowd of Comanches, *vaquero*s, and women, and some half-naked slaves, holding torches, surrounded the Comanche at the door. Segundo, his upper torso naked, covered in black paint up to his neck, his head now hairless covered in white, with black paint used around his eyes and cheekbones to make his head look like a floating skull, stood grinning at me like death back from the grave.

Segundo said, "Good. You stand. We won't have to make you crawl to see the great Chief of Ghosts, Sangre del Diablo, who calls you and the One Who Limps to his fire, there to look in your eyes, and deliver judgment for the evil you have done. Come!"

He stepped back from the doorway and motioned me out, the crowd parting to let me follow Segundo down a hall and out a doorway toward a snapping, crackling fire outside the gate. The fire was in the middle of a circle of spears ten feet long stabbed upright in the ground with pitch burning on their butt ends to make torches. Near the far edge of the circle, I saw a dark outline of a man hobbling between two tall men painted like Segundo. Still feeling a little unsteady, I walked erect, my chin up and staring straight ahead, between the two lines of men, some painted, some not, and women, some naked above their waists, their bare feet stomping to the drum rhythm. Somewhere outside the ring of torches, the pounding drum took up a new rhythm, boom ta ta boom, boom ta ta boom, and the crowd again began its chanting and ululating.

When He Watches reached the fire, two Comanches, painted like my keeper, took me by the arms and walked me to a log the size used to make corral fence posts. It had been adzed smooth and straight and planted upright in the circle of spears with a long crosspiece across its top eight or nine feet off the ground. A similar pole and crosspiece stood diametrically opposite the first pole on the other side of the fire.

Stools stood against the poles and He Watches, forced to climb on it, managed to rise up and stand with his back to the pole. One of his painted keepers climbed a ladder leaned against the backside of the pole and pulled He Watches' arms straight out along the crosspiece and tied them with pieces of wet rawhide at his shoulder, elbow, and hand joints. He Watches' face showed no emotion, his eyes, staring at his captors, calm, unafraid.

I was tied like He Watches on the opposite pole. The drum stopped and all voices in the crowd grew silent, the only sounds the hiss and pop of the fire giving off the tart, soothing smell of burning cedar.

A thing, a menacing specter I had never seen, even in my worst dreams, appeared out of the darkness and entered the circle of light. A naked giant lifted his arms high, a human skull in each hand. Strange swirling symmetrical signs in black tattooed all over his torso disappeared into orange and red flames painted around his waist and long streams of red and white flames covered his big, muscular arms. His legs were covered in red paint from his breechcloth crotch all the way to his beaded moccasins. The swirls on his body grew steadily wider and more intricate until they converged at his shoulders and merged with black glistening paint covering his bald head. A huge owl, its wings slightly extended for balance and a leather hood covering its eyes, rode on the specter's shoulder, its talons dug into a thick leather roll held in place with straps across the specter's chest and back, buckled together in gleaming silver, and connected to the owl's silver chain leg leash.

I shook my head, unsure this wasn't a dream. I realized I was awake, still among the living, and felt icy fingers of fear reach inside my belly and grab me. For a moment, I thought that those before me were evil spirits come to take me. The idea filled me with rage and the need to scream a war cry to vent my anger and drive them away, but I didn't make a sound, for there was something familiar about the painted flame and tattoos on the specter's arms. I remembered seeing points of the flames on the arms of the hacienda headman when I watched him make his hand chopping motions before sending the three men with the wagon off to Casas Grandes. The specter must be Sangre del Diablo, without his strange hair, come to torture us, playing his witch role, keeping his band and his prisoners believing he was the Chief of Ghosts. Except I didn't fear him now. I only wanted to kill him, and I thought, *He may be evil and a witch, but he's a man. I'll send him to the land of the grandfathers blind and ugly.*

I glanced at He Watches and noticed he

kept his eyes on every move Sangre del Diablo made as he swayed in front of the fire, the Comanche skull men on either side of him. The drum began a low rumble in a different rhythm as he slowly lowered his hands and held out the skulls, one to each of the skull men, who held them so the eye sockets stared out from their chests. They began to dance, Sangre del Diablo between them, in a three-step shuffle around the fire. Each time they reached a cardinal direction point, the Witch threw up his hands and shouted, "Ho!" When he reached the east, he practically screamed his chant, and the Comanches and even the *vaquero*s made wolf calls, and the women screamed their ululations.

Sangre del Diablo circled the fire four times this way and then stopped in front of He Watches, who, showing no fear, stared down at Sangre del Diablo. There was no sound except for the crackle of the flames as Sangre del Diablo took his time looking at every inch of He Watches, even twisting his head to look closely at his shattered knee. He looked in the eyes of He Watches and spoke in a guttural, rasping whisper all heard.

"Apache, why are you here?"

He Watches stared at him and said nothing.

"Why does a limping old man come to the Chief of Ghosts? Perhaps you want your leg healed? Perhaps you want to serve me? Apache, why are you here?"

He Watches raised his chin, looked toward the stars on the edge of the ragged, black horizon, and was silent. I felt my heart swell with pride at his courage.

"It doesn't matter that you're silent. I, Sangre del Diablo, Chief of Ghosts, know why you're here. You come for revenge. You murder my fierce ones. You murder my slave women. Murder them out of revenge. Are you from burning villages filled with hairless dead east of the great river? Are you from the ones I took in the Blue Mountains to the west? Are you from the smoking ruins of villages to the north or south? It makes no difference. Now you hang before me. Revenge makes you blind to my true power; you're too blind from revenge to serve me. Blind you are, and blind and hairless you shall be in the land of the grandfathers."

Sangre del Diablo held out his right hand, and the right side skull man handed over a skull, placing it upside down in his palm. Sangre del Diablo in a smooth, graceful motion lifted the jaw like lifting the top of a box and the skull came apart, the top of the skull in his right palm and jaw in his left. I saw that the skull top was filled with a powder so black it had a purple sheen in the flickering firelight.

The Witch hurled the powder on to He Watches, who coughed and wheezed as its cloud swirled about him and settled on his head and shoulders, leaving them splotched and streaked in large purple-black patches. He coughed again, a ragged gagging kind of cough as he squeezed his eyes shut and shook his head. He clenched his teeth, gagging and then wheezing and coughing again. Blood ran from his nose and his lips and he began twisting his head in agony.

Sangre del Diablo replaced the jaw back on the skull, handed it back to the left skull man, and slowly, deliberately sliding a heavy leather glove over his hand and wrist, lifted his right wrist to his shoulder touching the owl's talons. The owl turned and took hold of the glove and was brought face-to-face with the Witch who removed its hood. It was a great horned owl, its feathers a dark gray, its talons immense, its eyes yellow. The owl immediately turned its head toward the sounds of He Watches' distress. The Witch in his loud, raspy whisper said, "Death comes for you, old man." The Witch unsnapped the leash to the owl's feather-covered leg, and swinging his arm up shouted, *"Ataque!"* (Attack!) The owl flew off his gloved arm in great beating flaps of its wings and swooped out into the darkness.

The warriors and women waited as if a single beast holding its breath. I strained, helpless against my bonds. In a few seconds, the outstretched talons of the great owl swooped out of the night and stabbed into the eyes and face of He Watches. He jerked his head from side to side trying to throw off the owl as the raptor tore at his face and eyes and made sharp thrusts with its beak at the back of his neck near the base of his skull, ripping and tearing flesh. He Watches made no sound as he jerked his head from side to side, attempting to throw off the thing tearing at his face and head. His struggles grew weak. Watching death come to my grandfather, I strained in cold fury against the rawhide holding me, vowing the Witch's death and asking *Ussen* for his promised power.

He Watches blinded, blood streaming from many rips in his face and eyes, bowed his head and struggled no more. The owl with its great beak tearing at the base of his skull had finally broken his neck and released him to the land of the grandfathers. The owl hopped to He Watches' shoulder and facing Sangre del Diablo screeched his kill with outspread wings.

Sangre del Diablo raised his gloved arm and shouted, "Vengan!" (Come!) With a single flap, the owl jumped from the crosspiece and glided to his arm. Sangre del Diablo gave it a piece of bloody meat, which it tore apart and gobbled down. When it finished, Sangre del Diablo returned its hood. The drum began again its booming tattoo, and warriors and women resumed their howls and screams. With the owl still on his arm, Sangre del Diablo began again, with the skull men at his side, a whirling dance around the fire until they faced me and stopped.

CHAPTER 42
ESCAPE

Sangre del Diablo and I locked eyes, mine filled with roaring flames of anger and hatred, Sangre del Diablo's filled with smug pride and satisfaction. He said, "The old one goes to the land of the grandfathers blind and with a crooked leg, but he did not suffer long. He couldn't resist death when it flew to him. You, too, must suffer before you follow him. You haven't lived long enough to know true suffering. Hanging there through the night and day to come, you'll lose the use of your arms, and then before all my people, I'll tear your legs apart and geld you and make you eat your man parts. Then I'll put out your eyes before I leave you hanging there for death to come. Warrior, do you think you will enjoy the Happy Land blind and without arms and your man parts? I'll take them from you. I'm stronger and better than you. I'm the Chief of Ghosts." He turned to his skull men and yelled, "Bring water!"

The skull men stepped on benches brought for them and poured water over the rawhide ties. By the time the sun reached its zenith in the coming day, the green rawhide, shrinking as it dried, would have closed into ever tighter loops slowly separating my joints, causing excruciating pain in my shoulders, arms, and wrists and making them useless and dead.

After they poured the water and took away the benches, Sangre del Diablo said to his skull men, "Take the stools from their feet, and let the dead and the living walk on air. How does revenge against me taste now, you stupid, foolish Apache?"

The stool was yanked out from under me. My feet dropped a few inches and left me dangling by the rawhide ties that cut into my flesh, especially at my shoulder joints where most of my weight was supported, cut into the muscle under my arms, and my weight, pulling against my arm joints, made them slice at my flesh and joints like dull knives. I knew the pain would only grow to something much worse, but I made no sound as my mind formed a plea to *Ussen* for strength and courage to face the evil that stood before me.

The Witch turned to the crowd and said,

"Children, I, Sangre del Diablo, the Chief of Ghosts, will return again. Tomorrow night this warrior will pass to the Happy Land without arms, without eyes, and without his flesh to enjoy women. You'll see me take them from him. Warriors enjoy this night with any woman you choose. Take your pleasure, for when the sun rises, you'll go to find the two who escaped us. I'll have all these miserable Apaches who wanted revenge against us, and they'll go to the grandfathers screaming like the women we take on our raids. Now go! Take your pleasure before I call my ghosts against you."

The crowd yelled with one voice, "Ho! Ho! Hi-Yah!" The warriors and *vaqueros* took their women, some even taking two or three, and headed for the dark, black shadows under the groves of trees just beyond the circle of light made by the torches.

Sangre del Diablo turned to Segundo and said, "You're my strong right arm. You'll lead the men at first light to find the other two, so go and rest. We'll return to the hacienda, and I'll take my body back. Do not disturb me. Before the sun rises, this Apache will be groaning in pain. By noon, he will be screaming. Let the skulls watch them and make sure the old one has left for the land of the grandfathers." With the owl relaxed and still riding on his arm and Segundo following, he turned and walked back through the compound gates toward the hacienda. The skull men squatted by the fire, their eyes focused on me and on He Watches' body.

I felt the rawhide ties growing tighter, my fingers feeling like thousands of needles were being stuck in them. I bent my knees and placing my feet flat against the pole raised myself enough to take the pressure off my arms. The watching skull man said, "Enjoy the little extra time your legs give you, Apache. Soon even your feet and legs will grow too weak to rest you from the rawhide chewing you apart."

The night wore on. The rawhide drew tighter. Sounds from under the trees trickled to nothing, and the two skulls squatting by the dying fire appeared to be fighting to stay awake. I raised my eyes to the stars and saw the top of the night was past.

Then the skull facing He Watches stood and said to the other, "I make water," before disappearing into the shadows.

The other nodded and said, "Hmmph. I'll go when you return."

Five minutes passed. Ten. The skull watching me grew impatient, and muttering how the first one must have found an unused woman, picked up a small piece of burning firewood and walked the path the other skull took.

I closed my eyes and used my feet to push up once more against my own weight. Then, in a dream-like state, I thought I heard the voice of Klo-sen whispering in my ear. "When I cut these ties, can you keep from falling?" I shook my head, my arms too numb to hold anything. I dreamed. *Ussen saves me. Klo-sen has Power.*

Klo-sen, on a ladder against the back of the pole, slashed my wrists free, cut the rawhide at my elbows, and my arms, numb, flopped down by my sides. Klo-sen slid his arm around me, clamping me against the pole, and cut the rawhide holding my shoulders. He whispered, "Now I'll drop you. You won't fall much."

No longer dreaming, I said, "I know. Drop me. My arms will return soon." I hit the ground like a sack of corn and dropped to my knees before I fell over on my side. Klo-sen jumped off the ladder and gave me water and washed the blood from my face while Beela-chezzi carried the ladder to the cross of He Watches and cut him down.

I whispered, "The skulls?"

Klo-sen's black marble eyes glittered in

the dying light, and he said, "They are no more. Many in the bushes are no more. They believed they'd chase us in dawn's light. Fools! Now let's go!"

I shook my head. "No. The Witch must die. His helper Segundo is also a witch. He too must die."

Beela-chezzi grimaced with impatience. "Some sleep inside the walls. We must be far away before they are ready to ride, or they will take us all. Klo-sen and I are lucky to live. We go!"

"No. I know a place to hide in the compound. Bring He Watches. I'll show you. When my arms return, I'll kill the witches. Those left in this band will scatter without them, and then we'll return to Juh's camp. Help me stand."

Klo-sen stared at me, shook his head in disbelief, helped me up, and motioned to Beela-chezzi to bring the body of He Watches and follow them.

The torches on the spear butts were burning low when I led them through the compound gates and back to the windowless room where Segundo had kept me prisoner the day before.

Klo-sen and Beela-chezzi laid the body of He Watches against a wall and squatted close together with me in a corner where we could whisper our plans. Though the rawhide had begun to cut into the muscle under my arms, and though my joints were burning, they had not yet separated. Streamers of blood from the cuts made by the rawhide ran toward my fingertips where I felt its sticky warmth and the tingle of circulation beginning to return.

Beela-chezzi said, "Tell us what we should do in this place of witches and their evil."

I said, "I watched the Witch come and go with the *Shináá Cho.* He sleeps in the back corner room of the hacienda. The Comanches prefer to sleep outside the walls and not be closed in. The *vaquero*s stay near the Comanches, but they don't trust them. Comanches learning witchcraft stay in the hacienda. You'll know them because they have no hair. When they are not doing witchcraft, they wear hats that look like hair. The Witch does this too.

"The Witch calls the second chief, 'Segundo.' He sleeps somewhere here in the hacienda. He took me prisoner and has much skill. I never heard him coming. I must have my rifle back to kill the Witch. Segundo said he plans to sell it in Casas Grandes. Perhaps he keeps it in the place near the corral outside the wall gates where they keep supplies and load wagons for Casas Grandes. Will you go and look while my arms return and gain strength?"

Beela-chezzi nodded. "I'll go."

"When you return, close and lock the gates to keep any others out while we make things right with the witches."

Like morning mist on the wind, Beela-chezzi disappeared out the door.

The door to the room where Klo-sen and I hid creaked open enough for Beela-chezzi to slide inside. Klo-sen pulled his rifle to full cock.

"It is you Beela-chezzi?"

"I come. I cannot find the rifle. It is not in the place of supplies or where the men sleep. I have brought us pistolas and a rifle and bullets."

Making fists and flexing my arms, I sighed. "Then either the witches have it or know where it is. I am grateful you looked and brought me another. Feeling returns to my hands and arms." I held out my hand, and Beela-chezzi gave me the rifle and a bag with cartridges. In the dark gloom, my hands caressed the weapon and smelled the fresh gun oil. "You chose well. It feels and smells well cared for. Have you tried the bullets? Do they fit?"

Beela-chezzi shook his head. "Dawn

comes, so I hurried."

I took a cartridge from the saddlebag and slid one into the loading gate. I cycled the lever twice, and the bullet flew off the loading elevator and tinkled against the floor. "They fit. *Enjuh!*" I loaded the rifle, and we buckled on the holstered pistols Beela-chezzi had found.

"I'll find the witches and kill them. You go to the top of the compound walls by the gates and kill any warrior you see moving inside or out. We'll let the slaves go when we're done. I want the story of what we did here to go among the *Nakai-yi* and other Indians. When they hear it, they will fear us more than the Witch. Agreed?"

Klo-sen and Beela-chezzi nodded. "Agreed."

CHAPTER 43
BATTLE OF THE HACIENDA

We were in the courtyard when Segundo stepped into the cold night air. He surveyed the courtyard and its shadows and paused to stare at the big double gate to the compound. He must have known it had been open the night before. He must have seem the dim outline of Beela-chezzi kneeling on top of the wall next to the gate because, silent as a snake, Segundo glided forward, keeping in the wall shadows. He snapped my Yellow Boy to his shoulder and fired, the shot sounding like a huge explosion as it echoed off the compound walls. Our friend disappeared over the far side of the compound wall.

Segundo ran for the gates, but Klo-sen separated from a black hall entranceway and swung his rifle like a club into the back of his head. He sprawled forward, landing hard, face down on the walkway leading to the gates, the Yellow Boy flying from his hands.

Klo-sen drove his knee down between Segundo's shoulder blades, drew his knife, and grabbed his hair to yank his head back, but the hair came off with a weak tearing sound, braids and all. Klo-sen stuffed the hair in his belt as I ran to the Yellow Boy, picked it up, sighed with relief, and whispered, "My rifle! Quick, let's open the gate and help Beela-chezzi."

Outside the gate, we found Beela-chezzi sitting by a water barrel in dark shadows against the wall. Segundo's bullet had grazed him just below his ribs on the right side.

He said, "I'm slow moving, but I've had worse in arrow games we played before my first raid. I was crawling to the barrel for some water to splash on the wound when I saw movement in the trees." He pointed at two brushy spots under the trees north of the gate. "Our knives missed them."

I checked the Henry. It had a round in the chamber, and the loading tube showed six cartridges. Kneeling in the shadows by the gate, I sighted down the barrel and used it to scan the courtyard but saw nothing. "Segundo's shot must have awakened the Witch. I'll watch for him here. Be ready. He comes. Watch the trees for others."

Klo-sen and Beela-chezzi stretched out in the dust by the water barrel and sighted their rifles toward the trees.

The sound of many feet running and the crying of babies and small children echoed down the hacienda hallways leading to the courtyard. Above them, the bellows of Sangre del Diablo, "*Ejecútese! Maldígale! Ejecútese!* (Run! Damn you! Run!)." Women, some with babies or small children in their arms and slightly older children running beside them and crying in fear, poured out of two courtyard entrances and ran for the open gate.

I dashed through the gate to the shadows around another water barrel against the northern wall and again dropped to one knee, my attention on the courtyard entrances. The women and children strung out across the courtyard as the faster ones in front ran through the gate and headed for the stream. Two hunched-over Comanches, rifles at the ready in one hand and whips in the other to hurry stragglers, ran behind them.

I stood, snapped off two quick, booming shots, and dashed to my left back toward the gate. The first Comanche, already a quarter of the way across the courtyard toward the gate, took two more steps and collapsed; the second, to the left of the first, dropped in midstride like a poleaxed ox.

Three brilliant flashes with loud, sharp, rolling thunder from a single rifle on the top of the back courtyard wall sent bullets smashing into the hacienda walls behind the water barrel where I had stood only seconds before. I snapped off a shot toward the flashes and moved again to the other side of the gate, charging up the steps to sprawl flat on top of the compound wall. There was no return fire. I saw nothing on the back wall before raising my head to look over the wall and see Klo-sen, rifle in hand, running toward the spots Beela-chezzi had pointed to in the trees. A running hairless figure he did not see closed in behind him. Beela-chezzi fired three times and missed the juking, ducking figure. I glanced into the courtyard. Segundo was gone. I whipped the Henry in the direction of the hairless figure, but it had disappeared into the trees with Klo-sen.

Dawn's light came fast, and shadows following shifted and changed. The two Comanches who had chased the women and children lay in the middle of the courtyard, one face down, the backside of his left shoulder blown away, and the other lay on his back, one eye socket black, the other open, staring at the fading stars. No sounds at all came from inside the hacienda.

I waited on top of the wall for the coming light, straining to see anything move in the changing shadows on either side of the wall. A brilliant, yellow ball rose above the mountains sending golden beams like stage lights thrusting through the brush, tall cottonwoods, and drooping willows.

Yells and shots flashed in the tree shadows, their roar on top of the fading background screams of the women and children as they strung out running across the *llano* toward the watchtower hill. A pause and another shot exploded in the trees, a long pause, and then two more shots and another long pause.

Klo-sen staggered out of the trees holding his left hand in blood flowing from his side and collapsed. Segundo, blood smeared over his face, a knife in his hand, screaming a ghost-raising Comanche war cry, ran for Klo-sen. Beela-chezzi's shots knocked limbs off brush and trees all around Segundo, but none hit him.

On top of the compound wall, I rose to my knees and whipped the Henry to my shoulder and bellowed, "Segundo!" Reflexively, Segundo looked toward me. In a snapping boom, his left eye disappeared, and his head snapped back; his momentum took him another step, his head turning toward the sound of the rifle. His right eye, wide open, suddenly disappeared in another crack of thunder, leaving only a black socket, and the remaining back side of his head disappeared in a spray of blood, bone, and brains. He fell backwards and lay still not three yards from Klo-sen. Beela-chezzi, his face twisted in pain, holding his side with one hand and his rifle with the other, ran as fast as he could for Klo-sen.

I ran down the stairs and out the gate toward Klo-sen. I saw milling horses raising dust in the corral whining and snorting, but no one disturbing them. Beela-chezzi dropped to his knees by Klo-sen, whose face was twisted in pain. A round black hole just below his ribs leaked bright, red blood.

I helped Beela-chezzi by wrapping my arm around Klo-sen's back from the other side. We stood Klo-sen up. Comanche howls came from somewhere amid the horses, which ran out of the corral and pounded straight for us. Dragging Klo-sen between us, we ran for the compound gates. Howling like specters out of hell, two Comanches and the Witch rolled up from their horses' necks where they had been hanging. Bullets from the Comanche rifles raised little plumes of dust around us, and the ground shook from the pounding hooves of the horses running for us.

Klo-sen raised his head and looked at the horses. With the last of his strength, he bellowed, "Drop me, you fools! Run!" He jerked his arm off Beela-chezzi's shoulders and twisted out of my arm to land in the dust, our momentum carrying us a couple of steps forward. When we turned to pick him up, he screamed again, "Run!"

Beela-chezzi looked at me, nodded, and ran for the gate. I dashed for the gate, screaming, "Revenge will be yours, Klo-sen!"

The horses passed over Klo-sen and ran on as I cleared the gate and ran up the steps to the top of the wall for shots at the Witch and the two Comanches with him. But I could not find them in the dust cloud, soon a distant plume.

CHAPTER 44
CARMEN ROSARIO

We said nothing as we wrapped Klo-sen's broken body in a heavy blanket and carried it into the compound to rest in the same dark room with the body of He Watches. We quieted our raging thirsts, washed ourselves from water in the barrels, and sat down exhausted on the steps leading to the top of the walls.

Beela-chezzi said, "You've killed a witch, but not the giant who led the killing and scalping of our people. What will we do now? Wherever you go, I'll go. We must end this evil."

I leaned back on the steps and raised my face to the light. "We can't track the Witch now. There were three of them, and many horses running around them will destroy their trail. Which trail of prints in that herd of horses do we follow once they spread out wild and free on the *llano*? Who knows where they'll go? But the day comes when we'll find them again and *Ussen* will help us destroy this evil one. *Ussen* gave me Power to kill him. I'll do it one day. I know *Ussen* makes things right, makes life balance. This place is no more one of witches. It's a place of the dead. Now we must bury our grandfather and friend and return to the camp of Juh."

Beela-chezzi nodded. *"Enjuh!"*

A boy, no more than four or five, walked through the gate and stopped to stare at us. He said in Spanish, "Sangre del Diablo goes away. I have hunger. Let my mother make something to eat. Are we your slaves now?"

I smiled and shook my head. "Bring your mother; bring all the women and children. Ask her to cook for you, and maybe she will cook a meal for us."

Without a word, the child darted out the gate.

Soon a young woman came through the gate, the child peeping out at us from behind her skirts. The woman faced us and said, "Señores, I am Carmen Rosario. I pray, as our new masters, you let us back in the hacienda to serve you. We will die trying to live on the *llano*. My child says you want something to eat. I will cook it for you."

I said, "We're not your masters. We've decided not to keep you slaves. Go and tell your families and friends what happened here. Say that we Apaches have destroyed the *Brujo*'s hacienda and we will destroy him. *El Brujo* (the Witch) is gone and won't come back. You're free. We're hungry. Will you make us something to eat?"

The woman's eyes grew wide, and her hand covered her mouth as though her breath might leave when I told her they were free. Water from her eyes rolled down her cheeks, and she said, "*Muchas, muchas, gracias, Señores.* Sangre del Diablo had told me soon he takes *mi muchacho* away and sells me in the City of Mules (Chihuahua). *Mi muchacho y yo* (my child and I) will return to our mountains, but my husband and village, the *Brujo* and his Comanches wiped out."

Her head lowered, she asked, "You eat tortillas, chilies, frijoles, y filete (bread, chilies, beans, and steak)?"

Beela-chezzi grinned and said, "*Sí, Señora, esta muy bueno* (that is very good)."

"*Gracias, Señores.* I cook now. *Mi muchacho* comes when your meal is ready."

She turned and yelled out the gate, "*Vengan! Hay libertad!*" (Come! Freedom!) Holding the child's hand, they ran barefoot across the courtyard, leaping like jumping

486

ponies over the bodies of dead Comanches and disappearing down a hall leading to the back of the hacienda. Soon women, children, and babies began drifting through the gates. All paused at the gate and said to Beela-chezzi and me, "Muchas gracias, Señores."

We ate like starving men, as the children and their mothers, not saying a word, stood and watched us. When we finished a second pot of coffee, we left the kitchen with the big, iron stove and sat in the courtyard listening to the women, children, and babies scrambling to eat big meals. It was mid-morning, and the still air and bright sun promised a hot day.

Beela-chezzi took my offered *cigarro* and puffed to the four directions. He let the smoke drift away and said, "We'll take bodies of our friends when we go and bury them in a canyon where none will find them. What will we do with Comanches and *vaquero*s?"

"Nothing. Their ghosts will stay here, and their bodies will feed the buzzards and coyotes. The women and children will go back home. They won't stay here."

"Hmmph. How will they go? They have no horses. Will they walk? Many will die on

487

the *llano* before reaching Casas Grandes. Carmen Rosario is a good cook and a good mother with a strong child. It's not good for them to go to the Happy Land on the *llano*."

I looked at Beela-chezzi out of the corner of my eye and smiled. "We'll leave 'em ponies. The ponies that ran off with *el Brujo* and Comanches will come back because there's grain and water here. Ponies are no fools. Give the women the three wagons here. They're enough for all of them to ride. We'll harness teams for the wagons so the women can drive them to Casas Grandes. We'll take the rest of the ponies and use them to carry those gone to the land of the grandfathers and the bounty we take from the Brujo's supplies. What do you think?"

Beela-chezzi shrugged and shook his head. "I don't know. Maybe the Brujo and the Comanches will attack the women when they go to Casas Grandes. The road across the *llano* is very dangerous. There are witches and banditos everywhere."

I laughed aloud. "Why don't you just ask her if she wants to come with you rather than go back where maybe no one wants her now after she was a slave to the Brujo?"

Sheepishly, Beela-chezzi grinned and looked at the ground. "This I'll do."

"*Enjuh!* Come, amigo. We have much to do."

We went to the Brujo's place of crosses, pulled up the long spears stuck in the ground, and burned them. We put pitch on the posts where He Watches and I had been tied and set fire to them. The smoke from the fires billowed up ominously, making plumes tall and black, which would be seen for miles, I hoped maybe even by the Witch.

The women showed us the places where the Witch and Segundo slept. In Segundo's room, we found a skull filled with dark, black powder and one empty from its contents being thrown on He Watches. On a table lay jars of red, black, white, and orange body paints, and a straight razor and strop. A big mirror hung on the wall behind the table. Comanche weapons, a long spear, a bow and quiver of arrows, a gleaming sharp skinning knife, and horse gear were stacked in a corner within easy reach from a fancy, Mexican style bed. On a long table by the bed was a long barreled pistol in a holster and a roughly used and little cared for Winchester carbine.

Two doors down the hall from Segundo's room was the giant's room. Its bed was longer than others I saw, and a table held the same body paints and shaving supplies as Segundo's room. Several skulls were lined up side-by-side along the back of another table that held jars of dried plants and powders, bottles of stinking liquids, a mortar and pestle, and several mixing bowls. On a wall rack hung a hair hat with long braids and another carefully groomed to look like the hair worn by a hacendado, a *Nakai-yi* of great wealth. An armoire held a couple of gentleman's hats, suits of clothes, fancy shirts, and gloves used to handle the owl. In the far corner, its foot tied to a thin rawhide leash and roosting on a chest-high perch was el Brujo's owl. Beela-chezzi brought his rifle up sighting on the bird, but I pushed the barrel down and shook my head before he could pull back its hammer. The owl's yellow eyes followed me wherever I moved in the room before I turned, crossed my arms, and stared back at the yellow eyes following me. *Are those the eyes of death,* I thought, *or just those of a bird's trained to attack and to kill anything?*

Beela-chezzi said, "What will we do with death?"

I shook my head. Turning to the women who showed us the rooms, I said, "Bring buckets of oil used for the lamps. Leave one in each of the witches' sleeping places."

The women looked at each other,

frowned, and then nodded, saying, "Sí, Señor."

Beela-chezzi and I carried buckets of water, two fancy blankets, and thin rawhide rope to the room where we had left our friends. We straightened and washed the bodies, wrapped them in the blankets, and tied the blankets close around them. I sat back against the wall with Beela-chezzi, feeling the rips of storm and thunder in my bones and flesh and the wounds in my soul from hanging on *el Brujo*'s cross and loosing my friends. I thought over the lives of my friends, proud that they had been great warriors, and I was glad that He Watches had adopted me years ago and taught me many of the skills I used as a man.

As we had guessed, the free ponies, among them my paint and Beela-chezzi's roan, that ran off with Sangre del Diablo and his Comanches came back to the stream for water and stood around the corral waiting for their grain when the sun was low over the western mountains. The women spent most of the day at the creek washing clothes, themselves, and their children. Beela-chezzi and I found the harnesses for the work-horses to use with the Witch's three wagons we planned for the women and children to use to get back to Casas Grandes. Earlier in the day, we had found and loaded panniers in the barn with cases of ammunition, rifles, blankets, and axes and hoes. We knew Juh and his Nednhi Apaches and our women believed these were the best of presents.

Then, as the day turned toward evening, Beela-chezzi found Carmen Rosario and asked her to walk with him to the stream. She was hesitant at first, but he assured her he just wanted to talk, so she left the child with another woman and went with him. When they returned, he announced that she and her son would be traveling with us. I smiled and was glad for them.

CHAPTER 45
ENDINGS

All the women and children going to Casas Grandes were able to sit or stand in the wagons. Several of the women already knew how to drive a team and nodded they understood when I told them to stay on the road ruts. The ruts would lead them to Casas Grandes. They would be in the village before the sun rose if they drove the teams at a steady pace.

We carried the bodies of He Watches and Klo-sen to the place by the trees where we planned to load the horses, and then I took a lantern and went to the rooms of Sangre del Diablo and Segundo. I splashed the buckets of lantern oil left by the women earlier in the day all over the rooms. While the oil soaked into wood and cloth, I looked in the armoire, found a falconry glove, and pulled it on. I let the owl hop onto my gloved wrist, slipped on the hood without it protesting, pulled the knot loose that held the leash on the perch, and using the lantern, lit the oil in both rooms before running down the halls and out into the courtyard. The fires I started soon roared, snapping and popping into big, brilliant yellow flames, sending thick, acrid black smoke rolling along hall ceilings toward the courtyard.

The owl was relaxed and balanced comfortably on my wrist as I walked out the gate, across the circle where the Witch had hung He Watches and me, and down to the trees by the stream. I straddled an ancient cottonwood log with bark peeling off in long strips, leaned my rifle against a notch formed by the trunk and a large bole from a hacked off limb, and looked across my left shoulder to feel the sun's last yellow glow and view oranges, reds, and purples on the clouds over the Blue Mountains. I reached behind my back and pulled my knife, its edge sharp and gleaming, the hunting knife I had carried for years, the knife He Watches had given me when I first began training.

I looked between the knife in my hand and the owl on my wrist, and thought, *One swing of this blade, and this ghost is no more. It would be so easy, but, first, as my father taught me, I must think about what I do.* I stabbed the blade into the log so it was within quick, easy reach. Frogs, tree peepers, and crickets practicing their harmony for their night songs grew silent. The hacienda compound began to glow in flickering, yellow light against the black smoke roiling out the windows and doors.

I pulled the owl's hood off and looked at its big, yellow eyes blinking in the early evening light. I said, "What are you, Búh (Owl)? Are you death, a ghost of some evil man? Is that why you killed my grandfather? Was it you who caused the death of my friend? Is evil sleeping inside you like a rattlesnake in a rat's hole? When I had my dream, I saw a ghost; it was big and ugly and had big eyes. Was it the giant or you, Búh?" I stared at the owl for a long time, the pendulum of my thoughts marking the limits of its life.

At last, I shook my head and raised my wrist to look in the owl's eyes again and said, "You're not death. No ghost sits on my arm." I pointed at my eyes with my right hand's middle and forefingers. "I see you, feel you on my wrist. *Ussen* says my Power kills ghosts, kills witches. I don't kill you. My Power stays with me. One day, again I'll find the Witch who murdered and scalped my people, no matter if you're dead or free. If you warn him, Búh, I'll find you and kill you, too."

The night sky with its glowing, myriad stars, and the burning hacienda lighted the night. Pulling my knife from the log, I cut the anklets and leash thongs. When the leashes fell away, the owl made a low cooing call, and, looking at me, raised one unfettered foot off the glove and then the other while rhythmically ducking its head in a kind of dance.

I held my arm out and said, "My People fear you and say your tribe is evil, but *Ussen* has given me Power over you. Go, Búh. I give you life." I flipped my arm up in a launching motion. The owl spread its wings and, in long, sweeping strokes, sailed away into the night, a black form outlined against the stars before disappearing. I walked back to the hacienda and threw the glove, anklets, and leash into the hungry flames.

We saddled our ponies, including one for Carmen and her little son, loaded the pack bags on the packhorses, and silently tied the bodies of Klo-sen and He Watches across their mounts. By the time we had finished, a bright moon had floated above the eastern mountains, and the burning hacienda compound was nearing nothing but glowing embers. Beela-chezzi took half the pack-

horses and led the way back along the trail
we had followed to the big, green lake that
fed the stream running by the hacienda.
Carmen and the boy followed him. Leading
the other half of the packhorses, I followed
them.

In the early morning light, Beela-chezzi led
the way into a high-walled, narrow canyon
in the Blue Mountain foothills a few miles
from Juh's mountaintop fortress. We
stopped, and Carmen made a fire and baked
bread, using ground corn from a sack, while
Beela-chezzi and I disappeared to hunt for
burial sites along the cliffs. Near the end of
the canyon, we found two deep places under
rock shelves above the talus and returned
for the horses carrying the bodies.

Carmen offered us bread, but we refused,
Beela-chezzi telling her that we must bury
our friends first and then purify ourselves
before we ate. She said nothing, only nodding her head as we left camp again, leading the horses with Klo-sen and He Watches.

The morning air in the black shadows and
brilliant sunlight was cool and refreshing
and helped us keep our strength as we carried the bodies to the rock shelves and slid
them, heads pointed toward the west, far
into the deep places, leaving their rifles and

pistols with their bodies and using stones from the talus to cover their graves, careful to make the stone piles look as if they had formed naturally in the accumulating talus.

We led the ponies of He Watches and Klosen close to the graves, positioned them where we wanted them to fall, and then killed them with our knives, quickly and mercifully. He Watches' pony was getting too old and slow for raids and wars, but he wouldn't part with it when we had left to kill the Witch. Now he took it to the Happy Land, and Socorro would not grieve for him every time she saw it. Taken in a raid only a few years before, Klo-sen's pony was what every Apache warrior wanted, fast, with high endurance, and very easy to train. It was a shame to destroy such an animal, but Beela-chezzi didn't hesitate, laying him down with his head pointed toward Klo-sen.

Walking back down the canyon toward Carmen's fire, we found sage and herbs used in a purifying smoke and carried them back to the camp. Carmen had found a small natural tank and had brought a bucket of water back to camp. When she saw us smeared from the blood of the horses, she covered her mouth with her hand. When she learned why we were bloody, she sent us to the tank where we bathed and smoked.

For the rest of the afternoon, we sat by a small fire and bathed in the purifying smoke. Carmen and her little son watched us, apparently curious about the meaning of the purification and surprised at how spiritual we seemed to be. With the coming of dusk, we finished our purification and ate the corn she had baked into bread.

Chapter 46
New Beginnings

As we approached the foot of the mountain, I saw five tiny figures of horsemen descend the winding trail down to the *llano*. I stopped and pulled the *Shináá Cho* to study them. The man in the middle was big, powerfully built, and clearly dominant. I knew without guessing Juh came to greet us. Of those with him, I recognized two who had accompanied Juh when he showed us the place of the Witch's hacienda.

I called to Beela-chezzi and said, "Juh comes to greet us."

Beela-chezzi dismounted and checked the panniers and other packing rigs on the horses to ensure they weren't lost when we went up the steep stronghold trail. He grunted and said, "Hmmph. Juh will be happy to use the Witch's bullets he was afraid to take. Let's wait here for them. There will be less for each of us to manage going up the mountain trail, and I can better look after Carmen and the boy."

Carmen smiled and said, "I can ride the trail up that mountain, but perhaps you will keep an eye on our son."

Beela-chezzi looked at her, his eyes sparkling. "Sí, I will help our son . . . if he needs it."

Juh stopped before us and said, "*Dánt'e,* Killer of Witches and Beela-chezzi. So, you return with a *Nakai-yi* woman and child and loaded packhorses. I don't see your amigos, the grandfather with the stiff knee and the warrior, Klo-sen."

My face an iron mask in front of my feelings, I said, "They are gone. The Witch nearly killed me. We killed most of the Witch's band, but two Comanches and the Witch escaped. The rest are no more. His second in command went blind to the Happy Land. We gave his slaves their freedom and sent them on the road to Casas Grandes. We burned his hacienda. Beela-chezzi has taken a woman and her son from the Witch. His tipi is full of life again. Bullets and other supplies ride on these ponies. A few we need, but most are for your people. I will hunt and find the Witch. One day, I'll send him blind to the land of the grandfathers."

Juh grinned and nodded, his eyes sweeping the packhorse loads. "Presents will be welcomed by the People. Your band is free to stay long among us, Killer of Witches. Come, we'll ride with you to the stronghold."

I looked at Beela-chezzi, who was smiling. He nodded and said, *"Enjuh!"*

Juh sent word of our return on the legs of a young messenger. It was midafternoon when Juh and his warriors led us to the edge of the tall trees where our women and children stood proudly, arms outstretched, chanting, "They come!"

We rode to the camp's center fire near our tipis, where the wood and brush were piled high, and dismounted. The tipis of Klo-sen and Beela-chezzi, those of men not married, sat on the edge back from the others. Klo-sen's tipi and all his possessions would be burnt or thrown away so his ghost would not come back. I dismounted and walked first to Socorro's tipi where she stood waiting and looking expectantly back down the trail for He Watches. I said, "Grandmother, he is gone. Beela-chezzi and I have buried him. You are in my care now."

She raised her chin and looked in my eyes. "I hear you, Grandson. I go to the other

502

side of the mountain and mourn him. Go to your woman's tipi. Think no more of me."

"Stay in camp, Grandmother. There are many dangers on the mountain. Mourn here. I'll look after you."

"I go. If I do not return, burn my tipi and all that is in it."

"Grandmother, I hear you, but I want you to stay."

She put her hand on my shoulder and looked into my eyes. "You've been a good son. We were proud of you. Kill the Witch who took him. Now I go."

She turned from me and disappeared into the trees. I sighed and watched her go, knowing I would never see her again.

Sons-ee-ah-ray approached me from her tipi. "My son returns, and my heart is glad. I know one day you will avenge your father. What happened to the warrior Klo-sen?"

I looked into my mother's eyes, and my heart sank, realizing for the first time why she asked. "He is gone to the happy land of the grandfathers. He saved the lives of Beela-chezzi and me. He was a great warrior. I was proud to ride with him."

Her eyes were wells of great sadness. "When he returned, he would have been my man. Now I can only grieve for him."

■ ■ ■ ■

I sat smoking by the fire with Juanita, who sat with hands in her lap waiting for me to tell her my story. At the feast with the Nednhis, Beela-chezzi and I had little to say except that we destroyed most of the Witch's band and his hacienda, that I had sent Segundo, second to the Witch, blind to the land of the grandfathers, and that the Witch had escaped with two Comanches. I promised to hunt for him again and take vengeance for the murder and scalping of the Guadalupe band and for the deaths of my grandfather and Klo-sen.

When I changed my shirt to wash for the feast given by the Nednhis, Juanita saw the bruised and red rawhide marks around my wrists and elbows, the deep burns running around my shoulders, and the raw, red cuts in the flesh under my arms. She made me let her apply a mixture of fat and herbs she made for skin burns. Her powerful hands were gentle and rubbed the ointment into the wounds, lifting their burn and ache away from me.

We could hear the drums and chanting at the feast in the Nednhi camp several hundred yards away as our band gave away the booty we couldn't use. The night insects were in full song, and nearby in Beela-chezzi's tipi, we heard Carmen's full-throated laugh.

Juanita said, "Tell me of the scars on your wrists, elbows, and shoulders. How did the Witch do that to you?"

"Hmmph. You know how the *Indah* killed their God? You know they nailed his hands to a crosspiece that they tied high on a pole and then nailed his feet to the pole. You have seen this in the *Indah* holy places kept by the black robes?"

Her eyes grew wide, and she slowly nodded her head.

"The Witch did something like that to me, except he let my feet dangle and tied me to the crosspiece by my arm joints and lay the crosspiece across the top of the pole stuck in the ground. He planned to let me hang there the rest of the night after he killed Grandfather and all the next day before he came the next night and told his owl to kill me. If not for Klo-sen and Beela-chezzi freeing me, I would be in the land of the grandfathers, and you would be looking for another man."

She covered her mouth with her hand for a moment, and then she said, "Tell me all the story of the battle you had with this witch."

"This I'll do, but tell me first, why is Gourd Girl, your new slave, with Sons-ee-ah-ray and not with you?"

Juanita giggled. "She is no longer a slave. Your mother wanted a daughter, and she adopted her. She is called Lucky Star because you did not kill her shooting at the gourd."

I stared into the fire and shook my head. "It seems all we do is free slaves we should be taking." I looked in her eyes and smiled. It seemed she held a secret. "Tell me."

She laughed. "Tell you what?"

"You look different. I can tell when you hide something from me. What is it? Have you found new tipi poles or traded a basket to a Nednhi woman for a new pot?"

"No, no. Nothing like that." She coyly bent her head to look at her moccasins and then looking in my eyes, smiled, and said, "By Next Season of Little Eagles, I think you will have a son."

My eyes sparkled as I held her and whispered, *"Enjuh!"*

The morning air was cool and felt good on my skin as I ate Juanita's morning fry bread and watched the shadows change in the

506

morning light. I saw a young boy leave Juh's tipi and run toward mine. He came to our fire and, puffing a little from his run, said, "*Dánt'e,* Killer of Witches, my father asks that you come to his tipi. He has news for you."

I found Juh on his blanket under the tall pines. He waved for me to join him. After I sat down, he said, "A Mimbreño warrior with a message from Victorio came in last night. He told me a story I know you'll want to hear. He said he was hidden in the bosque resting his horse on the Rio Casas Grandes when he saw a ghost, or maybe a giant witch, riding with two Comanches, wipe out three wagons filled with women and children on the wagon road to Casas Grandes. A baby survived and the Witch didn't let the Comanches kill it. He took it and said he was leaving it with a woman in Casas Grandes. They burned the bodies with the wagons, and the warrior heard the Witch say the stupid *Nakai-yes* would believe the Apaches did it, even though the horses had been killed. He told the Comanches to go to the camp of Elias and he would meet them there in three moons."

I stared at the blanket under me, rage burning inside my mind like hot, fiery coals dumped on my head. I worked to keep my voice steady. "Where is the camp of this Elias? Who is he?"

Juh crossed his arms and shook his head. "Elias is Apache. He has his main camp on the western side of the Blue Mountains, north of the pass the *Nakai-yes* call El Paso Pulpito. Mostly he raids the villages and hacendado herds on the Rio Bavispe. Sometimes he goes north and crosses the border when he can get enough banditos to ride with him or when Geronimo sends word."

"Will you show me the trail to the camp of Elias?"

Juh studied my face and slowly nodded.

"Yes, Killer of Witches, but you need time with your family. In four days, I will send a warrior to show you the way to the camp of Elias."

I saw the faint smile breaking on Juh's lips and knew *Ussen* was giving me another chance to destroy the Witch.

ADDITIONAL READING

Austerman, Wayne R., *Sharps Rifles and Spanish Mules: The San Antonio–El Paso Mail 1851–1881,* Texas A&M University Press, College Station, TX, 1985.

Ball, Eve; Lynda A. Sánchez; and Nora Henn, *Indeh, an Apache Odyssey,* University of Oklahoma Press, Norman, OK, 1988.

Ball, Eve, *In the Days of Victorio: Recollections of a Warm Springs Apache,* University of Arizona Press, Tucson, AZ, 1970.

Blazer, Almer N., *Santana: War Chief of the Mescalero Apache,* Dog Soldier Press, Taos, NM, 2000.

Bray, Dorothy, editor, *Western Apache–English Dictionary: A Community-Generated Bilingual Dictionary,* Bilingual Press/ Editorial Bilingue, Tempe, AZ, 1998.

Cremony, John C., *Life Among the Apaches,* University of Nebraska Press, Lincoln,

NE, 1983.

Haley, James L., *Apaches: A History and Culture Portrait,* University of Oklahoma Press, Norman, OK, 1981.

Opler, Morris, E., *Apache Odyssey: A Journey Between Two Worlds,* University of Nebraska Press, Lincoln, NE, 2002.

Opler, Morris Edward, *An Apache Life-Way: The Economic, Social, & Religious Institutions of the Chiricahua Indians,* University of Nebraska Press, Lincoln, NE, 1996.

Robinson, Sherry, *Apache Voices: Their Stories of Survival as Told to Eve Ball,* University of New Mexico Press, Albuquerque, NM, 2003.

Sonnichsen, C.L., *The Mescalero Apaches,* University of Oklahoma Press, Norman, OK, 1958.

Thrapp, Dan L., *The Conquest of Apacheria,* University of Oklahoma Press, Norman, OK, 1967.

Worchester, Donald E., *The Apaches: Eagles of the Southwest,* University of Oklahoma Press, Norman, OK, 1992.

ABOUT THE AUTHOR

W. Michael Farmer, a member of the Western Writers of America, learned about the rich mosaic of historic figures depicted in his books while living in Las Cruces, New Mexico, for fifteen years. He has a Ph.D. in Physics and has conducted atmospheric research with laser based instruments he developed. He has published short stories in anthologies, won awards for essays, and published essays in magazines. His first novel, *Hombrecito's War,* won a Western Writers of America Spur Finalist Award for Best First Novel in 2006 and was a New Mexico Book Award Finalist for Historical Fiction in 2007. His other novels include: *Hombrecito's Search; Tiger, Tiger, Burning Bright: The Betrayals of Pancho Villa;* and *Conspiracy: The Trial of Oliver Lee and James Gililland.*